SHE BA

Julia had bee   had abandoned her   who now in turn ha   defenseless in a world turned cold and hostile.

There was one way only for her to win Kingsley back—a way she had always hesitated from taking.

Standing before him, she felt as shameless as a woman of the streets as she made him her promise —to be his in any and every way he wanted her, if he would take her again as his wife.

Then, to seal the bargain, she reached out to Kingsley, avoiding his cold, mocking gaze, feeling the heat of his face through the frailness of her gown. Taking his hand, she placed it on the fullness of her breast as she met his imperious kiss and felt him stripping her, stroking her flesh with a skill she would never have dreamed . . . leading her toward the heaven he promised and the inferno she feared. . . .

THE HOUSE OF KINGSLEY MERRICK

In this book you will find a stirring excerpt from This Is The House, *the first enthralling novel of this romantic historical trilogy, available in a Signet edition.*

Big Bestsellers from SIGNET

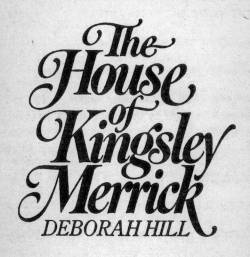

The House of Kingsley Merrick

DEBORAH HILL

A SIGNET BOOK

NEW AMERICAN LIBRARY

TIMES MIRROR

In the interests of narrative, I have taken liberties with the Australian gold rush and the South African diamond strike. I have used the American Civil War and its pressures on Cape Cod to suit myself (although I suspect I have not wandered far from the truth), and I have abridged many of the permutations of the Cape Cod Central Railroad. I have made up the Cape's woolen industry, at least to the extent of its size, time, and place, and I have created a whole society inhabiting a part of the Narrow Land not known to real estate agents or the Internal Revenue Service. It is true that my characters are inspired by people who lived in a setting such as I describe, and the detail of that setting is as authentic as my research can make it. But while I have allowed "my people" to be guided by fact, their personalities and their personal relationships, their inner selves are brought into being by me; they are my creations.

For the fact is that no evidence of their inner selves exists.

A sort of blanket censorship seems to have been exercised one hundred years ago in the name of the respectable, and what one generation allowed to pass the next carefully finished off so that only a monumental collection of trivia is left behind. There is a huge mass of impersonal fact about our Victorian forebears, and we know a lot about what they did, but we know nearly nothing about the kind of people they were. It is a fact that they lived through the events of our national history that tested to the breaking point the American Dream—events that shook to the core the entire country and were watched by the whole civilized world—but the American Victorian emerges unruffled, dignified, correct, weeping but never tear-stained, amazingly clothed in intricate garments that are never wrinkled, voicing platitudes in elegant prose.

Indeed, it is indisputable: the Victorians were shaped by

different ideals and expectations and measured by a yardstick different from our own, upholding a standard of behavior alien to us now so that failure to attain perfection might never be discovered. . . .

But despite the obscurity imposed by the passing of years, despite a different code of conduct, and despite the determination to obliterate themselves, even the Victorians reveal the day-to-day heartbeat of an era important in our history. It is all there in the record, if that record is searched in the light of known differences, and viewed in the light of the common bond which even the Victorians share: the bond of the human heart. It has been my aim to cherish that bond and to render it accessible to the contemporary reader. If I have succeeded, I will have rendered accessible as well an understanding of American social and political history of a century ago as it was lived by people in a small segment of the American continent, and revealed by people who, regardless of the very real divergence between generations and regardless of their protestations to the contrary, were in the final analysis no different from ourselves.

D.H.

One
Kingsley

The War of 1812 was done.

There were years ahead in which to reach and reap, in which to dream and plan. Now with the royal weight of Britain cut loose, the threat of French imperialism gone, Americans of enterprise looked with increasing interest to the manufactures given impetus by the war, to cotton which thrived astonishingly, to the west and the untapped wealth of a whole continent which stretched, limitless, to the Pacific, while on the eastern coast Americans turned again to their business upon the seas.

If the nation now looked elsewhere than the Atlantic Ocean for its well-being, that was no concern of those who knew that upon the bounteous bosom of the deep lay a well-being peculiarly their own. The yet minuscule incursion of steam-driven vessels and machines did not alter the belief of the mariner that supremacy lay in sail and would ever remain there. The War of 1812 with its embargoes and blockades had devastated the economy of New England. There was nothing now, with the Peace of Ghent signed, to stop the thrifty, vigorous Yankee from rising once more to his rightful place. Whatever happened west of the Alleghenies or on the banks of the Merrimack or even in ports to the south—notably that of New York—these things were not the business of the deep-water captain nor of the villages whence he came, nor of the men of business in Boston whose faith still rested in the fleet. For the task at hand was to carry more freight in larger vessels in the shortest possible time—the accomplishment of which would offset the newly (and unfairly) imposed tariffs, the success of which would restore the health, riches, and pride of a tradition and heritage so well begun after the American Revolution.

And so in the uncertain years that followed Mr. Madison's War, while the fleet was refitted and the disrupted business of the mariner gradually set to rights, the coast of New England waited for that breath of confidence which would signal the dawn of a new prosperity, and along with the rest, the village of Waterford on Cape Cod Bay waited also.

The Ne'er-do-Well

For as long as he lived, Kingsley Merrick never forgot the day when strangers entered his parents' house in Waterford and carried every piece of furniture to a platform in the backyard, where it was sold to the highest bidder. He would never forget seeing strangers poking and pawing through his home; he never would forget the folk whom he knew and had known always bidding on the furnishings of his young life: the clocks and the crystal, the mahogany tables and inlaid chairs and the cabinets in the dining room with their little panes of leaded glass, and all the china they contained, the woven rugs on the floors—everything but the clothes the Merricks wore and the mattresses they slept upon.

He had hidden in the bushes near the privy; he had seen it all, and when he went back to the Grays' house, where his family was waiting for the ignominy of auction to end, he had said nothing. He was fourteen years old, and fully able to comprehend the magnitude of misfortune when his father's ship was scuttled off Boston harbor, two years after the close of the war, and he did not want to talk about it.

His father had been trading off the African coast; the men in the crew sickened and many died; the Boston Port Authority condemned the ship for fear the plague infesting it would contaminate the mainland. The vessel, cargo and all, was towed out and sunk.

Kingsley had not known before, but he understood now that his father had borrowed heavily on the ship in order to undertake a South African route; its success would recoup the losses incurred during the war when captains could not sail and the savings of a lifetime slowly ebbed. Kingsley's father, Captain Elijah Merrick, known and respected as a man of outstanding ability and accomplishment, had used every cent he could get his hands on to buy his ship, and every cent went down with *Sweet Charity*.

At fourteen Kingsley was old enough to see clearly that the Merrick family, which had once been rich, was now poor.

7

And while being poor was not a terrible penalty in and of itself (for who, in America, in the year 1818, would be so undemocratic as to hold this against a man in a land where all were created equal?), there were penalties of a tangential sort to pay which were more than Kingsley Merrick was willing to tolerate. It was bad enough, surely, to see his father, once the master of the sea and of men, tending salt vats and plowing the thin, sandy soil in order to wrest subsistence for the family. It was bad enough to see the hopes of his sisters scuttled, hopes of genteel courtship and marriage which once Kingsley had scorned but of which he understood the importance now, because it was part of the girls' pride. Having lost his own, he was swamped with pity for them.

But worst of all was the Merrick store. Its presence in the stripped, bare front rooms of the house, its counters and shelves replacing the fine mahagony and gleaming elegance of the dining room and parlor, its crates of goods and its smells of raw wood and coffee beans, molasses and herbs replacing the scent of wax and polish and cleanliness—these were a perpetual affront, unavoidable, a monument to his father's monumental catastrophe. Even the house, with its gold-painted clapboards and its fenced porch on the roof and its graceful elms—the house which was once the pride of the Merricks' and Waterford, too—seemed shrunken and shriveled in the face of this disaster, becoming dingy and unkempt and reduced in stature because there was neither time nor money to spend on its appearance.

And to make the affront even more painful, there was Kingsley's mother, whose appointed task it was to run and manage the store, as though being poor were not enough, as though the degradation were not complete unless Molly Merrick, too, were reduced and her talents and grace ground to dust beneath the juggernaut of misfortune.

While America yet respected worthy women in trade and would continue to do so for another decade, Kingsley could not reconcile this contradiction in terms: his beautiful and charming mother who had led Waterford society ever since he could remember, now tending a counter over which she sold thread and needles, buttons and fishhooks, sugar and molasses, spermaceti candles and ordinary ones, cinnamon and cloves, while her hands became rough and red. The fact that his mother never complained and always carried herself proudly seared Kingsley's very soul. She was a martyr, in the truest sense!

The store was intended to provide a steady, if modest, income which would tide the Merricks over the lean, cold months; Kingsley was required, with his three sisters, to help his mother there, and every minute that he was not at his bench in district school number three he was either taking his place behind the counter or, if he were not needed here, hauling manure for his father. He hated the menial work and hated knowing that Waterford watched him doing it. How he envied his oldest sister Sarah, safely married already to Captain Josiah Denning and protected by him from this catastrophe! How he envied his brother Lije, who had left for Boston long before this misfortune, to seek his future as a merchant. His brother Lije did not have to wait upon people he had known all his life; his compatriots in the city would be strangers, unaware of the depths to which the Merricks had fallen. And Lije would never have to lug dung from one end of a field to the other!

Yes, Kingsley hated it all, hated the people who came to the store much in the same manner that folk might gather around a horse that had dropped in the traces, to see if it would be able to get up again. Would the Merricks rise? It was a question Waterford often asked itself, and a question that Kingsley pondered incessantly. For if the Merricks did not—or could not—it was clear they would be left far, far behind. The female reading society, which Kingsley's mother had organized a few years ago, held its meetings without her; she had no time to attend them, nor energy to read. The Lyceum, not so sophisticated as the later ones which would host traveling lecturers, yet much in advance of its time, had been set up by her during the war in order to occupy the foundering spirits of Waterford captains. But the Lyceum, too, now housed in a pillared building of its own, functioned without the presence of Elijah and Molly Merrick. They were too tired to attend. A new packet line was established, a committee formed to see about founding a new academy, petitions delivered to the General Court urging more frequent and regular delivery of the mail; the life of Waterford was surging forward, but Kingsley's father, once a leader of such activity, was no longer a part of it. There were no brilliant gatherings in the Merricks' parlor where once the cream of town might be found, nor could there ever be with a store there. Nothing was the same anymore, and Kingsley wondered if it ever would be, even if his parents finally did succeed in reestablishing themselves. They would be too late, too old, too worn-out to care anymore. Waterford would have passed the Merricks by while Elijah Merrick shoveled salt into barrels and Molly Merrick sold life's smaller necessities to fishers and farmers and gatherers of clams who traded at her store because she charged a cent or two less than any other store in town.

But she also sold these things to the established, more respectable people who had been her friends before the demise of the family position. The Blakes and the Crosbys, the Pollards and the Grays loyally came to her because she did not let the status as a woman in trade interfere with the unquenchable essence of her own personality, and the coterie of companions who had warmed their spirits before the flame of her lively conversation and ideas warmed them yet over the counter of the store instead of the tea table in the parlor of old.

Yes, if any one thing could have bridged the widening gulf between the Merricks and the families with whom they had once been intimate, it would have been Kingsley's mother. Her outstanding, strong, vital character and charm was certainly going a long way to keeping open the paths of friendship and respect that had so long existed between the Merricks and the society of mariners which led and controlled Waterford—but she could not counteract the machinations of Elijah Merrick. What ailed the old man, Kingsley did not know, but within the year of his permanent return to town, Elijah Merrick turned his back on the best in Waterford, withdrawing from the Church of the Standing Order, Congregational, patronizing the Inn of the Golden Ox on winter evenings, where he whittled and spat with farmers and fishers and tradesmen from the West Waterford mills, the tannery and leather goods shop, lampblack and ax factory, smithy and forge. Old Elijah Merrick cultivated the friendship of every undesirable person he could, completing the job of isolation which his scuttled ship began and inexorably drawing Molly Merrick into that isolation, too, forbidding her to attend the Congregational Church just as he did not and, by his refusal to enter the parlors of former friends, making it well-nigh impossible for her to go there, either. If any man wished the company of Elijah Merrick, he had to go to the Golden Ox to get it, and any woman who admired Molly Merrick must seek her in the store.

Captains did not frequent the Golden Ox; they had not done so for years, ever since its old proprietor had taken his stance on the side of Thomas Jefferson. And they did not propose to do so now, even for the sake of bygone times when Elijah Merrick was one of their own. The wives of captains did seek Molly Merrick but it was a strain for them, a situation growing more and more awkward as the months went by, and it was only a matter of time, Kingsley supposed, before they would stop, the gulf too wide anymore for them to cross.

He did not understand his father's attitude, and he resented it even in the face of his mother's quite wonderful acceptance. Kingsley could not accept, nor did he have any intention of trying. He was not going to be a second-class citizen because of his father; the Merricks did not need to be left out of everything important, not if Kingsley Merrick could do anything about it. And there was a lot he could do, yes, a lot!

He was fifteen when he went to sea. The panic that invariably followed the War of 1812 (as invariably panic follows any war) was settling down sufficiently so that trade was picking up and raw boys might be hired for cabin chores. He was nearly too late, even as his brother Lije had been too late at war's end, and he resolved to make up for it by industry, application, determination; he did not come back to Waterford, nor did he take a day or an hour away from the pursuit of his master's papers, until he got them seven years later.

In the interim there were changes.

In Waterford, Elijah Merrick, hand in glove with his new friends the farmers, mechanics, and fishermen, and one or two of Waterford's more substantial citizens who had remained loyal to the Merricks, began agitating for a new religious society. Universalists, they called themselves. In a detached manner his mother's letters told Kingsley all about it.

Universalists did not believe in Hell. They did not believe in the election of saints nor in the predestination of the elect, and they did not believe that they ought to pay the ministerial tax in support of the Reverend Mr. Simmonds, perennial pastor of the First Church, Congregational. They sealed their heresy by deducting the ministerial portion, and they were not willing to negotiate.

Since matters of religion, faith, and taxes were a primary concern of Waterford—indeed, of any town like it—there was considerable acrimony raised, beneath which lurked the suspicion that the Congregational Church had seen the last of its exclusive domination over men.

How Kinglsey's mother stood on this issue her letters never revealed, but he could easily guess. Matters of town and par-

11

ish government were not the concern of women, but the Universalist Society surely was the intimate concern of Molly Merrick. The husbands of her patrons and friends were bitterly opposed to this new notion of Elijah Merrick and his cronies at the Golden Ox, and surely it would serve to close with finality the few doors of acceptance and past respectability open to his mother.

There was nothing he could do about it except to continue as he was, working ever upward toward the quarterdeck, from which elevation he might rescue his mother and himself.

In other areas of change, progress was more dignified. The political squabbling along lines of national concern was settled quite easily by admitting to the Union the territory of Missouri as a state that countenanced slavery, balanced by admission of the free state of Maine, a solution that satisfied everybody. That there was even the necessity for compromise did not alarm anyone but the professional pessimist, and no one noticed that the southern portion of the Republic was drifting, drifting away from the mainstream of the American dream; certainly nothing of the kind occurred to Kingsley Merrick, busy upon the high seas and not even finding out about the Missouri Compromise until it was an accomplished fact. By then he was an able seaman, moving along the prescribed course set for the training of captains.

Waterford, too, traveled a course of its own, now with the panic of 1819 over, moving out steadily to meet its destiny. Within the next decade more Waterford men would master the sea than had ever done so before, and the face of the village slowly changed because a new style of house was built now to accommodate the comfort of the captain, a style inspired by and reflecting Grecian history, dear to the hearts of Americans because ancient Greece was a republic, just like the United States of America.

When Kingsley returned at last, his master's papers secured, the year was 1825 and already a new house rose majestically on the main road, two stories high with a sharp pitched roof, not unlike the colonial farmhouses of old, a granite-flagged porch running its length, held up by pillars of exquisite proportion; a wing of equal size was attached at a right angle, so that the pediment of its gable might face the road. It was magnificent, and Kingsley determined on the spot that one day soon he would have one like it.

Carefully as he could, he set about ascertaining the position of the Merricks in Waterford, and believed that there was reason to entertain some hope there.

Molly Merrick, the year before, had artfully persuaded her husband to change the character of the family store. With the marriage of the youngest daughter and the last left at home (all three girls having married men bent on going elsewhere) it was sensible for her to deal with the materials of clothing. A box of thread, a bolt of cloth, spools of braid and ribbon were more suitably matched to her accumulating years than heavy goods, and fashion, with its accoutrements, suited her abilities as well. Molly Merrick had an eye for style, and everyone knew it.

The Merrick Fashion Emporium was an instant success because Waterford had money enough now to consider more lavish apparel and because Molly Merrick was the kind of woman who could make the wearing of it (modeled by herself) seem an absolute necessity. When she opened the Emporium, the notion of trade now seemed a positive good, rather than a necessary evil. The moment it was inaugurated the nicest ladies came there to drink tea and discuss fashions and fabric and pore over the latest magazines depicting these things, and to discuss the latest books as well, for Molly Merrick had time to read again, and was not one to let conversation stagnate.

She was so successful that Kingsley could fairly feel the turn of the tide she had caused, and his father, busy and happy with the Universalists who were building a tiny chapel across the street from the Congregational Church, where it thumbed its nose at the citadel of tradition, seemed not disposed to interfere with his wife's growing leadership among Waterford's nice ladies. Molly Merrick even contrived to enter their parlors occasionally, to drink tea and converse pleasantly, carefully giving offense to no one but notifying all, by her presence, that her company was desirable even if her husband's was not. The ways of his parents seemed to have diverged a good deal in the seven years he had been away, as though each had tacitly agreed not to notice the activities of the other, and Kingsley was delighted. Surely he, too, would be able to make his way unmolested, just as his oldest sister had. Sarah's husband, Captain Josiah Denning, was even now building a new-style house for her to live in, and as far as Kingsley could see, Sarah had been able to keep clear of the quagmire created by the old man out of failure and arrogance and downright cussedness.

It was time now for Kingsley Merrick to make his way, stake out the territory he meant to make his own. With the secret blessing of his mother who reigned happily, if tenuously, in the Emporium, he went about securing the image of stability.

To prepare his way for eventual inclusion in the society of Waterford respectable, he sat righteously all day long on the Sundays he was home (and he came home frequently now) in a pew reserved for him in the Congregational Church. Neither his father, involved with the Universalist Society, nor the Congregational Church, busy opposing it, questioned his choice, as he knew they would not. A man's spiritual home was his own concern—this was his father's point of view. And certainly the Church of the Standing Order was not going to question this marvelous defection in their favor!

He contributed grandly and conspicuously to the new hearse house then being promoted by the First Parish Church, and he was satisfied that his support and presence in the portals of the elect effectively neutralized the bedrock animosity against Elijah Merrick. He contributed also to the new academy then abuilding, vigorously supported the purchase of the old Warden place for an almshouse, and most important of all, he bought a smart piece of land on Main Street and made it known that soon he would build himself a splendid new house of the sort now in fashion, which naturally would need a wife in it. The admiration of Waterford for the imposing new homes was boundless, and for the men of success and means who lived in them. For all that everyone was hell-bent on equality, the old appeal for distinction lingered, and Kingsley rather thought that most Waterford girls would welcome the opportunity to share such a house with him. Already their smiles were more suggestive, their eyes more alert when they looked his way!

Yes, things were falling nicely into place when he left one March day in the year 1828 to take a ship to Cadiz for a load of wine.

While he was gone, his mother went out riding with her friend, Olive Gray, and the Grays' new trotter bolted when Sam Crosby's hound raced out to the road to bark and chase them. The chaise struck a pothole and overturned. Mrs. Gray was crippled after that, but Kingsley's mother was killed.

By the time he returned in August, slack winds having slowed him abominably, and learned of this tragedy, Kingsley's mother had been in her grave three months. When he went to Waterford, grieving, to pay his respects, he discovered she was not interred in the First Parish cemetery. Instead, she was resting in a new burying ground far down the low road, and that in itself had occasioned quite an uproar.

14

The committee of the Congregational Church had offered space in the churchyard, provided old Elijah Merrick were to return to the fold and forget this Universalist nonsense, but the old man would not, and did not. He declared his wife would not care to spend eternity with the elect of Congregationalism; she had never belonged to them; she belonged only to him, and he was going to see to it that her remains rested free, under obligation to no one. That was the beginning of the new town burial grounds where old Elijah Merrick spent considerable time sitting under a tree next to the grave of his wife, until Barney Stone of the Universalist Society died and was buried nearby, and Molly Merrick might have permanent company. And then Elijah Merrick had gone to work on the Universalist cause with a vengeance that made what had gone before appear ephemeral and insignificant. Using the attempted bribe on the part of the Congregationalists, as well as the tax relief that belonging to an unorthodox faith might yield, he successfully solicited members, drawing into the society men and women from all walks of life and, worst of all, taking four of the elect with him, too. Much hustle and uproar filled Waterford and Elijah Merrick reveled in it. Dismayed, Kingsley could only stand helplessly by, viewing his father's merciless drive to usurpation of authority and tradition. When he returned later that year to learn that Elijah Merrick had risen in town meeting, to stand on the side of Andrew Jackson for the presidency of the United States, he knew his difficulties were grave indeed. Andrew Jackson and the Democrats denied everything that conservative New England stood for, and with Merrick's support of him, the tolerance of Waterford snapped, the breach wide open with the Universalists and Democrats on one side, Waterford's respectable on the other, and Kingsley Merrick caught in the trap of his family name. Waterford was downright suspicious of him, even hostile! It would take years to defuse such antagonism! What girl would marry him now! He would be an old man before he convinced anyone that he neither admired his father's ideas nor cared to emulate them, and he was not even home long enough to do it!

Forlorn, swamped with self-pity, angry at life, unsure of his next step (should he go ahead with his plans for a house on Main Street, or should he not?), he walked aimlessly in the gathering nightfall, noting the guarded, uncomfortable greetings of townsfolk as they hurried home to settle in, the glow of their oil lamps and the slow fires on their hearths soft and mellow in the tender evening air; he walked further than he

15

realized, all the way to Mill Village on the west edge of town. It was dark when he got there and he couldn't see the grist mill and the cotton mill, nor the tannery or the lampblack factory. Hardly could he see the small houses that line the road—but he couldn't miss the one from which came the sounds of merrymaking and laughter. Was it the house of Jonathan Stevens? Kingsley believed it was. He paused outside and was seen; he was invited to share the spontaneous gathering, and he was happy to do so, to put behind him for a while the despondency of that night. He enjoyed himself, for the Merricks were held in high esteem among the mill workers, Democrats to the last man. The Stevenses and the Stones and the Slaters and the MacFaddens went out of their way to ensure his entertainment.

When Susan Slater showed herself interested in him, pouring his hard cider into a mammoth mug and seating herself on the sofa beside him, looking up in admiration, he had taken it as a gesture of friendship much like the friendship of the others. When the group decided on a hayride, Susan invited him to sit by her in the wagon, and he understood then that she was willing for more than friendship to pass between them, and when she pretended not to notice his tentatively wandering hand, he was sure of it. Later, in the Slater barn Susan crept from her father's house and met him, to lie with him, to bare her breast and offer it, willingly to spread her legs for him, and Kingsley, for the whole night, forgot Waterford and the house on Main Street. But when he returned from his next trip to eagerly seek her out again, it was her father who met him at the Slater door, glowering and determined to make an honest woman of his daughter.

He married Susan Slater. Between the wrath of Susan's parents and his own upbringing, which insisted on gentlemanly conduct in situations such as these, there was nothing else he could do. Three months later a girl child was born, and a year after that a boy, whom Susan dutifully named after him. With the birth of his son, everything changed. In an ugly scene in the Slater kitchen, Susan's father told Kingsley to stay away, lest Susan drop a child every year for the old man to feed. Kingsley Merrick had debauched the Slaters' daughter, but he was not going to make her into a brood mare, with a constantly swollen belly hanging out for everyone to laugh at. All Susan asked was to be left alone, Jake Slater declared, and all Jake himself wanted was money for the maintenance of her children.

Was it true? Did Susan feel so little regard for him that she would agree to his simply disappearing from her life?

Susan did. Cowed by her father and thoroughly repentant of her initial transgressions, Susan would do whatever she had to in order to ease her guilty conscience. And it would be immeasurably eased without Kingsley Merrick, whose very presence caused quiverings and quakings and spasms of lasciviousness which she could not subdue. She told him only that she did not regard him highly anymore.

Somehow the will to succeed was gone. He took the money he had saved for the house on Main Street and bought a small schooner which required a crew of only three; abandoning deep water, he set about coasting, part of the apple-tree fleet which was never out of sight of the mainland and its orchards, delivering bricks and lumber, fish and potatoes, nails and bars of iron for the forges of coastal smithies. Defiantly he planned to live aboard the snug craft the rest of his life. Vaguely he pictured himself sailing, sailing about, his own master, and dreamed of the day when his son would sail with him, and he waited, waited for the boy Kingsley to grow, for the day the boy would fill the gaping, empty places that pockmarked his life. He drifted about, drinking more than was good for him, he supposed, but there was no reason not to. He took comfort where he could find it, enjoyed it while he had it, and often took it aboard with him to share his cabin, and eliminated completely, for the space of a few hours at least, the hurts and ills of his life. There was a prostitute at every port.

Before long, Waterford found out.

Shocked and offended by this terrible breach, this denial of public morality and the standards of decent people everywhere, Waterford and Mill Village protected themselves against Kingsley Merrick with their greatest, most invulnerable weapon—silence. He was neither spoken to when he came to town nor spoken of when he left it. For all Waterford knew or cared, Kingsley Merrick did not exist. His brother Lije avoided him assiduously, and his brother's wife, Elizabeth Gray, regarded Kingsley as she might a sea worm discovered in a clam shell. Elizabeth had nursed her crippled mother through her last days and had married Lije before Kingsley's reputation became common knowledge. She would have married Lije anyway, she assured her husband, but Lije was not so sure. Kingsley's public image was a hard one to conquer, and Lije would spend nearly a lifetime at it.

Their sister Sarah Denning, so embarrassed by Kingsley's

reputation, simply took to her bed with a sick headache whenever he came to town, and their father suffered his presence in the family homestead without question—but without warmth. Elijah Merrick would forgive and offer his love on the day that his son signed the Washingtonian pledge of abstinence, and not before. And Susan declared that she would never forgive him, no matter how many pledges he signed. She hated to see him coming, because he only renewed the shame of their marriage.

An isolation such as he had never known existed settled around him, and only his little ship contained warmth and comfort. He slipped further and further until the day his daughter died, succumbing to throat fever, and only the little boy in Mill Village was left. Kingsley Merrick knew remorse then, and fear. His daughter had neither known nor loved him; surely his son would never love him, either. It was a thought he could not bear; the boy was all he had. He must claim his child!

He went to Mill Village resolved to take his son away; he was greeted with a rifle, pointed directly at his chest.

"You get out," Jake Slater said stolidly. "Don't come back. Ever."

"I've come for the boy," Kingsley announced firmly. "I'll leave when I have him."

"You'll leave now," Jake Slater told him, and spat contemptuously. "You are a whorin' son of a bitch; if you think I'd let you take the boy to ruin you must be stupid as well as sinful!"

"He's mine!" Kingsley stormed. "There's no court in Massachusetts that would deny me custody."

He was right, of course, and even old Jake Slater must have known it. But Jake Slater also knew that the wretched man before him would never carry the case to law; he'd be doing well to carry a case of gin to the hold of his ship, and that was all he was good for. Jake Slater waved the rifle, indicating that it was time for his son-in-law to leave. He cocked the firing piece, and there was no question, in the mind of either man, that Jake Slater would have been happy to pull the trigger.

It was done. It was over. There was nothing left to hope for. He left, beaten; he did not fight, because there was nothing left to fight with. He left, walking out of the life of his son in West Waterford; he continued his downhill run to oblivion and returned to Cape Cod only once, five years later, to die in his father's house and in his father's arms, and never did he understand the nature and extent of the scars left upon the soul of the little boy.

The child Kingsley grew to manhood.

For a decade it had seemed that nothing, ever again, could suppress or diminish the ascendancy of New England shipping. Climbing out of the financial morass of war and embargo, the persistence and sheer energy of the merchant marine had, indeed, restored the Port of Boston to the lead it had once held, second only to New York and a vigorous second at that, destined one day to catch up! Boston and the villages whence the captains and crews came, all those who were involved in commerce on the sea were ready to dig in their heels and make that final bid for their goal—yet even as they pulled and pulled, its erosion began.

Subtly, tenuously, from so many different sources that it was hard—nay, impossible—to know where the trouble started, coastal, maritime New England sensed, rather than saw, the lustre fading from its star. That the textile industries on the Merrimack, begun after the War of 1812, were so profitable that the wealth from them exceeded that of shipping was not in itself disturbing. Any poor fool who owned a factory instead of a ship surely needed a rich reward to compensate himself. But to protect him by tariff was disquieting. The shipping of cotton, raw and finished, both to New England factories and to British ones restored the balance of trade that Boston so desperately needed—yet it caused maritime commerce to depend increasingly on manufactures for that balance. And in the ships more and more of the crew was of foreign origin, men who were willing to work for a pittance and who replaced the Yankee boy of old, who went west taking with him all his spunk and daring.

Steam locomotion was beginning to take on a threatening aspect and could no longer be laughed away. The railroad, once considered the toy of a few addlepated geniuses, clearly would one day be able to move all the goods that the appletree fleet carried. Steam-driven vessels on the inland waters could go upstream at will, which a sailing ship could not do; more and more steam-driven ships were being tried upon the sea, notably by England. In fact, England was changing her policy of continuous monopoly on behalf of the Honorable John Company, and the British merchant service was slowly, insidiously, rising to a more competitive level of operation.

And in time it became clear that Boston never, ever would

surpass New York, which possessed all possible natural advantages and was, unfortunately, peopled with men who knew how to use them.

Well, if anyone wanted to go live in New York—let him! Second on the list though Boston might be, it was yet a thriving little city, and it bred the best of America. It was beautiful and busy and fortunes could yet be made there, and a captain from New England was the best anywhere, his services in demand in any port he cared to visit. If Boston wasn't first anymore—well, perhaps it didn't need to be. Quality counted, and in terms of quality, nothing in America could touch Boston, and everybody knew it, no matter how much they pretended otherwise.

Yet—how far could Boston slip before that precious quality was lost? How much tonnage could England carry before the mariner was out of work? How much wealth could be concentrated in New York before its drain from New England would be felt? How many more Irish (now arriving in droves) could be absorbed before the heritage of Boston was diluted and washed away? How many more mills would be built before the industrialist took the reins from the Merchant Prince—forever?

These were questions New England could not answer, and so they were not talked about. They were portents of a future that had not yet arrived—and, perhaps, with a little luck and help from Divine Providence, could be postponed indefinitely.

On the twenty-fourth of January, 1848, the Divinity did indeed lift His Almighty Hand. In the barren scrubbiness of Sutter's Mill, in distant California, a nugget of gold was found.

No shot was ever heard 'round the world faster than that one, and in New England, with a whole vast continent separating men from their new hopes of fortune, speed was the only answer. If, in order to achieve it, carrying capacity was sacrificed, why, the enormous demand for passage and goods to California and their commensurate rise in price more than made up for it.

Builders of ships had tinkered with vessels designed for speed, vessels heavily sparred and rigged, but too streamlined to suit the needs of commerce for cargo. But now those daring, sleek, and rakish models were exactly the answer to the gold rush. They had style, they had speed, and the Yankee shipmaster knew how to make them fly. They must be built instantly, bigger, longer, stronger!

The builders of ships could do it!

The captains of New England were eager to try their hand.

The shipyards of the Atlantic Northeast surged into action, and with the gold strike in California, the day of the clipper dawned.

The Return
1854

Under the early sun, upon the face of the sea the packet schooner *Manhattan* raced through the Cape Cod Bay with a bracer of spray thrown up, every now and again, to refresh the watcher, and above it a gull hovered, treading air as a man might tread water. Its shadow on the deck was clear and sharp, nearly motionless in the sunlit June morning, and from the rail young Kingsley Merrick watched it with a measure of envy and admiration. He had always thought that gulls had the better life, and he could not help wishing at this moment that he were free, like the bird above the deck, to enjoy the blessings of so glorious a day. It was a shame not to be able to simply accept and be at one with the wind, the sun, the water, instead of being locked into worry and tension so firmly that the day was as good as lost. It was foolish to look ahead only with trepidation and he knew it. But knowing it did nothing to relieve his anxieties.

The gull slid down the bias of the sky to the water, swooped high again with a raucous shout, and, tiring of the packet, it flapped back toward Province Town, leaving Kingsley alone with his growing apprehensions.

Now that he was so close to his destination, he was glad—very glad—that he had decided to take the New York packet to Yarmouth, instead of one to Waterford. He was glad that Waterford would slide by on the port side, and relieved. He had opted to hire a chaise at Yarmouth's Inn, so that he could ride into town at his own leisure, absorb it again at his own pace instead of abruptly arriving at the Waterford wharf to be overwhelmed by it. For Waterford could easily over-whelm him, that he knew. It had overwhelmed him before, and, try as he might, he couldn't shake off the feeling that it hadn't been so long ago that he had lived there, not so long ago that the town had looked down on him with secret and not-so-secret scorn, sapping his belief in himself and his own abilities.

Ten years separated him from the childhood that was spent

there, but the miseries of the vulnerable boy had not been laid to rest, he discovered upon his decision to return. They came flooding back, despite the ease with which he was conquering the world that did not touch and bear on Waterford, and those miseries were undermining him now even as Waterford had once done. That he did not need! It would only get in his way, at the very time he must have a clear head. He must not let Waterford threaten him, he told himself firmly. He was making a fuss and causing himself unhappiness when there was no need for it. Waterford, by God, did not matter!

The town could not be distinguished from this distance; were the packet closer to land, Kinglsey knew, he would be able to see Grandfather's old, square house with its double chimneys and the porch on top of its hip roof, a house which was not Grandfather's any more, but had gone to Uncle Lije upon Grandfather's death in his old age. Further west along the shore, were he closer, he would have been able to spot the Grays' house where his Aunt Elizabeth had grown up, and further west there would be the old Warden Mansion, which was now the almshouse of Waterford, deserted by the Warden heirs when they decided they would rather build to the east of the meeting house and further away from the Waterford mills. Had he been closer to shore he would have been able to see the spire and the golden ball and vane of the Congregational Church.

His stomach knotted in a cramp and he found that his hands were sweating, the back of his neck ramrod stiff.

Yes, he was afraid. He had to admit it. He, who looked at life cheerfully, embracing it with enthusiasm—and, all things considered, getting along with it pretty well—he was afraid. It was no good telling himself he was not a child, but a man of twenty-four making his way in the world with as much chance as the next fellow of succeeding at it. It didn't help because he was far from the place where he was judged on his merits only, and approaching that place where his merits didn't matter, never had, never would. He was approaching Waterford where old terrors, he uncomfortably discovered, tracked him as mercilessly as ever they had. What a revelation, to discover their existence! And what dismay. . . . Even now he was cursing himself for going back to Waterford—but there had been two reasons, both compelling.

The first, ostensibly uppermost, was the dedication of the new Universalist Church, and wild horses wouldn't have been able to keep him away from that! The whole Merrick family would go, seated in a special pew at the front of the congregation, a pew which would be held in perpetuity for them even if none of them were Universalists. And all the founders of the church would be honored and praised, and none of the rancor which the church had once stirred up would be allowed to show because the church had prospered. It delighted Kingsley to be welcomed somewhere in perpetuity. It delighted him even more to know that Grandfather was being given recognition and homage. Grandfather had worked hard to help establish the Universalist Society, and now the society had grown in such numbers that it could build a large meeting house of its own, replacing the little chapel that had contained it until now. It was as though Grandfather's life was vindicated, justified, and had achieved excellence beyond the ordinary run of men. Grandfather had been a splendid old fellow, and there was no one in the world that Kingsley had loved better. The new church was a triumph for the old man, and he was sorry that Grandfather had not lived long enough to see it.

Besides, if Grandfather were alive, Kingsley would not be so apprehensive about entering Waterford today. . . .

He brought himself back to the deck of the packet. It had been an incredibly fast voyage up from New York, and an outstandingly pleasant one. The mild day, fresh and perfect in every respect, might be taken as an omen, he thought. Surely only good fortune could befall a man on such a day as this! And the pursuit of fortune was as responsible for bringing him back to Waterford as the dedication of the new church. The dedication was a screen—a worthy one, to be sure—for Kingsley's real purpose, which was to secure an interview with his uncle and, hopefully, to secure a loan as well. Uncle Lije was rich. Rich enough to spare Kingsley a bit of money, if he could but be persuaded. . . .

But it had to be done quickly. The loan must be got before he left next month for Australia, and Kingsley couldn't be sure that Uncle Lije would move that fast—if he moved at all. He was a conservative old fart. . . .

A quick surge of impatience gripped him there on the deck and then, replacing it, a prickle of tension as he pictured himself facing his uncle, man to man.

The family of Lije Merrick had always been polite to Kingsley—painfully polite, in fact, and his uncle had always been polite, too. But beneath that politeness, what scorn! What condescension! The memory of it chilled him now.

The family of Lije Merrick had invited him to stay at their

27

house while he was in Waterford, and he had put down the urge to refuse their invitation and lodge at the Inn of the Golden Ox instead. It would have been an act of outright rudeness, and he had not quite the courage for it—especially since he had a favor to ask his uncle. But he did not look forward to it. Not at all. The only shred of comfort he could derive from the whole situation was his cousin Tony, who would be going out to Australia, too. Tony was a decent fellow, and perhaps having a share of the same sort of adventure would serve to bring about a measure of camaraderie. As for the rest of them, the family of Uncle Lije, the citizens of Waterford itself . . .

He must simply bluff it out, he knew. He must put aside former fears and old hurts; he must shake off the past; at least he must behave in such a way that the past would appear to be shaken off. After all, it didn't matter anymore what his uncle or his uncle's family and Waterford thought of him if only he could secure that loan. They would be left far behind, because with the money he needed in his pocket the future would be his to shape and fashion. He knew he could succeed. He knew it! Nothing could stop him, Waterford least of all.

Still, despite the manifest unimportance of his native town, he was happier than ever to come upon it on his own terms and in his own time! He would trot through its center, viewing the new church as he did so, and on to his uncle's house, which had once been Grandfather's. And perhaps by the time he got there, having seen Waterford once again after so long a time, and seen it at his own pace, he would be feeling less nervous about it, and better able to present Uncle Lije the picture of assurance that a man must certainly have, in order to gain confidence and a loan. . . .

The coast of the Cape drifted on by. They were coming closer now to shore but Waterford was behind, and strain his eyes though he might, he could not so much as catch a glimpse of the golden vane and ball. Only an occasional wisp of smoke, floating above the trees far back from the shore, was evidence that the town lay hidden there at all.

The Yarmouth wharf was a scramble of luggage, wares, and people, but Kingsley was well dressed, top-hatted, complete with a cane (an expensive one, which he could barely afford), and he had no trouble securing a boy to take his valise and the presents he had brought his cousins. The youngster cheerfully led him through the mob, elbowing an opening when necessary, confident his prosperous gentleman would give him a good tip. They made their way up to the center of Yarmouth and to the inn where the parcels were left on the porch, the boy paid, the rig obtained.

"The nag looks pretty tired," he observed to the stable man. He looked the mare over critically. The innkeeper, flustered by the hint of scorn in the city man's voice, became belligerent.

"You don't know your horses then," he said sulkily. "This one will get you to Waterford and back, no mistake about it."

Kingsley knew horses very well, and he knew this one was the dregs.

"I want another," he insisted firmly. He was not going to Waterford looking like a peddler!

"You'll have to pay more."

"I never told you I wouldn't," Kingsley explained. "I merely asked for a rig. I'm not trying to get the cheapest you have. I'd appreciate a horse I don't have to worry about, for fear she won't make it and I'd have to pay for her burial."

"Very funny, very funny," the innkeeper growled, and shouted for the stable man to bring another horse. The new one was backed into the traces, the old one led away, and Kingsley looked after her with regret. It was a shame to treat an animal so, he thought, but there was nothing he could do about it, and it was no business of his. He paid the extra dollar, put his parcels on the seat, and checked the bit, loosened it, fondled the ears of the new mare.

"What's her name?" he asked.

"Her name!" snorted the innkeeper. "Good God, man, she'll go no matter what you call her!"

"The name?"

"Elsie," called the stable man.

He climbed up, depositing his cane carefully on the floor. "Sooooooo, Elsie," he crooned to the new horse, who waggled her ears and trotted off smoothly with only the slightest flick of the reins on her back. The innkeeper stared after his disappearing rig, the amazement clear upon his face. That nag had never behaved so smart before! He shrugged and pocketed the extra dollar.

It was pleasant, once he left the busy center of Yarmouth. On the left the bay was often in plain view, the tide ebbing now so that in some spots he could see the sands of the flats. He drove through the heart of Dennis, which had once been the eastern edge of Yarmouth village, and on past it toward the western side of Waterford; along the beach lay an occasional salt vat, bleached and weather-splintered and abandoned, for the most part, because salt was no longer profitable. There were few trees along the open road and the sun beat with increasing warmth; judging from its height he'd have to make good time, lest he be late for the dedication. He ruffled the ribbons a bit, and set the mare into a pacing trot that ate up the miles in incredible time. She was a good horse, her strides lengthening and her body settling closer to the ground as she reached for the road ahead. In the driving and observing of the horse he was at last able to relax and enjoy the day as he had been unable to do in the packet. It depended where your heart was, he decided. Horses and rigs were his love; were he a mariner, he supposed, the schooner and the wind would have done for him what Elsie was doing now.

A few modest homes appeared on the road, and he guessed he was approaching the outer limits of Mill Village which some people called West Waterford, in order to confer greater dignity upon it. Yes, there was Seth Stevens's cabinet shop, and there was the smithy of Nathan Hall. The smell of the tanneries was growing stronger, rapidly overpowering the faint and pervasive odor of low tide, and the house where he had grown up—the house of Jake Slater—was just around the corner . . . there . . . huddled among three others, its eaves low front and back, its shingles nearly black with the passing of time. Upstairs, under the roof, had been Kingsley's own domain. The little window he could see now was the very one he had lain beside, on his cot, where he watched the road on rainy days, the rivulets running down the pane distorting his view, the patter on the roof blending into the monotony that was a northeast storm.

Someone else lived there now, he guessed; there were geraniums in the windows, scraggly and sick, but sure evidence of habitation. A mill worker, no doubt.

He was sorry now that he could not stop, seek out the companions of his youth, his cousin Jerry and his friend Jon and the boys with whom he'd played (when there was time), with whom he'd netted herring and shot blackbirds for the bounty and trapped muskrats and skunks for their pelts in order to get what pocket money they could. With those boys he had run after the coach when it swung into Waterford from the south, stopping at the old mansion by the mills that served as a tavern, and with them he had idolized the driver and his mastery of the reins and his ability with the horn which he blew far away in the distance as he approached, warning the inhabitants of his arrival. With those boys he had thumbed his nose at the children of the rich and aped their manners in derision (who could do so better than he?). With those boys he'd spied on the packets from behind tuffets of beach grass on the dunes, to watch the captains coming home, men of erect and lordly bearing who were masters of the sea and objects of worship, whom the boys of West Waterford would rather emulate, when they grew up, than the drivers of coaches. They'd have to come in through the hawsehole, to be sure. They were not the sons of captains who could, if they were good enough, be trained for the quarterdeck by right—but they'd attain it anyway, through sheer skill and ability, and they'd be richer than any man who drove a coach!

And if they mastered clippers, Kingsley reminded himself, they'd be richer yet. A man could make a killing with a clipper, so he had been led to understand. He wondered if any of his old friends had reached the tantalizing goals they used to dream about, but there was no way to find out now, no time to stop. He'd be lucky to make it to the church before the dedication started, and had the packet been delayed, he'd not have made it at all. No matter. He *had* made it, and were he a bit hurried now, it left less time for pondering imponderable things, just as he had hoped it would.

He drove past the cluster of small cottages, past the mills and over the ford, past the peeling almshouse, putting the noise of the factories behind him. The houses were more grand now, the further away from Mill Village he went, the grass and fences in front of them neater, even the trees that lined the road taller, and despite himself he was getting tense again. Soon he would pass the Academy with its pillars and pediment and its motto, in gold leaf, inscribed above the door: *Lux et Veritas*—wretched place!

He had complained to no one about the miseries inflicted on him at the Academy. Mill Village would have had no sympathy (What, after all, was wrong with district school number four?) and Grandfather, the only other alternative, would have been too upset. Grandfather understood very well the hazards and pitfalls that Kingsley faced, had always done his best to help, laying out lunch for Kingsley in his kitchen and encouraging him to mime and laugh at Waterford Center boys who would not eat with him, walking to the Academy to meet him, lest Kingsley be accosted on the way home. He stayed with Grandfather at his square yellow house during the week, rather than risk the long trip back to Mill Village every night, where so many opportunities for ambush lay.

The Academy had been one long, unmitigated hell, one hell among others brought on him by his father who returned to Waterford when Kingsley was ten years old, to die of delirium tremens and probably a cancer, who left his meager life's savings to Kingsley, and whose dying request it was that the money be used for Academy tuition.

He had stuck it out grimly. He was not going to be forced out of the Academy when he had a perfect right to be there! He was not going to relinquish a superior, if hateful, education that was bound to help him; he was not going to be intimidated by anyone nor hamstrung by his fears, nor by Waterford's objections to his father (by virtue of which Grandfather's defections took on an aura of mildness). So he told no one that at the Academy there was sand in his inkwell, that his pen nibs were ground under anonymous heels, that he was tripped every time Master Starling called him up to work on the chalkboard or with the hemispheric globe, that upon return to his seat his neatly sewn copy book would be soiled with ink blots or the lessons carefully written in it smeared with spittle. He did not complain when no boy stepped forward to befriend him, when he was not invited to join games nor asked to anyone's house to play, nor when the little girls, cautioned by their mamas, would not speak to him. Nor was there anything that could be said when on examination day the Academy children recited and spelled and orated for their parents and the Slaters refused to come to town to see his performance, when the applause for him was perfunctory and feeble, contrasting with embarrassing clarity to the acclaim given the others. When it was his turn, he orated for Grandfather, who was his only support in the audience, or in Waterford, for that matter! And he knew Grandfather admired his spunk and was proud.

A year and a half later he was able to defend himself fairly well, and he no longer stayed the night with Grandfather. Though he loved the old man dearly, it was important to spend as much time in Mill Village as he could, so that his friends there wouldn't forget him nor believe he thought himself above them; often Jerry and Jon walked to meet him halfway in the hope that Academy boys would be lingering nearby—but by then the Academy boys had learned to leave Kingsley Merrick alone. Though their encounters with him had often been to their advantage, certainly Kingsley's confrontation with Sears Bradley convinced them they had better not push him too far. Once his blood was up there was no way to stop him, and Sears Bradley, beaten to a pulp, was proof of it.

Young Bradley, in front of a group on the Academy steps, blocked the passage to the door.

"His mother was a whore," he whispered loudly to his henchmen who gathered close behind, their faces cruel. "His father was a son-of-a-bitchin' ne'er-do-well out for a piece of ass, and he found it. And now we have to go to school with the bastard they made. . . ."

That was the last time anyone challenged Kingsley Merrick openly. The henchmen let the two of them fight it out without interference (as was the code among boys), and after that the warfare went underground, among the inkpots and copybooks and anonymously thrown stones, and Kingsley stuck it out.

His mother remarried when he was fourteen. Grandma and Grandpa Slater were both killed by an epidemic of throat fever which struck Mill Village that year, and Susan Slater, without their protection, took the first husband she could find when she went to Boston in hopes of finding work. The new husband owned and operated a sail loft and was not averse to Kingsley's working there, and Kingsley happily did so, dizzy with the relief and joy of being free from the Academy without having run away from it. Though he had faced up to it squarely, he had never defeated nor vanquished it, and sorry as he was to leave Grandfather he was sure, quite sure, that he would get nowhere by remaining in Waterford. He did not return even when Grandfather died. He mourned at a distance; his presence could not help Grandfather nor could Grandfather help him, ever again. And when his mother died in a belated pregnancy the year Kingsley was sixteen, he left the sail loft of her husband in which he had no interest, and took up the pursuit of his own destiny aided by a boot in the backside by his outraged and offended stepfather.

"Here I've been training you in trade!" the fellow bellowed. "For her sake. Now it's not good enough for you. What kind of thanks is that!"

"I'm sorry," Kingsley told him. "It's not enough. A man can't get rich making sail."

"I'm doing well enough," his mother's husband cried. "These new ships want sail by the square mile."

"I'm sorry," Kingsley said again. "There's no future for me in it."

"Well, there's no future for you in my house, either." The fellows face was pure purple; Kingsley left hurriedly.

And he had followed the star of an old love—coaching.

He went to work for Hartland's Express in Boston, sleeping in the huge stables where Hartland's horses were kept until he'd made enough to rent a room; he lugged manure and curried the animals and oiled harness and helped to keep the wagons of Hartland's land-bound fleet immaculate. Later he swept the office floors, copied letters, worked on the accounts. Promoted to the New York office, he mastered the intricacies of routes and rates and delivery schedules of parcels and light freight that Americans sent in increasing volume throughout the country, and he traveled to many of the cities where Hartland's had offices, learning of the inner workings of the express lines. Now, having learned them, he was off to Australia—and if everything went the way he hoped it would, his prospects were as good as—or better than—those of any mariner.

Yes! They certainly were, and despite the uneasiness that still nagged him, his head was high as he trotted into the center of Waterford, where silver poplars and the grand houses of captains lined the road, the square ones of old, pillared ones of the present. He trotted past the Congregational Church with its ball and vane and the national flag fluttering from the foremast on its training field, and past the new church opposite, standing grand and many-windowed and high, with a simple graceful spire that, if not so tall as the one on the Congregational Church, did have a gold ball on it and was fit for any main street, anywhere.

It was nearly time to turn, he judged. In the distance, close by the intersection of the Rockford Road which crossed the main street and went on down to the packet landing, he could see the old Merrick place where Grandfather had been born. It was humble and shabby in comparison with the rest of Waterford, shut up and disreputable and huddled low, like a toad or a mushroom in the flower bed of Main Street. No doubt Waterford would like to see it taken down and removed from sight, but no one could do that because Grandfather had willed it to Kingsley and if Kingsley had no use for it, still he was pleased to know it sat there, offensive and unpolished in the midst of so much grandeur. He had refused his uncle's offer to buy it, and other offers, too, that arrived occasionally in the mail. It gave him pleasure to do so, just as it gave him pleasure to see it today, unkempt and frowsy. But now it was out of sight as he turned down the low road; now he could see Grandfather's square old captain's house with the porch on top, the clapboards painted yellow still, as they had always been.

It was well shaded by huge twin elms in front and was much neater than had been the case when Grandfather had lived there. The driveway that swung past the entrance was snugly contained by a border of box, trimmed and shining in the shafts of sun that reached down through the trees, and the clamshells were well raked and smooth. Its lawns were close-cut, and an urn of fat, healthy geraniums guarded the stoop, brilliant spots of glowing red. It was impressive in a way it had not been when Grandfather was alive, and he debated as to whether he should pull up to the front door as surely the rig warranted, or drive to the back closer to the barn where he would be less obtrusive.

Why should I not intrude, he asked himself. I have been invited here, have I not?

He left the rig in the driveway and, tightly gripping his valise, marched himself up to the front door, rattling the knocker briskly.

"So you've finally got here."

It was none less than Uncle Lije, fat and prosperous, who opened the door and upon discovering Kingsley on the other side thrust out a hand with a heavy ring on it that pinched under his hearty clasp. "We were afraid you weren't going to make it, my boy!" Uncle Lije's shrewdly appraising glance saw in an instant Kingsley's fashionably cut suit, his hat which was the correct height for that season and his straight shoulders which, while neither broad nor deep, bespoke nonetheless a young man confident of himself and quite different from the callow youth last seen in Boston.

"We'll have to hurry," Uncle Lije said, herding Kingsley through the entrance hall, past the parlor where the murmur of many voices told of guests entertained—so quickly that Kingsley couldn't tell how many people were there—and into the kitchen that lay at the back of the house. On the table there was a plate with a chicken wing and cornbread on it and a mug of milk alongside; the kitchen was quite changed, he saw. A new iron cookstove was planted in front of the old hearth, which was handsomely bricked in, only one opening left to accommodate the chimney pipe, and the furnishings of the kitchen were new, replacing the odds and ends of old pine that had been Grandfather's.

"A little different than you remember, eh?" Uncle Lije chuckled. "Well, one day soon it'll be more different yet! I plan to make this room into a back parlor, so we'll have more space—put the kitchen further back. . . . You've cut it a bit fine," Uncle Lije went on, removing his watch from the pocket beneath his paunch. "I'm sorry to rush you so. Have a bite to eat, then best you freshen up quickly as you can. Your room is in the middle of the upstairs back hall. I'll have Tony take care of your carriage and bring up whatever's in it. We have an attached privy now—go through the back room—" Lije indicated it "—and you'll find it, all right. Later on we'll have to renew our acquaintance! Just now I'd better get back to our guests—Universalist higher-ups, don't you know, and the Duncans, our friends from Boston whom I'm sure you'll remember. . . . Your Aunt Sarah is having a dinner tonight; you can eat hearty then. I'll call you when we're ready to go."

Uncle Lije strode purposefully from the kitchen, leaving Kingsley to stare at the scrawny chicken wing and drying cornbread.

He did not know the Duncans, who boarded at Bowdoin Square in Boston along with the Merricks. The Duncans were always somewhere else the few times Uncle Lije had bade Kingsley to call, and Kingsley had never believed that to be accidental. The upstairs room he knew well—it was the smallest in the house, sandwiched in between two larger ones. But perhaps the house was quite crowded, he told himself, and he'd at least been given privacy, instead of having to share a bed with a stranger.

Well, he'd take the plate of food up in one hand, his valise in the other, and eat there while he freshened up. Presumably they'd at least have given him water and some towels.

He picked up the plate and heard Uncle Lije calling to his cousin Tony to take care of the rented horse; he reached for his valise and was nearly at the narrow flight of stairs which separated the kitchen from the pantry when light footfalls started at the top and a cascade of steps clattered down. He backed away just in time to avoid collision with the young girl who shot into the kitchen, who wheeled then to face him, her hand covering her mouth in horror at the accident so narrowly averted.

"Oh, I'm so sorry!" she gasped. "Please excuse me! Surely you are Kingsley?"

"I surely am," Kingsley told her.

"I'm Julia." She smiled in an attempt to seem gracious despite her haste. "You probably don't even remember me."

36

"I do remember you, of course, Julia," Kingsley bowed. "But I would not have known it was you."

She had been a little girl when he had seen her last, but now she was old enough to be out of short skirts. She was startlingly tall, handled herself like a colt, and was just as awkward. She was not pretty, but her face was lively and arresting with large eyes—green eyes, he saw—and a generous, smiling mouth. Her hair had been curled in corkscrews and pinned in bobbing, shining masses above her ears, reminding Kingsley of a parade horse with plumes attached to its harness. She dipped him a curtsey.

"It's nice to see you again, King," she said politely. "Please excuse me if I keep on going. Hetty says I may not use her flowers because she doesn't have enough of them, so I am on my way to the garden to get some for my bonnet."

She turned then, rummaging about in a cupboard, a handsome, massive oak one that had replaced Grandfather's pine hutch. She separated the scissors from the tangle of utensils within. "Here they are. I hope lilacs will do!" She smiled again, though it was evident she wanted to seek out the nearest bush and attack it. "Everyone will be wearing flowers in the rim of their bonnets," she explained in a mature manner. "And I don't mean to be left out, even if Hetty is nasty and won't give me any."

"The color would become you, I'm sure," he said kindly, though he could not imagine that with her rather pale complexion they would suit her at all.

"Oh, I hope so!" She rushed away into the courtyard to the west of the house where lay Uncle Lije's gardens.

He assayed the steps again, to the small back room in the center of the upstairs hall, a room which had only one window and no fireplace at all, wondering if they would have given him the same room in the dead of winter, even without heat. No matter! It was June now, without need of any; there was a narrow cot upon which he'd sleep well enough and a commode with water and towels and a chamber pot in the compartment below it, in case he didn't care to journey out to the new, attached privy.

He refreshed himself as the conveniences of the house permitted, changed into a fresh shirt, brushed his suit; he hastened back down the stairs to the kitchen and then to the front of the house and the parlor without waiting to be called, as Uncle Lije so obviously wished.

"Why, you're ahead of time!" Was Uncle Lije displeased at his unheralded appearance? He gave no sign of it, although

37

there was a certain tightening around his mouth. "Elizabeth, my dear," he called to his wife. "Here's Kingsley, at last."

The small parlor was so jammed with people and furnishings that it took Aunt Elizabeth several minutes to extricate herself, and in the interval Kingsley saw that his cousins Hetty and Ellen and Clara were there, with flower-decked bonnets, that at least half a dozen people unknown to him were wedged in between little dark tables (upon which knick-knacks were strewn with careful abandon) and blackly upholstered chairs; in the center was a round table with a lamp and a Bible and the week's accumulation of reading material. Over the shoulders of the mob smiled the lovely portrait of his grandmother who had died before he was born. It was one face too many in the small room, but it was a face fresh and lovely, and despite the impossibility of examining it closely, Kingsley had the distinct impression that the portrait, which had been unfinished when he saw it last, with Grandmother surrounded by mists of swirling gray, was now complete.

Aunt Elizabeth, bearing down on him with welcoming words on her lips and a properly auntlike kiss, shook his hand and exclaimed over the fitness of his appearance and was relieved from taking him into the parlor to meet the guests (a feat that would have been difficult to accomplish, in any case, by the density of the crowd there) because Tony came in the front door just then, the rented horse stabled and the packages for the family under his arm, Julia charged down the hall from the kitchen, lilacs bobbing from her bonnet, and Uncle Lije announced that it was time to leave.

Amid the scuffles and flurry of locating shawls and parasols, top hats and gloves and canes, Tony said, "Well, Kingsley! It's good to see you after so long! I'd shake your hand if I could."

It was a reminder that Tony would enjoy being relieved of Kingsley's parcels.

"Here! Let me take those," he said quickly, and just as quickly Tony passed them over. "You can throw 'em in the parlor when it's cleared out," Tony grinned. "What's this I hear about your going to Australia?"

The strangers were filing past, busily talking to one another and nodding politely to Kingsley, to whom they had not yet been introduced; Hetty slipped by without acknowledging him, a tall and angular girl; Ellen and Clara paused briefly and smiled at their unknown cousin.

"Welcome to Waterford!" they murmured before they moved by. "Do come along, Tony," they urged.

The parlor had emptied now and he put the parcels in the nearest chair. When he turned, Tony was gone and Julia, her lilacs caught in an impossible tangle with the corkscrew curls, waited by the door.

"We can walk together, if you like," she said artlessly. "We seem to have been left behind."

His gold-headed cane had been left behind, too, in the carriage, and it was too late to retrieve it.

"My pleasure." He smiled and fell into place at her side. "What a crowd you have at your house."

"I'll say!" she exclaimed. "They claimed all the best beds, too. We girls are relegated to the attic, and Tony is staying at the Grays' until tomorrow, when—thank goodness—everyone will leave."

"The dedication is quite an event, then?" They rounded the corner, trailing the procession of Merricks and their guests.

"Everyone in Waterford is celebrating it," Julia told him proudly.

"Even people who aren't Universalists?"

"Certainly!" she exclaimed. "After all—*we* aren't! But we're the guests of honor! Everyone who counts will be there, and I'm very glad you could make it, Kingsley," she said simply. "You knew Grandfather better than we did, and this day really honors him most of all."

"Your father mentioned that Aunt Sarah is giving a party later this afternoon."

"Oh, yes!" She nearly skipped in her excitement, and caught herself in mid-bounce. "I can hardly wait! I've never been to a grown-up party before, but Mother has given me permission to go to this one."

"Splendid!" It would be rather a relief to have this ingenuous child at his side. Grandly he extended an arm in invitation for her to take it. "Will you permit me to escort you?"

"Oh . . ." She drew slightly aside and did not rest her hand on his arm; flustered, she spoke quickly. "Oh, I don't think so. I mean, I think my parents would object because I'm not old enough."

He had embarrassed her completely and he smiled at her inexperience. "How old do you have to be?" he teased.

"Older than I am," she explained gravely, widening the gap between them.

"I only meant that I'd hold the door for you, silly

goose!"—he laughed—"so that it would look as though you were grown up."

"Well, all right," she said. "*That* might be rather fun! Besides, if no one talks to me, you would."

"Maybe I would," he agreed, "if you're nice to me."

"I am! Already!" she exclaimed, too young to know he was flirting.

Ahead he could see the new church, across the street from the old, and the highroad was clearing fast now; the Merricks were going to be nearly the last to arrive, he guessed, staging a dignified march to the front of the congregation so that no one in Waterford could miss seeing them. He was becoming more and more uneasy at the prospect.

"There's going to be a play tonight, at the Lyceum Hall," Julia was saying. "It's called *Poor Popinjay*. Mama says I may go to that, too."

Hurrying toward the church from the opposite direction, whisking up the steps ahead of Aunt Elizabeth and Uncle Lije, a young man with broad, braid-festooned shoulders smiled down at an attractive young woman on his arm and Kingsley heard her laugh, softly, as though amused to have so narrowly escaped being late and last.

"That fellow looks a lot like Sears Bradley," Kingsley remarked.

"It is," Julia said. "Did you know him when you lived here?"

"Aye." He remembered Bradley only too well! Seeing him now, even at a distance, caused something unpleasant to stir, something Kingsley could not quite put his finger on, a ghost belonging to the day that Bradley had insulted Susan Slater and Kingsley had whipped him.

"Who is it with him?" he asked, seeking to divert himself.

"Angelina Winslow—he's her escort for the day, no doubt! The dedication is like a party, you see," Julia explained. "The boys who are home from sea have asked girls to accompany them to the church this afternoon and to the play tonight. So it would appear that Sears Bradley has asked Angelina. The broken hearts of Waterford are past counting!"

"Because Sears Bradley is so desirable?"

"Because there are so few boys home! Not nearly enough to go around. The girls will have to go to the doings with their parents, those who have no escorts, and most will not have, since most of the boys can't just skip back when it suits them. No one asked Hetty, and I am glad," she announced, tossing her lilac-tassled head saucily.

40

Aunt Elizabeth and Uncle Lije had already passed inside; he took a deep breath and followed the guests and Tony and the girls, entering the new church which still smelled of plaster and paint and fresh wood. They were ceremoniously led down the aisle to the pew in the front, which had been reserved for them and where Aunt Sarah and her husband were seated already. The crowd in the church was hushed reverently, but an indecipherable rustle and hum rose up at the procession of Merricks.

He was tense now, he knew. His hands were wet and his face was hot. He steeled himself to keep his eyes front, to concentrate on walking erectly, proudly, to look only at the new pulpit on its lofty height and to the box on the left, also high above the congregation, where the Universalist choir would sit. He waited while the family filed into the pew, courteously helping Julia, and found, as he prepared to enter also, that there was no more room. Quickly he checked the pew, instantly suspicious that they had deliberately taken up more space than they needed. But they were well packed, he saw, and he turned to the usher who stared uncertainly and with embarrassment and who held up his hands in mute apology.

God help him! Just when he would have liked to settle down and out of sight in the shelter of the pew, there he was on his feet while everyone else was seated, and he couldn't have stood out more plainly had he perched in the pulpit, which appeared to be the only place available. Resolutely he continued to stare at the usher, demanding that he do something about it. From her seat Julia looked up at him and then at the full pew. She hopped nimbly to her feet.

"Kingsley and I will sit with the choir," she announced firmly, her voice too loud in the hushed church, easily heard by every person in it. Her mother looked at her, aghast, and her sisters stared up in alarm. Tony was hiding a grin beneath his hand, and Uncle Lije frowned and assiduously paged through the new hymn book.

The usher was overcome; wordlessly he led them to the loft where, like it or not, Kingsley awkwardly climbed up the set of steps that led to it and handed Julia in, sat himself beside her and bowed his head as if in prayer as she did hers. But it was not the Lord that occupied his mind. No, the memory associated with Sears Bradley was flooding him instead, for being up there in the choir loft, singled out and set high for all to see, to be examined and scrutinized while he

41

himself could do nothing about it, was now very poignantly reminiscent of something else. . . .

"Hold out your hands, Merrick," he heard Master Starling say, and felt upon his knuckles the intolerable pain of the cane cracking down on them. He heard the master say, "Climb up on this chair, here by my desk, and face the room."

The sneering, scornful faces of his schoolmates pinned him in disdain; his hands ached and stung and throbbed, and from their desks, the henchmen of Sears Bradley nudged one another triumphantly.

"I will not tolerate fighting during school," the master announced. "Merrick, here, has abused Sears Bradley; he shall pay for it. He shall stand here for the morning, and I urge you all to let him be a reminder. . . ."

The prospect of being exposed there for so long, of being punished when he was in the right, of being defenseless and helpless, unable to hide his pain, overwhelmed him. To his horror he found that he was crying, tears that he could not stop, while silently they laughed. . . .

For a moment he was paralyzed by the shock of remembering it; for a moment he thought he might cry again, and he struggled, there in the choir loft, sudden sweat bursting out on his brow. Yes, the memory of the day he whipped Bradley had returned now in full force and he willed himself to face it once again, stand steady before it, and defeat it before it defeated him. Gradually the pain of the small boy and his humiliation ebbed; gradually, gradually Kingsley made himself relax, mastering by sheer will himself and his memories, and took a deep breath and reviewed his present. It was quite a way to enter Waterford, after all! Hating the place as he did, he might just as well make the most of it. He might just as well sit there easily, comfortably, as though it did not make the least difference whether they were watching him or whether they were not, and deliberately he slung an arm over the back of his chair, sliding a little sidewise in it so that he could cross his legs, and hoped it looked impudent. He regarded the program the usher had given him, scanning the lineup of events as though they interested him. He was glad when the processional started, for it helped to disperse the sadness that the recollection of the child had left him. It helped to disperse the nagging worry that there would not be enough space for the choir, that he would be ousted, that he would drift from one corner of the church to another throughout the afternoon, as out of place there as he was in the rest of Waterford.

"I hope there will be room for everyone," Julia at his side murmured. "Because if there is not, two members of the choir will have to sit on the stairs. I shall not move!"

He was enormously comforted by this child who was not going to be pushed about by anyone. The chances were good, he reflected, that she had never been.

The choir climbed in over them, accommodating themselves with aplomb and smiling at the young Merricks as they squeezed their way by, two of them, indeed, sitting on the steps when Julia outstared them. The service commenced.

During the interminable prayers, anthems, hymns, and homilies and praises of Old Elijah Merrick and his cronies Kingsley found himself able to put Waterford aside. Lulled by the endlessly droning ministers, he thought about the horse he would like to have one day, about Australia and his prospects there, about how he might go about getting that loan from his uncle. Then he glanced over at Julia, and nearly laughed aloud when he saw that her lilacs were drooping badly in the accumulating heat of the afternoon so that, if the service of dedication were to take much longer, her face would surely be hidden by them. Facing the pulpit as the choir seats did, the rim of the straw bonnet shielded her from the congregation so that only he and the dignitaries seated behind the altar could see her face. The speakers must have seen it, too, for when they glanced toward the choir in their attempt to include everyone in their remarks, he detected a flash of surprise, and he wondered how long it would take before Julia herself would become aware of her rapidly accumulating disarray. With amusement he watched as less and less of her came to view through the next hour; and seeing the disaster that was her hat, and seeing her dismay when at last she realized she was peering out through a hedge of lavender bloom, he forgot the last traces of the discomfort that the afternoon had brought back to him.

The congregation rose for the final hymn, and Julia, peering up at him through her lilac blossoms, looked ready to weep.

"What'll I do?" she whispered. "Everyone will laugh at me."

"Take it off," he whispered back.

"I can't," she quavered. "I am still in church."

"Pick your poison," he said. "Either alternative looks equally bad to me."

"You're right!" She slipped off the offending bonnet and clutched it to her so that none of the blooms would fall out, and taking his arm, marched away with him after the benediction, with a glance neither right nor left as she and Kingsley led the procession of Merricks who were ushered out before the rest of the congregation.

The afternoon was cooling, there on the porch of the church, and Julia giggled.

"What a fright I must have looked," she laughed. "It took me the longest time to understand why you kept peeking at me."

"Not very gallant, was I?" he laughed back. Her good humor was infectious. "But you are a sport about it."

"Mama won't be," she remarked, and hastily threw the withered lilacs beneath a newly planted bush beside the door, turning to face the rest of the family piling out after them.

"You've disgraced us, Julia," her mother's voice was low-pitched so no one else would hear. Aunt Elizabeth glared at the girl's unadorned head. "You know a lady never removes her bonnet in church—nor anywhere else, for that matter."

"I'd have disgraced you the more if I had left it on! Truly, Mama," she explained earnestly, but the image of herself disappearing in a blush of lavender was too much. Despite her need to placate her mother, Julia burst into laughter and turned helplessly to Kingsley. He grandly offered his arm and led her down the steps, at the head of the Merrick procession even as they had trailed it on the way up.

"I'm afraid she is angry," Julia worried, though unable to suppress an occasional giggle.

"Don't worry about it," he commanded. "Tell me the procedure instead. What comes next on the schedule?"

He wanted to figure out, among the lineup of events such as Julia had described, when he might most likely see Uncle Lije alone.

"We'll go to the house, to freshen up," she told him. "And stretch a bit after so long an afternoon. Then we'll all go to Aunt Sarah's where there'll be food enough to pass for supper. Back to the house to change our clothes and then on to the play at the Lyceum Hall. It ought to be great fun, King."

But she was not allowed to go. Her mother, mortified by her conduct in the church, decreed the moment the front hall was reached, in her gentle voice so full of steel, that Julia had given evidence that she was yet a child and thus was not eligible to go to Aunt Sarah's party. Julia's disappointment was

44

so painfully evident as she dolefully climbed the stairs that Kingsley could not stay silent. Having hustled his packages from the parlor to his pallet, he drew Aunt Elizabeth far back into the hall where they could speak without being overheard.

"I'm afraid I'm the cause of this, Aunt. Were it not for me, Julia wouldn't have been sitting in the choir loft. And if she'd been in the pew with her back to the congregation, she could have removed her flowers unobtrusively, before her departure. But it was the hat or nothing because she was so conspicuous up there with me."

"It is not the occasion so much as the attitude that troubles me," Aunt Elizabeth said stiffly, offended by his interference. "Julia is far too headstrong and high-spirited; she needs taming, needs to consider her actions more carefully before she lets her impulses run away with her. This is just one occasion among many, I assure you."

But Kingsley was not deceived. His aunt had not liked her daughter up there in front of the congregation, sitting beside him. Julia had not considered her actions; she had stood by Kingsley with a generous impulse of her childish nature, so that he need not sit alone, as though she were as strongly attached to him as she was to her own brother, with whom such behavior might be expected. It cast Kingsley in a role closer to the family than Aunt Elizabeth liked. . . .

Uncle Lije strolled over then, apparently without purpose or direction.

"Well, King!" his uncle chided. "For a while there I thought you would be giving an oration, too, sitting in the lap of the clergy as you were."

"Very uplifting," Kingsley grinned, and was rewarded with a chuckle from his uncle. "I'm afraid it was the cause of grief to both Julia and my aunt."

"Women!" Uncle Lije brushed them aside. "They make a tempest in a teapot. Julia is only thirteen. Elizabeth expects too much of her." He shrugged. "They have to settle it themselves. It's not a man's job, bringing up daughters." Such camaraderie was surprising, and Kingsley wondered how far his uncle meant to carry it. "By the way, I, ah, have a little supply of cheer laid by," Uncle Lije murmured, astounding Kingsley completely. "I'm obliged to stay here with my guests, but there's no reason for you to have to put up with them. It's in the bottom of that oak cupboard, by the back door. Help yourself, if you like, before we carry on the festivities at Sarah's place." Uncle Lije looked as though he could have done without the impending fete at the Dennings.

"Thanks, I'll take you up on it." Kingsley smiled, delighted to have a place of refuge. "Send Tony in, too, if you think he could stand a bracer."

"I'll see how he's getting along," Lije said noncommittally.

"The social schedule seems a little thick," Kingsley put in quickly. "And, if I may, Uncle, I'd like a chance to speak with you privately."

"Oh?" Lije's affability wavered infinitesimally. "Well, now, I'd planned to go up to Boston soon as possible. Let me see. . . ."

"Have you any enormous desire to see tonight's production of *Poor Popinjay*?"

"I can't say that I have," Lije admitted dourly.

"I shouldn't like the fine folk of Waterford to feel I was uppity and couldn't be bothered to see their play," said Kingsley. "But it does look like as good an opportunity as any, doesn't it?"

"It looks like a relief to me," Lije chuckled. "I'd like to chat with you, King. Your promotion sounds splendid, and I'd like to hear more about it, especially in view of the fact that I mean to send Tony to Melbourne soon."

He had not been promoted; he was not even employed by Hartland's any more, having given his notice a month ago, but Uncle Lije, heretofore in ignorance about Kingsley's life in general and his job in particular, did not know this. Kingsley did not enlighten him.

"Possibly Tony and your male houseguests could escort the ladies to the performance," Kingsley suggested. "If you think it's possible to work it that way."

"Anything is possible," Lije beamed comfortably. "I'll see to it. Meet me in the study when they've gone."

With a nod Lije left him and Kingsley, hastening to the kitchen, cast about as to where Uncle Lije's study might be. The only possible place for one would be in the small back room attached to the kitchen, but when he peeked inside, he saw only a piano and a few chairs.

Perhaps the attic space above it? Certainly small, but after all, private. In a houseful of so many women, privacy must be very desirable. He poured a dram of brandy, sat at the kitchen table with it. The noise from the parlor and occasional rising up of laughter there told him that everyone was happy, and as he stared at the glass in his hands, it occurred to him that his uncle had offered him this place of refuge because he had wanted his nephew out of the way, lest he behave in a manner that would embarrass the Merricks in front of the high potentates of the Universalist Church, out there pontificating in the parlor, or their precious friends, the Duncans. What exactly Uncle Lije thought Kingsley might do to embarrass him was a mystery. Perhaps Uncle thought he might wipe his nose on his sleeve? Belch loudly? Curse in the presence of ladies?

Kingsley nearly laughed aloud. Any more of this brandy and he just might! Quickly he poured another dram. It would be a good idea to be as relaxed as possible before he bearded the Waterford lion in Aunt Sarah's den. He did not look forward to meeting Waterford any closer than he had already—but there was no help for it. His presence there would be expected, and having come this far, he had no intention of reneging.

No, sir! he thought. *I have never run from Waterford, and I'm not going to start now.* He downed the brandy, poured another, and wished that Tony would come out to the kitchen. But Tony would not. In all likelihood Tony didn't even know he was there; probably Uncle Lije had not mentioned it to him.

So much the worse for him, Kingsley thought, yawning and stretching, with the brandy running warmly, smoothly in his veins. *That he is stuck in there with all that hot air is no concern of mine!* He smiled to himself, and decided that with the aid of one more brandy, he might just be able to enjoy Aunt Sarah Denning's party, after all.

In the Dennings' garden, Waterford's deep water captains clustered.

"I really did think she would be too tender," Elnathan Blake said earnestly. "But I was dead wrong. There was nothing she couldn't do. Mastering her was like riding a fine horse—the smallest touch registered; she'd turn on a silver dollar."

"Couldn't be any better than *Unicorn*," scoffed James Pollard. "Why, I'd have made it to California under ninety days in *Unicorn* had it not been for a storm at thirty north, thirty-three thirty-five west. It drove me two hundred miles off course."

"*Unicorn!*" sneered Elisha Crosby. "You should see her now! So hogged you could walk upright under her keel, were she on land." That this was an exaggeration of the greatest degree did not trouble Crosby's listeners, who understood well enough that any vessel whose bow and stern drooped lower than its center was unwieldy and sluggish in response to the helm.

"Has anyone sighted Freeman or Richardson?" asked John Gray. "Last I heard they were spotted neck and neck at thirty south, thirty-five twenty west."

"That's the last report I heard," said Sears Bradley. "But I'd appreciate it, fellows, if you'd offer up a prayer on behalf of Freeman, on whom I've got a hundred dollars."

"Well," drawled Blake Stevens, "you should know better. I've a hundred fifty on Richardson myself."

"I know *Shooting Star* is a better vessel."

A discussion arose immediately on the respective merits of the clippers *Shooting Star* and *Witchcraft*, comparisons of their deadrise and hollow, dimensions of their spars, and then drifted to the talents of the designers and builders of clipper ships whose work all mariners had inspected carefully, tested, and compared.

Slightly on the outside of this group Kingsley Merrick stood, close enough so that the casual observer might not notice he had no part in the discussion, nor had even been invited to join it. He had run the gauntlet of introductions in Aunt Sarah's double parlors where the older generation clustered. He had forgotten most of their faces and just about everyone's name, but he could see that they remembered him very well, and that through him they had remembered other unfortunate things, too. Concealed beneath cool courtesy, revealed by the swiftness with which they resumed the conversations Kingsley's introduction had interrupted, it was clear they preferred to put him out of mind, although in deference to Elijah Merrick, Boston Merchant, whom they admired, they had been as discreet about it as was possible for their sort of person to be.

He hadn't let it bother him; what difference did they make? And he hadn't let the assembly of young captains in the garden bother him, either; they were, after all, only the boys he had known once, men now, who had changed little, their turned backs reminding him of the shooting matches with marbles, many years ago, in which he had not been permitted to compete.

But their great interest in themselves to the exclusion of all else left open the whole gamut of girls who were demure and retiring, as they had been trained to be, shyly following Kingsley about with their eyes when they thought he wasn't looking (girls always liked Kingsley Merrick), blushing and looking down at the grass when he caught them at it. Only Angelina Winslow did not blush nor avert her gaze when he found her watching and smiled at her. Presumably escorted by Sears Bradley who had deserted her now for his manly discussion of clippers and their great potential, Angelina stood with the girls, twirling her parasol.

"Well, old fellow, it's about time we had a chance to chat!" It was Tony, joining him on the edge of the discussion of the race to San Francisco.

"So you're off for Australia," Kingsley rejoined promptly, happy to have someone to talk to.

"You bet I am!" Tony laughed. "And I don't mind telling you, King, though I'd sooner you kept it to yourself, that it will be very nice indeed to be out from under Father's thumb. Needless to say, I was delighted to learn that you'll be going to Australia, too," Tony added politely. "I hope we shall be seeing something of one another there."

"You'll be working for Baker and Company?"

"Right. Father thought it would be just the thing to get my feet wet, so to speak. Later, if I'm doing well and the conditions are right, we'll open a branch of Merrick and Son in Melbourne."

"Does Baker and Company know you're using them as a training ground?" Kingsley asked noncommittally.

"Who can say?" Tony laughed. "There's a terrible shortage of labor in Melbourne. You must know that! Every able-bodied male wants to dig gold. They'll no doubt be glad to have me for as long as I will stay."

"When do you leave?"

"In three months."

"Why so long?"

"Father wants me to learn all the aspects of bookkeeping in his office before I go, so I'll know what I'm looking at when I get there." Tony made a sour face. "What a bore!"

Kingsley had known all about Hartland's bookkeeping, even before he left Boston, gleaning it from the books in between copying letters, and he couldn't help thinking that Tony was a little slow about it, considering he had always planned to go into Uncle Lije's business some day. No doubt he had thought there was plenty of time, until now. Tony, Kingsley reflected, had never been particularly alert to opportunity. But then, the need to be had never arisen.

James Pollard, gesturing widely, backed up a step, out of the circle of mariners, and knocked Kingsley's arm, causing the punch in his cup to slop down the front of his suit.

49

"Oh! So sorry, old man!" Pollard apologized. "Can I help?"

"No need, don't bother!" Kingsley brushed it off as quickly as possible, reaching for a handkerchief in his pocket while the captain watched. "I'll be more careful next time," Pollard said by way of further apology. "Send me the bill for cleaning it." He returned to his conversation.

Angelina Winslow had wandered away from the girls now, quietly investigating Aunt Sarah's roses.

"Well," said Kingsley, replacing the handkerchief and glancing over his shoulder at the captains. "At least they leave the field open. If you'll excuse me, Tony, there's a young lady whom I would like to know better."

"As a matter of fact, I'd like a chance to talk to Nell Denning," Tony said, his face lighting up with an animation notably lacking when he discussed business. "Who is it you're after?"

"Miss Winslow—out there in the rose garden."

"You'd better be careful," Tony cautioned him *sotto voce*. "Sears thinks she's his property."

"He isn't taking very good care of it, is he!" He meandered off in pursuit of Angelina.

Ah! If anything made that party worth the effort it took to stand it, Angelina Winslow did! She was the most lovely young woman Kingsley had ever seen—or was it the June afternoon, throwing red and golden stars in her hair? The brightness of the late sun caused her blue eyes to be cool and deep, reminding him of shady, mossy places. She smiled and spun her parasol gently as she talked; her bonnet was perched well back of her head, trimmed in lavender as was her white, billowing dress.

They admired Aunt Sarah's roses and he picked one for her. They discussed Mrs. Stowe's book which had, two years ago, caused such great indignation and furor and had raised a white heat of anger against the South and slavery (fairly or unfairly)—a heat which had abated somewhat now and allowed for more mature consideration. They discussed whether the South should, or could, free its blacks right away or do so gradually, over a span of time, or whether the best solution was not to ship those unfortunate black folks back to Africa where they belonged, as a group of highly placed men had wanted to do now for years. They discussed the theater in New York—the only city in all of America where it prospered—and Kingsley told Angelina about the Australian gold rush that was well underway now, and how the clippers were

50

speeding for Melbourne with as much haste as they did to San Francisco. He described, without detail, the opportunities he hoped to find there, and she was the first person he'd found so far who seemed to think the challenge of coaching might approach that of sailing. She was delightful.

Her eyes shone as she exclaimed, "What an exciting prospect, Mr. Merrick! Surely you must be looking forward to it! But I will be sorry to see you go so far away when I have only just met you," she pouted prettily. "It is very unkind of you, Mr. Merrick."

"Perhaps I shall return another day," he ventured. "Perhaps we could renew our acquaintance from time to time."

"It would be a pleasure," she smiled.

"Perhaps we could further our acquaintance before I leave," he said hopefully. "I can linger in Waterford another day or two." Swiftly he revised his plans, which had included getting out of Waterford as soon as ever he could.

"I'd enjoy that," she said. "I will be at home tomorrow afternoon."

"May I call on you then?"

"If it pleases you," she said demurely. There was laughter in her voice as she responded with the proper formula. "I could show you my pressed flower collection." Then she laughed outright, her eyes twinkling, as though she understood very well the opportunities a pressed flower collection could be made to yield—the sitting close, the occasional brush and touch of hands as the pages were turned.

"I'd like to see it very much," he responded, also according to formula, happily picturing himself exclaiming over her pressed flowers and allowing his eyes to travel from them to the lovely face that would be so close to his, letting her know he admired more than the dried husks of a summer day.

He was well satisfied with his afternoon, even though Aunt's party had been abysmally boring and offered no more compensations when he handed Angelina back to Sears Bradley who, discovering that Kingsley had made off with his girl, retrieved her with a scowl. He had drifted about for a while, listening to one conversation or another, none of which concerned him, all of it being ships and storms and without any attempt to include him. Deliberately or not, the captains and their wives (who discussed fashion and the garden) behaved exactly as though Kingsley were not there, and he was damned if he was going to loiter any longer.

Looking about, he discovered an exit via a hedge of bridal wreath. Quickly glancing around to assure himself no one was watching (little chance of that!), he dived through a parting in the cascades of flowers and made his way down the road to the packet landing, walking up the beach until the fields behind his uncle's house and the old saltworks of Grandfather's came into view. He crossed the field and came to rest on the knoll behind the house, behind which lay Grandfather's orchard.

The bay and the flats shimmered in the sunset; the sky was velvet and the swallows swept through it; the throbbing of the crickets rose up from the grass. Seeing it now, standing on the knoll, Kingsley remembered that he was born to this land, that it was part of him. He had forgotten, so long had he been gone from it, how lovely it was, how its beauty could make a man's heart ache.

Jesus! Who in his right mind would rather attend a party than stand before this sky, now preparing for sunset with banners of red and gold and purple hung up across the western horizon!

He was well out of it, here on the knoll, and glad that he'd left when he did, content as possible, under the circumstances, to renew his friendship with the swelling, gentle land that was growing dusky lavender now in the distance. He stood still, listening to it, still for a long time, watching the sky and the start of stars, when the music began. It was floating, quiet as the twilight and as peaceful, lovely as a dream, effortless as bird song pouring out into the deepening night. Softly he crept toward the little room in back of the kitchen where he'd seen the piano earlier in the afternoon, and within the room was Julia, seated with her back turned to the window, her lithe and supple body swaying slightly as the music swayed, a beautiful etude. Entranced, Kingsley waited by the open window, leaning on the sill, listening as he beheld the quiet fields and the shadowy orchard.

My God, how the girl could play! He was amazed, for although she was young, her touch and interpretation were fantastically mature, as though she and the music were one and there could be no separating the two. If she could play like that, only thirteen years old, just think what maturity could do for her! Or to her, he reflected sadly. A woman was not encouraged to shine, and Julia, still a child, would one day be a woman. One day soon.

"Julia! Julia!" he called during a long pause, softly so that he would not frighten her. But he did. She jumped from the piano bench, whirled about, and regarded Kingsley with terror. Then, seeing it was he, she relaxed all of an instant, and broke into a smile.

"For a minute I was afraid it was the family," she gasped. "But it is only you, Kingsley. Permit me to express my relief!" She came over to the window and leaned out, smiling.

"I didn't think they were as bad as all that!" He laughed. "Why are you so relieved?"

She hesitated. "Mama would be angry if she heard me play like that. She believes I play with too much . . . passion." Here Julia blushed deeply, so deeply that Kingsley could see it even in the dimness of the dusk.

"Passion might well describe it," he said. "I've been listening, and I have rarely heard anything I liked better. Where the devil did you learn to play like that, Julia?"

"I didn't learn," she protested. "I've had lessons, of course. All us girls have. But it just always does come out like that, and Mama gets very upset and says it's unbecoming. I usually wait for a time when she isn't home to play the way I want to. For the rest, I try to keep it simple so as not to offend her."

"It's a shame," he commiserated. "Come, Julia, walk on the beach with me and forget about it." Impulsively he reached for her hand; as quickly she drew it away.

"I can't," she said. "I'm supposed to stay inside and be a lady. I'm supposed to read my dull old Bible. I wish I wasn't a girl, Kingsley! I wish I was a boy! Don't you think I'd make a jolly good fellow?"

"I like your personality just the way you are. You're already a jolly good fellow whether you're a boy or not. It was damned decent of you to sit on that choir loft with me, and I appreciated it, Julia."

She smiled. "It was fun," she said. "You are fun. Unlike my mother," she added dryly. "My mother wants me to be a lady, and to tell the truth, I'd rather not!"

"I don't blame you," he said, "if sitting around singing psalms is the measure of success. But one day, Julia, you'll be a woman as well as a lady, with all the delights of womanhood at hand."

She regarded him blankly, so naive, so untutored, so innocent she had not the faintest idea that it was to the rewards of the senses he referred. He laughed, quickly changed the subject.

"I've brought you and your sisters a present from New York. Would you like to have yours now?"

"A present! I'd love it!" Instantly her face brightened, and she forgot her woes. "What is it, Kingsley? Do tell me!"

"Maybe you won't like it," he teased.

"Of course I will like it!"

"Maybe it's just a dull old fan or a stupid lace hankie."

"I would love it anyway," she gulped gamely. "But I hope it is a puzzle."

"How did you guess!" He laughed. "It *is* a puzzle. I got one for Clara and one for you, and your elder sisters get the dull old fan."

"Thank goodness!" She giggled. "Quickly, King, do get it! I'd love to start working on it." She was fairly jumping up and down in her eagerness.

Her delight in the puzzle was sincere and heartfelt; he helped her turn the pieces over and arrange them on a convenient table, and further stayed to help her begin to fit them together, exchanging remarks in the desultory manner of puzzle piecers. When he heard the Merricks approaching, he hurried to his feet and prepared to steal away through the kitchen and up the back stairs.

"Why are you going?" she asked. "It's much nicer when you're here."

"I've really meant to rest," he said. "And it would be difficult to excuse myself the moment they all troop in. Tell them that I'm upstairs, should they ask. And here are the parcels I have brought your sisters. Perhaps you would give them out, with my compliments."

"Yes, I'd be glad to," she smiled, but her eyes immediately dropped to the puzzle to find the next piece, and he rather thought she would forget the other presents.

He lay on his bed upstairs for a long time, listening to the chatter and preparation for the theater that night. How Uncle Lije was going to manage to get everyone out of the house without him, Kingsley didn't know. But he certainly was not going to intrude himself upon the scene, perhaps interfering with Uncle Lije's maneuvers.

He would lie there, he thought, until the house was quiet, and he would think about his conquest of Angelina Winslow. He would think over his Australian plans so that he'd be able to state them succinctly, though there was scarcely any need for that, so much had he thought about them already. He would compose himself for the pending interview with his uncle so that when it was done, his future would be assured, and so that once Australia was reached, Kingsley Merrick would be in the spot of a lifetime. . . .

He glanced around the small attic room that lay above the one where Julia that afternoon had been playing away her sadness and melancholy. It had been quarters for servants once, when Grandfather had been rich, long before Kingsley was born. Uncle Lije, like the rest of Waterford, had no servants, it being both undemocratic as well as impossible to find anyone willing to serve, and so he had taken the room for his own, smoking and reading in leisure there while his wife and daughters took care of the domesticity of the house. It was small, with only one window at its gable and just enough space at the peak for a man to stand.

"Rustic, is it not?" Uncle Lije smiled and offered Kingsley a cigar from a box on the corner of the desk. Two comfortable chairs and a low bookcase were the only other furnishings, because there was no room for more.

The smoke from his uncle's cheroot filled the place, and Kingsley took one from the box and lit it, although he was not a devotee of cigars. It seemed as good a defense as any.

"Open the window, King, or we'll suffocate," Uncle Lije directed from his great chair. "And then sit down, boy, and tell me about this Australian junket of yours." His voice was jovial, if slightly patronizing, but Kingsley warned himself to see how the land lay before launching into the subject of a loan.

"Well," he began, matching his tone to the affability of Uncle Lije's, "I doubt there is much I can tell you about Melbourne that you don't already know, from the standpoint of the Australian gold rush and its affect on business possibilities. You have probably investigated all the prospects from the point of view of merchandising. But you may not be aware of the possibilities in the moving of goods, of getting them from the port to the city and on out to the gold fields—or of getting prospectors themselves from port to city to the fields."

"True enough," said Uncle Lije. "I have mostly considered goods, the sort of thing that Merrick and Son might trade in if I ever do set up a branch."

"Actually, the moving of freight and passengers is quite profitable," Kingsley informed him. "There's nothing like a gold rush to encourage folks to get somewhere in a hurry—and of course, once they're where they want to be, goods and clothing and equipment must be moved quickly, to catch up with them. There are express companies operating now, out of Melbourne, very successfully. And with the lode promising to be a better one than ours in California—well, the possibilities are endless."

"Indeed," Uncle Lije nodded happily, picturing those possibilities as they might apply to his proposed branch office.

"Now! The mode of moving these goods and people! As you no doubt realize, sir, the day of the stagecoach has passed here in the United States with the advent of railroads."

"Coaching is still a going thing in the West," Uncle Lije remarked from behind his cigar.

"And will continue to be, until the railroads reach that far."

"Think they ever will?"

"I do, indeed." It was a certainty, and every man in coaching circles knew it. "And when it does, coaching in the West will be condemned to running lines between connections of the railroads just as it is now, here in the East. The more branches of the railroad there are, the less will be the need for coach lines at all. But Australia is so new that there may be many years before the railroad takes hold. In Australia there is good opportunity yet for coaching."

"Yes, yes. And for many other endeavors as well, which a man would be foolish not to capitalize on," Uncle Lije nodded sagely. "That is why I am eager for Tony to go out, too, to see about the possibility of my opening an Australian branch of Merrick and Son. It is harder and harder all the time for a small outfit like mine to compete successfully here in Boston. Money talks, boy. Money talks, and I don't have enough of it to secure the biggest contracts and the fattest profits. So it would be stupid of me not to expand if so sure an opportunity presents itself as seems to be the case in Melbourne."

Uncle Lije puffed a bit, and Kingsley decided he was waiting. After all, who had asked for this interview?

"Perhaps you'd be interested in learning more exactly the manner in which I'm going out," he said tentatively, resisting the impulse to clench his fists.

"Why, I assumed, naturally, that Hartland's Express is starting an Australian branch!"

"No. They aren't. They should—but they don't want to risk it, and I've been unable to persuade them. No, Uncle, I and my associates are going out on our own. I am no longer employed by Hartland's, and my associates aren't either. And whether I remain long in Melbourne or not depends on whether the express line we hope to set up is successful."

"You? You and your associates are going to start an

express line—a coaching company?" Clearly Uncle Lije thought him daft. "Who are they, your associates?"

"Six men who used to work for Hartland's in various capacities."

"What sort of capacities?"

"Well—two managed the wagons and horses that Hartland's used in the city. Two worked in the Philadelphia office. Two are drivers."

"And so six former employees—two of them whips—and you are going to start an independent line?" Uncle Lije's incredulity was amusing.

"They are very good whips," Kingsley assured him. "The best. Between them and those of us who have worked in the office we are qualified to run every aspect of an express line. In the past two years, since word of the strike in Victoria got out, each of us has been studying up on the requirements. Each has taken on a phase of the business at which he has specialized, and which he will oversee when we get underway. The Philadelphia men will handle supplies and equipment; the other two, New York men, will handle way stations; the two who've worked as drivers will take on the animals. I shall manage the bookkeeping and the overall operation. We can all take the reins when necessary, and in the beginning, until we have built up a sound organization, we shall."

"I declare I am astounded," Uncle Lije said. He could not truly believe that his nephew had it in him to start a new business in a strange land by himself, singlehanded, as it were. "You are quite confident, I perceive."

"Quite. I am sure we can secure the backing we need, one way or another." Kingsley was not so certain as he sounded, for the backing they could get might well depend on whether he could swing his part of the bargain now. "And I think my confidence is well placed. We will buy Concord coaches; they're the key. They're fast and strong and smart, and in Australia, where they are nearly unknown, the old English coaches can't hold a candle to them. A Concord is a clipper in comparison."

"Expensive," Lije observed.

"Necessary. They are the best thing on wheels ever made. If we are to keep a schedule, it's the Concords that will permit it. And keeping schedules will ensure the success of any express line."

"Won't it take a while to get them?"

"They are already on order with Abbot and Downing,"

Kingsley told him, enjoying profoundly the look of astonishment on his uncle's face.

"Good grief!" Uncle Lije exclaimed. "You are very impetuous, Kingsley!"

"No, I'm not," Kingsley chuckled. "We can sell them to another line if we fail, and the investment will be returned. Because there are so few Concords in Australia as yet, they are even more valuable down under than they are here. Even with depreciation, the investment can be recouped."

"And who shall pay for them?"

"That, Uncle, is up to you," Kingsley said slowly, meeting his uncle's eyes steadily. "If you would like the opportunity to invest in a line of coaches in Australia, now is your chance."

Uncle Lije did not move, nor did his face change. In silence he smoked a long, long time. "You'll need a lot more than coaches," he said after a long while. "You'll need horses . . . and many of them. Harness. Grain. Buildings. A good express service ought to have availability for many runs."

"I know, Uncle," Kingsley said firmly. "My associates are raising funds for animals and grain and such. We reason that if we can get to Melbourne and set up a line, however modest it may be, we'll have no trouble in building ourselves up. There are speculators by the dozen with gold in their pockets, waiting to see how they might increase their gains. One look at an operation running smoothly, with all the equipment it needs to put two coaches and teams on the road, will be enough to gain confidence, and we shall be able to finance more. And the Concords will clinch it! They'll demonstrate to all concerned that we really know what we're doing. It's not exactly an amateur operation, Uncle."

"Of course, I see that." Uncle Lije waved it away as being too obvious to even discuss. In his mind he was weighing the probabilities. The probability that Kingsley, if grateful to his uncle, might be helpful in the interest of Merrick and Son; the probability that if Kingsley were well enough funded, he would more likely succeed than if he were not. The probability that if Kingsley were to succeed in Australia, it was not unreasonable to suppose he might stay there. It would be pleasant to have Kingsley on the other side of the world where he could not hobble Lije Merrick's own image of himself. The fewer reminders of the elder Kingsley Merrick, the better. Lije had seen, only too clearly, what young Kingsley's presence in Waterford this day had done; things better forgotten had been suddenly remembered. The old man was clothed in respectability now, the laurels heaped upon his memory this day sufficient, Lije thought, to bury once and for all the animosity he had once stirred up. But it would take a lot more time before Waterford's abhorrence of a reprobate would be forgotten—time in which nothing—absolutely nothing—must be allowed to suggest that the elder Kingsley Merrick had even lived.

"Tell you what, King," he said slowly, as though he had only just now thought of it. "Suppose I were to give you enough money for coaches, even a few horses. Suppose it weren't a loan, but a legal transaction in which the money were to be yours, without interest to be paid on it, and without any possible interference from the lender, because it wouldn't be a loan."

"You mean you would give it to me outright?" This was more, much more, than Kingsley had hoped for!

"Not quite," Uncle Lije frowned. "Unfortunately, I am not in a position to just give money away. But I would give it to you as proceeds from the sale of the old house."

The old house had not entered his mind. "You mean you would buy it from me?"

"It is legally yours. There is no one else I can buy it from," Uncle Lije reminded him.

"It isn't worth much," Kingsley protested. "It isn't worth as much as I'll need."

"It'll be worth it to me," Uncle Lije remarked dryly. "How much do you want?"

Somehow it stuck in his craw, and he told himself he was being foolish to let it. He had no use for the place; he had only clung to it as his contribution to being a thorn in the flesh of Waterford society, a continuation of the tradition of his grandfather, who had been a thorn ever since Kingsley could remember.

His uncle had only thrown the house in now because it was as good a time as any to pry the place away from Kingsley at last, and it would be stupid to demur, he told himself, on the basis of one old, decrepit cottage which apparently would secure his stake in the future, a place he would never use and did not need.

"Four thousand dollars," he managed to say. It was far more than he needed for the wagons, far more, in fact, than the old house was worth.

Uncle Lije looked at him coolly. "All right," he said quietly, and Kingsley firmly quelled a faint stirring of remorse.

"I'll draw up a legal bill of sale when I get back to my office," Uncle Lije said. "Have Abbot and Downing send me the bill for the coaches, why not. I'll see they're shipped right away, from Boston. You can draw on my account for the rest."

"I'd be much obliged," he gulped, stunned by the ease and magnitude of his success.

Still his uncle sat quietly, making no move to terminate the interview. There was apparently something more that he wanted, and Kingsley waited to see what it might be.

"You are aware that Tony will arrive in Melbourne shortly after you do?"

"Yes, he's told me so."

Lije scowled. "Perhaps, King, you'd do me the favor of keeping an eye on Tony when he gets there." Lije coughed. "You've been in the business world and on your own long enough to know what the score is. Tony, unfortunately, has not. He's quite green, you see, and I'm a little concerned about him."

It was an understatement. Lije Merrick was extremely anxious about his son, although it would not do to say so. He had spoiled the boy, and he was paying for it now. He should have insisted from the beginning that Tony learn the business from the docks and counting rooms on up, but he had not because Tony had resisted. Tony had none-too-subtly suggested that he would rather work for Warner Hall, out in Mill Village, and learn how to run a mill, than to work for his own father learning the West India Trade. It had hurt! That his only son should admire a millwright—worthy, to be sure (his wife's mother, after all, was a Hall, from a long line of estimable millers), yet this boy would pass an opportunity such as Lije offered in favor of such a mundane employment . . . it was unthinkable. Acidly he pointed out that Hall was on the edge of closing his mill for lack of business (which shortly thereafter Hall did), that a man needed his son to carry forward what he'd begun, that if Tony knew what was good for him. . . . To soften his insistence, he had let Tony omit the basics, and Tony had warmed a comfortable chair in the inner office for two years—now Lije was cramming information into him as a goose for *pâté de foie gras*. How much of it Tony understood, there was no way of knowing!

"I'm sure Tony will do well," Lije Merrick insisted, more for his own benefit than Kingsley's. "I have no doubts on that score. But it will, naturally, take him a while to acclimatize himself and I am hoping you will—er—help him out if need be."

"Would you like me to write you from time to time?" Kingsley asked. "I'd be glad to. I might be able to give you a better idea than Tony can about the feasibility of opening a branch of Merrick and Son." He smiled pleasantly. "For all you know, you might be better off simply to leave him with Baker and Company."

Lije Merrick was not pleased that Kingsley had seen into the situation so clearly, and he rose abruptly to cover his exasperation.

"That will be unnecessary," he said, moving toward the door to indicate the interview was over. "I can judge that for myself. It's been a pleasure to chat with you, King. How long can you stay with us?"

"I was planning to go tomorrow or the next day—or the one after," he said. "I can hire a room at the Golden Ox, Uncle, if I am inconveniencing you."

"No, indeed! Certainly you aren't!" Uncle Lije exclaimed with false heartiness. He had planned to return to Boston as soon as the Universalist dignitaries could be packed off, and he wished that Kingsley would be gone by then. His family was going to linger a while in Waterford, and he did not want them subjected to anything untoward. In the back of his mind he pictured all the Slaters coming up from West Waterford to visit their kinsman in the big old house so much more grand than any of theirs. Or worse, he would picture a slight given one of his tender daughters, by the daughter of a mariner, a dig in the direction of Kingsley's unpleasant background—none of which was his fault, none of which could be avoided.

Yet this young man, he had to admit it, was likable and apparently very able. Lije was unwilling to be less than cordial; it might redound unpleasantly on Tony. . . .

"Naturally, you must stay as long as you like," he said firmly—so firmly that Kingsley rather thought he meant it.

"My thanks," he smiled, and extended his hand.

There was a door from Uncle Lije's lair to the back hall, and Kingsley quietly let himself into the small room that was his for the night, too excited to sleep and nearly too excited to rest, though he stretched out on the little bed, kicked off his boots, and crossed his hands beneath his head. He did not gloat over his success with his uncle, nor did he bemoan the loss of his house, his only inheritance. Both were way stations, at which he had no need to stop. Kingsley Merrick was not interested in step by step victories or miniscule defeats,

61

only in the final victory of succeeding where he meant to succeed.

He thought about Australia for a long, happy time, and then his mind swung to Angelina Winslow, upon whom he would call tomorrow (to the displeasure of Sears Bradley, he hoped), and then he slept, easily, peacefully. . . .

To be the recipient of his uncle's cordiality was a pleasant thing. To sit with him in the parlor, talking Australian prospects, the future of Merrick and Son and the Clipper Coach Line, as though he were welcomed there and had always been—it was sweet and heady, and Kingsley reveled in it. He chatted easily with Uncle and Aunt's friends, the Duncans, and with the girls hanging onto every word (except for Julia, who was too interested in her puzzle to leave it). He, with the rest of the family, waved good-bye to the Universalist dignitaries when Uncle Lije took them to the packet, and then he walked the beach with Tony, enjoying the waning morning and the sea and sand. The weather was deteriorating and promised rain, but the day was warm and the air soft; Tony, intent now to learn as much about Kingsley's schemes as he could, for once attentive to someone other than himself, had never been better company.

How long had he wished and needed to have something like this, something that he belonged to and that belonged to him as the family of Uncle Lije seemed to now. He was to depart soon and leave it all behind, but still he was at peace, at ease with himself and his situation. Now he was part of them, important to them. He had long needed a place to go, and from their behavior now Kingsley gathered that his uncle's family was willing that he be with them. Uncle Lije must have put a bee in everyone's bonnet!

How cordial Aunt Elizabeth had been this morning, no doubt as a result of learning from Uncle Lije that the old house was to be theirs, to dispose of as they pleased, and that Kingsley was no longer going to balk them on it as he had before whenever they had offered to buy it. She as well as Uncle Lije was relieved to know Tony would not be without aid, if he needed it, in far off Melbourne, and knowing Kingsley was agreeable in all things was sufficient, he supposed, to kindle that flame of kinship which had been so feeble for so long. He had proved his worthiness in all respects!

Perhaps, he wondered, much of his suspicion of Uncle Lije

and the family was unfounded, or imagined by himself as a result of the unjust and unkind treatment he had received at the hands of Waterford's elite. Perhaps he had simply assumed that the family of Lije Merrick also disdained him, even as did Waterford. Truly the grudging invitations to Bowdoin Square were infrequent, and certainly he had not imagined the many occasions when they had excused him from their presence, when they camped in Waterford and he was yet a child. . . . Still, what did it signify now? He might as well let bygones be bygones. It was the only way. A man did not travel far with a chip on his shoulder, and decisively he cast his off, permitting himself to enjoy his morning's walk with Tony (the talk turned to girls of easy virtue whom Tony hoped would be found in Melbourne). And he enjoyed the light luncheon Aunt Elizabeth prepared, gaily talking with his cousins about New York fashion and society, viewed by him at a distance, and when the meal was finished, he announced grandly that he would be spending the afternoon at Angelina Winslow's house and he hoped that they would excuse him, because it was high time he was on his way. Aunt Elizabeth stared in wonderment and his cousins gaped and Tony whistled softly, under his breath.

"You do move fast, King!" he exclaimed in admiration, and all in all, Kingsley was well satisfied as he let himself out the front door of his uncle's house, more at peace with himself and Waterford than he had ever been. For the whole visit had not been so bad, had it? If certain slights had occurred, they may well have been unintentional ones, and at Aunt Sarah's, more than likely, they had been brought on by the mutual interests of folk who lived here in town, their lives directed by ships rather than any design to make him feel uncomfortable. If he had been uncomfortable, it had been his own fault, he told himself as he set out for the Winslows' along the highroad, past the churches which glared at each other, and a half mile beyond them, where the Winslows lived. The sky was overcast now, and birds were singing loudly as they waited for rain; the colors and textures of Waterford, its gleaming paint and slate roofs and the road itself and the trees that hung over it were heightened, made deeper, given a richer weave, delightful to behold.

He nearly laughed aloud! His spirits were high, because he was going to Angelina's house, at her own invitation, and Angelina was a fair flower, indeed! He had not wanted to stay in Waterford any longer than he had to, but now it seemed there was no reason to hurry. Perhaps if the weather cleared, if the Winslows were willing and Angelina was, too, he might take her out riding with him tomorrow in his hired rig. Why, he had seen only a bit of the Cape since he had come back. There were many places he would like to reacquaint himself with, and how better than to go riding? Perhaps he would take her to Rockford by the West Gate, through the sheep pastures he had loved as a boy, and on to the south shore, so different from the north because of its paucity of deep water captains, but a refreshing change, with fishing important there and picturesque wharves and dories abounding, traps and nets and flakes of cod drying odoriferously in the sun. Perhaps Angelina would enjoy it, viewed from the respectability of a carriage, and perhaps on the way home, stopping to rest the horse under a tree overlooking one of the pretty ponds that abounded everywhere, perhaps from Angelina's pretty lips he might take a kiss, if she permitted it . . . or two. One had to proceed carefully with gently bred girls, he knew, though his acquaintance with girls of her kind was hardly extensive. Still, she could not be made of ice. In Kingsley's experience, no girl ever was. And Angelina, after all, had done her best to encourage his attentions. . . .

He climbed the Winslow steps.

"I'm sorry, Mr. Merrick. My daughter is not receiving today."

He stared at the plump, well-corsetted, richly draped person of Mrs. Winslow. "Are you sure?" he asked foolishly, before he got his wits about him. "She asked me here herself."

"Perhaps you misunderstood," Mrs. Winslow said firmly.

From the open door he could hear a low, masculine voice and the response of a gentle, soft one. It was Angelina, he knew, already being entertained, probably by Sears Bradley. Still, he could not take it in, so lulled had he been by his sense of well-being that had grown throughout the morning.

"Perhaps if you would tell your daughter I am here," he persisted, "she could make up her own mind as to whether or not she will receive me."

"Her mind is made up already. She will not receive you—now or ever," Mrs. Winslow said in icy disdain. "I have told her about you, Mr. Merrick, and she understands now that meeting you is unsuitable. Good day, sir."

A gaunt hollowness was creeping into him; a great cavern of emptiness was opening deep, deep within, its depths unplumbed and yawning wide.

Her steely glare dared him to argue the matter further. She waited for him to say good-bye, waited for him to back down and he did. There was nothing else he could do.

"Good day to you," he said feebly, and hastened off the porch before the door should be closed in his face.

Once in the road he kept on walking, because he could not just stand there, in front of her house. He did not look back to see if anyone were watching him from the window, and he did not glance at any of the other houses along the road, either, to see if anyone else were witness to his humiliation. He was not sure just where he would go, but he kept walking, steady and unhurried, as though a stroll were exactly his intention just then. Stalking him was despair, long-feared, long-fought.

The day had made up its mind for fog. Already mist was floating about on a gentle breeze, cooling his hot face and settling on his coat in tiny glistenings.

He had been too quick, acted too hastily in his confusion. He should have continued walking west, toward Mill Village, where he could have looked up his cousin Jerry Slater and his friend Jon Stevens—where at least the balance of the afternoon could be passed among the folk he knew best—but he could not turn around, past the Winslows' house again, possibly to be seen wandering around Waterford like the stray he was. He had to go somewhere, before the fog changed to drizzle, and he wondered if it would be possible to sneak up to his room at Uncle Lije's without anyone knowing he was there. It was imperative not to be seen, because he could not explain his sudden reappearance after assuring them all so casually, in so offhand and grand a manner, that he would be occupied for the balance of the afternoon. Perhaps, he hoped hopelessly, everyone would be going out later and he could sneak in. . . .

Oh, Kingsley Merrick, he told himself, creeping around the side of Lije's house farthest from the parlor, you have been such a goddamned jackass!

In the pantry, the window of which was above his head and opened slightly, he heard his cousin Hetty counting.

"Ten, eleven, twelve. There. That takes care of the forks. Well, at least *he* isn't here," she went on. "And I'd a lot sooner have the Blakes to tea without him."

"Now, now," came Aunt Elizabeth's voice in absentminded remonstrance. "How many slices of pound cake do you think I ought to cut?"

"Nine," Hetty said promptly, and there was a metallic bang as she set down a tray and put cups upon it, a rattling of silver as she counted out spoons. "Ten, eleven, twelve. If we cut a piece for everybody, then everybody will take one. But if there aren't enough to go around the ladies will refrain—good for their figures, too. If Kingsley were here he'd probably eat cake with his fingers. I'm sure I don't know why Angelina Winslow tolerates him."

"You're just jealous of her." It was Julia's voice; apparently she had been there all along. "Men like her, and they don't like you."

"Now, now," Aunt Elizabeth remonstrated without conviction.

"I'd rather be an old maid than have a scruffy character like Kingsley pay attention to me."

"He's not scruffy," Julia protested. "His suit looked brand-new to me."

"Bought for the occasion, no doubt," sniffed Hetty Merrick. "And isn't that just like a New Yorker? At Aunt Sarah's house he spilled punch all down the front of it, too. Doesn't even know how to handle a punch glass! Well, I suppose I can bear it, being nice to him for Tony's sake. He'll be gone soon enough."

Aunt Elizabeth's sigh was audible even from under the lilac, where Kingsley crouched. "I hope Tony doesn't see too much of Kingsley in Melbourne. I suspect his language and perhaps some of his habits are just a little crude."

"What habits?" Julia asked.

"Never mind, dear," said Aunt Elizabeth. "Will you take the tray in, please?"

Their voices trailed away. "I think he should have stayed with his cousins in Mill Village," Hetty's words drifted back. "Why the whole time, between the dedication and Aunt Sarah's party, he sat drinking himself silly in the kitchen. He's very declassé, Mother."

"Well, don't remind me," Aunt Elizabeth said irritably. "It doesn't help, knowing Tony . . ." her voice was gone.

The lilac blooms bending low nodded slightly as Kingsley stole away from them.

So, he thought, *that is how the land lies.*

Damn the family of Uncle Lije!

Damn the mother of Angelina Winslow.

Damn the whole of this damnable place!

He slipped behind the barn, where he would be hidden from

view; running from the barn was an old and nearly obscured path that he remembered led to the old Merrick place.

That was where he would go! Where else, but his own house, which would not be his much longer because he'd sold it. Well, it would do for now, it was a harbor, a haven from this blank, empty featureless afternoon with nothing to redeem it, nothing to soften the harsh pain in his gut, the foul taste in his mouth, the gnawing, eating anger and bitterness.

He let himself in at the back, brushing the mist from his coat and hat, looking about to accustom himself to the dimness of the old kitchen and trying to still the quivering tautness that gripped him. The house smelled musty and felt damp and was dark in all its corners. He fumbled for his flask and, leaning on a windowsill, fortified himself with a heavy swallow. Perhaps it would be better outside in the mist, after all. The house was terribly oppressive and even cold. Perhaps it would be warmer in the attic; perhaps the heat of yesterday's sun still lingered there. He climbed the steep stairs.

Yes, it was quite comfortable, though crowded with a jumble of dilapidated furniture, some of which he identified as belonging to Grandfather, insufficient for the style Uncle Lije deemed proper to himself, carted over here to moulder.

He dragged a chair he thought would hold him to the window facing west, and found a tottering candle stand on which to set his flask. The small window overlooked the west meadow across which was Grandfather's house, screened by trees, and the barn and outbuildings. There was no sign of life there, and he guessed the family were all busy with their entertainment of the Blakes, perhaps playing games or music or cards; there would be a fire on the hearth and the parlor would be warm and cheery, the girls' voices would be raised in happy laughter and from the kitchen would drift delicious smells of bread baking or the cake they would serve. It would all be very domestic and happy. It had always been.

Sitting there, the quiet of the old house suddenly intense, an occasional creaking here or there suddenly loud for the stillness, he remembered past years when Uncle Lije's family spent the summers at Waterford, staying with Grandfather or old Captain Gray, lighting their days with laughter and setting the hours spinning with their schemes and plans: a ride in a cart on the flats, perhaps, or a picnic under Grandfather's tallest salt vat. He remembered their pleasure in a swing that Uncle Lije had hung in Grandfather's orchard, the little girls like bright birds in their softly tinted dresses, flying in and out among the apple and pear trees, their delighted cries hanging in the summer air. . . . He had watched them from the barn loft, peeping out craftily so they would not see him and send him home. He remembered going back once in the autumn after they had left, swinging on that swing, hoping to feel for himself the effortless joy they seemed to find in it. But it was not there for him as he swung, back and forth, in the clear October day, the trees of the orchard golden and their falling leaves floating around him. He had gotten off the swing, then, and had stood under the trees, wondering what the enchantment had been and why he could not find it, too, and then Grandfather had come by, silently taking Kingsley's hand. They had walked down to the pond together and sailed small boats made of twigs, and Kingsley had been comforted, somehow, without a word being said, without having to tell Grandfather that he was lonely. . . .

The loneliness closed in on him now, inexorable, rising whole from those long-gone years.

Abruptly he moved the chair so that he would not have the house in his line of sight. He looked past it to the fields and the bay, shrouded now in mist so that only affirmation of them made them real. Across the bay he would escape this night! He would go back to Uncle Lije's house for supper because he must, but he would take the rig back to Yarmouth afterward. There was a packet run tonight, he was quite sure, and if he missed it there'd be another tomorrow morning.

He finished his flask quickly, deliberately, so that the warmth of the liquor would chase away the remainder of coldness that clutched at him; he leaned back, tipping the chair and putting his feet on the window sill, deliberately and with great effort putting Waterford and the family of his uncle from him, setting his mind to drift to that continent under the sea, on the other side of the world, where it was winter now and the days short. There would be no snow, he had learned, only rain. The trees did not drop their leaves there, he had learned, and the summers were torrid; he wondered if the ocean were a different hue and if the sky was a different blue from the shade he was accustomed to; the stars would be changed, he knew, and he fixed his mind on them and on the Australian earth beneath whose unknown texture lay gold and on which lay the future—possibly the whole lifetime—of Kingsley Merrick, a future he could claim wholly for his own, a land that would be wholly his. In that moment he yearned for it deeply, passionately, achingly and waited, waited for the

68

afternoon to pass, waited to quit Cape Cod, waited for the time that he would be free to go to that far-off land and do with it what he could . . . and put behind him the curse that was Waterford.

Two
Julia 1857

Sedately, Julia Merrick walked at Adam Levering's side, careful not to brush against him inadvertently, nor trip on the uneven cobbles of the street, nor on the frost-heaved bricks of sidewalks, because at any sign of unsteadiness Adam might well put a guiding hand beneath her elbow and she would rather he did not. She would rather he remained exactly as he was—beside her, with at least six inches between them, made happy by her presence, full of admiration for her and convinced that his admiration was returned in full. She was careful to let Adam do the talking, demurely following his lead, encouraging him when he needed it, and all the while she soaked up the sights and sounds of Boston in the spring, the happiest of all seasons. She walked slowly, as became a lady, even while her feet in their black high shoes itched to dance—for it was spring, when laughter and exuberance bubbled up and over. Wouldn't it be fine to be a colt put out to pasture, running for the joy of it!

Most of Beacon Hill was built in blocks of handsome brick with bowed fronts and little balconies above the street, but here and there a solitary mansion stood alone amid its lawns and gardens, which were greening up vigorously, promising their fulfillment of lilacs and primroses. Already the tulips were in bloom, with daffodils not far behind, and the edge of the breeze was rounded with warmth and gentleness instead of the raw sharpness of winter. When they turned onto Joy Street spring was on them in earnest as they looked down to the Boston Common blazing green with the arching trees overhead in bud. They breathed the soft, strong scents of the ground; the golden dome of the Capitol winked as they passed it by and the bricks of Boston glowed on Park Street and on the houses across Fremont Street and on those lining Beacon. Birds sang, and on the Common itself, along its paths and by its malls, thronged the citizens of West Boston, out to see the arrival of spring in the city, ready to ignore the occasional odors of the Back Bay now at low tide, wafting its stink toward the Common by an errant breeze.

It was Sunday afternoon, which accounted for the crowd, and which accounted also for Adam Levering's presence at her side. By day he worked at his uncle's office in the business district near the wharves of Boston Harbor, but this day, morning church and the dinner accounted for, he had called for Julia at Miss Easton's house at 3 Bowdoin Square where the Merricks lived. He had squired Julia about all winter, and because his family was a well-known and respected one, and because Adam Levering was a very model of courtesy and propriety, Julia was allowed to walk with him unaccompanied by any of her sisters, provided Adam handed her back to her parents by five o'clock. And Adam would.

"How fine it is to see the seasons change," Adam was saying. "And how fine it is to be walking in the springtime with you, Julia!"

"It is pleasant, isn't it," she agreed. "I'm so glad you enjoy walking, Adam! Ellen and Clara don't, and Hetty is too old to be any fun—I do very much enjoy going out with someone who is interesting to talk to."

"I hope," he said earnestly, "that it isn't only my conversational ability that causes you to come walking with me."

"Why, Adam," she teased. "What else could there be?"

His cheeks became quite red, and he grinned widely in an effort to seize and hold her banter. "Because I am good-looking?" he offered. He was not.

"I would never allow a person's appearance to determine my judgment about him," she assured him. "I would not come out with you just because you were nice to behold."

His smile wavered. "But this summer you won't be here," he said disconsolately. "Who will I walk with then?"

It was the third time—she'd been counting—that he'd brought up that fact, and it was very gratifying! Perhaps before summer he'd try to do something about it; certainly today he was full of personal allusions and suggestions that more lay in their relationship than met the eye—on such a day as this, with romance fairly hitting him over the head, he'd have to be numb not to! Julia thought everything was progressing very well. She refrained from breaking out into a skip.

"Ah, yes, summer," she murmured vaguely.

"Here we are," Adam declared, pausing near a tree on the river side of the Common. "On this very spot I first met you!" He looked over the ground with an air of satisfaction.

74

"And here," she tapped the soggy grass with her toe, "stood Sally!"

"And there, beside you, were your sisters. All because of that scoundrel, Charles Sumner, bless his benighted soul."

The well-born Sumner was not highly regarded among the upper echelons of Boston, from whence many of Adam's opinions came. Julia's own father opposed abolition, too, and so Julia understood this point of view although she did not share it. There was a tricky path to follow, between the sentiments of Adam Levering with which she did not care to argue, and her own conviction, which she had no intention of forsaking. But she was accustomed to the footing.

"Let's be glad a lot of people admired him," she said earnestly. "Else we'd not have brushed elbows long enough to get acquainted!"

Adam laughed. "I *am* very glad, Julia. And surely you are aware of it!"

She smiled for him, and demurely averted her eyes.

"Would you enjoy walking across the mill dam?" Adam asked.

"Perhaps it would be better to head up Beacon Street instead," she said regretfully. "We wouldn't have to hurry if we started home now, but if we detoured across the dam, I believe we'd have to run to reach Bowdoin Square by five o'clock. Besides, the dam is the most fun when the gates are open, and they'll be closed now."

"Sally likes it then, too," Adam said.

"My sister Ellen says it makes her afraid she'll throw herself in. She won't cross it unless she's in a carriage—preferably a closed one!"

"I don't blame her, if that's the way she feels."

Julia laughed. "But is it! I'm never sure. Sometimes I think it's only something she's talked herself into."

"She would fear it, nonetheless."

"Why, how right you are!" she exclaimed with admiration unfeigned. Adam, she thought, displayed considerably more sensitivity than she did, when it came to the feelings of other people. That was one of the things she liked about him. It was only a minor reason why she would marry him if she could—but it was, perhaps, the most decent one. As for the rest—well, was it indecent to marry someone because he provided an alternative—an escape—if he proved to be the answer to years of desolate wandering in her soul? Not because of himself, but because of what he could provide, the doors he could open, the people he knew? Perhaps it would

75

be indecent, she thought, if she did not like him. But she did like Adam (she told herself), and he had many fine qualities (she enumerated them frequently to herself) quite separate from what he might do for her if he chose. And she could make him happy. She *would* make him happy! The pall of indecency passed by.

Adam directed their meanderings along the river to Beacon Street.

"Sally is planning a cotillion," Adam said, in an offhand manner. "It will be a modest one as these things go. Business is rather at sixes and sevens just now, and doesn't warrant a big splash. But my uncle promised her a dance this spring, and Sally is bound to have one. Do you think you'd enjoy attending it?"

Her a heart gave a great bound, and it was difficult not to stop on the spot, clap her hands, click her heels in the air. "I don't know," she said casually, hoping her color wasn't rising. "Do you think I'd have a good time?"

"I can assure it," he promised. "I'll see to it myself that you enjoy yourself."

"My parents . . ." she began.

"They will be invited, too. Naturally."

Naturally. And would they, too, have an enjoyable evening? It was not a question she could put to Adam, yet whether or not the Merricks were made comfortable, welcomed, and waited upon would be very significant. It would be their opportunity to meet Adam's aunt and uncle and his mother, and if such a meeting went well, if all parties went out of their way to make sure that it did . . .

"Sally is drawing up her guest list now. Your name will be included, if you want it to be."

That would mean that Adam would ask Sally to include the Merricks—otherwise, Julia's name would be on that list whether she expressed a preference or not. Adam, bless his heart, was working things out in his own way and in his own time—and what could be more satisfactory than that?

"I think it would be very nice of Sally, were she to include me," Julia said. "And if you will promise me that you'll attend, too . . ."

"Oh, I'll be there," he said, and smiled at her in his sweet, benign way. "And if you'll let me, I'll claim three dances, too."

"I might let you," she prevaricated mischievously.

"Oh, please, do!"

"If you are very nice to me in the intervening time."

"I shall be."

"Will you write me a poem?"

"I shall write you dozens."

"Very well," she said. "I'll consider the three dances very seriously."

They walked slowly along Beacon Street, each happy if for differing reasons, and she was sure—just as sure as she could be—that he loved her.

"I'm glad we didn't have to hurry," he said as they approached the fenced-off trees and shrubbery that lay in the middle of Bowdoin Square. "Not on such a day as this. Isn't it lovely, that spring is here?"

She had not been happy when she had first met Adam, last fall when Charles Sumner rode into Boston. She was too old to go to school anymore. She had finished with Mrs. Hunt, and there was nothing to do after a pleasantly dull, idle summer in Waterford with her best friends, Caro and Prissy. Once back in the city there were lectures, of course, and afternoon tea and church on Sunday and the procession of young men, sons of Papa's business associates who came to call upon the Merrick sisters. There were the daughters of Papa's associates with whom to gossip and giggle and there were Clara and Ellen and Hetty, omnipresent, and if Julia had known discontent and restlessness before (she had known them, off and on, all her life), it was nothing compared to that time, when the barren sterility of life in the middle class stared her relentlessly in the eye. Now at seventeen she had come up smack against the general expectation that a young woman was pure of mind and empty of any purpose save that of domesticity, able with grace and loveliness to keep the fires burning in the hearth or to direct the energies of servants to do so, a virtual model of restraint and absolute in her devotion to her husband who would be a paragon of manhood, who could never make a mistake and who would deserve every ounce of devotion that his wife would lavish on him—and pretty soon Julia would have to find such a man. And when she married him, she would spend the rest of her life in gentle supervision of his children, in the performance of flawless needlework which was supposed to represent her highest attainment and achievement—and she would carefully adorn herself in expensive clothing and drink tea with other women of her class, like them absorbed in fashion and fancywork and the fiction in the multitudes of ladies' magazines now flooding the market, a woman interested only in her appearance and who cultivated idleness because she could afford to, and because her husband would insist upon it in order to demonstrate to the world that he was a success!

The Merricks spent long periods of time in Waterford, where there were no servants and idleness was not possible. Julia loved it there and always had—yet it was in Waterford she learned (to her sorrow) that domesticity was no more joyous than idleness! Washing and ironing, dusting and scrubbing, mending and cooking were not only irksome, but they left time for nothing else. Were she to eschew the upper middle class to which Papa aspired and instead marry a Waterford captain, if she could snag one, she would have everything she needed—clothing and good food and as many books as she wanted—but no time to read them, and no time to cultivate any interests at all. She would become banal, she would suffocate, stagnate, grow dull, for she would be no better off than if she married and lived in Boston, as far as the employment of her talents and abilities were concerned. She would be more independent, as wives of deep water captains had to be—but deeply mired by domestic chores. Truly it did appear that to be a respectable woman was the kiss of death—yet it was important to be respectable. No one, not even Julia in her wildest moments, doubted that!

Perhaps the answer lay in spinsterhood, even if that state implicitly admitted the failure to find her true place in life. But Julia was considering it quite seriously, that fall when she met Adam Levering. She would, after all, never have a place. She never had fitted where she belonged, though she had tried hard, very hard. With all her heart she had eschewed sliding down the banister at Waterford and climbing into the unused fireplaces at night to look up and see the stars, as though she were at the bottom of a well. She had refrained, after she'd been ten years old, from running when she was on the beach, letting her hair stream behind her in a wind of her own making; valiantly she had striven to remember always to wear her bonnet and gloves when she left the house and to restrain her gestures and modulate her voice; Mama was always upset when Julia spoke loudly, as she was so apt to do! She learned to play the piano simply and without emotion when Mama was there to hear, and to speak sweetly to her sisters even when their docility frustrated and maddened her. It was important to learn these things and keep them learned because Mama was so disturbed when Julia forgot, ultimately to resort to weeping when it seemed that Julia would never be able to take up the responsibilities inherent in her position as a Merrick daughter. Julia hated to see her mother cry. It made her feel so badly, so guilty to have caused distress. Her sisters, after all, seemed able to acquire the necessary graces (even if Hetty was a bit tart); the only person who had ever applauded her harem-scarum ways was her cousin Kingsley, whose kindness to her several years ago, when she was alone and in disgrace, she had never forgotten. But Kingsley's approbation was hardly desirable; if anything, it pointed to the error of her ways, because her family neither respected nor liked him much. If he were the only sort of person willing to abet her, why, then, something was very wrong—with her!

Miserably she had striven to follow Mama's precepts and example of decorum and ladylike behavior; uncomfortably she had mastered them with only occasional lapses now and then, convinced it was she who erred and that she must make herself want to be a lady, because that was the pinnacle of achievement.

Her whole life, until she was fifteen, was like a balance sheet, which recorded whether or not she had managed all the rules that day or whether she had failed in any, and if so, those were the ones to be worked on more diligently tomorrow. But the year she was fifteen—oh!—that year she went to Mrs. Hunt's school, and after that everything was different. It was at Mrs. Hunt's that she discovered the difficulty: it lay not so much in the rules for the conduct of a young lady as in the fact that life, as she had known it, provided nothing to relieve the frustration of restraint. It would not be so hard to fall into the proper patterns of behavior, she found, if the mind were occupied with things worthy of it and if the society surrounding it were stimulating, challenging, and eventful. For it was at Mrs. Hunt's school that Julia saw that the life she had lived until that time was suddenly, unbearably flat, like a portrait. It suddenly became a canvas on which was painted her family and herself and all the Merrick friends dressed properly and reading proper books, expressing proper sentiments and never, ever, uttering a single thought that had not been simply passed one to the other, dog-eared and with the most significant words underlined. Upon that canvas were painted no surprises, and there was no animation there. Everything, Julia came to realize, was static at Bowdoin Square and even in Waterford—but life was not of necessity bounded by these two places. She found that out at Mrs. Hunt's, too; it was there that Julia discovered Beacon Hill.

To be enrolled at Mrs. Hunt's school was rather a feather in one's bonnet, because the aristocrats of West Boston enrolled their daughters there. Mrs. Hunt was very particular about her pupils, and the difficulty attendant on going to her school heightened its desirability, and because of that, Mrs. Hunt's views passed unchallenged in the Merrick household: that literature was more important than needlework, that natural science was more necessary than dancing, that knowing arithmetic was more essential than watercolor painting. Mrs. Hunt insisted that girls had minds as able as boys and should know how to use them, and Beacon Hill believed her. No matter if no one else did! If the mamas and papas of Beacon Hill went along with it, no further recommendation was needed, no further investigation required. Papa had had no luck enrolling Hetty or Ellen or Clara, and they had acquired the usual education which included needlework, dancing, and watercoloring. But when Julia's turn came there had been a vacancy for her. Perhaps her parents' forsaking the Congregational church to become Unitarians had something to do with it. Mrs. Hunt was a Unitarian, too, and Papa had seen to it that the Merrick pew was in plain view of Mrs. Hunt, so that she could not fail to notice his daughter. In any case, Julia had been admitted the year she was fifteen, and it was then she met Sally Levering and other girls like her.

They had not become intimate friends, she and Sally. That could hardly be expected, for there was a big, big gap between a Beacon Hill heiress and the daughter of a West Indies goods importer who boarded at 3 Bowdoin Square! But Sally was a lively, high-spirited girl with so much confidence and poise that she had been more than willing to sit with Julia during the luncheon recesses, disregarding that gap because it did not concern her. She had willingly shared her desk and some of her secrets, too, and because of that friendship, however casual it had been on Sally's part, the other girls at Mrs. Hunt's had been nice to Julia, too, and through them she had learned a lot about the lives of people so wealthy they could have lived in style from the income of their funds alone. In the drawing rooms of those girls their mothers entertained Mr. Longfellow and Mr. Holmes, Mr. Agazziz and Mr. Emerson. There music was played and appreciated; neither politics nor fashion was discussed, but only books and art; business, Julia gathered, was relegated to the Somerset Club, next to the Gardiners' house, and there the men of Beacon Hill gathered, leaving their ladies free, for the most part, to work their will in the drawing room. When men and women met together they ate dinners with uncountable courses and danced in elegant surroundings and talked with one another in spirited, witty, uplifting conversation, in which the arts were primary and business forsaken.

She had not discovered all these things at once. She pieced them together from the scraps of conversation she heard from the girls at Mrs. Hunt's, from Sally's shared confidences (wherein Julia emphasized heavily the Merrick country estate on Cape Cod), and twice she had gone to a tea room with Sally, as though they were grown up, where Sally treated her to wonderful pastries and received the deference of the waiters with becoming modesty. Sally had seemed the most desirable friend in the world, and from Sally's artless conversation Julia learned all she needed to know. She learned that the men on Beacon Hill did not talk about money when in the presence of ladies—it was considered crude. She learned that if the men there did not personally admire the shining lights of New England cultural and intellectual attainment embraced by the Transcendentalists, by Brooke Farm, by Longfellow's writings and Emerson's notoriety, they did not interfere with the support, financial and spiritual, that their women contributed to it.

She learned that women on Beacon Hill were not relegated to the hearth, either to labor there on its behalf or in the adornment of it. Women, on Beacon Hill, were not fashion-plate advertisements of their husband's business prowess, nor did they pass their days vying with one another to outdo the last entertainment, thus to capture the leadership of society. Perhaps these things were done among the upper classes in New York City, but that only demonstrated the incontestable inferiority of New York City society. These things were not Bostonian, nor did they reflect the essence of Beacon Hill. Beacon Hill had better things to do, and went about doing them! And in the process, something very profound had occurred on behalf of womankind for there a woman might, if she wished, be entirely herself.

Herself! She might read poetry and write it and gather together poets in her parlor and invite everyone to listen to them.

Herself! She might read, and write vignettes or literary things, and invite writers to her drawing room where their brilliant, flashing minds might stimulate one another, and she could invite anyone else there whose talent might lend itself to the group thus gathered.

Herself! She might learn music and play it and gather to herself others who did the same, and they might even capture

81

a composer and exhibit him in the drawing room, and music was Julia Merrick's joy! Music was her undoing, her passion, the liberator of her spirit. Yes, upon Beacon Hill, her spirit might be liberated as a way of life! The understanding that upon Beacon Hill regularly occurred the brilliant, bantering, highcharged free flow of ideas as well as the expectation of excellence, after the countless hours of studied stultified conversation at Miss Easton's parlor, glittered in her mind's eye like the nativity star she'd read of in her Bible. Compared to Bowdoin Square and Waterford, the stimulus found in the drawing rooms of West Boston was enough to set Julia to longing for it with a nearly sickening intensity—to dream of it, and dream, and dream of a life uncluttered by small, petty convention, a life free to wander among all the ideas of man, and all his art, to fly as high as the human soul could fly—the freedom for flight secured absolutely by the millions of dollars salted away by Beacon Hill men in their counting rooms, to be used on the things in life that counted, really counted! Beacon Hill did not parade its wealth; money was not squandered on the appearance of things; its gatherings were private and its circle small, zealously guarded from public view, even hidden—but what a glow, what a patina covered it! And beneath lay quality.

When Julia realized that Sally Levering and her friends would soon prepare for courtship and that their fathers would give them grand parties peopled with cultured and interesting men and women who dined opulently at tables stretching so far you couldn't even see to the end of them—then, Miss Easton's dining room seemed awfully small. The patterns of courtship, as Julia understood them (patterns like James Duncan's wooing of Ellen, which required a certain amount of parlor-sitting and sighing and then an accounting with Papa, more parlor-sitting and perhaps a party with friends of the family)—well, it seemed downright limited.

As for marriage itself, well! On Beacon Hill the parties would continue after one married, musical afternoons and evenings would be arranged, balls and receptions and elegant dinners, too. Long journeys would be taken, children, servants, linens, and all, to New York and Philadelphia and the continent. The rising new talents of the city would be entertained, the cream of European culture welcomed, witty and enlightening conversation, laughter and gaiety would not stop on Beacon Hill after marriage, not for Sally or the girls at Mrs. Hunt's who belonged to that society. But when Julia married all she could expect was miles of needlework (if she married in Boston) or piles of ironing (if she wed in Waterford). Life for a married woman of respectability anywhere but on Beacon Hill was more confined, more hemmed in and bound by expectation than ever it was before wedlock—and the good Lord knew there were plenty of restrictions before!

Perhaps it was disloyal to think this way! Perhaps it was disloyal to find content no longer in the bosom of her family, nor to honor any more the standards and values it maintained in defense of the status quo—but the damage was done. It was too late. Sally and the girls and Mrs. Hunt and Beacon Hill and the quality of life one might find there took on the aura of absolute desirability, and so Julia had been disconsolate at the prospect of not going to Mrs. Hunt's school any more. Sally and the other girls would disappear behind the drawing room doors of Beacon Hill, and there would be little reason for them to remember their schoolmate, Julia Merrick. Without that daily contact at school there would be nothing to bind them together, and they would be gone. The shining image of Beacon Hill would be gone, too, and soon enough—all too soon—that was exactly what happened. Julia spent the summer in Waterford and returned to the city in the fall to find Boston empty without Mrs. Hunt's school and her friendship with Sally Levering.

All fall she had languished, dispirited, with so little to hope for that it wasn't hard at all to be a lady, according to her mother's standards, because there was nothing exciting or interesting to cause her to forget her manners.

She snatched eagerly at the diversion of Charles Sumner's entry into the city in the middle of November. It was by far the most exciting thing since the fugitive slave had been marched through the city in 1851, returned forcibly to his master and amid hoots and howls of protest from nearly everyone. Now Senator Sumner, who had been severely beaten by a Southern member of the federal legislature in the cause of abolition, was coming to the city of his birth and breeding, and all Boston was agog with excitement. Papa did not like abolitionists of any sort—not many merchants did because abolition would mean the demise of the South and of cotton, which northern mills needed and the American merchant fleet carried—but Papa did not try to stop his daughters from going to the Common that day. Everyone would be there to welcome the hero, and not simply because of his cause. The pride of Boston would be demonstrated that day, and Papa was tempted to go himself, except for pressing matters at his office. Mama, of course, was not up to it (Mama was never up to anything strenuous). And so armed with money for gingerbread to buy from the vendors who were sure to be present, Julia and Clara, Hetty and Ellen, sticking close together, joined the mob that November day.

Oh, did not Boston turn out to see its hero! Folk who had never liked Sumner adored him now, and many people who had opposed abolition now championed it, since their man in Congress had been abused for its sake. It must be worthy, because Charles Sumner had paid so dearly for his belief in it!

The Common was filled right up to the brim. Beyond the Common people were packed into the streets that led to it— West and Winter Street, Walnut and Joy, all along Tremont and Boyleston and Charles and Park—and from windows and even rooftops, Boston cheered and shouted and waved handkerchiefs and hats . . .

The crowd hushed when Charles Sumner's carriage stopped before the state house, where Mr. Sumner mounted the steps under Boston's golden dome, but his voice and the voices of the other speakers barely carried down toward the Charles River, upon which portion of the Common Julia and her sisters were standing, munching gingerbread, trying to hear.

Then there was a prodding right in the middle of her back and a girlish, gleeful voice said into her ear, "If you are a fugitive slave, I will arrest you!" Startled, she had glanced over her shoulder to see who might be poking, laughed to discover Sally there, and because the crowd was so dense, not allowing much room for an over-the-shoulder conversation, she had inched her way completely around so that she could talk to Sally face to face, and beside Sally stood Adam Levering.

Her sisters were still facing the capital, but Julia had her back to it, and so dense was the crowd that Ellen and Clara and Hetty hardly even knew there was a conversation going on behind them. It had been necessary to speak in a conspiratorial manner, so as not to disturb the crowd straining in vain to hear what Charles Sumner said, and it had been fun.

"May I introduce my cousin, Adam Levering?" Sally said instantly.

"Shhhh!" hissed someone nearby.

"How do you do, Mr. Levering?" Julia had whispered to him.

"How do you do, Miss Merrick?" Adam Levering murmured. "Forgive me for not removing my hat." Indeed there was nowhere he could have put it, even had he been able to take it off. To even raise his hand to his head was nearly impossible.

"Remove it later," she whispered. "I'll pretend I don't see it." She turned to Sally. "I thought your father was a cotton whig!"

"He is," Sally giggled. "He doesn't know I'm here."

"Will he be mad with you?"

"Father is never mad with me," Sally assured her. "He isn't home long enough to be mad with anybody. It's Adam who will come up for censure."

"Nonsense," Adam insisted. "I couldn't let you come alone—and surely nothing was going to stop you!"

"No," Sally agreed blithely. "Nothing ever does."

"Hush!" an angry voice was heard to say.

Sally wrinkled her nose. "Well, almost nothing!" She whispered into Julia's ear. "Do you think my cousin is nice?"

"He appears to be," she whispered back.

"Good! I think the two of you would get along capitally. Are those your sisters?" Swiftly Sally had changed the subject, brushing by it so quickly that Julia had not paid it much attention, indeed, had forgotten it, until the engraved invitation to dinner had arrived at 3 Bowdoin Square a week later. Sally, having sized up the Merrick girls on the Common, invited Clara, too (for Julia could not have gone unaccompanied to a house not known by her parents), and the excitement in the Merrick room the day that the invitation arrived was intense.

"You've known Sally Levering for two years," Hetty pointed out. "Why does she bid you to a party now, having never done so before?"

She remembered Sally's remark, that Adam would get on well with Julia Merrick, but it would not do to air it now. If it appeared that Sally were matchmaking, Mama would not let Julia go to the Leverings' house, no matter how illustrious they were. Matchmaking was common, Mama would say, no matter who does it.

"How should I know what passes through Sally Levering's mind?" she answered Hetty casually. "Perhaps seeing me elsewhere than at school placed me in a different aspect than before."

"I didn't know you were so intimate with her," Clara breathed in admiration, thrilled to the core at the prospect of entering the Levering mansion where the other half lived.

"We got along together very well at Mrs. Hunt's," Julia assured her sister. "She's a girl after my own heart."

"Then she must be a nice person," Ellen said, sweet and devoted as Ellen always was. No doubt Ellen did not experience even a pang of jealousy that the invitation did not include her, and the more she thought about it, the more Julia wondered why Ellen, much prettier than Clara, had not been chosen.

Mama was willing for her girls to go; a carriage was hired to carry Julia and Clara to the mansion; endless hours spent deciding on suitable dresses and altering the lines on the ones chosen because no party was complete unless this fussing about took place. Only five days separated Julia from the arrival of the invitation to Sally's dinner, but she was sure those days would never pass! She had never attended a party on Beacon Hill although she had heard about them through comments made casually at Mrs. Hunt's school. Now she was actually going to one! For once Julia, generally uninterested in what she wore, paid close attention to the goings-on in the sitting room. She was careful to dress modestly and to make sure Clara did, too. (In the better circles in Boston you were considered ostentatious if you did not. You would be considered brassy, as if you were a New Yorker.)

"Never, never mention money," she cautioned Clara. "Never tell how much a thing costs, whether little or a lot."

People in Mama and Papa's set forever were setting a price on things—but it was not done on Beacon Hill where, in the midst of millions, frugality was considered a virtue.

"And don't talk about fashion, either," she went on. "If you admire someone's dress, say why you admire it—because of its color, or line—but not because it is popular this year."

Boston society did not have to be in fashion if it didn't want to be, and often it was not.

"Good grief!" Clara exclaimed. "What shall I talk about?"

It was a problem! Clara never read anything more enlightening than Mrs. Edgeworth's novels or the fiction in *Gleason's Drawing Room Companion*. Instantly Julia began to understand the value of education in and of itself; Clara's genteel girls' school training would show badly.

"Your biggest asset is your painting," Julia counseled her. "You've had a lot of art lessons, and you know good composition when you see it."

"Perhaps," Clara mumbled dubiously. Her passion was painting roses on china, and it did not include much composition since she happily copied whatever was set before her.

"Pass the conversation to someone else, whenever it's your turn to speak. Do a lot of listening; you can admire the pictures and portraits—there's dozens of them there, Sally has told me that. I don't think you'll have any trouble, Clara," she added kindly. "We'll stick together."

"I hope so!" Clara exclaimed. "I'm getting more nervous by the minute."

Were it not for Clara, Julia would have been painfully nervous herself. But in the presence of her sister who depended on her, she could not afford to let her nerves show, lest Clara lose her head. Why, oh why, had not Sally chosen Ellen!

She tried her best to appear cool and calm, that late afternoon when she and Clara rode in the hired carriage to the Levering house, but her heart was pumping so frantically that she could scarcely hear the hoofbeats of the horse that pulled her. The hand that held Clara's was cold and wet as they climbed up the steps to the Levering front door, her voice low and a little shaky as the door opened and she told the formally clad gentleman standing there: "The Misses Merrick."

But she remembered to hold her head high and proudly and to keep her back straight as she and Clara were permitted to enter the entrance hall, on the wall of which was mounted a massive coat of arms with crossed swords and unicorns prancing upon it, the floor of which was alternating blocks of black and white marble, like a checkerboard, at the rear of which was a huge, beautiful circular staircase leading to the drawing room.

At the doorway to the receiving room adjoining the hall stood Sally (thank goodness!), who held out both hands to Julia and cried, "Here she is!" Impulsively Sally kissed Julia's cheek, as though their friendship was dear to her, and more formally shook Clara's hand.

"It's a pleasure to meet you," Sally Levering assured Clara. "Julia has mentioned you so often."

Julia had not, but it was a matter of no importance now.

"How do you do, Miss Levering?" Clara quaked. "Your dress is so pretty; the line of it is charming."

"Why, thank you," Sally smiled, as though the success of the entire event rested secure in this compliment. "I should like to introduce you to my brother Cabot, who has been eager to meet you both."

Cabot Levering, hovering nearby, came to Sally's side, tall and dashingly handsome, certainly more handsome than anyone Julia had before known. Cabot Levering listened closely to the introduction as though the Merrick girls were people he had long wished to meet. He bowed to each and smiled with confidence and ease, and for all her fluster Julia remembered to smile that way, too. Beyond Cabot, over his shoulder, she could see groups of young people chattering comfortably with one another. Her relief was enormous when she recognized many of the girls from Mrs. Hunt's.

"How do you do, Mr. Levering?" she heard Clara croak. "My sister has told me all about your lovely pictures."

Young Levering looked startled for a moment. "Oh," he fumbled. "How nice. Which pictures?"

"Which pictures?" Clara asked Julia helplessly, utterly snarled and unable to extricate herself.

This is going to be worse than I thought, Julia told herself. Brightly she smiled at Sally's brother and at Sally. "I told her about the Copley portraits you mentioned to me one day."

"Oh, of course," Sally sang. "We'll get to those later. Just now, Cabot will take you around to meet anyone you don't already know."

"I don't know anyone at all," faltered Clara.

"Many thanks, Mr. Levering," Julia said quickly, hiding Clara's mumbles beneath her own words, taking Clara's arm while they turned away from Sally, who was already greeting another guest. "Just shut your mouth!" she hissed fiercely. "Before your foot gets stuck in it!"

Startled and hurt, Clara clung to her side as she managed to stroll into the receiving room in proximity to handsome Cabot Levering. The girls from Mrs. Hunt's greeted her with warmth, the young men nearby with polite attention, and in the far corner, toward which Cabot worked, stood Adam Levering, alone.

"Why, hello again, Miss Merrick!" said Adam, apparently surprised to see her. "How do you do?" he said to Clara.

"Fine, thank you," Clara promptly said. "Do you already know my sister?"

"I met her on the Common last week, when we went to see Mr. Sumner."

"Really!" exclaimed Clara. "I was there, too, but I didn't see you."

"That's what comes of paying attention to the business at hand," Julia teased her. "I was paying attention to Mr. Levering instead."

"You never said so," Clara objected. "You only mentioned seeing Sally there."

"I couldn't say anything about Mr. Levering because we had not been properly introduced," she said with a sly glance toward Adam.

"Who could be more proper than Sally?" he demanded.

"You never tipped your hat!" she reminded him. "So it wasn't proper, at all."

"By Jove, you're right!" he exclaimed. "And I don't even have one now, to remedy the error."

"You're inside," Clara said practically, "so how could you?"

There was a butler bearing down on them, a tray in his hands with small goblets on it.

"Wine, Miss Merrick?" he asked. She had to do a lot of restraining not to look surprised that he knew her name, being unaware that he was trained to do so.

"Why yes, thank you," she said, taking a glass and warning Clara, with a glance, to take one, too, and be quiet about it and make no mention of the habitual Merrick abstinence at 3 Bowdoin Square.

"Excuse me, if you will," Cabot Levering said, having lingered on the edge of their little group. "I think I will fetch myself whiskey. Care for any, Adam?"

"Wine is fine," Adam said. "Whiskey is frisky. I'd enjoy some very much," he added roguishly.

Cabot went away with great purpose; Julia saw that his trail cut a great swatch through the room as all the girls in it strove to catch his attention. The butler departed.

"Now that we need not whisper, Mr. Levering," Julia said, "perhaps you will tell me something of yourself. I think no one will hush us now."

"Who hushed you before?" Clara asked. Julia nudged sharply. "I'll explain later," she scowled. "How do you pass your time here in our city?" She smiled at Adam Levering.

"I am employed by Sally's father," he said. "I work in his Boston office, learning his business."

"What is his business?" Clara asked.

"You've heard of the Levering Mills at Lawrence?"

"Why, yes, of course," Clara stammered. "Don't tell me that they belong to Sally's father! I never dreamed. . . ."

Julia moved to cut off Clara's ill-concealed astonishment which, if she knew Clara, was going to lead to effusive declarations about how impressed she was. "Does Sally's brother work in the Boston office, too?" she asked loudly.

"Yes, he does," Adam said. "The mills will be his one day."

"All of them?" breathed Clara.

He grinned. "Maybe Uncle Levering will hold a small one aside for me, if I'm good enough."

Julia rather thought Adam Levering would welcome a change of subject.

"How long have you lived in Boston, Mr. Levering?"

"Just since the end of summer."

"I hope you are enjoying our town. Have you been to a Lowell lecture yet?"

"I'm afraid there hasn't been time for that," he admitted sadly. "Right now Cabot and I are supposed to be concentrating on business."

"And we have our noses to the grindstone, for sure!" Cabot had reappeared, bearing a drink for Adam in one hand and his own in the other.

"Adam tells me that you are in training to be a tycoon," she said demurely to Sally's brother.

"It is true," Cabot sighed in mock sadness. "A crass and commercial man of business like all those new rich folk who live in Boston now. Wouldn't it be more effete to confess I am an artist in disguise, or a musician? But no, I am simply in business. A friend of mine from Harvard is in Europe studying butterflies, having been trained for the bar, but we Leverings must still earn a living. I, too, am a mere drone."

And heir to a fortune besides, Julia thought. "Oh, surely you have latent talent to redeem your crass soul," she laughed.

"No. Not a shred. But Adam does—perhaps my association with him will redeem me. He writes poetry."

"Do you, Mr. Levering!"

"I do," he bowed. "It is atrocious."

"I don't believe it!"

"It is," Cabot said. "I assure you, he's telling the truth, but at least he is trying."

"I paint china," Clara announced.

"My sister is very clever with her brush," Julia said quickly. "We should like to hear your poems, sometime, Mr. Levering. It's my guess that they are better than you're letting on."

"I'd show them to you, gladly," Adam Levering said with eagerness. "But you must share your talents, too."

"You can see my roses, any time you want to," Clara said.

"I'll play the piano for you, if you'll read to us!" Julia laughed.

"Then I'll come to your house whenever you say," Adam declared. "Name the day."

"Oh, any time at all," Clara giggled.

"No, we shall have to check first to see when we are free," Julia said sedately, glaring at Clara. It would not do to seem too eager.

"Well," Cabot said vaguely, "I'm glad to see that some of

us have talent." He drifted away to flirt with the girls, to chafe the boys.

It was a wonderful dinner. Adam stayed close to her side and was seated in the chair next to hers (little name cards marked the places), and even if it was supposed to be informal, it was more elegant than any Julia had ever beheld. Within the dining room there was ease and spontaneity. The conversation, shared by all, flitting about like a brilliant bird. The theatre, Longfellow's latest poem, the newly published *Atlantic Monthly* which promised a bright future for Boston's literary aspirations. After they had eaten, they decided to go out and down to the Common, there to listen to a tree, to see if it would talk to them as the Transcendentalists said it would. It was a hilarious stroll, and a loud one, too, their voices and laughter echoing in the now deserted streets of Beacon Hill. Julia had never laughed so hard as when Sam Higgins, with his ear to the bark of an old elm, declared it whispered warnings about the pigeons who roosted in its branches and instructed him to wear his hat. Back at Sally's there was mulled cider and little cakes, and Sally produced her mandolin and everyone sang. Sally sang a folk melody, without accompaniment, done so well and so sweetly that everyone in the room listened without breathing, and Cabot recited Mr. Longfellow's Indian poem as though he'd just thought it up, sitting there, and there wasn't one flaw in his presentation.

When the party broke up, Adam Levering walked with Julia and Clara back to Bowdoin Square. Tentatively he expressed the hope that he might return with his poetry, of course bringing Sally with him and perhaps Cabot, too (it would seem forward for him to simply arrive, all by himself), and Julia told him that he might come a week from Sunday; she would notify him if that was inconvenient with her family.

A week from Sunday!

It was clear he was taken with her, and Julia was too excited to sleep that night, wondering at it all.

As far as she could tell, Sally had invited her to the party with the intention of furthering her acquaintance with Adam Levering. She was not sure why Sally had done so, but there could be no doubt of her intention—Julia, in comparison with Clara, had shown up particularly well (which was probably why, of all her sisters, Clara had been the one Sally chose). But there were a dozen other girls Sally might have picked who surely would have seen to Adam's entertainment.

It was a little puzzling, but the outcome was certainly satisfactory, and she was not about to quibble over motives. She'd just have to wait and see how it all turned out, and it was a lot more enjoyable than the waiting she usually had to do, dawdling about the sitting room at Miss Easton's while up-and-coming young men of business called and insipid remarks about the weather were exchanged. She had had a firsthand glimpse of Beacon Hill, and it was just as delightful as she'd believed it to be. And if Adam Levering chose to further his friendship with her, it was possible—just possible—that she could see it firsthand again.

That was as far as she dared to let her thoughts go, just then. It was enough. Just the hope for one more chance. And perhaps one after that.

Adam Levering, looking not the least like a sophisticated Brahmin, stood before them, her sisters and Mama and Miss Easton and Cabot and Sally, who had been given the most comfortable chair. The papers in Adam's hands were filled with his carefully transcribed poems, and they trembled slightly as he plunged on with determination.

"O softly now the Frog Pond shineth," Adam droned,

> In the golden twilight ray.
> Round the stones green ivy twineth
> In the silent end of day.
> The robin to his loved one calleth
> As the veil of evening falleth.

Sally was looking positively pained, Julia observed, soundlessly tapping the arm of her chair with a finger, measuring the meter.

> Upon the face of darkness deep
> The lights of Boston, one by one
> Around and 'bout the Common keep
> Their cheery watch, though day is done
> And by their brightness shielding
> Against the night unyielding.

Cabot's handsome face was impassive, immobile, betraying no sign of his opinion of Adam's versifying.

> So may the beacon lights of home
> Teach us that where e'er we roam

We are guided in the right
As our footsteps are this night
Treading through the peaceful hour
To home, the source of quiet power.

In the silence that followed Adam's recitation, Cabot Levering cleared his throat and looked at his boots; Sally gazed with fervid absorption at an urn of Chinese porcelain.

"Why, Adam!" Julia murmured at last, for want of anything else. In truth, she didn't know what to say. After Longfellow, Adam Levering trailed rather far in the rear—but after all, Longfellow had had to start somewhere, hadn't he?

"Oh, Mr. Levering!" From her chair by the fireplace Mama was daubbing at her eyes. "That is lovely," she said, relieving Julia of the necessity for further comment.

"Oh, yes," breathed Ellen.

"Do you think so?" Adam asked, his face varying hues of scarlet, his brow wet with perspiration, his eyes pleading with them to like his poetry. He had been reading for twenty minutes in a monotone that faltered only when he delivered a line that contained what he considered an especially fine image and now his voice was quite feeble and rasping. "Did you like the reference to the beacon lights and their connection to Beacon Hill?"

"Oh, let me get you something to drink," Julia exclaimed. "You sound as though you are dry, Mr. Levering!"

"Yes," he nodded, "I am that!"

"I do think," Mama simpered, "that you should see about having your poems published, Mr. Levering. Why, they are far better than the ones here in *Gleason's Drawing Room Companion*"—Mama rapped the table beside her where that week's issue of the *Companion* lay. "I think you owe it to the world to share your great gifts."

"Mama is so right!" Clara said. From Miss Easton's pantry where she took the tray, balanced it, started back, Julia heard Clara babble on. "If you have a talent that gives people pleasure, why you should share it. Art has no other justification!"

"Art is not an object to be used and passed around like a silver dollar," Sally offered. "It justifies itself."

Julia set the tray on the round, centered table and paused at this challenge, and decided to take it up. The faces of Mama and Clara and Ellen were very blank, as though they

93

had no notion of what Sally was saying, but the girls at Mrs. Hunt's had thrived on such fare, and Julia loved it, too.

"If a tree falls in the forest but no one hears the sound of its fall, did it make any sound at all?" she asked Sally. "If there was no one to hear, then the fall was silent, was it not? And without someone to receive the outpouring of a pen or brush, is there anything which can be called art? It is only self-indulgence, until someone else can share it."

"The tree indulges itself," Cabot grinned.

"Drink! Drink!" croaked Adam. She laughed and poured the cider while Adam said, with becoming modesty, "I don't know that it's such a great gift that I have, but I do enjoy making rhymes."

Mama encouraged him to tell her how he first started composing, and his face was returning to its more usual shade. Gratefully he took the cider and a cookie which Miss Easton had baked that day especially for the reading of the poetry. Julia passed out the refreshments to the rest of the multitude.

"Now it is your turn, Miss Merrick," said Cabot. "I heard you promise Adam you'd play your piano if he read you his poems. You may justify your art by sharing it."

Well, I did promise, that is certainly true." Quickly she rose and made her way to the piano, chattering like a fool every step of the way so that neither Mama nor Miss Easton would notice that she had neglected to ask Miss Easton if she might use it. Invariably she asked; invariably Miss Easton assented; but to ask would betray the fact that this house was not the Merricks' own. She had never told Sally that she lived at board, and she certainly did not want the Leverings to discover the fact just at that moment, when in Mama's inhibiting presence she could not stretch things out a bit to make them more palatable. "You see," she babbled in Miss Easton's and Mama's direction, "this has all come about because Mr. Levering insisted on being shy about his poems. I told him that I would play for him if he would read to me—"

"And I said I would show him my painting, too," chimed in Clara, upon whose painted plates they now ate their refreshments. For once Julia could be thankful for Clara's talkativeness which, once under way, was difficult to stop. Clara was going on now about composition in painting, sounding not too dumb about it, either, and Julia, as she seated herself at the piano, decided on the spot to play her best, even though Mama would not like it. Mama insisted that it was unfeminine to play well. But Julia had been about Beacon Hill girls long enough to know that excellence was admired there. If they saw, these Leverings, that she too maintained a standard of excellence, perhaps the ignominy of living in a hired house (it was bound to be discovered!) could be offset. It was a risk she would take, a gamble on the values that she believed Beacon Hill held dear.

She began slowly, tentatively, and then let the music take her. The baroque staccato notes of the Bach fugue broke onto the stilled surface of the room and shattered all complacency there, held the audience spellbound at the precise and dignified delivery of the old music, and when it was done, she lulled that same surface into a shimmering stream of liquid sound with a Beethoven etude and then stirred it again with the lovely *Moonlight Sonata* which, she knew, could not fail to work on the romantic yearnings of those who listened.

When she was finished, there was silence longer than customary in any parlor or drawing room.

"Fantastic," murmured Adam Levering, his eyes mirroring admiration.

"Excellent," Cabot proclaimed. "Why the deuce haven't you played before, Julia? You should have, the night of our dinner."

"I didn't think of it," she confessed. "I was having too much fun."

"Quite remarkable," Miss Easton was saying to Mama, wondering why she had never heard Julia play that way before, and Mama could only nod helplessly, wondering why Julia, after all the coaching she had received, should be so persistent in unsexing herself.

"And now, Cabot Levering will entertain us with something," Julia announced, anxious to divert attention from herself.

"I will?"

"Why should you not?" Julia demanded. "Here you are, sitting about all afternoon while Adam and I perform for your pleasure, and you haven't done a thing to enlighten or amuse us. You have not paid your way at all, Mr. C. Levering."

"Julia!" Mama reproved. Really, was there no stopping her? "Mr. Levering is our guest."

"But she is right," Cabot smiled. "I must pipe for my supper, like everyone else. I will declaim!"

"I will sing," Sally announced. "And so, I hope, will the sisters of Julia!"

"Oh, I couldn't," Ellen blushed. "But I will accompany Hetty."

Hetty sang and Sally did, too, and Cabot recited a passage from *Hamlet,* complete with gestures, in a manner Edwin Booth would have been proud of.

The Leverings left, then, amid merry farewells and laughter. Adam shook Julia's hand shyly on his way out and pressed into it a folded piece of paper. "I wrote these lines this week," he whispered. His face was all aflame again. "I hope you will like them."

Mama and Clara and Miss Easton waited expectantly as she unfolded the note and scanned its contents.

"Won't you read it to us?" Mama asked. "Or is it personal?"

There could be nothing personal, of course; she was obliged to read it aloud in order to satisfy the expectation that nothing ever happened in the lives of young people that they could not share with the world at large.

> How well, so well, I remember when we met
> When your gentle smile and floating curls of jet
> Became for me the image of the womanly ideal,
> And tight upon my heart your laughter set a seal.
>
> Pray look upon me kindly, turn me not away,
> Thy presence shines upon my soul as the sun
> upon the day,
> And were I not to see you, upon me night will fall.
> It is my fondest hope, that upon you I might call.

"Well!" snorted Hetty, very upset that her younger sister was so well advanced in romance.

"How lovely," Clara murmured, more generous than Hetty, and Ellen wore a smile of syrup sweetness, recalling similar sentiments (if not so schematically expressed) from her special friend, James Duncan.

"I should think you must be very flattered, Julia," Mama said.

"Oh, yes, I am," Julia assured her.

"Well, come along," Mama said to the girls. "We must get ready for supper."

"Oh, supper!" Miss Easton exclaimed. "I swan I have been so enchanted I forgot all about it." She hurried off to stir up her kitchen help.

"Would it be all right, Mama, if I linger here a while, and play a bit more?"

Mama sighed. Now, she supposed, there would be no stopping this daughter of hers—and perhaps there was no reason to stop her, since the young folks of the Levering house had so clearly admired her performance. "For a while, then," she said in resignation, and led the girls away.

Was Adam Levering in love with her, she wondered as she seated herself. If he were not very much attracted to her, he was giving a remarkable performance, and there was no need for it. He would have been welcomed to the parlor at 3 Bowdoin Square without such signs of devotion. He need not have given her a poem of her own. He need not say or do the things he was saying or doing unless he meant them. It was all very flattering, even exciting, and she was pleased that she had opted for him instead of running after Cabot, as apparently every girl within range did. It was pleasant to think that such a man as Adam might love her.

And more than pleasant—it was important. For now her hopes might have a fuller rein. Adam Levering had called, had liked what he saw (else he would not have given her his poem), and it was possible—quite possible—that he liked her well enough to see more of her, possibly to court her. And if he did—Oh! if he did!—the way out of the mediocre expectation of her life, a way to escape the portrait, opened wide, through Adam Levering. She could only cross her fingers and hope, hope, hope. If he came again soon, alone, she would know. . . .

Everyone had been there in Miss Easton's parlor, because it was late Saturday afternoon: her mother and her sisters, the Huelett family who had recently taken rooms at 3 Bowdoin Square, Miss Easton herself, and Papa and the Duncans, even the Duncans' son James, who was home from Dartmouth and dressed respectably for a change (He was apt to look seedy!). Julia suspected that James had come down to ask Papa for Ellen's hand in marriage, but all afternoon he had only sat there on Miss Easton's couch, sweating, and looked very much relieved when there appeared a distraction from Beacon Hill.

Everyone was impressed to receive a Levering at 3 Bowdoin Square! Her sisters—except for Ellen—fell all over Adam in their attempts to be enchanting, but Adam concentrated on being charming to Mama and Papa. He succeeded so well that they did not object when he asked if he and Julia might go walking on the Common before supper. Naturally Clara came, too—but not before Julia warned her, in the closet where they scrambled for their capes, to listen and say little.

"Your family is delightful," he remarked as they crossed Bowdoin Square and over to Bullfinch Street from whence the Common might be gained.

"Thank you," she smiled. "Clara and I think a lot of them." Clara smiled, too, and discreetly said nothing.

"I am only sorry you couldn't meet my brother," she went on. "He's a fine fellow, and I am sure you would have enjoyed him."

"He is not home at present?"

"No, he's in Australia." She hoped the image of that far-off land would intrigue Adam, so that he would think her family interesting.

"Australia!" he exclaimed. "Does he like it there?"

"Very much, from the sound of his letters."

"What's his line?" Adam asked, happy to have something to talk about.

"He's operating the Melbourne branch of Papa's business," Julia told him importantly. "But don't ask me what the business does, because I don't really know." *Imports and exports sounded so dull*, she thought. She did not wish her family to appear dull! She cast about for something else to offer up that might seem even more glamorous than Tony. "I have a cousin in Melbourne, too," she added. "He started a coaching line that ran to the gold fields, and my brother says it was very successful. So successful, in fact, that my cousin sold his business—recently, I believe—and is even now loitering about the Continent and looking at cathedrals in his off moments. He has even been to Egypt, to see the pyramids."

"Amazing." Adam seemed suitably impressed, and Julia was glad she had thought of Kingsley, who made her family seem exotic. She tried to think of other exotic things. "I have another cousin who is a clipper captain," she said, remembering her Aunt Sarah's oldest son—so old he was like an uncle to her. "Once he sailed to California in ninety-nine days."

Clara, on Julia's far side, nodded affirmation. "Yes, indeed!" she said.

"Remarkable!" She was gratified that Adam seemed to find it all interesting. "What an unusual family you have, Miss Merrick! Such a variety of experience and talents! And certainly very large, too. Why I counted at least twelve people in your parlor!"

Clara giggled, and Julia knew she must laugh, too.

"They are not all my family," she said with as much dignity as she could.

"Oh? I naturally assumed the Duncans and the Hueletts and Miss Easton were your relatives."

"No, no. The Duncans and Hueletts are boarders at Miss Easton's house, just as we are. But very congenial ones, as you saw. James may marry Ellen—that's how congenial."

He was clearly taken aback, nonplussed even, at the idea that the Merricks lived at board, and she thought she had done badly to let him know it so early in their acquaintance. But there was no choice with Clara present. "Our home is in Waterford," she said quickly, hoping to convey the impression that it was a grand one, a veritable mansion. "We spend a great deal of our time there in summer, and so we board here in Boston where we can leave Papa alone easily because there is Miss Easton to look after him." This, she thought, sounded especially fine, because the Beacon Hill wealthy had summer places at Nahant, too. Everyone else was stuck in the city in hot weather.

"Ah, yes," he faltered. "And where is Waterford?"

"My dear Mr. Levering, are you telling me you don't know?"

She could not believe it, and thought he was teasing, wishing she had what it took to poke him with her parasol in gay flirtation. "I shall pay no attention to you, if you don't do better than that!"

"Truly, I am unacquainted with the place."

"Waterford is on Cape Cod," she informed him.

"Oh, indeed," he said politely. "Where they fish a lot. Is Waterford a fishing village, Miss Merrick?"

"Hardly!" she exclaimed. "It is the residence of deep water captains, well known as such here in Boston, and along the seaboard, too. You are not a coast dweller, Mr. Levering. You have given yourself away."

"I am from Connecticut," he admitted, "western Connecticut. I moved to Boston with my mother in order to learn Uncle Levering's business. We live with Sally's family."

Ah, she thought. *He too lived at board. So much the better.* He would not be stuck-up as a boy Boston-born, but his prospects must be good if he were a Levering.

"Sally is having a picnic next Saturday," Adam said. His voice was low, so that Clara would not hear. "It's to be an informal affair, strictly for the younger generation. Would you care to accompany me, Miss Merrick?"

Her little world rocked for a moment, at the shock of such an opportunity.

"I might," she parried, "if you would care to call me Julia."

"I would be happy to—Julia," he smiled, and looked like a sheep. "Are you sure it will be all right with your parents?"

"I expect so," she said. "Let's go home and find out."

It had been fine with Mama and Papa. They were not at all averse to Julia's seeing a member of the illustrious Beacon Hill society, and to top it all off James Duncan had finally popped the question to Papa, and everyone at 3 Bowdoin Square was so excited that Julia could have gone to dinner with the man on the moon, with only a brief moment of persuasion.

It didn't take too long, after that, having accompanied Adam to several small, intimate, informal gatherings in the backyards of Beacon Hill, to discover why Sally had been so zealous on her behalf. Adam did not fit on Beacon Hill and he was awkward there. He had not attended Harvard College, as had everyone else, but had attended Yale University instead. He was not a Bostonian, and had not discovered yet how to be one. But he was a Levering, under the protective wing of his uncle, cordially welcomed wherever a Levering was, loyally befriended by his family, and Sally astutely had seen that Adam would be more at ease with a young lady who was not enmeshed in Boston kinship and heritage and who was unfamiliar with both, even as he was. Once he accommodated himself to Boston and acquired a suitable amount of requisite polish—well then, that was something else again. By then (probably Sally thought), Adam would no longer be interested in Julia Merrick, who had not so much to offer as an heiress.

Julia Merrick was exactly the girl for Adam to begin with, well educated, quick and bright and unlikely to discomfit the Connecticut cousin. Whether Sally had foreseen Adam's falling in love with Julia, or would have chosen otherwise had she known of it, was a moot point. Adam *was* in love, and carried Julia with him wherever he went—with no evidence that he wanted to drop her in favor of a girl more highly born, and it was a lovely, delicious winter, the finest of her life. Adam took her walking with Clara or Ellen in attendance, at first. Later he took her alone. On Sundays they strolled to the waterfront where clippers, the pride of New England, came into and went out of the crowded harbor, where the masts of hundreds of vessels rose like a leafless forest, swaying in the swells as though a breeze had stirred their barren tops. It was fun to go there with Adam, more exciting than it had ever been before when she'd gone there with her family, with Adam pointing out his uncle's ships and the ones he held shares in which carried cotton, and the busy, bustling scene amid piles of wares and barrels and miles of ropes took on a zest it did not have before.

Once he took her, with ten other couples, on the great sleigh once owned by the Perkins family but now available to anyone who wanted to hire it, and with Adam's friends and three young matrons she rode all the way out to Milton where dancing and games and delicious refreshments awaited them at a great house, the group singing and laughing all the way home in the brisk night.

Adam Levering continued to write poetry which he dedicated to Julia, and he wrote her rambling letters, if a week went by when he did not see her. Adam took her to sleighing parties when winter held Boston tightly, when the young folks from the Hill rode out together in the snapping bright air, the harness and bells jingling and chiming and groups challenging one another to races across Boston Neck. Racing was not legal and resulted in fines which the young men cheerfully paid, and it continued as long as snow covered the streets.

She went skating three times on the Frog Pond with Adam and Sally and Cabot Levering and Sam Higgins and Mary Abbott and Jackson Curtis and the other folk of Beacon Hill, and afterward she went to the home of one or another of them, where they all drank hot chocolate and got warm again, chaperoned by a matronly sister scarcely older than themselves. There she played for them because Adam begged and the others insisted, and she listened while the others displayed their talents, too. For the young people of Beacon Hill were all well trained in one art or another as their fathers had not been; they appreciated life's finer things and happily garnered the fruits of the harvest of the older generation, themselves stars shimmering in the firmament of the Hub.

In their company Julia Merrick found herself fitting comfortably, easily, like a hand sliding into a glove so well sized that you didn't even have to wrestle with its wrinkles: she belonged. She belonged! She did! Like a combustion her dreams grew more elaborate, more elegant, more enticing, and hopelessly ensnarling, catching her in their nimbus of allure, nurturing her lively imagination and the sensitivity of her own artistic temperament, and causing her to see only what she wished to see. Surely Adam would be rich someday, through his uncle. Already he belonged to society through his birth. Surely he did like her, and surely Beacon Hill would accept her as his wife. His friends were very cordial, the ones whom she saw while in his company. They liked her, even though there was a certain restraint because her family wasn't known to them nor were her antecedents, and nowhere could kinship be claimed. But they overlooked that, for Adam's sake, and Julia saw no reason why everyone else should not do the same. Cabot Levering spent a lot of time laughing with her; Sally and her friends adopted Julia as one of their own, almost a protégée, showing what would happen in the future when she belonged in their company permanently.

The excitement over being squired about by Adam became more exhilarating than ever, but freighted with significance, too, now as she saw in him the passport to something so exquisite. Eagerly she counted up the occasions when she went out with him and the gestures of esteem he proffered, adding them, like trophies, to her collection, prized as evidence of her progress to the summit of Beacon Hill. Like the lace handkerchief he gave her for a New Year's present, straight from Paris. The valentine candy he brought in a pretty box shaped like a heart, with red satin on the cover. His poems which eulogized her. The rapture with which he listened to her play for him on Miss Easton's piano, the deference with which he treated her, his timid joy when occasionally, if reluctantly, she allowed him to hold her hand. The pretty bouquet of spring flowers he had sent recently, and now! Now the invitation to Sally's coming-of-age ball, which he had obtained for her. It could only mean one thing—the time was ripe! Adam was ready and the ball was his tool presenting the Merricks to his aunt and uncle Levering. With this accomplished the way would be open to speaking with Papa—something he could not do until the Merricks and the Leverings met.

Perhaps the evening of the ball would never arrive! Certainly time had stood still since the engraved invitation arrived while she dreamed of dancing and laughed with joy and waited, waited, waited while Adam, faithful to his promise, cranked out a poem a day in her honor. Time stood motionless while the seamstress fitted and sewed a dress for Mama and a marvelous blue silk one for Julia, the skirt flounced in three fluffy tiers with tassels on them, held out to the fullest extent by the new watch-spring hoops held by tapes to her tightly pulled-in waist. A great expanse of unadorned shoulder and bosom was set off by the fashionable bertha flounced with a fall of lace, and above it her breasts, pushed high by her new corset, swelled into smooth milky fullness, suggesting a ripeness of figure which nature had not originally given her. Dismayed by this suggestiveness, Mama saved the day by tucking Adam's Parisian lace handkerchief into the edge of the dress, where its froth obscured what bodice and corset would reveal. The effect was ravishing! With her sisters clustered about her, watching, Julia played endlessly with her hair to see what might be the very best, most sophisticated and charming way of accommodating the little clusters of seed pearls and blue wax flowers that exactly matched the blue silk of her gown. And she waited, nearly unable to contain her excitement at the ball, and the promise it held.

What a lark it was, to ride in a hired carriage to the Leverings' house, a closed one with a driver out front and Princess Julia inside, accompanied by her parents. She watched the gas lamps coasting by as the horses trotted along, the wheels of the carriage clattering on the cobbles and her heart fluttering joyfully. She did not know that Papa was unhappy about hiring a rig, and unhappy about paying the seamstress so high a fee for the dresses made especially for this night. His own business had fallen off, along with the general decline everywhere, but he did nothing to hinder Julia's happiness, so pleased was he with the success she was enjoying, and so hopeful was he about its outcome. . . .

The receiving line was something she was not prepared for, and she quailed as Mama's and Papa's and her own name were announced, and they must approach the array of Leverings to shake hands and murmur politely. Uncle and Aunt Levering looked at a loss when the Merricks came up, but Adam was instantly there, and somehow the Merricks made it through. Adam's mother was expecting them, Julia thought, because her greeting held an air of scrutiny and interest that could not otherwise be explained.

Her dance program filled with admirable rapidity; Adam claimed three, which was all propriety would allow him, and handsome Cabot two, and the Thayer boy and Sam Higgins and Ned Abbott asked for the others.

It was joyous, standing there in the Levering second-floor drawing room which had, by virtue of enormous sliding doors, been opened to yet another drawing room of equal size so that the dance floor was tremendous. There were flowers everywhere, over the windows and doors and mirrors; the polished floor gleamed, and at the far end was an orchestra, already playing background music. She introduced Mama and Papa to the young people whom she knew, by virtue of having been in Adam's company all winter, and she enjoyed receiving their compliments and their introductions to their mamas and papas.

If anyone glanced askance at the sight of the Cape Cod Merricks standing in the halls of the mighty, Julia did not notice. Mama and Papa looked wonderful, Papa so dignified and handsome, his moustache full and glossy and the hair on his head still abundant, his vest rounded like a dome and his watch chain describing a gleaming arc. Mama was lovely—a little faded, perhaps, amid so much elegance, and perhaps looking a little frightened as well, but her hair was done up becomingly and her dress concealed her scrawniness, and Julia was pleased with them, pleased with herself, pleased, after Sally's presentation and the first dance began, to have Adam quickly at her side, his mother in tow, and his uncle and aunt. Above the music the elder Leverings were left with the elder Merricks while Adam waltzed her away, leaving no time for awkwardness.

"You look so lovely, Julia," he whispered, holding her correctly three feet away, whirling her so that her voluminous skirt swirled out and swayed like a bell.

"Thank you, Adam," she smiled at him while the ballroom swept with dizzying speed around her. "You are very handsome, yourself!"

She thought she saw Papa disappearing with Mr. Levering in the direction of the card tables, though it was difficult to be sure of it, because suddenly, with great daring, Adam wisked her out onto a balcony where the night air was cool, the lights of the house throwing square and rectangular patches on the street below.

"Let us hope they adore one another," he said, taking her hand in his and leading her to a railing over which they both leaned.

"And why need they adore one another?" she asked archly into the darkness, knowing full well that it was to their parents he referred.

"Oh, Julia," he stammered. "If our parents liked and approved of one another . . . why, perhaps—if it is all right with you, Julia . . . I do so hope that all of us can reach an understanding."

"An understanding?"

"If our parents agree and there are no objections, perhaps then, Julia, I might speak with your papa about our being betrothed . . . if, my dear," he gulped over that word, "if you would consent to being betrothed to me."

She glanced up to catch his face, then bashfully looked away.

"Why, Adam," she murmured, as became the situation. "I had no idea . . . this is really quite a surprise . . . forgive me if I don't quite know what to say."

"I realize I cannot hope that you should love me now, dear Julia." His words were quick and sure, and she was nearly certain that he had memorized them. "But in time, perhaps you could learn. I would surely be made the happiest man in the world if you would consent to try."

"Perhaps we had better wait to see if our parents do get along with one another," she prevaricated, coyly and correctly. She could not let him know that she had been awaiting this moment! "I am not sure what to think, Adam, especially until I know Papa's feeling on the matter."

"Oh, quite!" he cried, relieved to have finally gotten off his chest what he had wished to say for weeks.

"Come what may," she looked demurely at him. "I am sure we will always be the very best of friends."

"Oh, I do hope so, dearest Julia!" he cried, just as Cabot strode onto the balcony in search of her. He was next on her program.

"I thought I saw the two of you disappearing out this door," he laughed. "Come, Miss Merrick, now I have my chance with you!"

Adam frowned, but Cabot, appearing not to notice, whirled her away and out onto yet another balcony which overlooked the rear of the mansion and its garden. There were several other couples at whom he made a face and, taking Julia's hand, led her toward an unoccupied corner.

"How ravishing you are, my lovely Julia," he said in the darkness, taking the hand he still held and sweeping it to his lips to kiss it.

She curtseyed with a giggle. Cabot was forever doing ridiculous things like that. A jolly sort; she would be happy to belong to his family and him, and through Adam, she would!

"You do say the nicest things, dear sir," she laughed, looking up at him with coy appreciation.

"I suppose we must get back to the dance floor," he said, "but I did want to steal a moment to tell you how admirable you look. And to tell you that there is a favor you could do me—and yourself."

"Oh? Do tell me! I would love to grant you a favor."

"I wish you would take away that dratted handkerchief," he grinned. "You would look prettier without it, and I could admire you the more—or that much more of you. It ruins the line of your dress," he added quickly, so that his remarks took an inoffensive cast.

"Oh!" she murmured, glancing down at the hankie, although she had to cross her eyes to do so. "Do you think it is ruined, Cabot?"

"It's a stunning gown," he said earnestly. "And you wear it far better than a woman of shorter stature could. It's perfect just as it was designed, and surely does not need anything extra."

"Adam gave me this hankie," she said. "I'd like to have it on display, to show him how much I appreciate his gift."

"You can hold it, daintily, or tuck it into your glove so the lace shows between the buttons."

How clever he was! It was just the right touch!

"Then I shall," she said. "And thank you for the advice."

Turning her back to him, she removed the hankie and stuffed in partway into her glove.

"Just as I thought," he nodded in satisfaction, appraising her from tip to toe. "Truly stunning."

He had never behaved this way before, and she was warmed. Could it be possible that he had conceived an attraction to her? Flattering, in the extreme!

He handed her over to Ned Abbott who seemed, everytime he looked at her, to have his eyes fastened on her bosom and she chattered furiously, seeking to divert him. Mama, she noticed, was sitting on the edge of a group of ladies, but she could not tell whether anyone spoke with her or whether Mama was only watching because there was no other course open to her.

She danced with Adam again and on his arm went into the dining room where an enormous buffet was laid out—fish and turkey, mutton and veal, ham and sweetbreads, duck and grouse, quail and salads and jellies and fruits and nuts and sugar-frosted sweets and row upon row of wines, which an attendant poured at request. She picked at the food on her plate in the prescribed manner, not minding because her stays were far too tight to allow real eating, and they laughed together over the vicissitudes of Jackson Curtis who had, from a source he would not reveal, become sedately, hilariously

106

drunk and was fighting a losing battle with an oyster which persistently slipped away from his grasp. Everyone pretended that this was the customary method of eating oysters; no one chided Jackson—and no one copied him, either.

"We shouldn't laugh," Julia said softly to Adam. "It is unkind. But really," she chuckled, "he is awfully funny."

"You are a kind person," Adam said, his eyes mellow in adoration as he looked at her. "Compared to the girls I have known, you are very kind, and I hope you will be kind to me."

He took her hand and squeezed it, and she guessed, judging from the stories she read in *Gleason's Drawing Room Companion*, that she should have been all atremble by then. Adam Levering did not have what it took to make a girl tremble, but no matter!

"When are you going to write me a poem?" she asked in a manner indicating that she thought his rhymes were marvelous.

"Tonight, when I get to my room," he promised. "I'll bring it to you soon as I'm satisfied it's worthy of you."

She smiled and saw that the Thayer boy was looking for her. "I declare!" she said brightly, examining her program. It dangled from her wrist by a fine silken cord with a tassle on the end of it. "There is Jules. Do excuse me."

He rose and helped her to her feet. "My loss," he said bowing gracefully and handing her over.

Mama sat quite alone now. No, there was Papa, coming to join her, and Julia felt better about that. How long had her mother been sitting there alone, she wondered uneasily. How unkind, that these folk should let her!

Cabot, when his turn came again, chafed her about the hankie.

"What did Adam say when he discovered it was gone?"

"It isn't gone," she said. "It's right here in my glove where you told me to put it."

"You mean he didn't notice that it was no longer part of your dress?"

"He didn't say so."

"Perhaps he was offended after all," Cabot suggested.

"If so he has no right to be. There is no understanding between us at present; he is hardly in a position to dictate to me."

"Delightful!" Cabot said, and laughed heartily. "That information lightens my heart."

"Oh, pshaw," she chided him gaily, tapping him with her fan. "As if it mattered to you."

"Of course it does," he said smoothly. "Why, the thought of one more pretty girl taken out of circulation is enough to prostrate me."

He did not look the type to prostrate easily, and she couldn't help laughing, perhaps louder than she should. He led her to Adam, who was her last partner for the last dance.

"What were you and Cabot so jolly about?" he asked, and she guessed that beneath his bantering tone he was disturbed.

"Inane things, like Curtis and his oysters," she told him with a smile.

"Cabot is a handsome fellow, Julia, but he is also irresponsible and his reputation is not untarnished."

"I can't imagine anything unsavory going on between him and anyone in this room," Julia said lightly.

"Oh, certainly not with anyone here, nor anyone in society," Adam protested, blushing. "That is unthinkable! But there are plenty of others, and Cabot likes to try them all. The girls here on the hill know how to handle him, but perhaps you don't. I am only warning you."

She had seen those selfsame girls turning inside out to attract Cabot's attention, and she did not believe they would be cool in their handling of his attention. In fact, she believed Adam was jealous!

"You need not warn me," she said gently. "How could he have any attraction for me, Adam, when you are my friend?"

The gratitude and humble happiness on his face were amazing, she thought. She surely had him where she wanted him, did she not? And it hadn't hurt a bit, flirting with Cabot. It had merely moved Adam to greater distraction over her. So much the better. She smiled tenderly at him, took his arm while he led her to Mama and Papa, while their wraps along with those of everyone else were brought and the carriages driven around. The Merricks, having thanked the host and hostess, were safely tucked in and driven away.

"Did you enjoy the Leverings?" she asked Mama and Papa, leaning back on the carriage cushions, her feet beating with exhaustion, a delicious flow of fatigue coursing through her.

"Very pleasant, very pleasant," said Papa jovially.

"Charming, I am sure," Mama murmured, her voice weary.

And did the Leverings like the Merricks? It was not a question Julia could ask with any delicacy. She forbade herself to think about it. Instead she thought only of the wonderful evening, her first ball in society, her progress with Adam. . . .

His new poem did not come, and he did not write a letter. She heard nothing from Sally, either, even after she sent the proper note of thanks for the delightful evening she'd enjoyed so well, and by the end of the week she was frantic. What had gone wrong? Had she behaved badly, without realizing it? Was she going to be simply, humiliatingly, dropped? Then, at last, a note. Could Adam see her, please, quickly as possible? Might he come around at three? He would do so unless she sent him word it was inconvenient.

She managed to get everyone out of Miss Easton's parlor by three, including Miss Easton, and she met Adam at the door herself when he rang the bell. She did not like the look on his face as she led him into the parlor and seated him on the couch, herself beside him with an appropriate space between. His face was pale and his eyes were tired and his hands were shaking. *Possibly he is only smitten with love,* she thought, but somehow she didn't believe it was so simple. And it was not.

"I must go to England," he said at last. "I am due to leave next week."

"To England!" What was she to make of that?

"My uncle wishes me to learn more about the cotton mills there, in order to improve our own. He thinks there's no better way to do it than to learn it all firsthand."

"Oh," she said faintly.

"I . . . I do hope, Julia, that when I return, we will be able to resume our friendship. Would you write to me while I am in England?"

"Yes, of course," she murmured. "How long will you be gone?"

He looked more uncomfortable than ever. "Uncle refuses to be pinned down to that point," he said finally.

"You mean you would like me to be your friend whenever you get back, although it could be months from now?"

"Oh, I do hope you will, Julia. Is it asking too much?"

It was! It was! Surely Adam did not expect it from her! Not without a definite understanding between them!

"I cannot say at present," she declared, remembering the formulas required. "You ask a great deal, Mr. Levering. I am sure I will always entertain for you a most warm regard, but whether or not I will be waiting here indefinitely I cannot say."

"I was afraid of that," he said sadly. "But Julia, surely you know that I love you!"

Ah! That was more like it.

"Perhaps," she said primly, "it is Papa to whom you should be talking."

"I can't," he said sadly. "I am in no position to. I shouldn't even be asking you to wait for me, but I am asking anyway, Julia, because I can't see anything else to do. I am very dependent on my uncle's whim, and his whim at the moment is to pack me off to Manchester." When she said nothing, he turned to her in sudden despair and said with heat, "I told him I wouldn't go. . . . We've done nothing, all of us, but argue about it all week. But nothing moves him, neither my protests nor Sally's tears. He told me that if I didn't go to England as he requires, I'll be out on my ear . . . and then what prospects have we, Julia, you and I?"

She stared at him in disbelief as the designs of Adam's uncle became slowly and unpleasantly clear to her, and the more she understood them, the more stunning they were.

The Merricks were not good enough! Incredible as it was, it was the only possible conclusion she could draw.

"Perhaps we had better speak frankly, Adam," she said, masking her dismay beneath a voice that to her ears sounded calm. "Is your uncle trying to get you out of Boston so that you won't see me anymore?"

The misery on his face was answer enough, but she persisted. It was humiliating enough to be scorned by the Leverings, without being meek over it.

"Is it? I must know." She drew herself up proudly.

"I'm afraid so."

"Why has he not done this long ago? We have kept one another company all winter."

"He didn't know it," Adam said. "And certainly none of us—my friends, or Sally—were about to tell him. So Uncle Levering knew nothing about you until the night of Sally's ball."

She remembered only now that when she had seen Adam this winter in the company of his friends, the only chaperones had been very young—nobody's parents had been in evidence, and it must have been a prearranged conspiracy, all of them in on it. She, Julia Merrick, was a well-kept secret!

"Your mother?" she asked coldly, keeping a firm hand on her humiliation.

"She didn't know, either, until just before you and your parents arrived, when I told her."

"And now that your mother and your aunt and uncle have met us, they have found us wanting? Is that the story?"

"I wish you wouldn't state it quite so harshly, Julia. It's not so simple as that. There must be two dozen family lines on Beacon Hill, and my uncle expected that I would marry into one of them. A family he doesn't know—why, it will take him a while to get used to the idea. Sally is furious with him—we've all enjoyed you so, Julia; one day he will, too!"

She remained motionless and admired her own icy poise, which, she was sure, masked her hurt and growing anger. Adam was sweating now.

"I am sure he will come to his senses, when he sees we have remained loyal to one another throughout a separation." His eyes were full of pleading, and he looked very much like a hound begging for a biscuit.

"Oh?" She laughed bitterly. "And you believe your uncle will not devise another mission for you, and another, and another?"

"I hope not." He sighed plaintively. "Won't you wait, Julia?"

She could not just sit beside him on that couch! She rose with all her dignity her height gave her, looked down at him with all the hauteur she could muster, walked to the far end of the parlor, away from him, and stared out the window at the brownstones on Bowdoin Square which were not adequate in the view of Beacon Hill. She should have known—how stupid not to understand from the start that among Lowells and Laurences and Leverings a Merrick would be ever unwelcome, that only from a position of power could a Levering take a Merrick to wife. And Adam was powerless.

"It is hopeless," he mourned from the couch. "Hopeless. If you don't stand by me, then Uncle has me where he wants me."

"If you do not stand by yourself, that is most certainly true."

"But Julia, I have no means of making a living aside from my uncle's business."

It *was* hopeless, and she understood it so to be. But she would not—no, never would she admit to it.

"There are other businesses," she said remorselessly.

"I would have to leave Boston. If I incurred my uncle's displeasure, he would make certain of that."

She was filled with wrath at his uncle who had spoiled it all.

"I find this discussion distasteful, and you may tell your

111

Mr. Levering so," she said her eyes flashing. "The day you quit him is the day you may return here. Not before. Whether I will be waiting or not, I cannot say. Certainly not without more assurance from you that you are willing to fight him. There can be no future for you and me unless you are willing to do so."

By now Adam Levering had regained some of his poise, some perspective, enough to see that he was cutting a poor figure, deserved nothing from her but the scorn he saw in her eyes. He came to stand beside her in the window, to look out on the square with her.

"Perhaps, in time, I will have acquired enough skill, enough contacts, to set up for myself in some way," he said, determined to rescue some of his flagging self-esteem. "If our talking this afternoon shows me nothing else, it shows me that I am foolish to let myself become so dependent on the Leverings, and I swear to you, Julia, that somehow I shall break away from them, if only to lay claim to my soul." He might have said more, but there was no point to it, no point in discussing the day that Adam Levering might be free of the Leverings, because that day was too distant, too nebulous to make any difference.

"Do that," she said softly. "Claim your soul, if you can." Abruptly she turned and offered him her hand. "It has been a pleasure knowing you, Adam," she said stiffly, resolving not to cry.

He looked on the edge of tears himself. He shook her hand limply; he shifted from one foot to the other, staring at her profile as she turned again to watch the street, refusing to look at him, and then he left. When he looked up from the sidewalk to the parlor at 3 Bowdoin Square, there was no one at the window.

Secretly Julia sulked, bereft of comfort and bitter against life. She must pretend everything was as it had always been, for hardly could she tell Mama that the Merricks had not measured up to the Levering standards and that she had lost Adam on account of it! It was depressing to understand that Mama and Papa had failed to pass the test the Levering ball now seemed to be. She was sorry for them and embarrassed by them, filled with a protective sort of love for them which was quite new to her, such as she might feel for a wounded bird whose broken wing fluttered in her hand. She must never, never let them know.

But beside her compassion, rising to engulf all other considerations was the crushing knowledge that everything was lost—that her marvelous alternative to staid boredom or mundane drudgery was gone. There was the searing mortification of Adam's request that she wait patiently while his uncle sent him away—perhaps many times—meekly waiting for old Levering to acquiesce to the presence of Julia Merrick in his family, as though his uncle might swallow her like a bitter pill. As if he ever would! That Adam might declare his freedom sometime in the distant future did not comfort her, nor even his willingness to do so. It would do her no good if it were true that his uncle would close Boston's doors to Adam; there would be no more balls at anyone's mansion on Beacon Hill and no way to gain entry to them. There had never been, even when he had been at her side, but she had been too dazzled to see it. It was enough to make anyone cry, and she did her share of weeping whenever she could excuse herself from the family circle—but even that was difficult, for one was always supposed to be doing something with somebody, companionship following one even to the privy. Never had she been so aware of the lack of privacy in the life of a young girl; never had she needed it more!

Ahead lay vast expanses of days, with the portrait waiting for her face to be painted on it—and everything was hopeless, hopeless!

Then, as the second day of mourning lingered into the late afternoon, she was drawn suddenly out of her unhappiness by a rattle on the door knocker downstairs, by the running footsteps of Ellen who hurried up to find her.

"Here's a message for you, Julia," Ellen panted (for running upstairs tightly laced was not easy). "The Levering footman is out on the steps waiting for an answer."

The Levering footman! Quickly, her hand trembling, she opened the envelope. "Will you come out riding with me at seven and a half? C.L."

Cabot!

"Well?" asked Ellen.

Quickly Julia saw it all, laid out flat like a puzzle awaiting a skillful hand to fit the pieces all together—her hand. There would be no questions asked if her family assumed she was going to ride with Adam—but with Cabot? Mama and Papa, quite naturally, did not know him as well, and if they allowed her to go at all, they would surely want Hetty or Ellen or Clara to go along, especially since it would be dusk. She did not want them! Here was her chance—perhaps her last change—to again find hope. Here was Cabot Levering, and certainly she would be hampered by the presence of her sisters in captivating him; his attention could not possibly be focused exclusively on her, and that was where she meant to have it. Cabot Levering could unlock any door on Beacon Hill that he chose.

"The footman is waiting," Ellen reminded her.

"What shall I do?" Julia asked. "Mama isn't here to tell me. He wants me to go riding this evening at seven and a half," she added, without mentioning who "he" was.

Adam, Ellen knew, had been at 3 Bowdoin Square but once that week, and Julia had been looking very peaked; perhaps she and Adam had got themselves into a lovers' quarrel—and now there was an opportunity to make it all up. Ellen, herself betrothed, wished happiness on all mortals less blessed than herself.

"Oh, do go ahead," she said. "I'm sure Mama won't mind. I'll tell her that I encouraged you to say yes without her permission. I'm positive she'd be agreeable."

Gleefully Julia got from her escritoire a single sheet of heavy paper; in copperplate script she wrote the single word YES, folded it, and sent Ellen back to the footman.

Cabot!

She hugged herself! Oh, how suddenly rosy everything was! Cabot, for all she knew, had liked her all along. Cabot, because he was a gentleman, refrained from any demonstration of interest other than a distantly friendly one because Adam was his cousin; Adam loved Julia; Cabot, therefore, would not put himself forward (though he had hinted much the night of Sally's dance).

But Adam, whether he liked it or not, no longer contended for Julia's affection, and Cabot, overcome by his infatuation with her, was now free to make his bid. Hardly could he invite her to a party, with all the ruckus in the Levering mansion yet so recent; he could not ask her to walk with him in daylight because they might be seen and the ruckus rolled up again. But he could ride with her at dusk, when neither of them would be recognized, and secure for himself the knowledge that she would allow him to press suit; armed with her acceptance, he could then storm the Levering fortress of exclusion. Surely if *he* wanted Julia Merrick, his father would not banish *him* from Boston.

And through Cabot—whom she had always thought so handsome, whose very smile caused similar reactions within her as described in the tender breasts of the *Drawing Room Companion* maidens—through Cabot the life on Beacon Hill, which was her passport to living itself, was again attainable.

But how was she going to get out of the house and into that carriage! Alone and unaccompanied! Perhaps Ellen, who seemed so sympathetic, would help. Immediately she went to find her, beckoning her out of Miss Easton's parlor and into the now empty dining room, upon which she closed the doors.

"Ellen," she began, "I need your help with . . . Adam." Her distress over this lie caused her voice to tremble and her eyes to fill.

"Oh, poor Julia!" Ellen exclaimed softly. "So you have had an argument with him! I am sorry." Her own eyes filled with pity for Julia, whose beau was not as steady as her own, faithful, decent James. "How can I help?"

"I'm afraid that Mama—if she agrees to let me go—will insist on one of you coming along. I wouldn't blame her, it being dusk and all, but how can I patch things up with someone listening?"

The problem was instantly clear to Ellen. Only since James had become engaged to her had Ellen been allowed any time alone with him—and precious little at that. It was pretty hard to accomplish any personal business that way! It was not proper to ride alone with a young man at dusk—but Julia knew Adam very well and he was extremely courteous. Perhaps the rules ought to be stretched on special occasions? "I think," said Ellen slowly, "that perhaps Mama need not know you were going." Her heart quailed at such insubordination—but in truth she knew no other course, and love was the most important thing of all. "Mama and Papa are dining tonight at the Mallorys' house; we are invited, too, but you might not be up to it, and have to stay home."

It was as far as Ellen dared to go. The sisters stared at one another as Julia thought it over. Then she laughed, a pure and joyful laugh. "I feel dreadful," she declared. "Adam has not sent me a poem all week and I have a headache, just thinking about it. He was angry when I wore his handkerchief unobtrusively and I was angry because he was trying to tell me what to do, and I am pouting while I wait for him to come to his senses. I am in no shape to go out to dinner. I would rather pout here, alone."

She hugged Ellen and whisked back upstairs. Now, who would have thought that a spineless creature like Ellen Merrick would abet such a thing! Promptly she shucked off her dress and underpinnings and made haste to put on her nightclothes, in case Mama should come back early.

It worked beautifully. Miss Easton would be at home and

the Hueletts, too, so there was no problem in leaving Julia behind. Mama felt her forehead and tried to urge her to come to the Mallorys'—but Mama did not insist on it, was gentle and kind, and Ellen must have done her work well. The only problem was that they all might not leave in time—that Cabot would come charging up the steps at the same instant the Merricks went charging down. But it did not happen, and Julia was dressed and waiting at the front window of the sitting room upstairs when the closed carriage (oh! closed!) drew up.

Pushing back her quickly aroused trepidation (a closed carriage *was* a bit compromising), Julia fled downstairs and opened the door before Cabot could raise the knocker, and slipped out and closed the door quietly behind her. Whether she could get back in or not, undetected, she resolved not to worry about now, nor the questionable nature of the Levering conveyance. If the outcome of tonight's meeting went as she planned, she'd pay the consequences of disobedience gladly, atone endlessly, if only it worked!

"Good evening, Cabot Levering!" she murmured, slipping her arm beneath his, causing him to turn in mid-stride and go back down the steps in the same motion as he was climbing them. "What a nice evening for a ride!"

The coachman was holding open the door and Julia scrambled into the dark interior before any inhabitants of Miss Easton's saw her. Cabot murmured instructions to his man, who touched the brow of his cap and set himself onto the driver's seat out front.

It was a much nicer carriage than the one Papa had hired to take her to the Levering ball, upholstered in velvet and polished leather with brass fittings that gleamed as they passed each gas lamp, rugs piled on the floor to warm the feet if need be, but the evening was warm. She put her shawl beside her, between herself and Cabot; as yet there was no need of it.

"Where are we going?" she asked, leaning back into the comfort that Levering money could buy.

"Would Brookline suit you?" Cabot asked. "The air is so fresh there, yet it's close by. I get tired of smelling Back Bay at low tide, don't you?"

"Ugh!" she exclaimed. "It's awful. I wish they'd fill it in." The lights on the mill damn were flashing past.

"I expect some day they will," Cabot said. "Some day soon perhaps." The carriage paused while the toll was paid, and then it was dark; they were in the country.

"I'll bet you know all about a land scheme already," she teased. "I'll bet there's plans going on right now to fill the bay, and shrewd as you are, you've already invested in it."

"That would be telling," he teased back. Out of the dark came his hand to fold around hers. "It's certainly very pleasant, driving out here with you."

"The pleasure is mine," she said politely, withdrawing her hand. "I enjoy being with you," she added boldly, to offset the removal of the hand.

"Then Adam's departure has not broken your heart?"

It was delicate, whichever way she answered.

"I think it very inconvenient of him, to just up and leave," she said. "I'm too angry about it to know whether or not my heart is broken. He might have given me more warning." There! That should satisfy Cabot that she knew nothing of Adam's struggles, nor of his intentions, thus she was not being fickle. The affronted damsel could seek her revenge through Cabot Levering himself, if so he chose.

"It certainly was inconsiderate," Cabot said, taking her hand back. "Perhaps you'll permit me to make it up to you. Jack Curtis is having a picnic next week. Perhaps you'd like to come."

"Why," she drawled. "I might. I enjoy Jackson very much."

"I hoped you'd come because you enjoy me."

"You know already that I do!"

"And I guess you know that I have admired you."

"Why, I can't say that I do," she said pertly, very satisfied, indeed, with the way things were going. "You never paid any more attention to me than you did anyone else. Why, I guess I've always thought you were the roving sort."

"I suppose I am," he chuckled. "But, then, someone comes along who makes you want to stop roving. Someone like you, Julia, and then someone else generally gets there first, like Adam did."

"Adam is a fine fellow," she asserted stoutly.

"So am I!" Behind her, his free arm crept over the seat back, hovering above her shoulders. She moved away a little, but to her dismay, Cabot Levering moved over, too, with her shawl squashed up in between them. "Maybe I am just as fine as Adam. Do you think so, Julia?"

"I . . . don't know," she laughed feebly. "After all, I don't know you as well."

"There are ways to get acquainted, like now, alone together at our leisure."

"It won't happen again," she promised him. "Mama doesn't even know I'm here. She thinks I'm in bed with the pouts over Adam, and I can't imagine another occasion will arise. We'd better make the best of our time, Cabot! Tell me all about yourself."

He laughed. "What a delightful person you are, Julia," he exclaimed. "And desirable as well. Very desirable." He reached out to play with a tendril of her hair and instinctively she drew back, to find her shoulder jammed up against the door of the coach.

"Do you think," he murmured low, "we are well enough acquainted that I might kiss you?"

Kiss her! She nearly leaped from the coach in alarm.

Oh, she thought, her mind darting in a dozen directions at once. *How did it work? Romantic stories were devoid of details. Did he think it due him, considering they had known one another quite a while?*

She did not want him to kiss her. She did not want him anywhere near her—yet if Cabot expected that sort of intimacy, and if she refused, would he then disappear and not ask her to accompany him again?

"You haven't said yes or no, Julia," he persisted, the hair discarded in favor of her ear, its outline traced with his finger.

"Very well," she whispered, her heart beating loud in her ears. She took a deep breath and held it.

He turned her face toward his own. He put his lips firmly, squarely on hers. The unfamiliar hardness of them meeting hers so deliberately was not especially pleasant, and his cheek was like a wall against which her nose was pressed, threatening to smother her. Then his lips left hers and she could breathe again.

"There." He smiled. "That's wan't so bad, was it?"

His body radiated warmth, and she was painfully, acutely, aware of its bulk, its breadth, the vitality of it. And she was afraid, afraid of his body, afraid of his eyes which laughed down at her and the mouth which had touched hers, and which was coming down now for another kiss.

"Was it?" He paused in the descent, his lips only inches away from hers.

"Oh, no . . . indeed," she whispered gamely, clenching her fists and screwing up her courage for what appeared to be a second round. She must give it another chance!

"Your lips are lovely," he murmured. "Sweet and tender and delicious, just as you are, dear Julia."

She tried to smile, as though she were flattered. She wished that his eyes were not so intent. She wished desperately that he were not so close. He was talking, low and soft, as the top button under her chin gave way under his expert fingers.

"Why, I've wanted to kiss you for a long time," Cabot was saying. "Every time I saw you with Adam, when we skated, when you played the piano for us all . . . we all surely enjoyed your company, Julia, and no one can play as well as you. Why Mary Lowell was telling me, just the other day, how much she admired . . ."

She froze.

Mary Lowell was very important on Beacon Hill.

Her bodice hung open and Cabot was gently pushing aside her chemise, the silken top of her corset and she shrank back against the strong and muscular arm that had slipped, unannounced, behind her. "Mary Lowell's circle will be an important, enjoyable one," he said. "She told me how much she wished you could be part of it."

His eyes never left hers as he busied himself first with her clothing and then, tentatively, herself.

If she said no, he would take her home. He would go back to Beacon Hill alone and her chance would be lost. Wasn't it worth letting him touch as much of her, beneath the layers of feminine apparel, he managed to find? Would it kill her?

The arm behind her was as steel as were his eyes. She made her hands lie passive in her lap as she endured his touch, unable to deny him. She sat there inert until, crushing the froth of lace and linen, Cabot Levering expertly revealed her breast in its entirety while his thumb urgently stroked her pink and innocent nipple . . .

"No!" she cried out, the writhing within surging up and over the top of her self-control. "No!" she shrieked, clawing at his hand with both her hands, and she would have screamed again but could not because his lips sealed hers now, not allowing her protest, while the arm behind her caught her inexorably and the hand on her breast pressed tight and hard and its fingers squeezed and pinched as though she were a lump of clay.

There was nothing she could do to stop him, no protest her lips could make because they were hurtfully pressed beneath his and her fingers were as nothing on his, as though they were mere wisps . . . it was frightful, and it hurt—he was hurting her—*her*—working now on her other breast, the fabrics of her dress and underclothing tearing as he exposed and kneaded and pinched that one, too, and she let herself go limp in an effort to make him stop hurting her. For if she didn't fight him, perhaps he would not hold so tightly, nor press on her mouth so hard that his teeth, on her lips, were surely cutting and her mouth surely bleeding. . . .

She dropped her hands and, sure enough, his touch became more gentle, just as she had thought it would. Without resistance she bore the hands which firmly now, but without pain, caressed her and motionless, waited as his lips left hers—at last!—and lowered themselves and in the dark she felt them on her breast, whispering over her tormented flesh, felt his lips on her, his tongue, and then in agony, despair, revulsion, felt his teeth rake her—

She gasped, flung him away, a hand on his handsome face and the other on the handle of the coach door, which she flung open, allowing the night wind and the dust of the road to gust in. His hold was broken, and she could at last get out from that band of steel. She leaped to the opposite seat, her hand on the doorframe as the door banged crazily against the side of the carriage and across from her heavily breathed Cabot Levering, changed into the beast she had always heard lived beneath the surface of men—a beast she had never seen before.

The coach slowed, stopped, the coachman climbed down, closed the door without looking at the occupants, climbed back onto the box, waited.

"Do you mean it?" Cabot asked sardonically, his breathing returning to normal now.

"I mean it," she said, trying to hold back her tears. "Please take me home."

"You are in earnest, then?"

"I am," she said coldly as she could, trying to control the tremor in her voice. "If you don't get this rig turned around this minute, I'll jump out of it."

"Well," Cabot said, breaking a lengthy silence. "I can see you don't like me as well as I'd hoped you did."

How could he think so ill of her? she wondered despondently.

"You have misjudged me, that's all," she shot back with as much spirit as she could. "You must have thought I worked in one of your father's mills, Mr. Levering."

"I know a social climber when I see one," he retorted. "Usually your sort will do anything required."

He stood up to put his head through the small trap door in the roof that permitted him to speak to his man. The carriage turned in a wide arc, resumed its journey in the direction

120

from which they had come. The distance which had seemed so short going out now stretched to an aching infinity as Julia huddled miserably in her corner, refastening her garments as best she could, waiting for the lights strung like a necklace through the night that would signal the approach of the mill dam.

Throughout the endless ride to Bowdoin Square they both sat silently on separate sides of the coach, and she tried to understand why such humiliation, such mortification should be heaped on her. Once back at Bowdoin Square she jumped from the carriage before either Cabot or his man could move.

If only her family were not back! Quietly as she could, in spite of her haste, she let herself into Miss Easton's house, shut the door behind her, listened. From the parlor came the drone of conversation, from the kitchen the clatter of the girls doing the dishes. No one heard. She stole up the stairs, willing none of the boards to betray her presence, into the sitting room of the Merricks, which had not changed since she had left it. She fled to her own room, closed the door, and leaned against it, swallowed up in this moment of silence, and by the enormous portent of this night.

She had deceived her dear parents and had been duped by a person she had been warned about—Adam had told her Cabot was unreliable! Oh, she had not understood what sort of thing might come from that unreliability, but she had been warned, and had chosen not to listen, had chosen to lie and cheat, and now she was pure no longer. She had been tainted by Cabot Levering, her purity stained forever—for once a girl was stained, there was no way to erase it. Everyone knew that, and Julia knew it, too. Until now she had been so pure that she hadn't even known lust existed, just as she was not supposed to know. Now that she knew what it was all about, she longed to be innocent again—lust was a terrible thing to behold, and to be the victim of. Awful! Awful! Her panic rose as she thought about it; she was becoming frantic. She must do something—now—to stop it so that she would be under control when the family returned, for they must never know what had happened this night. It was bad enough being forever stained, without dear Mama knowing about it, for Mama would rather be dead, Julia was certain, than know of her daughter's taint.

And Julia, herself, must forget that Cabot Levering had touched her intimately! Panic flared up at the very thought of it, and shame, and anguish; her tears became urgent and her body shook violently; if she didn't get herself in hand, stem the run of terror that shot deeply through her being, she would faint on the spot. . . .

Somehow she must put away this dreadful night, where it could not haunt and torment her! She must put the memory of Cabot's hand away where it would not cause her to be afraid. She must close her mind to it—instantly! It was the only way to escape her torment and the dreadful circle of recrimination so justly deserved! She must, or she would go crazy!

She must go back! She must be what she had been before she had given over to her dreams of Beacon Hill, she must take her place in the great canvas, the flat and lifeless portrait, she must fill the space allotted for her there as it had been meant to be filled from the beginning, before she was foolish enough to try escaping it.

She must return to the safety of Mama and Papa and Ellen and Clara and Hetty, and their secure, dependable world, and she must do it quickly, before she got lost forever in this swamp of self-accusation and humiliation, and once there she must be everything that Mama had always wanted her to be, put down her restlessness and rebellion, banish and repudiate her dreams, and in that way redeem herself. Going back would surely quiet her guilt and atone for her errors; surely if she sank out of sight, into the manners and rituals so familiar to her, she would be restored, made whole, and Cabot and Sally and Adam and the Levering family would be left behind, closed out of that studied, predictable world. She would have Papa's protection, Mama's comfort, her sisters' love. How she needed them now!

Yes! She would help in getting the household ready for its summer move to Waterford, she would tell Ellen that nothing had been resolved between Adam and herself, and she would say nothing to remind anyone that she had been courted by a member of society. She would mend her dress so that Mama wouldn't discover it had been torn and she would take upon herself all the tasks and duties that as a daughter were hers, and perhaps the whole thing would get buried just as she would be buried beneath the meaningless and inflexible and blessed routine of her family. Perhaps the pain of her ruined dreams, the pain of her ruined maidenhood would—somehow—grow less, fade, lie recumbent. She would have to make sure that it did. She must gain the upper hand over her mind, and she would start now, this instant.

She climbed back into bed, to pretend she slept in case her family should return sooner than she expected. She lay there

122

stiffly, concentrating sternly on the ways in which she would please Mama and Papa, carefully blocking any other errant thought with the enumeration of those ways. She thought a long, long time. . . .

"Julia! Julia! It's time to get up!" It was Mama, gently shaking her shoulder. Instantly Julia was awake, instantly she remembered the torn dress and for a moment was filled with panic until she remembered she had stuffed it under her bed, where no one would see it. She blinked and yawned, to cover any distress that might have shown, and looked up at Mama's gentle face, smiling down at her—Mama who loved her and was so patient! How Julia in that moment longed to unburden her heart which she found now as full of anguish as it had been when she climbed into bed last night! But it was a luxury an erring child like herself could not afford. She looked away from Mama, so that Mama would not discover her guilt, saw that midmorning sunlight was streaming into the room.

"Oh!" she exclaimed "Is it late?"

"I thought you might be tired," Mama said. "You have seemed upset, dear, just lately. I thought it would do no harm if you were to get some extra rest." She could not remember having ever been allowed to sleep late! Respectable people did not. Mama's kindness reminded her that she was not respectable either.

"Oh, yes. Thank you, Mama," she gulped.

"Papa has come home from the office," Mama said, now that the amenities were disposed of. "He wants to talk to you. Here." Mama took from the dresser a tray which Julia had not noticed and set it on the table beside her bed. "I've brought you a little tea and toast; you can eat while you dress. I think Papa is a little in a hurry, Julia, so perhaps you had better get along with it."

Papa had come home from the office to talk with her? Julia could not imagine why, unless someone had seen her in the Levering coach last night and had mentioned it to Papa and Papa had hurried home to see if it were true. Oh, she thought, that has got to be it! How could she possibly face him!

Mama had left the room now, so that Julia could dress privately, but her hands were trembling so badly that she knew she could not dress. She tried to eat the toast, but it stuck in her throat, gagging her until an enormous swallow disposed of it, leaving her weak and shaking all over. She brushed her hair and tied it back with a blue ribbon, and because there was no help for it, she put on her robe of quilted calico and her slippers of the same material. It was not suitable to approach her father in such garb, but if she were disgraced and dishonored in his eyes because she had left the house last night, the robe would only be part of the whole, unsavory picture. . . .

I can't go out there, she thought. I can't.

But she must, and somehow she did, quietly opening her bedroom door and stealing down the hall, peeking into the sitting room where Papa stood by the window watching the street below. No one else was in the room, she quickly ascertained, and it was far worse that way, for clearly he had chased them all downstairs into Miss Easton's parlor so he could have at her without anyone present to defend her or take her side. As if anyone would! Not even Ellen would, once she found that Julia had ridden out with Cabot, and not Adam!

"Come in, Julia!" Papa called when he saw her at the door. He crossed the room and took her hand, seated her in a chair by the window and took one across from her, pulling it up closer to hers, apparently not noticing she was still in her nightclothes. He did not look angry, she saw.

In fact, she could not determine exactly what the expression on his face did tell her. It was bland, yet strained. Tensely, she waited.

"This morning at my office I received a letter," he began, and her heart sank. Someone had informed him in writing! "It will be of great interest to you, I know, so I came right home to show it to you." Now his face contained excitement, and she did not believe that it would have, had he known about her defection. She allowed herself to relax, just a little.

"There are some things I'd like to ask you first, before we talk about this letter."

Instantly her alarm rose up again.

"Yes, Papa?" she asked, hoping that he did not notice the tremor in her voice.

"How do things stand, between you and the Levering boy?"

"Adam?"

"Is there another?"

"No! No!" she stammered. "The fact is, Papa, that Adam is being sent to England. I won't be seeing him any more."

"Never?"

Why was he watching her so carefully? She wished he

124

wouldn't, because she had no control over the hot blush now spreading all over her face.

"I don't think so, Papa."

"Why is that, I wonder?"

This, too, she could not divulge for the sake of her parents' pride. She could not tell them that they had not measured up to the standard of Beacon Hill.

"Really, Papa!" she protested, hoping that he would believe his question offended her maidenly dignity. "We—we are not well suited, Adam and I."

"That's a pity," he said. "I had hopes . . . but never mind. It makes the letter doubly important, and I was only curious to know whether or not my immediate appraisal of it was accurate. I see that it was. Let me tell you a few things, Julia my dear, that will allow you to understand the significance of this letter, especially now that your young friend appears to . . . er . . . no longer interest you."

He would drive her mad if he did not get on with it! She clenched her teeth and waited.

"You knew, of course, that Tony and I had set up a branch of Merrick and Son in Australia?"

"Oh, of course, Papa. And isn't it nice that Tony has enjoyed Melbourne so much!"

"He has enjoyed it too much," Papa said ruefully. "He has enjoyed it so much that he has failed to be attentive to the demands of the business. When Kingsley was still in Melbourne, he was able to give Tony advice and sometimes a line of credit, but now Kingsley is gone and Tony has not done well with the branch. In fact, he has done very badly and has run me into debt over it. If I am to repay the indebtedness, I must liquidate my holdings here in Boston. That has become very clear to me this week."

She had not the slightest idea how a man might liquidate his holdings, knowing neither concept at all, but it was clear to her that Papa had not come home to discuss any activity of hers last night, and she relaxed at last in her chair.

"I know this is not something that a young and tender girl such as yourself would be likely to understand," Papa went on. "So let us change the topic of conversation to another phase of it. Are you aware, Julia, that financial conditions just now are very unsettled?"

Surely this was a very strange conversation! She frowned in an attempt to follow it. Women were neither expected nor required to understand the man's world of business.

"I think I remember hearing something of the kind," she

murmured, recalling that Adam had told her the Beacon Hill social season would be more limited this year, because of business being bad.

"I shall not bore you with the details," Papa said, and his face was white. "Suffice it to say that my business here in Boston has suffered badly. My resources are at a low ebb and I am not sure that I can cover Tony's indebtedness."

"Oh, I am sorry to hear it," she cried with genuine concern. "Perhaps my ball gown was too expensive! You should have told me, Papa! I'd have been satisfied with less!"

"The gown didn't help, but I considered it a kind of investment. Lost now, like the rest. I shall miss the place in Waterford," Papa sighed. "I expect, we all will miss it."

"Miss it?" She tried very hard to understand him, but it was difficult.

"Yes," he said sadly. "Unless something happens—some sort of reverse in the present business cycle, I will have to sell the house and the land, too."

"Sell it!" In a daze, she saw the beautiful house with its pretty rooftop porch—the fields, the orchard, the terrace, the pond—the bay beyond—whirling about and whisked away. "Sell it?" she whispered. "Oh, Papa, no!"

"I'm sorry now I tore down the old place," Papa went on, as if he had not heard her. "We could have lived there—but now we don't even have that to turn to."

She pictured the musty, dreadful dark cottage, bought from her cousin Kingsley, sagging in every seam, and even if the Merricks might not be able to return to it now, the realization of having to live in such an awful house brought to her clearly the situation that Papa faced.

"Father," she said. "That's terrible! You must mean that we shall be poor!"

"Yes," he mumbled, looking at his hands. "We will be poor. Your mother, your sisters, you and me—and Tony, too. We will all be poor. I can hardly believe it myself. I have wanted all my life to provide you and your mother everything you needed and wanted." He watched her, judging the effect of these apparently humble words, but Julia, rising to the bait, did not notice.

"Oh, Papa!" she exclaimed. "You have been a most kind and generous father. The best of all papas!"

He jumped to his feet and began to wander about the room. "Yes, yes, I have been a good provider, and it has been a splendid life's work. You girls are the flowers in my garden, the flowers I have nurtured since your first dear breath. To see you wither now, from want of care . . ." He paused by the hearth, propped himself on the mantle, held a hand to his brow and massaged it, as though it were tight. He glanced her way, to see if more were needed. "To see your wonderful mother shorn of all she holds dear, after the magnificent years she has given us her devotion . . ." He allowed his voice to break, and Julia ran to him, throwing her arms about him.

"Papa!" she cried. "Surely something can be done!"

"There's only one thing I can think of." He did not look at her, but continued staring disconsolately at the mantle. "There's only one way I can see out of the whole mess, the only way I can see to maintain the kind of life we have known always and loved. And that is if you, Julia, were to marry Kingsley."

Her breath was suddenly lost, somewhere deep inside her. Her heart suddenly did not beat, and in her ears was a hushed stillness, within which she could hear the most minute sounds—the brush of a tree branch that touched the house, the plink of a teacup downstairs in Miss Easton's parlor, where gentle voices spoke in words she could not distinguish.

She backed away from her father. "If I married Kingsley?" Her heart began to pound fast now, as if to make up for lost time. "I? Marry Kingsley?"

He took her hand, and led her back to the chairs they had occupied when the interview began.

"Here." He dug into his pocket and brought out the letter. "I would like you to read this now."

It was written in a beautiful, flowing script which was better, Julia noticed, than her own. But her hands were trembling as she reached for it, and she folded them tightly.

"Perhaps you had better read it to me," she said weakly.

"Very well." Papa cleared his throat, glanced at her to make sure he had her attention. "I'll skip over the amenities and commence at the point that concerns you." He scanned the page, and began.

I have been touring the Continent this year, as you know, and I have seen about all there is to see and done about all there is to do, and I confess I am tired of it and bored with it.

I have written to Hartland's to ask if I might take charge of their Boston office, and although I have yet to receive their reply, I am confident that the position is mine for the asking. I return home with what would be called a tolerable fortune in Boston or New York, and Hartland's knows it. There is no one in the New York office disposed to argue with success; the Boston branch, as I understand it, needs new blood. I believe they will welcome me.

So I shall sail soon for home. I cannot stay away. Despite myself and all my resolutions, my heart will revisit the scene of my unhappily spent younger years, and I am eager to see it once again. I cannot crowd old associations out of my memory, and indeed, I hardly even wish to. I believe they can be turned, now, into pleasant remembrances. . . .

Remember me to my Aunt Elizabeth and to my cousins, especially to Julia with whom I once shared a choir loft and who played lovely music for me, whom I recall so clearly and with such delight—

> Your Humble Servant,
> Etc. Etc.,
> Kingsley

"There," Papa said in triumph.

She sat quietly and stared at him, her mind a perfect blank.

"He does not speak of marriage in so many words, that's true," Papa said into the silence. "But there is room for interpretation, is there not?" He was speaking fast now. "He mentions you specifically, Julia, and he is coming home soon. I wonder, the more I think of it, if he is not coming home just to see you. Surely he must be thinking of marriage—to someone! He is twenty-seven years old, and ripe for wedding. He is a rich man, Julia! You are old enough, and you, my dear, possess all the accomplishments and graces proper to the wife of a wealthy gentleman. You would be a fine wife for him, Julia, and I am sure he would give you a good life. And I am sure he would not let his wife's family perish in destitution."

Surely Papa must be jesting! Surely he did not expect her to take this seriously—but as she looked carefully at him and tried to make some coherent pattern of the difficulties that he faced—all of which seemed quite jumbled now in her confusion—she saw that he was very much in earnest—had the whole thing plotted out in his mind—his salvation and Mama's and hers—through the beneficence of Kingsley Merrick. A beneficence she herself was to secure.

She was suddenly very cold.

"Naturally, Kingsley has not said that he wishes to marry

you. It would be unbecoming to say so in a letter—but we can hope. And when he arrives, we can do our best to show our pride and joy, our precious daughter, in the true light of her sweetness and purity, her accomplishments."

"Papa!" she cried, unable to listen to another word of it. "For heaven's sake, why not just ask him for a loan?"

Papa looked at her for a long moment. "I'm afraid it would be more than that," he said. "I'd have to ask him for virtual support, if the present state of things continues. I am nearly bankrupt. Considering that we have not put ourselves out to be especially kind to Kingsley in the years of his youth—years which he remembers yet, I would gather from his letter—I think that would be asking quite a lot, don't you?"

"He might do it. I remember him as a kind person."

"He might. He might not. I don't know why he should if there is nothing in it for him. But if you are his wife, Julia, I think our manner of living might continue on the plane that we are accustomed to. Naturally I would retire, and live in the house at Waterford—our expenses there would not be so very great a strain—though more, I am sure, than Kingsley would care to underwrite out of sheer generosity. . . . Our family is yet quite large; only Ellen has any prospects, but I don't really believe James will prosper, not as a teacher, which is what he plans to be—and there is still Tony, who will have to be given another stake to get going again. Clara will want to continue her art instruction, and lately Hetty has been talking of attending the Franklin Academy, so that she might qualify herself to teach school, even though, at present, I would prefer she did not. Her chances of getting a husband would be nil then—but either way, provision will have to be made for her, for a while, at least. . . ." He went on and on, enumerating all the things that the family would like to do, and Julia was beside herself by the time he finished, wishing only that she might get away from him, and away from the implication of his plans upon her life. Marry Kingsley!

"Naturally," Papa was rambling on, "we cannot let him know how precarious our situation is. It might discourage him—might it not? We shall have to carry on as we usually do, but we shall be nice to him, make him see how pleasant it is to belong to our family—how lucky he is, really, to be in a position where he might easily belong to it for the rest of his life. . . ."

Anger rose in her then, and momentarily she forgot her

vows of obedience and docility of the night before, and her reason for making them.

"I thought Kingsley was considered something of a black sheep," she said acidly. "I thought he wasn't good enough for us—that the only reason we were even nice to him was to wangle his house away and so that he'd look after Tony's interests. That's what you said at the time, Papa."

"I wouldn't put it quite that way," Papa began. "Kingsley's father was a renegade of the first order, and caused us much embarrassment. Naturally we were not eager to be intimate with the son who served to remind everyone of certain unfortunate facts."

"That was not very charitable of you," she said. "It was mean, Father."

"I know," he admitted. "That's why we have to be especially careful now. Hopefully Kingsley was never aware of how assiduously we tried to avoid him."

"You've already indicated that he does know."

"It's delicate," he agreed. "We can't really be sure how much he has understood. We can only be cordial now."

"It's a rather dishonorable course, Father! One of which I have no wish to be a part. He wasn't good enough for us before, and from the sound of it, we aren't good enough for him now!"

"We certainly are," Papa said loudly, springing to his feet, pacing. "I have worked, all my life, rising from nothing to a position of respectability and some affluence, so that you girls would qualify for good, sound marriages. Now Tony has run me in debt. If business weren't so bad I could pay it—an evil turn in events has led me to this impasse, none of my own doing. I'm as good as the next fellow, better than most, and no one can say I haven't worked hard. Would you deny me, Julia—I who have labored so long on your behalf?"

Her anger faded and taking its place was the remorse she'd felt last night, the guilt over betraying her parents, and everything they stood for, her denial of their standards, their love—and here was Papa, asking for her help. Who was she to deny him, cast aspersions on his character? Denying him was causing even greater guilt to rise now, and it was an impossible burden, a crushing cross, heaping dread upon her which she could not face. To betray her father twice was impossible in the face of this remorse! Surely it must be very hard for Papa to ask! She should be making it easier for him, not harder. And to think of Mama living at the almshouse in Waterford—that was impossible! Yet just as cruel was her newly acquired understanding of the intent of men, the learning of which had brought on all this guilt and recrimination, the perception of which led her unavoidably to know that within young men—no doubt all young men—was caged the beast she had seen in Cabot Levering.

"Perhaps he will not like me," she faltered.

"There's no reason why he shouldn't," Papa assured her. "Frankly speaking, you far outshine your sisters, and I'll try to see to it that while he is in Waterford, Kingsley sees as little of anyone else as possible. There are, of course, added inducements you might offer, if you judge them necessary. Men are not such ephemeral creatures as women, Julia, and if need be, you might demonstrate to Kingsley that you are desirable not only socially, but in other aspects of your womanhood as well. It is no time to be prudish, unless you feel that Kingsley would admire you the more for it. Somehow I don't believe he will. He's no gentleman—though in time he may become one! I would suggest that if you find him becoming impatient with your modesty, you let some of it fall by the wayside. Not too much, of course. Just a little, without letting Mama know! Enough to show him how desirable you are. And my dear, you could be—you are—desirable indeed!"

She could only stare, scarcely believing what she heard. That her father could even hint at such a thing concerning her own attributes . . . Papa, it appeared, was not one hundred percent ephemeral, either! It was possible that the beast lay within Papa, too! It was a shock great as all the other shocks she had endured.

"Just remember your mother," he said. "And her devotion to you all these years. She loves you well, Julia; she would lay down her life for you. Is it so much to ask—that you sacrifice a part of yours?"

Yes! Yes! she wanted to cry. *It is too much!* He stood there unperturbed, satisfied, well pleased with his solution to the family problems, and she could not cry out. She could only leave the room, blindly, stumbling against the doorway to the hall, groping her way to her bedroom, locking the door behind her lest Papa decide there was more he needed to say and should follow her. The little room was barren and cheerless, and she hesitated in the middle of it, shocked and despairing, unable to turn one way or the other, or even to climb back into bed where she might get warm again.

How could it be? How could it be! In so short a time, everything in her life was being swept away, just when she needed it to remain exactly as it was! Now, just now, when she needed the comfort and assurance and safety that her family had always provided—now when she needed the bulwark of her family to shield her from her anguish and fears and make them go away—now it was on the verge of perishing unless she could save it—and if she did, she wouldn't be around to be sheltered and protected by it because she would be married to Kingsley.

She did not want to marry Kingsley.

She did not want to marry anyone, having then to confront what lurked behind the façade called man! No! She did not want to marry—not anymore!

Her dread grew, larger and more formidable—it surged about her, as though she were upon a rock in the middle of the sea, where an angry, ugly surf pounded around her and reached up to lash her flesh. Beneath the tattered edge of her self-control fear lunged, and her numbed brain heard Papa's voice saying, "Enough to show him how desirable you are . . ." Desirable. Cabot had used that word, and Julia understood now that desirability did not refer to charm, or talent, or even an attractive appearance. It meant something more—a great deal more. It meant the ability of a woman to make a man want to touch her body, and somehow, in some way, she must not only contrive to be desirable—she must also allow her cousin certain liberties! She must do it so that her family wouldn't be poor—so she wouldn't be poor . . . !

I won't, she thought desperately. *I can't. Perhaps Kingsley doesn't want to marry me at all!* Her spirits rose a bit at this ray of hope—only to sink again upon reminding herself that she must see to it that he did want to marry her, else Papa would have to sell the house and the land in Waterford, and the Merricks would have to depend on charity to survive. . . . A fine way to repay the years of loving care!

No! No! she nearly cried out. She could no longer bear immobility in the face of this onslaught—this catastrophe—and her inescapable dread. She moved about the little room, straightening a chair here, a picture there, and to distract herself, however momentarily, fetching her clothes from her wardrobe to put on for the day—remembering the dress beneath the bed which had better get mended. She reached under and retrieved it, carefully gauging how best to fix it, getting her thread and needle and scissors and thimble from the little japanned box that held her sewing things. She took them to the window and the chair there where the sun, now high, threw only a small streak of dancing light upon the floor at her feet. . . .

She couldn't do it.

She would have to do it!

Beyond the window, a tree which shaded Miss Easton's tiny courtyard in the rear of the house lifted its branches high, reaching for the sky above Boston. It was a bright sky, washed by an east breeze, where an occasional gull cruised like a kite, free and soaring.

I can't, she thought. *Someone else will have to. Clara will have to do it. Hetty will have to do it . . . But Hetty wasn't very pleasant and Clara was terribly homely. If only Ellen weren't engaged to James . . . but she was, and only Hetty and Clara were left. I'll have to play them up anyway,* she thought. *It doesn't give me much to hope for, but I'll have to try. And if it doesn't work . . . .*

She shivered.

In a branch of the tree a chickadee hopped and chattered, impervious to her misery.

She must not think of it! She must think of something else! *I remember him as a kind man,* she told herself desperately, reaching for something, however fragile, to salvage in the midst of disaster. I remember him as a sympathetic man, who stood by me once and tried to defend me and later to comfort me. . . . For all I know, he is a fine person. . . .

And yet the character and temperament of her cousin was, she knew, a minor issue at this point, a smoke screen behind which the crux of the matter lay.

The crux of it was too awful—too impossible—to contemplate, but she could not stop her mind, nor put from herself the understanding that Kingsley was indeed a man, with a man's body, a man's lusts, and if she must be desirable to him now, in order to get him to marry her, what—she quailed . . . she almost could not formulate the thought, even to herself . . . what would happen later, when they were wed?

I won't! she cried silently; fear rose to clutch her throat. The needle pricked her finger and a bright drop of blood blossomed and stood upon her skin like a glistening bead, and she stared at it, her pulse pounding and her finger throbbing and within, deep and mute, part of herself looked upon her pain and anguish calmly, invulnerable.

Perhaps, it said, voiceless, *you will have to.*

Sitting in the thin streak of sunlight which was all that remained of the morning, she felt her very being in retreat, withdrawing toward the safety of a protective shell which she had not even known existed, as though within the core of her self lay as a nautilus the curved, curled chambers of brittleness, of numbness, of merciful emptiness, over which now washed the tears of her despair.

I can't, she wept. *I can't.*

Three
The Native Son

The fiddlers scraped with vigor, their music soared and swooped as the dancers on the floor circled, barely avoiding collisions, while the drift of the dance rotated past the entrance of the Lyceum Hall and the convenient basket full of the evening's contributions, past the rose-strewn punch table where parched merrymakers clustered, down to the fiddlers on their platform, on by the multitude of chairs in the far corner where the older women might sit, and back again to the entrance. The waltz, danced by so many people, required more room than the upper floor of Waterford's Lyceum Hall offered, but the undaunted couples whirled, bumped, whirled on; in their midst stepped Kingsley Merrick, guiding with determination his cousin Clara, who responded to his lead as might the helm of the frigate *Constitution*. Clara, concentrating now on the music and her attempt to follow, had long since given up the pretense of conversation; on her upper lip were forming beads of sweat which mingled with the unfortunate dark hairs that grew there. She was certainly homely, Kingsley thought, and certainly heavy on her feet, and he could see why Julia had suggested that he dance with the girl. Surely no one else would! He had gallantly complied, leading the thrilled and nervous Clara to the floor, but he was well aware, as he did so, that Julia, in rescuing Clara from the wall where unclaimed girls generally stood, had used her sister to gain a respite for herself.

He guessed he had come on a bit too strong. He guessed, by claiming her for every dance earlier in the evening and by suggesting that they stroll in the moonlight when the revelry here was done, that he had alarmed her, that he had pressed a bit too hard. Yes, it had been a mistake! One he'd made because of Julia, herself. Julia, extraordinarily handsome in a gown of blue silk that swayed so gracefully when she walked, cut low in the front so that the gentle swell of her bosom was forever just at the edge of his vision as he danced with her. Julia, gentle and smiling subtly, listening to what he had to

137

say and asking, now and again, a question that indicated she had really heard him and was not simply playing up to him to gain his attention. Julia alone of all the young women of Waterford not playing up to him at all but waiting with quiet dignity which made him eager—too eager—to seek her presence. Now she was in retreat, her eyes which had sparkled were veiled, and she had found, suddenly, little to say except to praise her sister Clara who was a lovely girl, he'd find, once he got past her shyness and awkwardness— perhaps he ought to ask her to dance?

Well, he could take the hint! He was behaving like a gawky boy instead of the man of the world he was—he'd just got carried away, was all, exactly as he had the moment he'd first laid eyes on her. . . . It wouldn't do, not at all.

When he was through with Clara, he'd ask other girls to dance, girls whose eager eyes followed him as he had waltzed with Julia and were following him now as he shuffled along with Clara, upon whose foot he trod.

About the room mamas of eligible girls were fairly wringing their hands in vexation that Kingsley Merrick thus far had shown himself interested only in his cousins (really, the hospitality of the Merricks need not be repaid that plentifully even though young Merrick was a guest in their house!).

But he would not attend Julia any more tonight. He would not ask her to dance again and he would not even speak with her; when the dance was over, having applied pressure of the reverse order, perhaps she might find herself no longer fatigued. She might welcome the chance to again receive his attention, to walk in the moonlight, especially when she saw that she might lose out to others—for certainly there were others! Kingsley Merrick was in great demand!

There was nothing, he mused as he shoved Clara about, nothing that could compete with success, nothing to compare with it. Nothing could take its place in one's assessment of oneself, and now, with his triumphal return to Waterford, he had learned the corollary: that if those who had once doubted, even scorned, now understood that you had achieved success, then your achievement was double-fold. Did not Waterford admire him now! Oh, at this very moment, Waterford wanted him, all right. There had been men yesterday on the beach to meet him as he stepped off the packet, men glad to shake his hand, older captains, retired now, and some of the younger crop, waiting for voyages; the minister of the First Parish Church, Congregational, had been there and the minister of the Universalist Church, trying to elbow

138

his way in, and of course Uncle Lije himself, eager to hurry Kingsley away to his house, there to surround him with comfort and joy.

It was quite a reception, all right, quite different from the last! Just now there was only unabated goodwill flowing in Kingsley Merrick's direction, and he had the sense to enjoy it while he had it—a little scornfully, perhaps, because he knew the stuff it was made of and was not deceived. It amused him because he could afford to be amused now. He'd known favor won by his worth, not simply by his achievements; it sufficed to steady him, had done so for quite a while. He had done well not only financially in Australia, but he had found friends and comrades there, too, and the farewell party they had given him, complete with many elaborate gifts, was one that would be long remembered. It should have been recorded in Australian annals, except that it was too ribald. Hadn't they all had fun!

He regretted leaving them. With the agreement of his partners, he had sold the Clipper Coach Line at exactly the right moment, at the peak of its success but before the competition started getting rough—but he would miss those friends. As a rule he had always gotten on well with his peers; he anticipated doing so again, when he went up to Boston to take over Hartland's office. That was where he belonged! Not here, in this staid and respectable and stifling community of captains and their families, who thought ostentation was the mark of an ill-bred man, who hid their wealth (and there was a lot of it here) by dressing modestly, by remaining in the homes their fathers had built when the Greek influence was just begun (only a few of them building newer, larger, more lordly palaces now). They eschewed servants because they disliked and distrusted the Irish who crowded the cities and threatened to overwhelm the native-born; they got only occasional grudging help from the local farming and fishing community, and they settled for it rather than accommodating themselves to the challenge of an alien people with new ideas. The mariner packed into his attic priceless treasure from the ports of the world, displayed his artifacts sparingly in his parlor so that no one could accuse him of parading his success. . . .

Christ! Why succeed at all if you couldn't enjoy it? What was money for but to buy ease and pleasure! Whether it was ostentation or not, Kingsley Merrick didn't intend to bury his fortune beneath the floorboards! He'd use it well, as Abel Warden of East Waterford did, who employed servants and dressed like a New Yorker. But then, Mr. Warden was not truly of Waterford—no more than Kingsley would be, and so was not influenced by local opinion, just as Kingsley was not. Wealthier than the rest by inheritance and by acumen, Warden rose to lordly heights both here and in Boston—yet the rest were not far behind, Kingsley surmised, in wordly measure. More than one mariner owned ships—or shares in them—as well as mastering them. More than one owned stocks in textile mills and railroads (though these things, anathema to the sailing merchant fleet, were not acknowledged). There wasn't a mariner here who had not at least once taken out a clipper, the height of seafaring and the pinnacle of both achievement and remuneration. Yes, indeed, Waterford, for all its dowdy colors, was not wanting when it came to tabulating worth. . . .

Of course, all these treasures were slightly tarnished these days; stocks and shipping and nearly everything involved in the marketplace were slightly depressed, as he understood it, because the panic had stalled everything, but no one was seriously worried as yet. Things had a way of straightening themselves around, so Uncle Lije affirmed. What was down one year would be up the next. Only the improvident need worry.

Uncle Lije, he gathered, was not among the improvident.

Gad, would this dance never end? His arm about Clara's waist was going to be lame at this rate! No. It was now coming to a close. The musicians were winding down; soon they'd put their instruments aside and drink the punch that the young ladies of the library association sponsoring the dance would hurry to offer them. He and Clara were near that corner where chairs were grouped and Uncle Lije was there, just as Kingsley had seen him last, standing beside Aunt Elizabeth, sipping punch and watching the progress of the dance. He maneuvered Clara out of the mainstream despite her inability to understand what he was trying to do, and into the little eddy of respite.

"I thought you might like to rest," he said cordially to her, bowing to his aunt and reaching for a chair, all in one motion. "Won't you sit down?"

"Why, thank you," Clara said in an approximation of coy appreciation (a flutter of the thin eyelashes, a hand pressed to her flat chest). Heavily, she sat.

"Having a good time?" Uncle Lije asked. Several members of the older set, glancing up, smiled benignly. (Wasn't Kingsley Merrick handsome, and didn't he have the nicest manners? Been in Europe for a year, my dear. Europe would

140

put polish on a clam shell. Never know him for the same lad, would you?)

"A fine time, Uncle!"

"Been dancing with my daughters, I see! You've monopolized them, you rogue!" Lije winked slyly.

"Too much, perhaps."

"No, no," Lije said quickly. "I am sure that is not the case at all."

"Nonetheless I shall find out how the other maidens of Waterford dance. Julia is quite tired of me."

"No, no," Lije said more quickly. "I am sure she is not. She has mentioned to me already how much she enjoys your company."

"Oh? Well, good! Perhaps she might, if I ask her nicely, walk with me after the dance is done. That is, sir, if you and Aunt Elizabeth approve of it." (There was more than one way to get around Julia!)

"Certainly, certainly." Lije smiled broadly, nodded. "I'm sure you'll take good care of her."

"Oh, yes!" said Aunt Elizabeth in response to an unseen nudge from her husband. "Julia would be delighted, I am sure."

"That's good to know. I'll ask her, then, later on."

He bowed and departed; the fiddlers were tuning up again and he made his way to the side of Amanda Warden, who pretended not to notice his approach, who pretended to be surprised when he appeared at her elbow. She was standing with her father, and the honorable Abel Warden greeted Kingsley warmly. He did not come to Waterford much, but when in residence at his huge place to the east of town he made a point of being present on the local scene and of dragging his family along, so that Waterford would not think him too elevated for their amusements. His son John lolled in a corner, disdaining to dance and probably sneaking drinks from his flask, but Mandy was more than willing to do her part.

"I hoped your daughter would do me the honor . . ."

"I would be charmed to dance, sir," Mandy Warden smiled, although she did not personally know Kingsley Merrick, nor had she ever met him. But she was rich enough, spoiled enough, to be bold. He was a new and exciting face on the scene she found usually dull—and who had not heard of him since his return?

"How are you, Merrick!" Warden reached out to shake

Kingsley's hand. "Happy to see you home again. Amanda," he said to his daughter, "this is King Merrick."

"How do you do?" She dipped a small, pert curtsey.

"Do I have your permission, sir, to dance with her?"

"Indeed, indeed!"

With a nod, Kingsley whirled her off, narrowly escaping collision with another couple, the man of whom scowled in a manner reminiscent of times gone by.

"That's Sears Bradley, isn't it?" he asked Amanda Warden, who glanced casually toward the couple and back again.

"Yes, it is. He thinks himself very important, too! We have interrupted his step, now he is off balance, and very annoyed, I expect."

He looked again and saw that Bradley's partner was Angelina Winslow. At least, she had been Angelina Winslow once!

"Is that Miss Winslow he's dancing with?"

"No!" giggled Amanda Warden. "It's Mrs. Bradley. Tell me of your adventures, Mr. Merrick! I understand you have made Australia your home," she said, quickly changing the subject, steering it away from a woman other than herself. She, thank God, was a good dancer.

"I have lived there, yes. But the year past I have been in Europe," he told her. "So I can't claim to be a recent resident."

"Still, you know so much about it!" Miss Warden exclaimed. "Do, please, tell me about it." Her eyes, starry with admiration real or trumped up, gazed into his with the fervid appeal to learn of Mr. Merrick's Great Experience, to get Mr. Merrick talking about himself, which men so loved to do, to present him with an audience so rapt that he would call upon her at her house for more. Obediently he told her what he guessed she would want to hear—what most people wanted to hear—about the umbrella-shaped blue-gray gum trees of Australia, the sparse leaves of which did not fall in winter, and which filtered the sun and diffused it delightfully in summer; the bracing, invigorating air which made nothing of one hundred degree heat, the population of aborigines, fast dying out, whose language sounded like the babble of children pretending to be Indians; kangaroos and koala bears and brilliant birds—things he had described so much already that he could do it without thinking, his mind free to wander as he talked.

He did not describe the dust and flies and mosquitos of summer, the mice and mud of winter which made the acres of tents at the diggings a positive hell, cheerfully endured as men dug, deeper and deeper, squeezing into narrow shafts and lifting with a windlass bucket after bucket of dirt to be panned and thrown in a heap of mulloch. He said little about the men whom he had met there, who drank and cursed and ignored the tremendous and motley mix of nationalities, races, religions, positions in society, or lack of them except for their disdain of the Chinese. Around and over the maelstrom Kingsley Merrick assigned coaches and drivers and way stations and feed and moved passengers and goods from Melbourne to the fields at Ballarat, ninety miles away over a winding track, and a similar distance to Bendigo. Along the road to the gold fields were tents that served coffee and grog, and the fields themselves were a disaster area of pits and holes dug so close to one another that a wagon couldn't drive through lest it fall into a cavern.

He did not mention to his polite, attentive listeners the police force, auxiliary to the British army, that threw its weight around and pestered people for their permits, sometimes making a man climb out of his hundred foot hole a dozen times a day, the violence that erupted when men were pushed too far—these things he did not describe to young ladies or their mamas and papas; nor did he often describe the struggle to establish the Clipper Coach Line. It was not something the ladies were much interested in (except Julia, whose questions had drawn from him its whole story), and unless a man knew something of coaching, it was not something he'd likely appreciate. Few were the men to whom Kingsley had described it.

He arrived in Melbourne to find the city still raw, hip deep in mud, and scarcely any rooms available to rent. Tents were set up in vacant lots between buildings, and everywhere men milled about, eager to get to the gold fields and happy to walk if no other means of conveyance were available. It was a jocose crowd, a joyful one, and the bloody Yanks were as welcome there as the next man. There was no looking down a long nose at uncouth Americans, such as was too frequently the case in England. Australia, like America, was not concerned with a man's couth, but only with his ability.

From the port of Melbourne to the city itself struggled the heavy English wagons in the rain, floating through the quagmire on their floors, their wheels up to the hub in mud and the horses floundering gamely. He eliminated immediately the possibility of profitable ferrying of goods from the port of entry. Prospective passengers walked, as well they might; a

Concord would fare no better between Emerald Hill and the Yarra than the English wagons were doing now.

But between Melbourne and the diggings! That was where Concords had the edge over the steel-spring English coaches. Concords were slung on thick leather thoroughbraces and, instead of jiggling and jouncing and bouncing fit to put a man's head through the roof, they swayed to the roughness of the road like a schooner sailing downwind over the swells. They were so light in contrast to the British wagons that a horse could haul them further, faster, reducing the traveling time by half. The Clipper Coach here couldn't lose with its new Concord! With difficulty he rented an office on Collins Street, just as his partners and equipment caught up with him. They arrived with the Concord filled to the brim with Yankee harness and a whole gaggle of splendid, unbroken horses which, because they were green, had been bought cheaply. He hid his dismay at the sight of them. How long would it take, he wondered, before they'd be useful? The money wouldn't last forever! But it would not do to display misgivings. . . .

Cheerfully he left the job to the whips, and set out with the others to establish way stations along the track.

Hay and oats were at a premium. Even if a farmer wanted to produce them, everyone was at the diggings and no one was left to labor in the fields. So the Clipper Coach Line was obliged to bring them in from Tasmania at £35/10 a ton, and cart them from the wharf, besides. The stakes were rising, higher by the day—but Kingsley Merrick, a picture of self-confidence, smiling, cordial, set about promoting the line, promptly paying the accumulation of bills, and in three weeks every last raw colt was in harness, ready to go. He wouldn't have believed it possible had he not seen it with his own eyes.

The first Clipper Coach left the Criterion six weeks after the office was rented, Fulton in the box and Nash waiting for him at Forest Creek to make the return trip, the others at way stations with fresh horses to back into the traces the instant the coach pulled up, able to take the reins if need be, Merrick selling tickets, taking in the cash. . . .

He'd waited breathlessly in the office, waiting to see if the coach would return at eight o'clock the next morning as he'd advertised it would. The mail took two days, but the Clipper would take twelve hours to Forest Creek and twelve back, if only Fulton didn't get lost! Sometimes the road, what there was of it, simply petered out and you were off in the trackless bush, cutting cross country, and heaven help you if you got off course by even a slight degree! If only Nash, due to set out as evening fell, hadn't imbibed too freely at the grog tents at Forest Creek! He could drive blindfolded, but Kingsley hoped he wouldn't be driving blind. . . .

The coach, dusty but still splendidly red, the floral and gold ornamentation still in evidence after the night on the road, pulled up to the Criterion at seven and a half in the morning, parcels piled high in the rack out back, chock-full of passengers inside and more crowded onto the roof and beside Nash, the driver, all of them excited, merry, and quite drunk on grog and the excitement of the first run of the Clipper Coach Line which they had themselves witnessed every mile of. . . .

Success was unavoidable. More coaches were procured. They'd been furiously busy; between business and the pleasant friendships that arose so easily, why, there had been little time for his cousin Tony who worked, as planned, for Baker and Company and then opened a branch of Merrick and Son and did a little speculating on the side. Except for some last-ditch advice upon occasion, a loan several times when Tony had inaccurately judged a risk, he had seen little of him, nor did he care to!

"The little bears sound charming!" exclaimed Amanda Warden. "Do you think they'd make good pets?"

"Perhaps," he laughed, "but they smell bad! They eat only eucalyptus leaves, and the eucalyptus is very pungent, like a dose of spring tonic."

"Ugh!" she exclaimed cheerfully. "Let's leave the little bears there, where they belong! I should like to hear more, Mr. Merrick, any time you'd care to tell it. We plan to be in Waterford another week or two. In fact, my mother will come down from Boston soon to join us, and I know she will be eager to meet you to learn of Australia, too."

"Wonderful!" he exclaimed, as though this were the best news he had heard that night. "I would be happy to come to your place," he added, and he would be happy, indeed, because there was much he would discuss with Abel Warden.

He had steered her back toward her father and slipped out of the line of the dance. Abel Warden was talking to Captain Warner Gray who owned shares in several ships, and both men welcomed Kingsley into their conversation, concerning as it did the profitability of packets and shipping to Australia. Who had better information than Kingsley Merrick on such a subject? Were the crews of ships still deserting once Melbourne was reached, they wondered? They had heard men simply jumped overboard, once in sight of land, that ships were tied up two or three days just waiting their turn for a pilot.

That was in the beginning, Kingsley assured them. Now gold was no longer just lying on the ground, waiting to be picked up. It was hard work now, and the mania was gone. It was a business like any other—but a return cargo was very much a problem, though wool production was certainly on the ascent and might one day provide the balance in trade, much as cotton did for America.

He enjoyed to the hilt being so much in demand, his opinions cultivated so attentively by men and his attention so eagerly sought by women (cousin Nell Denning was waving, with a little twinkling movement of her fingers from behind the back of her partner), and he watched Julia, as he talked with Warden and Gray, when he thought she did not notice. Yes, she pleased him. She pleased him very much, and even her withdrawals, when he was pushing too fast, pleased him, whetting as they did his appetite for pursuit. Pursuit he had always enjoyed! Her reluctance, her hesitation (not a confused and girlish hesitation, either, but a more dignified one, as though playing for time, to see and decide whether he was fit)—it had him positively tingling—yes, she was very distinct from all the many young ladies who now seemed so eager to fall all over him. The fact was—his cousin Julia quite intrigued him.

Now she was watching him covertly from across the dance floor, perhaps having recovered from his asking for every dance which was Not Done. Quickly he turned, still in the company of Abel Warden and Warner Gray, as though he were listening carefully and only shifting his stance, and found beside him Angelina Winslow. Now wife of Sears Bradley, if Miss Warden were correct. Beside her Bradley watched the dance floor as a man might watch the sea looking for landfall, listening to the comments of the gentleman on his far side whom Kingsley could not place, though he looked familiar.

"Why, hello," he smiled, breaking off from Warden and Gray with a polite nod.

"Hello, yourself," she said softly. "And how are you, Mr. Merrick? It is so pleasant to have you in our midst once more." She stepped back, so that Bradley and the unidentified gentlemen could be included in the conversation. "You remember my husband, Sears?"

Bradley shook Kingsley's hand. "How are you, Merrick?" he asked without warmth.

"And this is my father, Captain Winslow. I don't know if you two are acquainted."

The captain also shook hands, but with more vigor than had Bradley. "Glad to meet you, Merrick," he said. "Expect to be sailing for Melbourne soon. Hear you've spent quite a while there."

"I have," said Kingsley. "Very enjoyably."

"Meant to ask you about the port."

"Not as good as Sydney harbor, I'm afraid. But protected from the ocean by the bay, once you're past Bass Strait."

"Don't, Father," laughed Angelina. "Not at a party. If you get to talking, he'll never ask me to dance—and dancing is what we're here for."

He took his cue. "I hope," he said to Sears Bradley, "that I may have this dance with your wife?"

"Why not?" said Bradley ungraciously.

He bowed in the direction of the two men, and carried Angelina away with him.

"I'm very annoyed with you," she smiled. "I thought, being old friends as we were, that I would not have to resort to forcing you to ask. All evening I've been hoping you'd come flying to my side to renew our acquaintance."

Hardly could he admit he had hardly noticed she was there, so intent had he been on Julia and so swamped with the attention of others.

"I was unsure of my reception," he prevaricated. "I wouldn't care to barge in where I'm not wanted."

"Oh," she breathed. "Of course—I should have understood instantly." She looked up at him, without hint of reserve or embarrassment. "Will you accept my apology, sir, on behalf of my mother and her rudeness when you last visited Waterford? I was most distressed about that, when I learned of it."

"I shouldn't like you to be distressed," he said gallantly.

Angelina smiled up at him. In the candlelight of the room's many sconces he could not tell if her eyes were as blue as he remembered them, and even the expression there was difficult to discern. He didn't believe, for a moment, that she hadn't known what her mother was up to and concurred in it—but it was of no consequence now. It was past and gone, even if Angelina Winslow Bradley treated it as a thing of the present.

"Well," she went on. "I told my mother what I thought of her behavior! But it was too late—you were gone. . . . You

147

do dance very well! I hope we country girls have proven ourselves equal to your ability!"

"Country girls, indeed!" he scoffed. "You'd all pass muster anywhere."

"Your venture in Australia was satisfactory, I hear. I congratulate you! Doesn't it seem like a long time ago, Kingsley, that you were telling me about the things you hoped to find there? And here you are, back again, having found them!"

Her use of his given name was deliberate; she looked at him closely as she said it, as though to gauge his reaction to this familiarity, excusable if the admission were made that she had known him, and known him fairly well, a long time ago.

He did not give her the satisfaction of an equivalent response. "Tell me about yourself," he countered. "What have you been up to, in my absence?" He swung her around now, and Bradley was in his line of sight, scowling as he watched them circling about.

"Well, I have married, as you see," she said, sounding none too thrilled about it. "And I have two little boys." Her voice grew warmer. "John and Todd. Todd is only a baby—John is three, or will be soon, and very handsome, too! Sears' unmarried sister lives with us, and she all but runs the house and the babies, too. It's like having house help, only better—she has nowhere else to go, you see, and I needn't worry about whether she's happy or if she'll stay." He could see that Angelina, instead of accepting the burdens as well as the joys of the married state, had cast off most of the drudgery and continued to exist as she always had when a pampered and petted daughter of her parents. Only Sears Bradley was doing the pampering now, and no doubt the petting, too, and from the look on his face at that moment, it was clear that Sears Bradley did not like his wife enjoying the company of other men.

"Perhaps, Kingsley," Angelina was saying, "you would do us the honor of calling at our house soon. My sister-in-law loves to receive!"

"And you believe she would receive me?" he asked wickedly, enjoying the confusion he saw spreading over her lovely face.

With some embarrassment she murmured, "It is up to me whom we receive. And I would be happy were you to find time to see us."

"I'm sure Sears would be happy, too," he remarked wryly.

"Oh, Sears!" She dismissed her husband with a toss of her head. "Sears is never happy unless he's on the quarterdeck."

"Possibly he is not happy that you're dancing with me?"

"Possibly," she smiled. "Which is too bad, because you dance better than he does."

"I trust you need not tell him so."

"Perhaps I will," she teased. "Maybe he'd try harder."

"Try harder to dance well?"

"And to please me, generally. I need a lot of pleasing. I'm very hard to satisfy." She smiled sweetly.

It was really quite preposterous, certainly alien to the laws of etiquette even as imperfectly as Kingsley Merrick understood them, and thoroughly enjoyable. The displeasure of Sears Bradley was a satisfactory thing; Angelina, in her undisguised, unwise admiration, was also pleasant, causing him to forget that once she had sloughed him off just as had the rest of Waterford.

"Are you tired of telling people about Australia?" she asked with a sly sparkle in her eye. "Are you tired of having everyone listen to every morsel, every crumb of information you have on the subject? Or would you like me to ask you about it?"

"Don't ask," he said quickly, laughing. "I tend to put myself to sleep the minute the subject comes up."

"Then I won't, and I won't ask about your travels in Europe either, unless you want me to."

"Other people's travels are pretty dull listening. But I will admit that seeing far away places is very enlightening, and well worth the trouble."

"Sears wants me to go on his next voyage," she said vaguely.

"You'd never regret it. A great opportunity. Plenty of women sail with their husbands, don't they?"

"Oh, yes," she agreed quickly, and he wondered if he missed a cue which required protest of disappointment at her impending absence. "It's considered quite the thing to do."

"Besides, there would be a surprise awaiting you upon your return."

"Truly!" The sparkle was back. "Tell me!"

"It wouldn't be a surprise."

"It would be more fun to anticipate if I knew what it was."

"Well," he said slowly, as though reluctant to part with his secret. "I intend to build a house here in Waterford—right in the middle of town where no one can miss it. Different than any other—no, don't ask me what sort of difference, because

149

I shan't tell. And when you get back, it will be up and waiting to receive you."

"How splendid!" she exclaimed. "And very good news. This must mean that you plan to live in Waterford."

"Heaven forbid!" he laughed. "My place here will be for summer use."

"I really can't bear it!" she exclaimed. "Kingsley Merrick is going to build a summer home in Waterford. And I suppose, m'lord, that you shall live on Beacon Hill when you aren't living here?"

"I plan to," he said cheerfully.

"Oh, Sears will be perfectly green," she crowed, and looked about with a guilty grimace, to see if anyone might have heard this questionable remark, and then back at Kingsley, to see if she had overstepped the boundaries of good taste.

In truth, Kingsley was unsure about the reception he ought to give this remark, and uncertain, too, about how to read Angelina herself, who was behaving outrageously for a married woman. Across the room Sears Bradley made as though to cut across the floor; a twirling couple barreled by and he withdrew, his face thunderous, as he worked his way around the edge of the dance, hopelessly to pursue his wife and Kingsley Merrick.

He pulled her deftly across the room, cutting across the axis of the dance. Quite a handful, she was. No wonder Sears Bradley wanted to take her with him in his ship, the better to keep an eye on her. She was damned attractive. On the far side of the floor Bradley had retreated, and Kingsley did not like the look of him.

"I'm going to take you around and leave you with your husband," he murmured to Angelina. "I should not like to cause trouble, and from the look of him, I'd say trouble wasn't far away."

"It's too bad," she sighed. "I've enjoyed your company. I'd like to see you again, but I don't suppose you will call on us." She looked at him wistfully. "I'm afraid that I can't blame you. But perhaps I will see you, anyway, at someone else's house or party. You must be very much in demand. If ever you're looking for a spot to have your privacy, I recommend the overlook just off the Rockford Road by the Flax Pond. It's very pleasant there. I'm sure you'd enjoy it."

Was she telling him she would meet him there? Gad! The woman must have nerves of steel; there her husband stood, not five feet away. He swung her out on his arm, gathered her in so that she was placed properly by his side, so they might approach Bradley in a conventional posture.

"Thank you, sir," he said, bowing to Sears but keeping a careful watch on Bradley's clenched fists. "Thank you for the privilege of dancing with your wife."

"A privilege you have abused, sir," Bradley said icily. "See that it doesn't happen again."

It was true enough; he had danced with Angelina, a married woman, a trifle longer than courtesy required.

"Really, Sears!" Angelina exclaimed, her voice a mixture of offended innocence and scorn. It did not help. Kingsley would not have liked to meet the man in an isolated spot at that moment, and rather than risk further antagonizing him, he turned quickly and walked away. If Bradley was so possessive of his wife, let him be.

He did not so much as glance at Angelina after that; between avoiding both her and Julia, he began to wonder where he might rest his eyes! But Julia stayed in the corner with her parents, Bradley took Angelina away soon after, and Kingsley described Australia five more times to five more willing, eager, urgent listeners.

The color of Port Phillip Bay and all of the Pacific, he told Sophie MacLaren, was deep blue, quite different from the grayish cast that the Atlantic so often took, and lovely.

The city of Melbourne was attractive now, he informed Melissa Blake, gentle terrain around it before the land rose to meet the Dandenong Range, and as he was leaving they were setting up attractive precast-iron houses, complete with filigree, that arrived, their pieces already numbered, ready to assemble—why, the place had already lost its rawness, and you'd never believe, looking at it now, that before the gold rush began, it could hardly be said to have existed at all.

Gum trees were grayish in foliage, he admitted to Elizabeth Warner, and scanty at that, tougher than a—very tough, hardy trees, indeed. Thick, ferny undergrowth, the hiding place of venomous snakes . . . . She squeaked in feminine horror, quivered in anticipation of hearing more later on, another time—sometime next week? At her house?

Indeed, it was enjoyable to be ardently cultivated, and he did nothing to discourage the enthusiasm of Waterford. Later, when it was gone, he would rest happy in the memory that Waterford had once courted and wooed him, just as he intended it should.

He returned Margaret Pollard to her parents before the end of the last dance, so that there would be no expectation

151

that he would take the young lady home, and made his way to the far corner and Julia. Her smile was polished and bright, as it had been earlier in the evening, and he guessed she had recovered from his overzealous pursuit of her.

"Mama and Papa say they will let me walk with you," she said, "if you are still inclined to take a stroll."

"It might be cool now," he remarked, as though that might be reason enough to forgo it.

"Julia can use my cloak," Aunt Elizabeth said, handing it to her. "It won't take me long to get home, and I shan't be needing it."

"Yes, yes, do take a walk," Uncle Lije boomed joyfully. "A bit of fresh air would be pleasant, I'm sure!"

He held out his arm for Julia to take, watching her carefully to see if she really did want to go. She took his arm, almost with eagerness, it seemed to him. His neglect had worked after all.

In the main street of Waterford the moon shook silver through the leaves of the poplars and elms and splashed it at their feet; through its shafts drifted other young couples on their way home, walking slowly as possible, taking advantage of this quiet, intimate moment so rarely given to the young, thus doubly prized. Several went off down the road to the packet landing, and Kingsley steered Julia there, too. Once on the beach the couples parted from one another, swallowed up by the empty night, the moon playing on the dunes and occasional boulders and the wharf so intensely that nothing could be seen in the shadows.

Beneath them the sauntering couples appeared, disappeared, appeared again in the moonlight, in the darkness.

"My sister Clara is such a lovely girl, don't you think?" Julia was saying. "She really has a lot of talent, too, in her art. Given the proper instructions, I think she could do a lot with it."

"As I remember, you have quite a bit of talent, too," Kingsley said. "At the piano."

"Oh," she said, modestly. "I suppose I have—but a picture! Well, you can look at it and look at it! Once a piece is played on the piano, it's gone."

"I prefer music to painting, personally," he said.

"Oh." That seemed to stop her! "Well, of course, I do myself." She was silent for a while, looking out over the bay. "My sister Hetty is an interesting person—have you talked with her enough yet to discern that? A really active and curious mind. It's a shame she didn't have the chance to go to

152

Mrs. Hunt's school, as I did. She could have done more with it than I ever could. Mrs. Hunt believed in training women to think. Directly in line with Elizabeth Peabody, who has done so much for the education of women. Hetty is really very smart," Julia declared.

"It doesn't strike me that you are so very far behind, Julia," he said softly.

"Hetty has virtually written the whole script for the Dramatic Display," she said quickly. "And she has done it brilliantly."

"Dramatic Display?"

"Next on the Select Library's agenda. The girls are raising money for books, you see." She spoke quickly, fairly raced along. "Tonight we made twenty dollars. The Display will be held in a week and a half, and perhaps we'll earn another twenty! Later we're going to have a tea, and then a fair where we'll sell crochet and embroidery. Why, if we keep at it long enough, perhaps one day we'll have enough to put up a building just for books, so the collection won't have to be kept at the house of the librarian, the way it is now."

"From the sound of it, you'll be kept very busy," he said politely. "You'll surely miss it when you go back to Boston in the fall."

She hesitated. "Has Papa said nothing about that?"

"Not to me."

"My understanding is that he may retire soon, and we all shall live here, all the year."

"Amazing!" he exclaimed. "No, your father hasn't mentioned such a thing. And I suppose Tony will run his business?"

"I suppose," she said uncomfortably, shifting her stance, pulling the shawl more tightly about her throat. "But if I'm going to stay in Waterford, I hope to start a literary society here. Prissy and Caro are very enthused about the idea already. They're my best friends," she explained. She looked about, glanced at him quickly. "You must have many plans, too, Kingsley."

"Oh," he said. "I do. My house, to begin with." It would be erected on the site of the old one which had been his inheritance. His house would be three stories high with a French roof after the style of Mansard, such as he had seen in Europe—a style very new in America, almost unknown. There would be a tower attached to it, rising another story, soaring higher in Waterford than even the steeple on the First Parish Church, Congregational. "I have my fine filly from

153

England, who should be here any day." Duchess should have even now entered the port of New York. "And I suppose, before anything else, there is the barn to consider." It would have to be a big one, because his new carriage, sleek and shining, would come soon from Connecticut; it would have to be large enough for the stabling of Duchess and the four matched blacks who would pull the green and gold Concord coach that had arrived from New Hampshire only yesterday, resplendent on Uncle Lije's side lawn, a commemorative token of the vehicle of his success in Australia. Traffic in front of Uncle Lije's house had increased considerably since the arrival of the Concord!

"They sound like pastimes," Julia observed, "not like plans."

"Oh," he laughed, gesturing negligently. "I have no grand scheme upon which I shall design my life." This was not true, but it was too early in the day to tell anyone yet the contents of his dreams, and certainly too soon to tell Julia, who perhaps had her part to play in them! "I shall live well, as it pleases me. I shall be surrounded by fine things, not because they are fine, but because I enjoy them. I shall do what I think right and proper, when the time comes, not because it is right and proper but because it's what I want to do."

"Why, Kingsley!" she laughed uneasily. "How very unpuritan of you!"

"Don't tell!" he whispered in a conspiratorial manner. "I might get run out on a rail. But I am not a puritan. Shall I tell you something else? A lot of people who pretend to be upright are not."

"I'd hate to believe that. Surely you wouldn't disillusion me."

"I might," he chuckled, and leaned over to kiss her, finding only empty air because she had moved so abruptly.

"These slippers!" she exclaimed, bending forward to unlace their ribbons, to take them off under the modest cover of her skirt, to shake them vigorously, sprinkling sand liberally over both of them. "They're absolutely *filled!*"

Had she dodged him on purpose? He suspected it, even though she was cheerfully continuing the conversation as though nothing had occurred to interrupt it. "You must put a weather vane on your barn. Everyone does, the handsomer the better. Everyone here uses a clipper."

"I shan't," he said. "I'll use a trotter, stretched out and pacing."

"Perfect!" she declared, having retied her shoes. "Certainly

154

more suitable for you than a ship!" How well Julia seemed to understand him! "You don't think highly of captains, do you?" she said softly as they began to walk home.

"What makes you say such a thing?"

"I watched you, looking around tonight. One after the other of them, you'd look them over stem to stern, and it did seem to me you found them wanting."

"I've given it away, then."

"To me you have—indeed yes. But I won't tell."

"They'll find it out, soon enough."

"What is it about them that troubles you?"

"Their arrogance."

She started to say something, checked herself, and he laughed. "You were about to say that I am arrogant, too, isn't that so?"

"Yes," she said boldly. Any other girl would have denied it. "And for the same reason as they. All of you are very successful!"

"But it is not enough, you see," he explained. "Here you must be successful at sea."

"They admire you now," she pointed out.

"Only because I made a lot of money. If I had been only moderately successful, they'd not even notice."

"Papa is admired here, and I think one would have to call his success modest."

How true, how true, my little duckling! He fell silent, musing on the veneration of Elijah Merrick in Waterford, a veneration he'd inherited along with Grandfather's house, a respect and nobility which the years had polished and which Uncle Lije, by never reminding anyone that Grandfather had once been the focus of unrest, continually applied gloss to.

"Tell me about your horse who is en route," Julia said into the silence. "You must think highly of her, to bring her so far when you could have bought one in this country."

He laughed, and extolled the virtues of Duchess in detail, and did not stop until they had reached the house of Uncle Lije. The oil lamp in the hall was low; beside it were two candles in brass holders, waiting to be lit. The house was silent; no one was waiting up for them. *Astounding*, he thought.

"I must go up the back stairs," Julia said (there was no connection from the front of the house to the back save through the bedrooms), "so I'll leave you here, and thank you for escorting me."

"It would be only a half-done job if I left you to make

your way in the dark." He lit one of the candles from the lamp, gave her the unlit one, and guided her down to the wide entrance hall, large enough to be nearly another room, led her into the back parlor which had been the kitchen when he was last here, and to the narrow stairs that separated it from the old pantry which was a pantry yet, connecting the new kitchen with the dining room at the front of the house. Expectantly she held her candle out to be lit, but he took it from her instead, set both upon the small table by the stairs, leaned on the post at the bottom. She looked questioningly at him as he barred her way, clasped her empty hands, unclasped them, clasped them again.

"I have most certainly enjoyed your company this evening," he began. "I hope you have enjoyed mine."

"Indeed I have," she said nervously.

"Do you think we might see something of one another in the future?"

"I don't see how we can avoid it," she smiled. "Living as we do in the same house."

"I had something in mind that didn't include the presence of your family. For instance, when my carriage arrives, would you do me the honor of accompanying me in it?"

"Alone?"

"Yes."

"As I recall, it is a closed carriage, Kingsley. I can't ride in it with you unless someone else is there." She spoke very quickly.

"I can see about borrowing your father's phaeton, then, if that would better satisfy appearance." He tried to coax a smile from her. "Perhaps I'll try to get it tomorrow." He took her hand.

"I imagine Papa will let you," she said, her face now strained and tense in the candlelight. "Why not ask him? But just now, Kingsley, I am very weary. I should like to retire." Her hand in his fluttered and he let it go, lit the candle intended for her use, handed it to her.

"Would you like to ride with me?" he pushed, caught her gaze, challenged her. This time she did not look away.

"Surely," she said, after only a second's hesitation. "Yes, I would be glad to," she added, and waited, her head high, her lips curved into a determined smile, until he stood aside to let her pass. She did so quickly, gathering her skirts in one hand while the other, holding the candle, trembled ever so slightly. Perhaps with fatigue.

"Good night, Julia," he called softly after her.

"Good night." Her voice trailed behind her fleeing figure, and her shadow followed her to her room.

He made his way to the front stairs, creeping up them stealthily so as not to disturb his aunt and uncle whose chamber was across the upstairs hall from the large guest room that was his. Nothing but the best would do for him now; no more little cubbyholes in which the cast-off nephew was stuffed. No sir, the finest accommodations of the house were reserved for Kingsley Merrick, elegant meals with the best of wines and the whole family on tap to entertain him. They had all deceived him once, when they were eager to secure his goodwill for Tony's sake—and he'd let himself believe they cared about him. Now, because he'd scored so outstandingly, they were ready to deceive him again, but he knew better than accept their gestures of goodwill at face value. Were he still poor, he'd not be put up in this lovely large room with its floorboards polished and shining, roses on its wallpaper and crisp white curtains at the windows and a layer of marble on everything flat enough to hold it. No—they were people who catered to the appearance of things. Kingsley had returned to Waterford rich and so could be respected there—the Merrick doors were open wide, just as he'd expected they would be. His family, like everyone around them, responded like barometers, indicating the pressure of wealth or its lack—all but Julia.

As a child Julia had befriended him without a thought to his rank or status. Now, as an adult, Julia regarded him as a man like any other, willing to receive him if he merited it, unwilling to do so if he did not, disregarding his new rank now as completely as she had before. That he was wooed now by Waterford made no difference to her.

He had come back with her in mind. He had never forgotten her ingenuous spontaneity, her unaffected enthusiasms, her childish sensitivities and her high spirits, yet he had certainly come to no hard and fast decisions about her. In the four years of his absence she could have changed dramatically; she could have turned out badly, graceless and haughty like her sister Hetty, homely and obtuse like her sister Clara, or so faded and sweet, like Ellen, that she was only a faintly reproduced copy of proper young womanhood.

But Julia was none of these. She was more, and it was immediately apparent, as soon as he saw her waiting to receive him with the rest of the family in the stuffy front parlor. She stood near the portrait of Grandmother, who smiled with an eagerness that suggested Julia's own enthusiasms; she'd turned out handsomely—not beautiful, as his grandmother must have been, but with many of her features, her green eyes, startling and fresh, and her abundant dark hair. She carried her height like a princess, and her slenderness made her seem nearly fragile; she wore her clothes with style, seemed poised and quick—and then, of course, there were other of her qualifications! She was city-bred, so that the chances were good that she had acquired the knowledge of city ways that a wife of his must have. She was of Waterford, belonging to the town as only the native-born could, yet slightly separate from it because of her father's reputation, which placed the Merricks a cut above the rest, in a position of respect and acceptance, a position that would be another tool in his hands when it came to bending Waterford to his will.

Yet Julia was not a means to gaining advantage. Any of her sisters would have been, had he been required to settle for one of them. But Julia had carried forward the charms of her childhood as well as adding to them her poise—yes, she was everything he could have hoped for. He'd served notice tonight that he meant to court her, and she'd accepted his notice. Exactly how he was going to do it, and attend to the other business at hand that he intended to accomplish before he went up to Hartland's to take over the office, he didn't know. But he'd manage it somehow. He'd have to be pretty careful with Julia, because it was obvious that not only was she innocent—she was also very proper, as might be expected of girls brought up as she had been, and for all that once she had chafed against the restrictions of convention, perhaps by now she was fairly conventional herself. Yes, he had better find out, because there would come a day when Waterford wooed him no longer, when he showed it his intentions. And he had better be sure that Julia understood, and that she'd be able to bear it.

Why not take her with him as he investigated Waterford's possibilities? He was not willing to show her everything of his intent, because some of it was too close to home to show anyone. But if she understood the direction he was taking, it might serve a double purpose—show her the sort of man he was, show her what life at his side might be like, see if she'd be a help or a hindrance there, if she wanted what he had to offer. . . .

Hall's house was more lofty than the usual low-swept cottage of the mill folks, as became the owner of mill property. Its gable faced the road, so that pediment and pilaster might be displayed, and it was a story and a half high so that it stood slightly taller than the others. But that was as far as Hall had gone in announcing to the world that he was a man of some means. The house was small, as such houses went; it had no adjacent wings as did those in the center of town and no porch, either, so that you were either in it or you were not, and he and Julia, poised on the stoop, stood there as supplicants until the door was opened by Hall's dried-up, spinster sister. He had not come across Hall by chance, as he'd hoped, but that did not stop him. He'd parked the carriage beneath the one tree in Hall's front yard, and came round to help Julia down.

"Why do you want to call on Mr. Hall?" she asked. "Is he a special friend of yours?"

"He was a friend of Grandfather," he said. "And I haven't see him since my return."

The door at last was opened a crack.

"Is Mr. Hall in?" he asked the old lady whose eye gleamed in the narrowness of her hospitality.

"He's here," she said. "Resting."

"I shouldn't like to disturb him."

"Let me see," she said, and closed the door again.

There was not much to examine besides the panels.

"You're looking very pretty today," he said to Julia.

"Thank you," she smiled primly. "You're quite dashing yourself. Seeing you handle the horse and reins reminds me you're a professional."

"As a captain knows his ship, an express agent knows horses," he said. "I'll teach you to drive, if you'd like."

"I would! All I know how to do at present is to steer."

"Adequate in most cases," he allowed. "Certainly with your father's nag."

She nodded quickly. "It's true Bessie is no challenge," she said. "But you make even her look smart. Papa's riding horse is more spirited, I think. Perhaps you should try him sometime."

"Mr. Hall will receive you," the old sister said, at last opening the door fully. "Come this way."

Warner Hall was sitting comfortably in a large chair which very much swamped him, so small and frail he had become, a swathed foot rested, propped up in front of him, on a stool.

He waved vaguely. "Forgive me for not rising," he said, his voice old and shaky like his hand. "Young Merrick, is it?"

"Yes, sir, and I've brought my cousin Julia, too. We were

out testing the fresh air, and thought to stop by on our way home. I hope we haven't disturbed you, Mr. Hall."

"Not a bit, not a bit," Hall exclaimed feebly, reaching out his dry, wrinkled hand to shake Kingsley's and then, in turn, to shake Julia's. "It's a pleasure to see young people. I have little opportunity these days. Mariah! Do bring up some chairs, girl! And fetch some tea."

"Please don't bother," Kingsley said hastily, relieving the elderly sister from further fuss, bringing up the chairs so that she would not have to. Warner Hall and his sister were people of Grandfather's vintage, too ancient for carrying chairs about. Surely, to Hall, the young Merricks must seem as chicks, newly hatched.

He seated Julia, and then himself.

"Well, young lady," Warner Hall announced. "I haven't seen you for a long time! You were a child when I laid eyes on you last! She's turned out pretty well, hasn't she?" he remarked to Kingsley, as though Julia were a child yet.

"She surely has," Kingsley said, joining Warner Hall on the other side of the age span.

"How is your good father?" Hall inquired of Julia. "He never comes to see me any more."

"He's fine, Mr. Hall," Julia assured him, apparently not put out to be the child yet. "If he'd known I was coming here today, I'm sure he'd have sent a message." This was not true, because Elijah Merrick was careful not to cultivate Mill Village. But when Grandfather had been alive Lije was equally careful not to offend men like Warner Hall, whom Grandfather esteemed so highly, and had been careful ever after not to offend them, either. It had worked well, because apparently Warner Hall had never been aware of being avoided.

His attention fastened now on Kingsley.

"Hear you struck gold in Australia!"

"My express service struck it for me."

"That was clever of you, young man, providing for others who went to grub instead of rushing out to grub yourself. Your family must be very proud of him," he said to Julia.

"We are," she smiled.

"Well, he deserves success. He's had to work for it. Nothing's been given him on a silver platter," Hall nodded, in oblique reference to Tony, and Kingsley was beginning to regret having brought Julia, if the old man was going to spend the afternoon in reference to things as they had been. Yet those things could not be covered up, he reminded himself.

He had returned in order to grow past them, not to ignore them.

"How's that brother of yours doing in Melbourne?" Hall asked Julia. "Has he made out so well as young Kingsley, here?"

"Hardly!" Julia laughed. "But then, his capacity there was agent to my father. He wasn't free, as Kingsley, to pursue his own interests."

"Ah, yes." That avenue having been explored, he turned once again to Kingsley. "What are you up to now? All that money burning a hole in your pocket?"

"I sit on it constantly, to smother the flames," he chuckled. "What would you have done with it, sir, were you to have had it at my age?"

"Put it in my mill, of course!" the old man snorted. "Still would."

"So would I," Kingsley said softly, watching closely to gauge the old man's response.

"What do you know of manufacture?" Warner Hall demanded, side-stepping any reference to the mill which was his.

"Nothing I couldn't learn," Kingsley said. "Clearly the future lies in factories, not on the sea."

"Or railroads," Hall reflected.

"Indeed, railroads."

"What sort of manufacturing do you envision the most profitable?"

"Wool, of course."

"Wool!" Hall would have spat had Julia not been present, nor his sister, sitting in watchful silence. "When cotton can so easily be had! I carded wool here, at the beginning, but I switched to cotton when I saw how fast it was being produced in the South. I'd be spinning it today were there more water here, but I can't keep up with Lowell, nor can I spin as cheaply. It's not even worth the try," he grumbled. "Industry is getting big. Too big. Inhuman. We lose a lot, closing these little mills, losing the solidarity of the small community, forcing families into the cities. Terrible. I suppose you like city life, young lady," he turned to Julia.

"Yes," she said without prevarication. "I like it very much."

"Waterford's good enough for me," Hall declared. "I suppose those abolitionists have everything in an uproar."

"They try. They made capital on the assault on Mr. Sumner, and when he visited Boston last fall, there was a furor."

"All sympathy, I expect."

"Mostly," she admitted.

"Well, we can't have slavery in the territories," he said loudly. "I'm no abolitionist, but it's unthinkable to allow slavery to compete with the labor of free men on free soil. There's only one outcome to that—who can compete with labor which is not paid!"

"You can't grow cotton in used-up land," Kingsley reminded him.

"Just whose side are you on, young man?" asked Hall.

"I have no side at present. I am only pointing out why the manufacture of wool will, sooner or later, be more profitable than the spinning of cotton."

Hall cocked an old man's eye on him, an old rooster's eye, with his old rooster's wattles fairly quivering above his stock as he caught the scent.

"So you think we will come to war," he said. He was quick, that was sure, despite his age. Many a man preferred to close his eyes to the collision course of the already divided nation, avoiding reference to it, or its implications.

"I do," Kingsley said firmly.

"Over slavery."

"Over its ambiguities which are inalterably in opposition to the pursuit of free men."

"The Dred Scott decision is an abomination," Hall said. "Carried to its logical conclusion, slavery is allowable anywhere. Packed court. Those Southern bastards are tearing us apart. Excuse me," he said to his sister and to Julia. There were tears in his eyes.

"One day we will need to clothe and cover an army," Kingsley said quickly, striving to fill the gap so that the old man could get himself under control. "And when we do, there'll be no cotton at all."

"We thought we could contain it," Hall said, refusing to seek refuge in Kingsley's change of subject. "We thought we could send them back to Africa; we thought if we didn't try to force the South, as the abolitionists wanted to do, that slavery would gradually ease out. We didn't understand how great the demand for cotton would become, how easily it could be processed once the machinery for processing it was perfected. *We* never wanted to free the slaves then—even some abolitionists didn't. Once I heard an abolitionist speak who wanted the free states to secede from the Union, so the curse of slavery wouldn't blight us all. People and their causes!" Hall snorted. "Before abolition it was temperance.

Or some fool who wanted us to eat Graham bread. Or more fools who wanted to give the vote to women. I suppose you think that's a good idea, young lady." He glared at Julia.

"No more than freeing slaves without training them for it," she replied promptly. "You can't expect a person to act responsibly who has never been given responsibility. Women and black people need education, Mr. Hall. Then, perhaps, their freedom makes some sense."

Hall nodded. "That disposes of that," he cackled, his admiration evident. "Now to Graham bread and temperance. Both good for the health, I'm told."

"And both dull as dust," Kingsley chuckled.

"Some folks could stand it," Hall said in a sudden peevish turn. "Your father was one, young man."

He was caught flat-footed at this sudden derailment in the course of conversation. "Oh, indeed," he said feebly. "Among the army of inebriates, he was top rank." There was an empty, resounding hollow in his gut which he ignored.

"Nice enough fellow," Hall mused. "I don't know how he came to be such a sot. Worst thing about it, in my opinion, was the waste of a good man's life. I hope you won't waste yours, young fellow."

"I certainly don't intend to." He stood up and took Julia's hand, leading her to rise, also. "Don't want to tire you, sir. Just wanted to drop in and pay my respects."

"Wish you'd do it again. It's a pleasure to talk to someone with his wits about him."

"For my part, sir, it's pleasant to talk with someone who isn't viewing the world from a quarterdeck."

"Hah!" Old Warner Hall was delighted, as Kingsley had known he would be. His interests tended to run counter to that of the mariner.

"I'll drop by later in the week, if I have time," Kingsley said. "Soon, I'm afraid, I have to go to Boston, but I'll get back to you before I do, if I can."

"I'll be looking forward to it!" Warner Hall's head bobbed in enthusiasm. "I'd be interested to know how much power you think can be generated here, given the proper setup. It's something I tickle my brain with every once in a while."

"I'll give it some thought," Kingsley said, shaking the sly old bird's hand. He hadn't missed a trick.

Julia curtseyed. "Good-bye, Mr. Hall. I'm glad to have seen you once again."

"About time, isn't it!" Hall agreed, and signaled his decrepit sister that the young folk might be shown out.

He helped Julia into the carriage, went around and climbed in himself, and set the nag Bessie to trotting home. Beside him, Julia watched the houses pass by, and her silence gave him the chance to order his thoughts around the knot of tension that gripped him. He had ridden out with her three times between the dance and now; he had shown her only the best of himself, his courtesy and conversational ability, his wit and his humor, and never once had conversation strayed into channels of personal concern, intimacy, or the hidden life of men and women that lurked behind the facade of manners.

I believe I had better change that, he thought. *Whether it's usual or not, I had better find out what she's thinking. She certainly appears to have a mind of her own—but how much does she reflect what is thought around her?*

Abruptly he turned off the high road and into a little-used track, far enough to gain privacy from Waterford. She looked at him quickly, alarm on her face, and he smiled to put her at ease.

"I want to talk with you," he said. "And I don't want to do it while I'm driving."

"Oh?" Her voice faltered, and she looked away, back at him. "What is it, Kingsley?"

"I wonder how much you know about my father," he said bluntly.

"I don't remember him," she said tactfully. "I probably never met him. But soon I'll know what he looks like, because Papa is having a portrait made. . . ." She gasped. "I forgot! It was supposed to be a surprise . . . and now I've given it away!" She was flustered. "Do pretend it's a surprise, won't you, King? Papa was so pleased to have found a miniature of your father, tucked away in Grandfather's things. He thought you'd be happy with it."

"Perhaps the miniature isn't my father at all, but someone else. Perhaps it's really Bluebeard."

She laughed uncertainly. "You are droll! Of course it's your father. The miniature isn't labeled, that's true—but Papa ought to know his own brother when he sees him!"

"My father was something of a reprobate," he said evenly. "I doubt that anyone has forgotten it. Your father can paint him in as many colors as he wants, but it doesn't alter anything; my father is part of me. I bear his name and, like it or not, his reputation as well. I am wondering, since Mr. Hall brought it up, if that troubles you."

Does it, Julia? he wondered, the hollow spot inside wider, deeper than before.

"It's the privilege of the old to be outspoken," she said. "But they always seem to forget that they might wound someone. I thought you handled Mr. Hall very well. There's certainly no point in apologizing for something that isn't your fault, or in trying to duck it, either."

Did she mean it, or was she only giving it lip service?

He took her hand and she flinched, but did not take it away.

"I'm wondering," he said, "if it embarrasses you, as it has done your father for so many years."

"What's past is past," she said simply. "Apparently Papa must think so, too, or he wouldn't have commissioned the portrait."

He kissed her hand, its blue veins delicately tracing their map beneath the white, smooth surface. He glanced over it and saw that she was watching in a kind of fascination, not knowing whether to draw her hand back or to allow it to remain in his.

"I had a purpose in mind, visiting Warner Hall today."

"You were not just visiting an old friend of Grandfather?" Her eyes twinkled a little, as though she were teasing him.

"He *was* Grandfather's friend," Kingsley said. "I wasn't deceiving you."

"What were you doing, then?" she asked.

"I was trying to find out if he'd like to see his mill converted to the processing of wool. Whether he'd be interested in seeing *me* convert it."

"Why do you want to?" she frowned. "I thought you were going to run Hartland's office."

"I am. Changing the machinery has to be done by someone who understands such things. Running it can be done by anyone who's been trained for it. It could be done by my cousin Jerry Slater, who is a wizard with machines."

"And you?"

"Why, I'd organize it, get it going, keep it going, handle the orders—which I can do from Boston. I'd oversee it—and I would profit quite well doing so."

"If there's a war."

"There will be a war," he said firmly.

She paused, smiled. "That's very enterprising of you, King."

"There is another reason, besides my profit."

"And what is that?"

"The profit that Mill Village would stand to gain."

"Why, yes, a thriving mill would do a lot for West Waterford."

"I am eager to see Mill Village prosper. I was born there, brought up there; I am a Slater; my kin are there. My friends tell me that the wage of a common seaman is so low that none of them can afford to learn the mysteries of deep water—but of machines—why, it's in their blood. I can give them a chance they were born to have. . . ."

"Very laudable," she observed, which did not tell him what she thought about it. In fact, she had not really told him how she felt about anything.

"I expect that not everyone in Waterford will be pleased at finding Mill Village prosperous," he probed further.

"What difference does that make?" she demanded. "Certainly your own convictions on such matters are more important than the pleasure of Waterford Center."

Dear Julia, with a mind of her own, just as he had thought!

"I have several other projects in mind, too, that may discomfit the citizenry. Not all of them will be well received, I think. Progress is always disturbing."

"Progress, in whatever guise, is bound to benefit everyone," she said. "Isn't it?"

"Certainly. And I pride myself on being progressive. Popularity isn't as important to me as using my time—and my money—constructively." He wondered if he should tell her more about the projects he had in mind. . . .

"Well, I'm glad to hear it," she said briskly. "Waterford Center is so mired down in tradition that it certainly could use a push forward. I can't imagine anyone here has had a fresh idea since the American Revolution. Hardly anyone has even read Mr. Emerson. The premise upon which Brooke Farm was begun is unknown here—and the failure of Mr. Alcott doesn't really deny the truth of his goal—to combine labor and intellectual pursuit. . . ." She warmed to the topic, which no doubt she had learned at her school in Boston.

"Then you, too, are progressive."

"Why, I never thought much about what I was." She blushed under his warm gaze. "I suppose if anyone is progressive it is my sister Hetty," she said quickly. "You ought to discuss your ideas with her, get her opinions. She's so smart!"

"I don't want to discuss them with her. I want to discuss

166

them with you, get your ideas. I think your opinions are admirable."

"Oh," she said faintly.

"In fact, I think you are admirable. And I am wondering what you think of me."

"Why . . . I think highly of you, Kingsley!"

"Do you think highly enough of me to allow me to kiss you?"

The pulse in her throat was lifting and falling very rapidly, like the heart of a tiny animal beating quickly to maintain the small, fast-burning life.

"I . . . I don't know," she said, striving without success to retrieve her hand which he did not let go. She was flitting around like a nervous, taut chickadee, and he almost felt sorry for her.

"It won't hurt," he promised. "You might even like it."

"Don't you think we should go home?" she asked piteously.

"Perhaps you don't like me. Perhaps I've offended you."

"Of course you haven't!" she exclaimed, and paused, and put on top of his hand her free one, and forced herself to look at him. "I do like you, King," she said, her voice low and a little unsteady. "Don't doubt it for a moment. But do I have to prove that I like you, when such intimacy is usually reserved for people who have known one another much longer than this?"

"You've known me all your life," he reminded her. "Besides, we haven't got long. Sooner or later I have to go to Boston, and a letter is no substitute for a kiss."

"It could be," she said levelly. "If the people involved willed it to be. If they believed that their qualities of character were what really counted."

She had him there! To persist would be to deny that her qualities of character were not the most important aspect of her! Not only was it untrue (as far as it went), but to a girl raised as Julia had been, it would be the equivalent of announcing that his intentions were not honorable. He might as well slit his own throat.

He laughed. "Very well, cousin. Rest easy, I shall not try to kiss you."

It seemed she breathed easier then. "I appreciate your consideration," she said. "Your delicacy."

"Happy to hear it," he said gallantly, untruthfully. "So I'll wait until you bid me. It's the best demonstration of the excellence of my character that I can think of." He laughed again, to show her she had not offended him, and she laughed, to show that he had done quite the correct thing, and they rode home, upright and proper, together regarding the road as it was framed between the upright ears of Bessie.

Julia, Julia, who is Julia? he mused as he sat with his uncle in the dining room, lit cheerfully with the morning sun. She had not been present with the family for breakfast—perhaps she had taken hers early, for she was up and about. He could hear her voice upstairs, probably helping her mother dust, their chitchat passing unintelligibly back and forth. *How uninteresting*, he thought, *to be a woman, but how interesting women are!*

Julia herself was very interesting.

He had ridden in the phaeton with her often these past two weeks and sometimes he took assorted members of the family riding in the Concord coach, up on the box himself cracking the whip. If he'd had a horn he would have blown it! Not that it was necessary. Waterford knew where he was, all right.

It was time he could ill afford, between conferring with Jon Stevens about his house and Warner Hall in Mill Village and other business he was determined to pursue in Waterford, and there were, of course, the unavoidable invitations to dinner, extended by Aunt Sarah Denning and the Grays, down the road, Aunt Elizabeth's family. There had been Abel Warden (who had only to crook his finger and all of Waterford, including even Uncle Lije, leaped, and at which Kingsley, too, had leaped because old Warden could be very useful), and he had dined there several times, basking in Mandy's admiration. He had badly wanted time to enjoy his friends in Mill Village and had little chance to do so. Duchess, now arrived and full of fidgets, wanted a lot of exercise, and he'd had his hands full with her, for he didn't want anyone else to ride her until he was sure that he'd trained her to his own requirements.

But he had, nonetheless, pursued his quest for Julia Merrick's affection, and had found himself more deeply immersed in admiration for her, an admiration she appeared to reciprocate. Yet for all her evident pleasure in his company, he could not be entirely certain of how she felt. There was a restraint about her, even in the midst of laughter, a certain watchfulness, even in the middle of conversation that engrossed her attention, and he wasn't entirely sure how to read it.

Tonight she was playing the piano for the girls' library

fund-raising project, and all this week she had seemed more and more tense—no doubt nervous about performing in public, though from what little he'd heard of her practice, he guessed she needn't have worried too much. But he'd been deliberately careful to bring no pressure of any kind to bear on her, careful not to increase the tension. He'd suggested a ride this afternoon, and she'd been delighted—but was it simply relief at diversion, or did she truly enjoy him? He could never be sure . . . and there was so little time left! Perhaps this afternoon, tension or no . . .

Meanwhile there was this morning, this moment, a bright one with the sun shining into the glass-fronted cabinets in the dining room, revealing that in the crystal cupboard Aunt Elizabeth allowed no mote of dust. Uncle Lije, replete with breakfast, sat blinking in the light like a turtle, and it was as good a time as any to nail down certain difficulties that Lije presented.

"The packet proprietors are meeting here later this morning," his uncle said from behind the cigar that accompanied his morning coffee. (Aunt Elizabeth would air the place out once he vacated it.) "You might find it interesting—would you care to attend as my guest?"

"I take it you are a proprietor," Kingsley remarked.

"I am. I have been, for twelve years. If you are going to be taking part in the Waterford scene, King, the business of the packet might well interest you. It's like Waterford's pulse—you can see how the patient's health is without having to get too intimate—if you follow my parallel." Lije ahemmed at the humor of his remark. "I haven't wanted to get too bogged down in Waterford affairs, since I have always been so busy in Boston—but I have been a proprietor—they meet infrequently—and I have found it very useful as far as sizing things up here goes."

"Julia tells me you may no longer live in Boston."

"She does?" Lije appeared disturbed. "What else did she tell you?"

"Not much. As might be expected of a girl, she seems to have little idea about what's going on—only that you are going to retire, and that perhaps Tony will run your business. I assume, sir, that you are closing the Melbourne branch of Merrick and Son."

"Why, er, yes, so I am," Lije confirmed, hurrying after the drift of conversation in order to head it elsewhere. "Yes, it's closed already."

"Tony must be on his way home."

"Yes, yes indeed, he's on his way." Lije ahemmed profoundly, worked on his cigar. "If I'm going to retire, after all, I'll need someone to run my Boston office—and Tony has, after all, had three excellent years of experience on his own."

Much of Tony's experience was far from excellent, Kingsley knew from firsthand observation—but it was not his business. "You are quite decided about your retirement, then." It was early; Lije was young, at the age of fifty-eight or so, to consider retirement.

"Well, business is dull," Lije said defensively. "I can hardly describe to you how dull it is! It is just not worth a man's time these days. So I'll see how things go. If trade picks up—well then, perhaps I shall reconsider, assuming it's all right with Tony. And if it does not—well! I shall live here, where money goes a lot further than in the city, and where a lot is going to occupy a man's attention, if he wants it occupied."

"Like the proprietors."

"Yes. Though I shall have to see if that is worth the effort. The church—I'd like to see it become Unitarian—I think the congregation is nearly ready—the school districts—offices of the town that need able men to fill them—there are dozens of ways a man may employ his God-given talents here. And for a while I shall do that. Anyway, getting back to the proprietors," Lije smiled, steering the conversation away from shoal water as casually yet rapidly as possible, "would you care to sit with us?"

The packet proprietor's meeting would actually be a good place to start, he thought—and it was about time to get started. He'd played long enough, relaxed long enough, was eager to jump into the fray now—but he did not care to seem anxious.

"I wanted to ride Duchess this morning and I hoped, sir, that I might borrow your phaeton again this afternoon."

"Ah, Duchess! How I do admire that horse!" Kingsley had not offered his uncle a chance in the saddle. His hands were heavy, too heavy. "If you took her out right now you'd make it back in time for the meeting—it's scheduled for ten and a half. And you surely may have the phaeton." Indeed, there had been no occasion that Kingsley had asked for it that Lije had refused, even though once Kingsley had seen him about town on foot.

"Should I see Jon Stevens when I ride, shall I tell him to commence my house and barn?"

"Why not, my boy! Why not!"

"Because we've come to no definite agreement—that's why not!"

"Why, I assured you that nothing would please me more than to see you put the house on the very foundations of the Merrick family homestead—even if I have covered them over!"

"Old habits die hard, Uncle. I am a businessman just as are you. I want money exchanged, a bill of sale signed. . . ."

"I know, I know," Lije laughed, waving Kingsley's enumerations away. "You want it done properly."

"You bought it from me."

"That's because I had to! You certainly weren't about to give it away." Lije guffawed, as though the time in their lives when Kingsley had been stubbornly annoying over such things was a phantom dispersed, never to reappear or cause disturbance.

"If business is slack, I can't imagine that at least four thousand dollars—which, if I remember, is what you paid for it—wouldn't come in handy."

"No, no." Again Lije waved. "I don't need money, boy. I've already told you, a man of foresight and common sense had nothing to worry about—and I pride myself on being in possession of these things. Surely you don't doubt that I am able to take care of my own affairs."

"Certainly not! I never meant . . ."

"I'm sure you didn't! Consider the subject closed. If it makes you feel better, I'll draw up the deed today, for a dollar and due consideration, etc., etc. But I don't want to hear any more foolishness about four thousand dollars."

He shrugged. He did not like it. He did not like being under obligation to his uncle that the dollar would impose, even one that was only morally binding, able to be broken if that was the sort of man he was, or if the situation required it. But it would be boorish to persist.

"Just out of curiosity," Lije asked. "Do you plan to live there alone?"

"Alone?"

"An eighteen-room mansion, and no hostess? A house on Beacon Hill, and no one to see it's properly run? A man up-and-coming as you are, no doubt involved with businessmen in the Boston area and certain to be involved here—with no one at his side? Unheard of! I am wondering, as you formulate your plans and move ahead with them, if you've given any thought to marriage."

"Why, no, I haven't," he murmured cagily. "I've been busy enough just thinking out what I want to do."

"Understandable, understandable." Lije leaned back in his chair. "Young men are so apt to get sidetracked! But you ought not to let yourself be sidetracked much longer, King. You're twenty-eight years old!"

"True," he agreed. "I am twenty-eight."

"A woman gives you a reason for coming home at night, Kingsley." Uncle Lije went on earnestly. "A reason to keep reaching, keep striving even when the will to do so is gone—as sometimes happens when a man becomes tired or misfortune stalks him. The right woman is the mainstay of a man—unobtrusive when things are going well, and a prop, a comfort when they are not."

"You are good advertisement for matrimony," Kingsley smiled. "But I don't know very many girls. We haven't mounted assault on the parlors of Waterford, as I think about it."

"Do you think a Waterford girl would be suitable?" Lije asked swiftly, steering rapidly away from the invitations he had turned down on Kingsley's behalf. "I mean, country-bred girls such as ours are bound to be would hardly fit the role you will require. For it will be a very taxing role, King. You are going far, and your wife will have to know how to handle all kinds of people, entertain them, make them happy in your home so that you have a better chance to work with them later."

"Perhaps," he laughed. "But if I don't work with Duchess now, I won't have another chance. She'll be wild, and I'll have to break her all over again."

It was not a subject he wished to discuss with his uncle just now; he rose, shook hands, hurried upstairs to change into older clothes, to hurry to the barn. For Uncle Lije was leading, chin first, into the heart of the subject that had occupied a considerable portion of Kingsley's thought and planning, and Kingsley was not going to let that lead get ahead of itself! He did not trust his uncle, despite all the loving, jovial familiarity exhibited these past few weeks in the bosom of the Merrick house. Kingsley was not about to assume it was genuine. There could be no doubt success had gone a long way to obliterating the hesitations, uncertainties about Kingsley himself—but how far? He could easily picture himself asking Lije too soon for his youngest daughter, presuming his success would gain him even that; he could picture Lije, leaning back in the chair that would creak under his girth, and drawl, *Why Kingsley, I have given you the land for your house—must I give you a wife for it, too?* It was just possible! Why else would his uncle give land away, but to use by way of discharging any familial obligation to his nephew, thereby relieving him of the necessity of consenting to marriage of his daughter as well! No, sir! Asking about his plans, so that the refusal could be firmly made even before permission had been sought! Hinting, possibly hoping to flush Kingsley out, nip the idea in the bud!

No, he would not risk Lije, not yet. He would have to win Julia first so that she would be at his side when he asked permission of her father—not the other way around, of asking permission to court her. This permission Lije might well refuse, but there was little likelihood he would deny his daughter the man she asked for. . . . He would play it safe and see what progress he might make before he left for the city. Once he was gone, there was no telling what harm the old fellow might do. Yes, perhaps soon, despite his lack of certainty, he had better speak to Julia—and just now he would ride to Mill Village and seek Jon Stevens there. . . .

"The meeting of the proprietors shall come to order," announced Elisha Crosby. He slouched into the chair provided for him at the head of Lije Merrick's dining room table, his scrawny neck rising from his old-fashioned stock; his cagey old eyes, hooded by the erosion of time, glared menacingly at the proprietors, all of whom glared back. "The minutes of the last meeting shall be read."

They were read and approved.

"Treasurer?" Crosby asked glumly. "We'll hear from you now."

The treasurer's report was read, showing a deficit of thirty dollars. There were no additions or corrections, and a deep, sad silence followed.

"Well, gentlemen," Crosby said, not moving from his slouch. "This is one of the few occasions that we are all gathered here together. Master Bradley is present, Mr. Merrick is here, and I think it as good a time as any to bite the bullet. At this time I am opening the floor to discussion as to whether or not this company shall dissolve."

"We can't just dissolve," said Sears Bradley, who had recently taken over his father's position on the board. "We perform a real service to the community, and even if it has shown us no profit this year, to abandon it would put the

173

town at the mercy of Snow's packet. I believe we owe it to Waterford to continue our service."

"That's right," said Captain Josiah Crawford. "Snow could simply raise his rates and we'd all have to pay them."

Uncle Lije stirred ponderously.

"We're paying now," he pointed out. "At least those of us in this room are paying." Sitting beside his uncle as a guest of the proprietors, Kingsley observed that Lije Merrick's words were heard, and held weight.

"I'd be interested to know how Snow has made out this year," speculated Captain Barney Blake.

"Since he carries stuff for his own store, it doesn't matter to him," said Captain Denning Blake, his brother. "Even at a loss, he'll gain. He has to get his goods in somehow."

"It isn't a question of just this year," Elisha Crosby pointed out. "And I think the gentlemen in this room know it. Every year profit has been declining. Running in the red has been in the cards for a long time now."

"Would it be in order to ask why?" Kingsley put in. He had not spoken before.

"Well, the current economy has made a big difference," explained Captain Blake. "Having been away from our shores for so long, Mr. Merrick, perhaps you have not been aware of the general situation."

"I am aware of it," Kingsley said. "But Mr. Crosby has stated that profits have been declining over a long period, and the depressed condition of the present is comparatively recent."

Silence followed while each man waited to see if another would say what they all dreaded to hear. No one did.

"Perhaps," Kingsley persisted. "I may ask if the Cape Cod Railroad's extension to Yarmouth has anything to do with it?"

"Of course it does," Bradley snapped. "That's obvious."

They all hated the railroad.

"Folks take the stage to Yarmouth," Crosby explained. "Or they are driven to Yarmouth by their families, to connect with the train. Everyone considers it a lark, damn them."

"Why not think about it more realistically," Kingsley urged. "Everyone knows when the train will leave, and when it will arrive, barring an accident. Isn't that so? And no one knows the schedule of a packet—nor can anyone ever know when or where the wind will blow or a storm arise. If there's a schedule to meet, the train is the way to meet it, and gentlemen! We all have schedules. We are businessmen, and business will not wait upon the tide."

More silence, scowls of displeasure, frowns of concentrated attention upon cigars and toothpicks.

"The Cape Cod Railroad Company established its Yarmouth branch four years ago. Perhaps your records will show how far back your own profits began to decline."

"Four years or so ago," Crosby said tonelessly.

"Well?" said Bradley. "What difference does that make? The question still hinges on whether or not we're providing a service and whether or not we ought to continue that service. Mr. Merrick's brilliant analysis doesn't alter that." His tone was scornful, his voice challenging. Kingsley reminded himself to forgo the luxury of responding in kind.

"Is Captain Winslow willing to serve another year?" Uncle Lije asked.

"Aye. But he wants twenty dollars more."

"Has anyone thought to ask Snow if our packet might mate with his, run alternate trips? We tried it some years back, as I remember; perhaps it's time to try again."

"I approached him on the subject yesterday," Crosby said. "But he didn't seem too eager."

That, Kingsley deduced, meant Snow had turned the offer down.

There was another long silence, in which the party seemed to have fallen asleep.

"Well, gentlemen," Uncle Lije said. "I, for one, am in favor of discontinuing. I, for one, have no wish to support an endeavor that isn't even breaking even. That is bad business practice, gentlemen. Our ship is going to need repairs soon, and the capital is going to come from us. Apparently there will be no way to float such repairs out of profit: I am unwilling to buoy up an endeavor which is obviously sinking."

The simile was too apt for comfort, and several members stretched their necks within their collars. Their faces reflected their dismay, and Kingsley had the impression that they had been depending on Uncle Lije, who was richer than they.

"I think we should sacrifice ourselves, to keep it going at least a while longer," said Sears Bradley. "For all we know, when this damned depression ends, we'll be making a profit again."

"That, of course, is up to this group," Uncle Lije said quickly—very quickly. "But since I do not care to be part of a bad business proposition, I shall offer my resignation if the proprietors see fit to continue this folly."

"You can't do that, Lije!" Crosby protested. "It wouldn't be the same without you!"

And your money, Kingsley thought.

"My mind is made up, Elisha. There is no room in business for sentiment—and it is pretty clear that only sentiment can keep our line alive." It sounded good; it sounded right; it sounded sincere and straight from the shoulder. Lije Merrick was listening carefully, and was satisfied with himself.

"You're being awfully hasty, Mr. Merrick," said Sears Bradley. "Surely the assessment won't be so very great—for a while."

"The assessment does not bother me, young man," Uncle Lije said brusquely. "It's the postponements of the inevitable that is troublesome, without a shred of gain in it."

It was quite a blow, Kingsley could see; the faces of the assembly were longer and longer. Another lengthy silence ensued.

"I don't suppose," Crosby said, "that Mr. Merrick's nephew would be interested in taking his uncle's place?"

"Mr. Merrick's nephew doesn't even live in Waterford," Bradley pointed out.

"Well," said Uncle Lije, "my nephew plans to build a house here and live here some of the time, same as I do."

"Does anyone object to extending an invitation to Mr. Kingsley Merrick to join us?" Crosby asked.

"I would welcome Mr. Merrick to the board," said Captain Barney Blake.

"And I," said his brother.

"And I," said Captain Josiah Crawford.

"And I."

"And I."

Bradley was silent.

"Any opposed?"

Bradley was silent still, his face set.

"How about it, Mr. Merrick?" Crosby asked. "Do you accept our invitation?"

It was time. Yes, it was time and his pulse leaped suddenly with the excitement, the anticipation of a man moving in on the kill.

"On one condition I accept it, and with pleasure."

"What is your condition, sir?"

They all waited with eagerness written on their faces. Kingsley Merrick was rich—so rich he could buy them a whole new packet if he wanted to. Surely he was the answer. How well they were prepared to love him, should he bail out their boat! And how well he was prepared to enjoy the next few moments.

"My condition is that while the packet is kept in service, the real point of this board of directors shall be to investigate and encourage the extension of the Cape Cod Railroad so that it comes at least as far as Waterford. Or else form a corporation of our own, to build our own line connecting in Yarmouth." His calm ultimatum detonated the hidden tensions of the meeting.

"What?" roared Bradley.

"He's crazy!" shouted Captain Crawford.

"What kind of a board would we be, to take with one hand and give with the other?" demanded Barney Blake's brother.

"It would mean we would be working for the eventual dissolution of the packet service, Mr. Merrick," Crosby pointed out gently, hushing the remarks with a pound of his gavel.

"Sir, the packet will dissolve in time, without any assistance from this group. To guide its destiny will put the proprietors in a position to be shareholders in the railroad, to their greater profit; the railroad will provide a far greater service to our citizens than the packet is able to do—I believe that concern was expressed about providing service?"

Sears Bradley's face was becoming very red, and Kingsley could see by glancing about the room that he was not alone in his anger.

Bradley pounded the table. "An express agent makes use of any and every method of conveyance! As long as his parcels and mail get to their destination, that's what matters, isn't it, Mr. Merrick? You are accustomed to rail, steam, stage, sail—anything that goes, and so naturally it doesn't bother you, or concern you either, that the railroads are making things mighty tough for us seafarers. But it is our business, and we'd better see to it that it remains our business, to keep sail ascendant wherever possible. The clippers have certainly established us on the high seas, but these encroachments at home are not to be tolerated! Mr. Merrick," he said, addressing the group at large, "has been promoting the idea of rail every since he came back here. Oh, yes!" He turned back to Kingsley. "I know you have, that you have discussed it with the honorable Abel Warden, and even with David Snow."

(It had been an excellent opportunity at Warden's, when he had dined there. How Bradley had found out about old Abel's interest and that of David Snow was something else— but it did not trouble him at this moment.)

"I believe there is no stricture about speaking to men privately," he observed politely.

"None whatever," Bradley said, his voice strained. "But there is no stricture about calling a spade a spade, either. You are deliberately trying to undermine this community, Merrick, and it wouldn't surprise me to learn that it's your reason for returning here."

"Extension of rail would cause Waterford to grow; ignoring steam will not make it go away. Vast numbers of people frequent steam-driven vessels; steamers from New York to Boston are always filled. Is that true also of sailing packets covering the same route?"

The faces of all of them began to show varying hues of scarlet now, but Kingsley was not diverted.

"I know you are mariners and I know what the threat of steam means to you. But whether sail can continue to compete successfully or not, the railroad is here to stay, and we can all make it work for us, instead of fighting it."

"And will you use steam to operate the industrial complex you envision in Mill Village?" sneered Bradley. "I tell you, gentlemen, there is no stone Mr. Merrick will not overturn to alter the character of our village. Why, without the packet, nothing would be the same. Can you imagine our waterfront dormant? And can you hear the clatter of machinery on the mill stream, picture immigrant labor teeming into our town to man those machines?"

"Really, you are quite hysterical, Mr. Bradley." It was gratifying to watch Bradley's rage. Kingsley suppressed a smile. "Mill Village hardly has the capacity of turning into another Lowell. As for the packet, picturesque as it may be, the fact remains that it is dying from lack of patronage from the village itself."

"Can you truthfully tell us, Mr. Merrick, that your reason for being so devoted to rail is not to serve better your prospects in West Waterford? To ship your materials in and out?" Bradley's challenging, belligerent face glowered malignantly.

"I don't have to tell you anything, truthful or otherwise. You can drag all the red herring across the trail that you like, Mr. Bradley, but it will not relieve you from having to face the fact that the packet cannon stay alive; you can squeal like a stuck pig all you want to, but you're a damn fool if you do."

Bradley was instantly on his feet. "I find your words distasteful and insulting, sir. Take them back."

"How can I?" Kingsley drawled. "When your stupidity and

blindness make so obvious the fact that you are an ignorant ass."

He had not risen at Bradley's challenge, but crossed his arms on his chest and leaned insolently back in his chair, balancing it on two legs; the packet proprietors, their faces white and their consternation rising, sat motionless for a moment while Bradley's face turned purple.

"You are a guest in my house, Captain," Uncle Lije said into the horrified gap. "Kindly be seated."

"I will not join this man at your table," Bradley said stiffly. "It is clear that he is a son of a bitch, and I, for one, shall tolerate his presence no longer."

"You are excused, Mr. Bradley," Uncle Lije said loudly, trying to cover his shock over the young captain's inexcusable lapse, his provocation to bloodletting.

The gentlemen in the diningroom, not knowing where to look, fastened their eyes carefully on the panels of the door which closed emphatically on Sears Bradley. Kingsley cleared his throat, folded his hands on the table before him, noting with pride that they were steady.

"Personally, I don't give a tinker's dam whether Waterford is on the line or not," he told their dismayed faces now turned to him at the sound of his voice. "You wondered what were the conditions of my serving on the board of proprietors of the packet *Patriot*, and I have told you. I will happily help to keep the packet afloat until such time as the railroad can take over its function—but only with the understanding that we pursue actively that takeover."

"Well, let's vote on it," Elisha Crosby said briskly. "I'll poll the members. Mr. Blake."

"Not yet," said Captain Barney Blake. "It's too big a question to decide in one morning."

"Mr. Blake?" Crosby asked his brother.

"No."

"Mr. Crawford?"

"Perhaps next year?" responded Crawford.

"Mr. Pollard?"

"No."

"Mr. Denning?"

"Opposed—inalterably."

"Mr. Sears?"

"Also."

"Mr. Merrick?" Crosby glanced at Uncle Lije.

"I'm for it," Lije said strongly.

"Me, too," Crosby said. "Two for, six opposed. That takes

care of that. All in favor of continuing the packet for the next year, fiscal 1859."

"Aye," came the chorus.

"Opposed?"

"No," said Uncle Lije.

"Abstain," Crosby said. "The ayes have it."

Swiftly the meeting conducted and concluded the rest of its business, the rates, fares, salary for the captain, necessary repairs, swiftly it adjourned, its members bowing in haste to their host and disappearing in all decent rapidity. Crosby, still seated at the head of the table, watched them go in laconic silence, and when the last had shut the door, he straightened up, pushed his chair back, rose, and extended a hand to Kingsley.

"I congratulate you, sir, on the astuteness of your observations. The enormous success of the clippers and their superiority over steam has rather blinded our good citizens, led them to believe so ardently in their cause that they are unable to see past it. My feeling is that Snow would welcome the railroad, as it would provide him with more ready access to his source of supply."

"Yes, I think he feels that way."

"Probably he opposed the mating of the packets in order to bring more pressure to bear," Crosby observed.

"Possibly," Kingsley assented.

Crosby let it pass. "Perhaps Hall would work for it, too. It might mean he could bring in raw cotton more cheaply, and get his mill in operation again. Unless it is true, what Bradley says, that you plan to run it yourself."

"Hall's support would be good to have in any case," he said, bypassing Crosby's incipient question.

"I'll support it myself," Crosby said gruffly. "Much as I favor sail, it's absurd to let sympathy interfere with the facts. The railroad is here to stay, and we might as well cash in on it. There may be considerable support along the line; there's money in Brewster, and in Dennis, too. Some in Orleans, more than you might suspect. Eastham would welcome a line closer to home, I think."

Crosby nodded to them both, clapped his hat on his head and left.

"There's a sharp man," Kingsley mused to his uncle. "I'm mighty impressed. He's been sitting there doping it all out while the others have been fluttering around like so many hens."

"You're fair sharp yourself, King," Uncle Lije said, and

looked at him with something like discomfort. "I wonder what exactly you have in mind to do to Waterford. Are Bradley's accusations true?"

He shrugged in nonchalance. "I have the time and the means to tinker with the workings of the town—it amuses me to do so. You have been encouraging me all along to take an interest in what goes on here, haven't you?"

"Certainly," Lije said uneasily. "But I didn't think you'd go about turning it upside down."

"Are you opposed?"

"No—no. I'm not," Lije said. "I admire your spunk. You have a lot of ideas, and I'm proud to see the way you go about projecting them. But for an old duffer like me—why, it takes getting used to, that's all. I'd be interested to know what you have in mind."

"At the moment I'm concentrating on how to get Warner Hall to lease me his water rights."

"So Bradley was right!"

"His facts are correct—but his interpretation leaves something to be desired," Kingsley smiled. "I'd like to convert Hall's mill to woolen manufacture."

"What do you know about wool?" Lije demanded. "Or a factory, for that matter!"

"All I know of wool is what I learned in Australia, where they're raising quite a lot of it," he admitted. "But I like to picture myself the owner of a mill, even if it's a small one. I like the idea of having a Village connection. All my friends are there."

"Surely you must consider the people here, in Waterford Center, your friends."

"I'm not sure that I do," he mused. "I am not sure that the men at the meeting this morning consider me favorably any more."

"Well, it's true that pursuing the railroad is bound to cause ill will," Lije said. "But if you kept your involvement minimal . . ."

"Which I don't plan to do," he said softly. "I don't do things by halves, Uncle. It's not my way. That's why I want to build my house on your lot. It's in the center of everything; there it will stand, unavoidable. And there I would be, also unavoidable. I saw Jon this morning, by the way, and he will order lumber today; already, I suspect, men are digging the foundation out and setting the sills for the barn. We'd better draw that deed up."

"Surely," said Lije, rising to lead Kingsley upstairs to his study. "Tell me, young man, has Hall been receptive to your ideas? Will he rent you his rights?"

"I don't know yet," he admitted. "All I can do is put the idea in his head, like a seed, and hope it sprouts. Like the railroad. If it grows, the time is right. If it doesn't, why, I shall have to wait."

"Hall's mill would absorb a lot of capital."

"I have a lot. But there's always room for more, Uncle, if you're interested."

There was an odd look in Elijah Merrick's eyes, a look Kingsley could not read. It was a gambling look, unless he missed his guess; at the end of his career with his nest egg secured, Uncle Lije had to decide whether or not he should risk any of it on his nephew's schemes—on his nephew, in fact.

"Count me in," he declared briskly. "And I dare say it wouldn't hurt Warner Hall to know I am interested. He would hold shares, too, am I right?"

"If I can bring him around, yes. He would accept shares in lieu of cash; he will lease me his rights and property so that he is assured a little income and stands a gain without monetary risk to himself and without cleaning out my pockets as well, leaving me nothing to put into the conversion."

"Excellent, excellent," Lije murmured. "I believe I could go it for twenty thousand, if that amount would help."

"It surely would!" he exclaimed, impressed by this demonstration of his uncle's confidence in him. Perhaps he'd misjudged the old bird!

He wandered about the sunlit study above the new kitchen, which had windows on three sides, cheerful and vigorous, while Lije fussed about with the proper wording for the deed. The north window looked to the bay; the tide must be halfway out now, judging from the amount of sand drying now in the warmth of the August sun. He'd go out to the barn and curry Duchess, he guessed, and then he'd hitch old Bessie up to the phaeton and whisk Julia out there, far away from prying eyes.

"Here you are," Uncle Lije said. "A dollar, please."

With a laugh Kingsley handed him a gold piece. "I'd pay more," he reminded his uncle.

"Yes, yes," Lije brushed him away. "So you've said."

They shook hands and he turned to the door, opened it and found Julia standing there, her hand raised to knock.

"Oh!" she murmured.

" I thought you'd be getting ready to ride," he chaffed her. "Ladies always take so long to get ready for anything."

"I don't," she laughed. "As a matter of fact, I was on my way to dress just now—this telegram has just arrived for Papa, so I thought I'd bring it along."

"Telegram?" Lije asked from his desk. "Bring it right in, my dear."

"See you soon," Julia said to him. "I'll meet you in the back parlor in half an hour or so." She slipped by, closing the door behind her.

He took the deed to his room in the front of the house, looked it over carefully to assure himself it was properly drawn. He'd have to see that it got to the county courthouse for recording. Just now, he guessed, a bite to eat was in order, and then on to the barn. Across the field he could see, through the few trees and abundant brush, a team of men with shovels and pushcarts already working at his house site, revealing the old foundation and digging it out, dumping the excavated trash to a low spot behind the house where it would be covered up, later, and a lawn planted atop. When he got back from taking Julia out he'd go over, see how they were doing; who could watch his house begin and not be on the scene! He looked there with satisfaction.

Oh, if he were properly ambitious he would no doubt take his hundred thousand and make a million of it—many a man would try, and never think of anything else. But was not Kingsley Merrick luckier than they, a man who understood that money and the accumulation of it was not a worthy goal in and of itself. No, the using of it, the spending of it, the discreet application of it toward goals you could lay your hands on and control absolutely, like a railroad, like a mill, like a town. . . .

The rich can have their speculations, their ventures, their schemes, he thought happily. *For me, this very thing that I am doing is meat and drink. Had life ever been finer?*

The Select Library Exhibition and Dramatic Display was cause for great excitement—greater, in the Merrick house, than even the dance had created. The girls talked of nothing else. Ellen, personifying Truth, was to be draped in a shimmering silvery toga with an uplifted sword in one hand and a banner in the other, the word TRUTH sewn on it; in the kitchen she was heating the irons for the final pressing of the banner, testing them carefully, worried lest in her state of high excitement she would scorch the fabric. James Duncan was on his way to Waterford; he would arrive by suppertime and would witness the Great Event. Thereafter he would remain, to teach in the Waterford Academy, his first position, and Ellen was excited at seeing him again, at knowing he would stay, at knowing he would see her on stage tonight—and nervous, as well. If she dropped the banner it would be a mortification from which she would never, ever recover.

At least she wouldn't be alone on the stage! Other Waterford maidens would be there, too, draped and armored and taking stances appropriate to their banners: JUSTICE, FREEDOM, and FELICITY. On the far left of the stage, Hetty would narrate her presentation of the True State of Happiness for Woman, couched in terms mild enough not to offend the sensibilities of the audience, yet deftly suggesting that there lay ahead for female kind a bliss not entirely encompassed by the attainment of perfect womanhood as wife, mother, and keeper of the hearth. Hetty had written the script herself, had arduously gone over it with the rest of the ladies of the library board, and while some thought it shocking—one vowing she would not attend the evening's production lest it be believed she harbored such sentiments—the rest were excited and enthusiastic about it. Hetty was hemming the skirt of the new dress she had made especially for her presentation—a dark blue bombazine that made her look quite old—going over in her mind the script she knew from memory but would pretend to read. Their cousin Nathan King, newly arrived from the port of Marseilles, would escort her to and from the event, and Hetty was unbearably pleased with the whole thing. Loftily she let it be known that she did so enjoy the company of an older man with whom a platonic relationship allowed for greater enjoyment of enlightened conversation.

"Captain King is your cousin, too," she told Kingsley as he sat there with the girls, waiting for Julia. "He was Grandfather's nephew."

A response of some sort was clearly in order.

"Doesn't seem likely," he said indifferently. "He's a little young to be a nephew." He was not conversant with the Merrick family tree.

"His mother was Grandfather's sister," Hetty said knowledgeably.

"You must be joking," Kingsley laughed. "If it's true, why, the captain's parents must have been in their dotage when Old Nate was born."

"He isn't so old," Hetty said stiffly.

But he was adding, subtracting. "Considering Grandfather would be ninety, if he were still alive, and Nate is how old?

Forty? Aunt Deborah must have laughed like Sarah in the Bible, when she learned of the expected arrival of the captain!"

Hetty scowled and Clara blushed at this oblique reference to childbirth and pregnancy. Really! Sometimes Kingsley was nearly coarse! Had he not, just yesterday at dinner, referred to a bird he'd seen in Australia as a "laughing jackass"?

"It's not so amusing as that," Hetty reproved him. "Aunt Deborah was Grandfather's youngest sister." Quickly she navigated away from the age that lady must have been when Nate was born, so as to avoid childbirth altogether. "We are very proud of our family. You ought to be, too, especially since you bear a derivation of the King name. Your ancestors are not people to laugh at."

"The Chinese people whom I met in Australia would certainly agree," he said affably, restraining his fidgets there on the couch.

"Why, indeed yes, Kingsley," Clara exclaimed, pinning a horrid bow onto the dress she was trimming, holding it up to judge the effect. "You are related to most folks in Waterford, just as we are."

"And to most of West Waterford, too," he reminded her. He was not about to be swallowed up by the Merricks. "And half of Rockford, as well. The Slaters come from there." Would Julia never arrive?

"West Waterford and Rockford are not so distinguished," Hetty said, forgetting momentarily her father's injunction to be pleasant at all times to their upstart cousin.

"Don't put on airs, Het," Clara rebuked her. "It really doesn't matter, so long as a person is honest and hardworking, where he comes from. Does it, Kingsley?"

"That's right," he said, feeling like a child in Sunday school.

"Our captains are as hardworking people as there are," Hetty flashed. "But they are also distinguished. Captain King is very distinguished."

"I'm sure he is," Kingsley said. He had not seen King in years and was beginning to wish he never would.

Hah! There was Julia now, slowly coming down the back stairs. Quickly he moved to meet her.

"Oh, Kingsley!" She seemed nearly surprised to find him waiting, as though she'd been so preoccupied with her thoughts she'd forgotten why she'd changed her clothes, or why he was there in the back parlor, lingering at the bottom of the stairs.

185

Clara held up her dress, displaying its awful adornment. "What do you think of this?"

"I told her it's too heavy," Hetty said. "But she wouldn't listen to me."

"Is it, Julia?"

"We'll fix it later," she assured her sister. "If fixing it is what you want, Clara."

"There isn't any later," Clara cried. "I'm going to wear it tonight."

"Well, then." She shrugged gently at Clara, meaninglessly, took Kingsley's arm. "I'm ready any time you are," she smiled.

"Then let's be off," he exclaimed, relieved to be excused from the sisters, their concerns, their stupid conversation. He put Julia in the phaeton, admiring the slenderness of an ankle as it flashed by. He took the carriage carefully past the packet wharf (was it just a little rickety? In need of repair? Ready to fall down?) and on by the breakwater, a few of its stones lying on the sand at its feet and not yet replaced. He set Lije's horse to pacing, the phaeton jolting across the wrinkles set by the tide, ridged as any washboard, and pulled Bessie to a halt before they reached the outer limits of the tidal flats, a mile from shore.

"The tide is low," she protested. "I'd love to go further out."

"Channels get too deep," he said firmly. "I shouldn't like to risk your father's horse, or you, either." As firmly, he took her hand.

"It would be easy to fly a kite out here, wouldn't it?" she said quickly, not resisting his hand. "We used to fly them in the back pasture before I got too old for such unladylike nonsense—but I always got tangled up in the only tree in sight."

"Next time we ride out, let's bring a kite and try it," he grinned.

"We'd look foolish!" she protested, glancing at him to see if he meant it.

"What difference does that make?" he asked.

"Why, none, I suppose," she laughed, after a pause. "Now that I stop to think of it. None of the things that usually matter seem to make any difference when you're around, Kingsley. The more time I spend with you, the more free I feel! I might just fly a kite out here—if you were with me." She sighed, looked shyly at him. "I surely do wish you weren't going to Boston," she said. "You're about the only

186

person I've ever known who makes me feel that I'm quite all right, just the way I am."

"You're very much all right," he assured her. "You have everything that counts."

"I'm too tall," she said. "But it doesn't bother you."

"No, it certainly doesn't."

"You are not offended when I use my head."

"Not at all offended."

"Many a man would be," she said. "Women aren't supposed to have any sense. But you don't depend on a woman's limitations to define your own strength."

"I know my strengths," he said. "And my weaknesses, too."

"You're a lot stronger than I am, in many respects," she mused. "You know your own mind; what other people think doesn't concern you. I'm not so independent."

"You've never been in a position where you could be independent," he said. "On the whole, I think no woman is in such a position, so you can't expect that of yourself. Not while you're so young, anyway."

"Will you write me, when you're in Boston?"

"I'm not a good correspondent," he said. "But I'll try."

There was a long silence as they watched a passing gull.

"Maybe," she said, taking a deep breath, "since you will be leaving, maybe you should—kiss me." She was blushing furiously. "I mean . . . you said you wouldn't unless I asked, and you've stuck to your promise very well. But if I don't ask, and you leave—why, the opportunity will be gone—and it'll all be my fault."

She had offered!

"Do you really want me to?" he asked. "Or are you only trying to please me?"

She was startled, staring at him, her lips rounded, as though an unspoken "oh!" had just left them, and he wanted badly in that moment to gather her to him, so innocent and lovable was she—but he resisted. It was not the way to gain this girl's confidence, he knew.

"I hardly know how to answer," she said. "You weren't supposed to ask."

He laughed, buoyant and carefree.

"I don't always do the expected," he said lightly.

"Well, you don't have to kiss me," she said with a small air of injury. "I didn't mean to put you in an awkward spot."

"You didn't," he assured her, taking her cold hand. "I'd

like very much to kiss you. I just don't want you to think you have to offer; I'd like you just as well even if you didn't."

"Why, that's very nice of you, Kingsley," she smiled. Was she relieved?

"But, of course, there is a difference between the affection of—say a sister and a brother—and a man and a woman who are not directly related to one another."

"I'm directly related to you," she observed, her hand very tight on his. "But somehow you don't seem the same as Tony."

"Indeed, I am not!" He looked out over the bay where there were many sails, far out, and a streamer of smoke trailing a steam-driven ship. *Ask her,* he commanded himself. *Ask her now.*

There was always a line that must be crossed, past which a man was committed and beyond which he was vulnerable because of that commitment. It was a line he must cross alone, on his own initiative and drive and then, looking back, must hope he would be joined there, and not left to stand alone, exposed. The more it mattered, the more exposed he was, and Kingsley Merrick found now that it mattered very much, that should she refuse him, he would bear a wound, a grievous one. He hesitated on the brink of leaping, because there'd be nothing to catch him if he fell. Yet this was the time—she had offered to let him kiss her—she regretted his impending departure—she found freedom to be her true self in his company—What more did he need? It was now or never!

"I'm a modestly rich man, Julia," he said. "One day I will be richer yet, if I'm clever enough. I view my wealth as a means of freeing myself from the restraint of convention because I can afford to disregard it if I choose. At this moment I don't need to curry anyone's favor. There will be times when I have to—to get where I want to go—there are times like that for just about everyone, I guess. But speaking generally, I suppose I'm as unfettered as a man can be—and I can unfetter you, too."

"Can you?" she asked, in what was nearly a whisper.

"If I offered you the freedom of my fortune, Julia, would you accept it?"

"Are you being hypothetical?" she asked. "I'm not entirely sure of your meaning."

"I think you are."

"It's not my place to guess at what you're saying, Kingsley," she murmured, and looked as though she might cry. "I can only hope I know what you mean—but you might be driving at something quite different."

"Will you be my wife?" he blurted, leaping at last on the strength of what she might hope. "Will you come to Boston with me and live with me there?"

"Why—I . . . I guess you'll have to ask Papa," she said, her face unreadable, though she tried to smile. "You'll have to ask whether he will let me go or not."

"I'm asking something of you, Julia, not of your papa. I am asking if you will accept me—and if you will, then your papa will accept me, too."

How important it was, how painfully important in that moment with the gulls wheeling and crying and the sand making little sucking and popping noises in the stillness between heartbeats. How important it was to get it from her, tear it from her, wrest it away.

Will you accept me? How odd it was that it seemed he had asked this question for many years, from many people. It doesn't matter, he told himself fiercely, waiting for her answer. But it did, and he did not stop to ask himself why.

"Yes, Kingsley," she said, her face white, deadly serious. "I will accept you." Her eyes were veiled, though somehow they seemed to be searching, reaching for an answer to a question she had not asked, for an assurance of a sort he could not fathom, but in his overwhelming relief to have traversed this great expanse of dangerous territory which made him so very vulnerable, he did not stop to look more closely. In his relief and his need to rid himself of the suddenly overwhelming load of tension, he became expansive, confident.

"My dear one," he said, grateful for the privacy afforded by the expanse of wind-driven flats, so far from shore. "You have made me very happy." He turned to her and took her in his arms, held her closely and tenderly, that he might kiss gently her soft mouth, as yet so innocent that it did not even know how to respond to his lips and lay without motion or life beneath his, which now he might claim, capture, teach. He stroked her cheek, looked deeply into the green and glittering eyes which were searching his now. "Would you marry me soon?" he asked softly.

"Unless I drown first," she said with a straight face. "The tide is coming in."

He laughed, not at all offended that she had chosen to lighten a moment that might have become very heavy. Heaviness was for later, when she had learned to be less reticent and could put her whole soul into it! When she had learned

189

not to fear his embrace, to come forward to meet it—and he could teach her. He would loosen the bonds so tightly fastened by decorum! He would teach Julia to live!

"Then I'll speak to your father at the first opportunity," he promised. "And may I tell you that you have consented already?"

"Well," she hesitated, but only for a moment. "It's true that you should have asked him before you asked me—but I think that in this case, Kingsley, he will raise no strong objection to the course you have chosen. Yes, you may tell him that we have discussed it already." She laughed strangely. "He may even be glad you have done so!"

Duncan had arrived. Ellen sat beside him on the couch in the back parlor, looking pleased with herself and proprietary. He had already been to the Academy, collected his necessary books which lay in a pile at his feet, untouched, unopened, because he had eyes for Ellen. Hetty was resting upstairs in order to refresh herself for the evening's ordeal; Julia had hurried up, too, after Kingsley brought her home. He'd gone to watch the digging at his lot for a while and now it was nearly dinnertime, and Clara was left with the chore of setting the diningroom table and helping Aunt Elizabeth in the kitchen which she did with more clatter and clashing of pots than was required, reminding everyone that she, at least, was willing helper to her mother.

Uncle Lije was there, chatting amiably with Duncan, looking unwell, Kingsley thought, but dinner was served too soon to lure the old fellow away from the house and into private conversation. At the end of the meal there was a knocking at the door, answered by Clara.

"Jerry Slater's boy has just brought this," she said importantly. "He's waiting for an answer."

It was from Warner Hall. "Would like a moment of your time this evening if possible."

So Hall would see him! Ah, that was good! Kingsley fingered the note speculatively. If Hall wanted to see him, it augured well, indeed. Until now, Kingsley had initiated all the contacts! But there was the confounded program tonight and he dare not miss it. Julia would be understandably hurt if he did, and perhaps angry. Balanced between her consent and the yet-to-be-obtained consent of her father, he could hardly risk her displeasure lest she tell him coldly that he need not speak to Papa at all. Yet he did not want to put Hall off. The old man, with the impatience and irritability of the elderly,

190

might well decide the whole thing was not worth discussing if Merrick couldn't be bothered to see him when he was sent for. He took the note and scrubbed about in his pocket for a pencil; he scrawled on its unused side: "Unavoidably detained until ten o'clock. I will come then unless notified inconvenient."

"If you'd give this to young Thad, I'd appreciate it," he told Clara, who looked impressed.

Mr. Hall wants to see me tonight," he told his uncle when the ladies departed to change clothes for the evening. "Want to come along? We'd have to leave before the entertainment was over, but I don't like the idea of putting Hall off."

"No, I should think it better to go when he asks. Sure, I'd like to come along," Lije agreed. "It might be interesting. We can steal out after Julia's recital."

Ah hah! On the way to West Waterford there would be ample time to discuss the marriage of Lije's youngest daughter! Perhaps, once arrived with the presence of Uncle Lije lending prestige to his plans, he'd find Hall amenable to his proposals—why else would he send for young Merrick unless he was ready to listen?—perhaps everything would get itself taken care of in one night!

Really, Merrick, he told himself, *you are just too damnably efficient.*

Uncle Lije and James Duncan drank coffee and talked about the Academy as Kingsley sat with them, making his plans and hearing nothing of what they said nor caring anything about it, either. Nathan King arrived then, a big, bluff, cordial fellow who shook Kingsley's hand with vigor.

"Hear you're all worked up about the Cape Cod Railroad Company, young man," King said heartily. "Hope you come to your senses soon. What we don't need is a cinder throwing, howling locomotive tearing through town." He did not seem offended by Kingsley's interest in steam; he treated the notion as he might that of a child who temporarily wanted one thing and was soon satisfied with another. It was a relief not to run into animus, especially since a good part of the evening would be spent in King's company.

James Duncan, small and spectacled, seemed minute in King's presence, and even Kingsley, though not so very small, felt himself so and found his own voice booming more loudly to compete with King's. He grinned at his own efforts, then found himself engrossed in Julia, who appeared with the rest of the Merrick ladies, quite lovely in a simple frock of green, who greeted him with a special sort of quietness which he found both appealing and satisfying. The group made its way to the Lyceum, where Clara stationed herself at the entrance to hand out programs (the horrid bow still in evidence) and the others disappeared behind the curtain of the stage, which twitched and danced with the activity of those behind it. A glance at the printed sheet told Kingsley that the Freedom Tableau would be first, Clarissa Gray would recite, Miss Merrick would play, and half a dozen young ladies would follow, presenting their varied talents and accomplishments.

They seated themselves in the last row, the better to sneak off.

The covert gaze of Waterford was on him as he sat with his aunt and uncle, Nathan King and James Duncan. It was not the open, uncritical gaze he had received earlier, at the dance. It was speculative now, and in a few instances hostile. Word spread fast in a town like Waterford, and he did not doubt that the meeting of the packet proprietors was already part of the public domain. As, no doubt, were his intentions at West Waterford, which he had not troubled to conceal; Kinksley Merrick now stood revealed as a challenge to Waterford and its tradition of the sea, and as he had expected, the challenge raised doubts and unease. He had known it would; he relished it.

The tableau was the first presentation; the lamps were turned low, one by one, upon the Lyceum walls, and the curtains upon the stage rustled and twitched until they were finally drawn aside to show the maidens in place, transfixed and unmoving, like living statuary. Hetty at the side began to read in her precise, clipped voice. He had expected to find it amusing, but the girls in their earnestness were impossible to laugh at and everyone else was taking them seriously, too. He folded his arms across his chest, thought about Warner Hall and how much control he should be allowed to have in the new mill. He thought about the fellow he'd bring over from England who knew machinery and who would oversee the conversion while Clarissa Gray recited with animation; he thought about the pastures of West Waterford that were nearly bare of sheep now, and while a piano was rolled onto the stage by three husky young boys following Miss Gray's performance, he pictured those same pastures swarming with sheep which village folk would sheer for the mill, to the profit of everyone involved.

Julia at last seated herself behind the piano, waited for the rustles and rumbles of the audience to subside. She lifted her hands.

Her recital was stunning. He found himself leaning forward, tingling and exhilarated as she played a scherzo, a polonaise, a mazurka and a romantic selection—all executed without the least flaw, all played as though they welled from her own being, more brilliantly even than he had heard when she practiced at the house, as might be expected with the stimulus of an audience to hear. *What a rare gift,* he thought, and wondered if anyone here, in this hall, was sufficiently aware of it.

Oh, she shall shine when she is my wife, he thought. *She shall play to her heart's content on the best piano money can buy! His wife!* She had accepted him, she had allowed him to kiss her, and suddenly, overwhelmingly, he needed her, a fullness swelling in his groin, his blood running swiftly hot and his body a massive aching as he pictured her without her clothes, imagined the body he had never seen surely sleek and smooth, long-legged and narrow of hip, her skin warm and fragrant and silky as he caressed it . . .

It had been long—too long—since he had known a woman! Thank God the Lyceum Hall was dark! He struggled to regain his control; with determination he forsook Julia in her nakedness and swung his mind to the interview that must pass between himself and his uncle. *How strange,* he thought, *that whenever I make a move, my uncle is always there and his approval, in one way or another, must be secured. The site for my house. The wife I would put there. The coaches I once needed. Now the mill, which would certainly convert more comfortably with Uncle Lije's contribution.* Like it or not, Uncle Lije was important to him in many ways, as important, in fact, as Julia, herself!

"Not bad, is she?" Lije hissed under cover of the applause for Julia, and they crept away quickly.

There was no sign of the moon which had so brilliantly lit the streets of Waterford the night of the dance. An occasional unevenness in the sky gave credence to its still being up there, rising behind the clouds; the air was heavy and damp. *Somewhere at sea,* he thought, *there is dirty weather. And not so far away.* They went directly to the barn to saddle their mounts; the hay sweet, the grain musty. *Now,* he thought. *Now.*

"Your daughter is truly gifted," he said, settling the saddle on Duchess, who stepped skittishly away.

"That she is," Lije agreed.

"Uncle," he said, following Duchess, reaching beneath her to find the cinch. "Julia and I find ourselves very compatible.

We have been able to see a lot of one another since my return, and we find that we share many values and interests." He pulled the strap tight. "I have been impertinent enough to ask her whether or not she cares for me, and she tells me that she does."

"Indeed," Lije grunted as he, too, pulled tight the girth.

"I have asked her, Uncle, if she would consent to being my wife, provided you also consent. I suppose I shouldn't have discussed it with her before coming to you, but the situation presented itself and I . . ."

"Yes, yes," Uncle Lije chuckled, breathless, slipping the bit into his horse's mouth, buckling it beneath his horse's ears. "Sometimes we must take advantage of situations as they arise. If we wait, sometimes the opportunity is lost and the game, as well!"

"Then you don't mind that I have spoken with her?" Duchess bridled, he leaned against the stable wall. There was no sense hurrying now, Warner Hall or no.

"Of course I don't! I know that Julia likes you because she has told me so herself. So naturally I am glad to see her sentiments reciprocated."

He was not sure he liked Julia's discussing the state of her heart with her father. *I suppose,* he thought, *that such discussion is impossible to avoid in a family like this one, where even the slightest trifle is a morsel to be shared. Perhaps,* he thought, *she mentioned it to him only this afternoon, since we talked, to prepare the way for me. Perhaps I should be grateful.*

A feeble flash of lightning cast the barn in momentary blue.

"That being the case, sir, will you consent to our betrothal?"

He held his breath.

"Consent? Why, Kingsley, I suppose I will. I hadn't really considered—it had never crossed my mind that things should ripen so soon—Julia is so young, you know. I hadn't really thought of her as marriageable! But I am confident you would be a good provider and a kind husband, have no doubt on that score, my boy. I must only decide whether or not her mother and I believe she is really ready to assume the obligations of the married state. I don't mind telling you that it comes as a bit of a shock—knowing that your youngest child has been courted and asked for!"

"But you wouldn't mind her marrying me, provided she is, in your opinion, ready to marry at all?"

"Bless you, no, Kingsley! I would be delighted if she married you!" There was no mistaking the sincerity in Uncle Lije's voice.

It was tempting to hug his uncle! Lift him off the ground in an expansive embrace! Kingsley's heart soared, affection rushed out, kindness, the urge to repay such generosity with generosity of his own.

"Well, that's swell, sir!" he beamed. "I can't tell you how happy you've made me."

"I'm happy too, King, very much so."

"I guess we had better be on our way, but thank you, Uncle, very kindly!"

"You are indeed welcome," Lije smiled into the shadows.

"Ride Duchess, if you like," Kingsley offered, greater magnanimity could be found nowhere else. "You'll find her a real treat."

"Why, thanks," Uncle Lije said. "I've been itching to try her."

"You should have asked!"

"I could see you were very particular."

"So I am."

"I'm cognizant of the great honor you've done me," Lije laughed.

"Even as you have done me," Kingsley bowed, and led Lije's horse out, followed by Lije himself. The gelding was a good mount, nothing like Duchess, of course, but Uncle Lije had the best of everything available.

"I think we'd better take the low road," Lije said at the foot of the driveway. "It might be a little awkward to pass the Lyceum again."

"Agreed," he declared instantly, and they set out, abreast down the narrow road with the trees beside it meeting overhead and then breaking way to open stretches where the meadows reached to the shore, breathless in the oppressive darkness, deep shadowed scrub and brush silent and sinister. Out across the bay thunder growled low and throaty, the breeze rising as the low road joined the high and they put the horses to a canter. It was really too much exercise for Elijah Merrick, at his age and with the strain under which he'd labored for so long, now apparently at an end. He could feel his heart pounding as though he, and not this splendid animal of his nephew's, were running; his ears began to sing and he could not find the necessary breath to call to Kingsley to slow down. *I am older than I thought*, he told himself sadly. *That telegram aged me ten years.*

Then it struck, the very air a sheet of glare and blinding white, with thunder a splitting crack, tearing the sky apart behind the lightning. Duchess leaped.

He had just finished crossing the ford (Thank God, Kingsley thought, as the lightning struck. Water was no place to be near with lightning that close). Joyful in the rising storm, he stopped to wait for Uncle Lije, to exclaim over the close strike, tried to calm the gelding who had not liked it at all. Then Duchess raced by in a streak, soundless in the noise of the wind, like a ghost, the whites of her eyes gleaming, her saddle empty, its stirrups flapping and banging into her ribs, goading her to further frenzy, shying away as she pulled abreast of him and pulling ahead so he couldn't get at the reins.

Jesus, he thought, *she has bolted . . . she has thrown him!* There could be no question of going after her. His uncle must be found and quickly. He wheeled his mount, rode back, able to see nothing in the pitching darkness, hearing nothing in the fast rising storm. He dismounted and began to search the sides of the road and found Lije close by a tree and some bushes where he'd rolled—unmoving, still. He put an ear on the old man's chest, but his own heart was pounding too loudly to know if Lije lived or not.

The wind would cover his calls for help; every house was dark, and although he disliked leaving Lije there in the elements, there was no choice. He dared not move him. He stripped off his coat and covered Lije with it, and with his linen shirt he pillowed Lije's head and ran to Jerry Slater's house, pounding on the door, half naked, the lightning flares gleaming in the sweat of his body.

A lamp was lit. Jerry, thick with sleep, fumbled at the latch and stepped back to behold his kinsman Kingsley Merrick scantily clothed and breathing hard.

"What in God's name are you doing!" Jerry exclaimed. "Where the hell are your clothes?"

"I've wrapped them around my uncle. He's lying beside the road back there—Duchess threw him," he gasped. "Jerry, help me!"

But already Jerry was running to get his trousers, into which he tucked his nightshirt, and came back bearing quilts followed by his wife who demanded to know what was being done with them.

"Tell Thad to get the cart ready," Jerry told her. "And tell him to fetch Stevens." Together they ran back to find Lije, tucked the quilts around him, and knelt, helplessly, by his side.

"What were you doing here?" Jerry asked. "Of all the Christly places you might be!"

"We were going to see Warner Hall," Kingsley explained, beginning to shiver in the wind. Where, oh where was the cart! "I must get word to him that I've been detained."

"I'll send Thad, if he ever gets here." Jon Stevens's lantern was bobbing in the black now, and the creaking of the old cart could be made out feebly in the wind. "I've lost my horse," Kingsley said, never feeling so helpless before. "She ran off after that lightning."

"We'll find her come morning," Jerry soothed. "We'll take care of everything. Calm yourself, King!"

It was not easy! He ran to Jon Stevens, back to Jerry; they lifted Lije up and onto the cart and sent Jerry's boy back with a message to Hall, and started out for Waterford Center. The cart, old and wobbly, the horse that pulled it just as old and decrepit, maintained a snail's pace through the night which was covered with sheets of rain now, pounding on Kingsley's uncovered flesh (*where had his shirt and coat got to?*) and soaking the inert blanketed form on the cart. He dared not remove one of the blankets to cover himself in case, by doing so, Lije would lose precious body heat. Lije's horse, tied to the cart, plodded, head down.

At the junction of the low road Stevens turned aside.

"I'll notify Dr. McLaren," he said briefly. "I can't be of much help just crawling along with you. I'll take your uncle's horse, King; I'll meet you by the time you get him home."

And crawl they did, past the silent and shuttered, scattered houses along the way, brooding in the rain. Even the Grays' house was dark now; whether they were still at the Lyceum or had been home so long that they were abed now, it was not possible to know. He had lost track of time entirely.

"You were going to see Hall?" Jerry asked, to divert him.

"He sent me a note. He asked me to come to his house tonight."

"Yes, Thad told me he'd been sent to you with a message. He got a nickel for it—tickled pink."

"I brought my uncle because I thought he'd enjoy it," Kingsley said woodenly. "I lent him my horse because I thought he'd enjoy that, too, and the lightning struck—Jesus! It was close! I'd just passed the ford—I remember being relieved that I wasn't in the water. It must have nearly hit them; there's no holding Duchess when she's scared, but my uncle is a good rider. It never crossed my mind. . . ."

"Bradley was down talking to Hall this afternoon," Jerry said quickly, to divert his cousin's distress. "They had a regular brawl."

"What about?"

"Bradley was trying to persuade Hall not to sell his mill to you, from what I hear. Got abusive, even. Probably got Hall's dander up. Maybe that's why he sent for you. I mention it only to warn you what to expect. Bradley has really dug in his heels over your railroad and your mill. He's not without influence and friends, Kingsley."

"Nor am I," Kingsley said scornfully, warm in his rising anger against Sears Bradley which helped to level his frenzy at the slow, slow pace of the cart and the chill of the slow, sad rain.

Up the road the lights of Lije's house probed the darkness in tentative, feeble winks.

"I guess I'd better run on ahead," he told Jerry. "Might be well to prepare my aunt for what's coming."

"Right." Jerry waved him on and he jogged off, grateful the lights were still on, that folks were still up and about so he would not have to awaken Aunt Elizabeth with such a shock. It would be bad enough, just going into the parlor!

He let himself in the front door. Down the hall were lamps, a fire against the dampness, the sounds of cheerful talk. *They are waiting up for us,* he thought.

"Elijah?" he heard Aunt Elizabeth call. "Kingsley?"

"It is I," he answered. He leaned against the newel post of the stairs, summoning his strength against the drain of his energies. He willed Aunt Elizabeth to come to him but she did not, and he walked to the brightly lit back parlor, framed in its opening, the hair on his chest dripping, curling down to his belt, his arms and back wet and bare.

"Oh!" cried Aunt Elizabeth, rising unsteadily. Duncan and King were already on their feet. The girls, after one look, shocked past words to see a man nearly unclothed, fled to the kitchen.

"There's been an accident," he told his aunt, once the girls' voices subsided in the other room. "Uncle is being brought home now; a place must be prepared for him to lie."

"To lie!" she whispered. Instantly Nathan King was by her side, ready to catch her should she fall.

"We've sent for the doctor," he said quickly. "He'll be here soon, too. Hurry, Aunt Elizabeth!" he urged, hoping that haste would help her keep her wits about her. He took the stairs two at a time, found a shirt in his room and pulled it on so his cousins would be able to look his way again, though no doubt not without embarrassment to have glimpsed him so intimately. *Christ,* he thought, *even at a time like this they worry about purity!*

Filling the gap of shock, everyone was flying about, running upstairs to turn back the bed, to the kitchen to stoke up the stove for water (was not hot water always needed?). Nathan King and James Duncan went out on the front steps, listening for the cart which was now within hearing distance on the road, ready to help lift Lije from its sodden interior and into his own clean bed. Jon was galloping in now, flinging himself from Lije's horse. "McLaren's on the way," he called, tying the horse to the nearest elm and readying himself to lift and carry as the cart pulled up to the door.

It was not easy getting Lije over the edge, through the doorway, up the stairs. The muddy boots of those who had been that night in West Waterford left blotches and clumps of earth on the polished floor and immaculate carpets but no one noticed until Lije was settled, rumpled and looking small, in his bed. Awkwardly Jerry Slater and Jon Stevens stood, unsure of whether they ought to leave without a word or wait for one. Kingsley steered them out with a hand on either shoulder.

"My thanks," he murmured, "and the thanks of those in this house."

"I'll rub your uncle's nag down before I leave," Jon promised.

"And we'll look for Duchess in the morning," Jerry said; together they went out.

In the master chamber Nathan King stood helplessly by to lift or roll Lije if the need arose while Aunt Elizabeth worked on his soaked clothing. Hetty was not there, he saw, although she had come up with her mother; no doubt she had been sent out the back way so that she would not behold her father in his nakedness as one by one Aunt Elizabeth removed the remnants of his clothing, but helpless at the last when his trousers would not budge, embarrassed by what lay beneath them.

"Here, Aunt," Kingsley stepped quickly to her side before she would be forced to call on Nate for help. "My friends say the doctor is on his way," he said, to distract her from her foolish fluster. "He'll be here soon."

199

"What has happened?" she asked piteously, just now aware that she did not know.

"Duchess threw him," he explained briefly.

She shook her head in disbelief, in dismay, bemused as she gazed upon her husband's unmoving face. "He looks terrible," she whispered. "Either he was injured when he fell, or something else has happened as well. Kingsley, we must send for Tony." She was not looking at him, only at Uncle Lije, gray and breathing slowly. "If Elijah should die and Tony not get here in time. . . . We must telegraph him to come home."

Telegraph Tony!

"Where is he?" Kingsley asked in astonishment that Tony was near enough to notify.

"Bowdoin Square," Aunt Elizabeth said. "Nathan, perhaps, would go to Yarmouth to send the message." The captain jumped instantly to her side, all eagerness to be helpful and to be released from his imprisonment in the bedroom. "Tell him to take the morning train," she instructed Nate. "We'll meet him at the Yarmouth Depot."

"I'll fetch one of the girls to wait with you, Aunt," Kingsley said to her, and closed the door behind him, slowly, thoughtfully descending the stairs.

Tony was in Boston.

How long had he been there? Why had he not come to Waterford before? How strange that no one told him of Tony's return—a return that must have been very recent, because Lije had said only this morning (how long ago!) that he was en route. . . .

Julia was waiting with the teapot, and he dropped into a chair beside her, having instructed Clara to go up to her mother.

"They're going to send a wire to your brother," he said as offhandedly as he could. "Apparently he is in Boston."

Julia stared at him, alarmed. "Oh, no!" she exclaimed.

"That's what your mother says."

"He must be there, then, if Mama says so," she faltered, bit her lip. "I think Papa has been very angry with Tony," she said at last. "He didn't make the branch in Melbourne the thriving success Papa hoped for, and Papa ordered him home, I know. Perhaps Tony arrived in Boston while Papa was here, in Waterford." She frowned, as though uncertain.

"Then why hasn't Tony come down here?"

It was certainly strange!

"Papa has been very upset, Kingsley," she said earnestly. "So upset that we girls were told not to mention Tony to him—probably, that being the case, Tony was told to stay out of sight until Papa cooled off a little."

"He must have failed badly," Kingsley observed.

"Yes. No. I don't know! Perhaps he didn't do all that badly," she said quickly. "Perhaps Papa is only disappointed that he couldn't do better. I can't imagine that seeing him now would do Papa much good, either. He'd just get angry, all over again."

"I think your mother has other things than Tony's restorative properties in mind," he said gently. "I think she believes Tony should be here in case your father doesn't pull out of this."

"You mean he might not?" There was fear in her eyes now. "You mean he might die?" Her voice rose, with an edge of panic to it.

"Your mother is upset," he tried to soothe her. "We won't know what his condition is until the doctor gets here. Perhaps she's jumping to conclusions."

She stared at him as though she had not heard, her eyes enormous, searching his for strength, for protection.

"Perhaps it's not time to say so," he said slowly, softly covering her hand with his. "But I spoke to your father before we set out tonight and he has given us his blessing. Whatever happens, Julia, I am here. I'll take care of you."

She stared, as though she had not the slightest idea of what he meant; her eyes wavered, came to rest upon the shirt he'd so hastily pulled on, as yet buttoned only partially so that the vigorous, bristling hair of his chest curled out above the unfastened collar.

"Thank goodness you did speak." Her voice was thin. "Perhaps there'll be no other chance." She tried to be brave, but her eyes were filling and she bit her lip; she shielded her face with her hand, which trembled, rested her forehead on it. He sat quietly with her, hoping his presence would in some way give her assurance.

In the kitchen Ellen was banging about, no doubt relieving her disquiet by whipping up a cake or pudding to restore those who might hunger in the night. At the front door James Duncan let McLaren in. Clara and Hetty drifted into the room, barely able to look at their cousin Kingsley; Duncan, after showing the doctor upstairs, came down and through and out to Ellen in the kitchen, and in silence they waited, waited.

It took a long time for McLaren to come down.

"It doesn't look good," he said, addressing Kingsley, with a

201

voice loud enough for all to hear. "He came to, when I examined him, but slipped back again. He's very weak; I think he has had a stroke."

"A stroke!" Julia gasped.

McLaren was pacing now, choosing his words with care.

"And, of course, he's thoroughly drenched and chilled. On top of a stroke, that's very bad, very bad. It's not unusual for a case of this sort to recover," he addressed the ceiling. "Unfortunately, it is not unusual for them to . . . slip away. You never know what it's going to be," he said, gesturing to the mantel, his hands, palms up, his shoulders hunched, to indicate he had not the faintest idea of Lije Merrick's chances. "Mustard plasters will help, and an extract of bee balm, good for the heart; I've bled him once so there's not so great a load on his system, and I'll bleed him again in the morning. Room should be warm, a little brandy, warmed up, every hour. I have some, if you don't. I repeat these instructions, girls, in case your mother—who is understandably distraught—doesn't remember. Perhaps yourself to spell her through the night. He mustn't be left alone. Nor should she." He cleared his throat in a mighty roar, causing them all to start. "I'd like to speak with you privately, young man," he said to Kingsley.

Kingsley led him to the front parlor and wearily lowered himself into a chair once McLaren was seated.

"He won't make it," McLaren said, his heavy Scot's brow drawn low in a frown. "He hasn't a chance. I thought you ought to know it. It's true he did recover consciousness when I was examining him, but I had the distinct impression that he didn't care whether he got well or not. It's as though he'd relinquished life already. A man who does not fight dies. Has he been under strain, that you know of?"

"Nothing he's said would indicate it," Kingsley told him, searching his recollections. "The market's been bad, of course, and I gather Tony has disappointed him, but it seems to me that if it's true, he's weathered it well enough." Or hidden it, a small, unbidden voice in his brain commented.

"I suppose the boy could have done it." McLaren's scowl deepened, nearly hiding his fierce, bright eyes. "Only heir, and all. The boy is weak, no doubt about it. But you can surely take his place, seems to me." The doctor shook his head, the silver hair flashing. "You're on good terms?"

"The best."

"Well." McLaren rose, examined the fastenings of his

satchel to make sure they were secure. "The Lord disposes. Don't get up, boy. I'll see my own way out."

Indeed he was too tired to rise. He leaned his head back on the smooth chair, feeling the muscles of his neck relax, his whole weary body relax, heard the jangling and clinking of the doctor's rig as it rolled out of the yard in the rain, heard the rain tapping, tapping, a branch of the elms in front of the house brushing the clapboards in the wind.

Yes, he thought, his mind dimming. *I can take Tony's place, if Uncle will let me. I can be as a son to him, better than the one he had.* . . .

The morning light, striking his face, woke him. He turned his eyes away, blinking, looked about and to the face of his grandmother whose portrait on the wall, where it had always been, smiled off into the distance where she eagerly saw something that delighted her. Now Grandmother possessed a wide skirt that draped itself gracefully about her hidden feet and trailed over polished floorboards; behind her a curtain parted, to show the bay and an impossibly large vessel riding at anchor there. He had always preferred the portrait in its unfinished state and still did, but naturally Uncle Lije, being the pompous sort, would hardly countenance an unfinished portrait.

He blinked, wakened instantly. *Lije. Jesus!* The whole night had slipped away! He must see how his uncle was, now that several hours had passed! He must find his horse, wherever she was; he must see Warner Hall, certainly, and he must see to something else, too, a nagging thought reminded him. Something that was simply not right. . . . *Tony,* he thought. *He must find out more about Tony.* . . . *And food!* Suddenly he was ravenous, and, pulling himself together, he let himself out into the front hall, went to the back parlor which had once been Grandfather's kitchen, passed on to the kitchen which had once been the little room behind the house where Julia had played her piano, but which was much larger now, and very up-to-date with a new stove, a new sink, and fancy plumbing that let the waste water into the rose garden. Behind that the woodshed, then the double privy.

On the kitchen table was cold johnnycake, and water steamed on the stove for tea. He sat there to eat, listening to the silence of the house resound ominously in his ears. Light footfalls on the stairs, a pause while the door to the front parlor opened, quietly closed, the floorboards creaking toward the kitchen where Julia at last found him. There were great

203

circles under her eyes and her usually straight shoulders slumped with fatigue.

Instantly he rose.

"He hasn't long," she said without inflection. "I was coming to get you."

"Is Tony here?"

"Yes, in your room."

"Why not at your mother's side?"

"We still don't know if Papa would want to see him, should he regain consciousness. So we thought we ought to have Tony out of sight but within reach. Tony hopes Papa will speak forgiveness, so he's waiting."

He helped her up the stairs, opened the chamber door to let her precede him.

Grouped about the bed were the family of Uncle Lije, Dr. McLaren, the minister of the Congregational Church, assorted Grays to sustain Aunt Elizabeth in her hour of need. The room was hot, stifling, and heavy; Kingsley found himself having trouble breathing, and did not doubt that Uncle Lije was, too. But one look at Lije told him there was no need to worry about it; Lije would not need air much longer. Ashen and apparently without life, the coverlet rising and falling only occasionally, and shallow at that, Elijah Merrick was on the edge of death. The girls with wet faces, the men with stoic ones, waited to see if Lije Merrick would waken before he died, give a message, ask for his loved ones.

Propriety required that he stay by the side of his uncle but the chance to see Tony alone was not to be missed. He let himself out and into his own room, where sat the heir, his elbows on his knees in front of the window, on the table beside him a bottle of bourbon half empty. A glance at the commode, under which Kingsley had stashed his supply, told him that Tony had helped himself, without bothering to close the small doors again.

He pulled up a tiny chair that he was not sure would bear his weight, sat gingerly in it, waited a moment for Tony to look at him, but Tony did not. The situation forbade saying the words uppermost in his mind; he settled for convention.

"I'm surely sorry, old man. If I hadn't had him out with me last night, I guess this wouldn't have happened."

Tony shook his head, still not looking up. He groped for the bottle beside him, took a huge swallow, still without meeting Kingsley's eyes.

"They won't let me in," he said finally. "Not unless Father asks for me. They're afraid the sight of me might make him worse. What a hell of a note. They're right, I'm afraid. One look at me and he'd have another stroke."

"And why is that?" Kingsley asked consolingly. Tony's eyes were vague despite the pain in them, and he was far from sober; much might be gotten from him now, and Kingsley aimed to get it.

"I'm not supposed to be here," Tony explained. "I'm supposed to be en route from Melbourne, so you won't have a chance to see me." Tony eyed him wisely. "But you have seen me, after all."

"So I have," Kingsley said. "Have another drink."

Tony did.

"Why is it that I am not supposed to see you?"

"Can't tell. Father would be very, very mad."

"Because you did so badly at Melbourne?"

"That's it," Tony nodded, pleased he had not let the cat out of the bag. The cat was out already, it seemed. The relief of that was enough to call for another drink. "I did badly at Melbourne, yes, indeed I did," he said while pouring. "Father's ashamed of me."

"And didn't want me to know."

"Right. Pride. Father is very proud." Tony's face crumpled up like a child's and he stared at Kingsley as if in hopes of finding redemption. "I told him you would loan him money if he needed it. Would you, King?"

"What did your father say when you suggested that?" he asked without bothering to answer.

"He only looked at me in the same manner he would have looked at a fresh pile of dung in the street. As though it should be evident, even to one as stupid as me, that never would you lend him enough to cover my indebtedness."

"How much?"

"Thirty thousand. Father can't cover it. The banks closed yesterday; I wired and told him so. He's finished, and it's my fault." Tony began to weep, and Kingsley, motionless, stared at the bent head, the quivering shoulders. Slowly forming in the back of his mind was the affable image of his uncle, these last few weeks, dispensing largesse, refusing to take money for his land because he didn't need any, airly disposing of Boston because it bored him, refusing to support the packet because it was bad business, asking for shares in the mill to the tune of twenty thousand dollars when he couldn't, according to Tony, cover an indebtedness of thirty.

Tony was mumbling now and Kingsley bent close to listen.

"He looked so haggard. He forbade me to leave Boston,

said he was coming here, arranged to meet you here, and if he could he'd arrange collateral. I was to keep out of the way until he sent for me—I could just rot there. If only he'd wake up long enough to say he loved me still, I could manage somehow," Tony grieved. "As it is, all that's left are harsh, bitter words to remember him by."

His mind working in a dozen directions at once, Kingsley said absently, "You are his son, Tony. Of course he loves you, whether he wakes up and says so or not."

"Did he raise the collateral?" Tony asked. "Can you tell me that?"

He'd given away a piece of land in the center of town. He'd supported Kingsley against the packet proprietors, given indication he believed in the mill, surrounded him with family and affection and provided a daughter to marry—consenting so very readily to the bethrothal of Julia.

"I suspect he has," Kingsley said slowly. "Yes, if it makes you feel better, Tony, I think I can tell you truthfully that he has done it."

An outcry strangely distant but loud in the silence of the house came to them from across the hall and Tony, leaping up and flinging his chair to one side, scrambled for the door.

"Something's happened!" he cried as he lurched. "I must go to him!" he wailed, and bumbled away.

He watched Tony's shambling, stumbling exit, unable to move, even to breathe. He heard Tony wrench open the door and close it again, the interval in between just enough to allow a snatch of ministerial prayer to escape: "Father, watch over these bereaved souls . . . ," and within this room rang Tony's words: Has he raised the collateral?

He was cold; gooseflesh stole over him and all the whirling minutiae of the last three weeks settled, fell quietly at his feet, so that he was farseeing, able to look now at the pieces and assemble them, lock them together.

His uncle had thrown Julia and himself together every chance he could, had carefully hidden away any sign of financial distress so that Kingsley would suspect nothing, presented a man of comfortable circumstance, magnanimous, filled with affection, happy to let Kingsley have his youngest daughter whom he had not considered old enough for marriage. His uncle had set a snare for him, the very same snare that Kingsley believed he was setting himself in order to catch and capture his cousin Julia. And he had won. Won with such ridiculous ease. Won Julia Merrick, whom Lije was so eager to give away!

He was a pawn, and he had never once suspected it. He'd been duped, and his rage was boiling now, like a seething surf; rushing toward him, towering high above him, and now crashing down upon him was the onslaught of humiliation, of mortification because it was not only his uncle who duped him—no, not only he, a man from whom, after all, such action might be expected—no, there was Julia, as well.

There was Julia, who must have known all along that Tony was hiding in Bowdoin Square: his presence there had come as no surprise to her.

There was Julia, who had brought Tony's telegram to her father, lingered in his office to such an extent that she was late for her afternoon ride, emerging from that office distracter and sober.

There was Julia who had asked him to kiss her before he left for Boston, because there might not be another chance. A request that was bound to raise his hopes if he had any, impel him toward a request of his own which—no doubt at all—had been her intention when she offered.

There was Julia, and twist and turn as he might, he could not escape the horrendous conclusion that Julia had duped him, too.

I can't stay here, he thought wildly. *I have to get out of here. When that damned minister is through praying she'll come looking for me.*

He did not want to see her. He had to decide, and quickly, what he was going to do. He had to decide it before he saw her next, and quickly he slipped out of the room and down the stairs, out the front door so that no one would hear him crossing through the house, and he circled past his Concord and out into the field behind Uncle Lije's house, past the old saltworks that lay dismantled and stacked in neat piles by the beach, the boards waiting there until better use could be made of them; soaked in salt, they would never rot.

He fled up the beach, only a small spit now at high tide, bent on putting as much distance between himself and the family of Uncle Lije as he could . . . but flight did not stop his mind, nor did he intend that it should. He must think! Clearly! Concisely! But his brain circled, dove in one direction, then another, like a gull fishing above the bay.

Why hadn't he asked for money?

Would you? he demanded of himself. Would you ask a man whom once you considered beneath notice, whom you favored only when it paid to do so, who was now more powerful than you? Would you ask for a loan, a gift of money—

207

outright maintenance? For if Tony were right, that was what Uncle Lije needed now. What the whole family needed, and would need for the rest of their lives.

Well, at least Lije had no use for money any more.

He tried to picture his uncle coming clean once his daughter was safely married, but it was impossible. He could not imagine his uncle so humiliating himself. *Why,* he thought, *the old fart has died just to get out of it.* He was a man willing to die. McLaren had said just that. Willing? Happy! What could he have possibly contrived, had he lived, to explain his financial ambiguities?

It was imponderable, and no doubt Uncle Lije had found it imponderable, too. No doubt Uncle Lije had been relieved to pass on to whatever reward awaited him, glad to leave his family the job of cleaning up after him the best they could, leaving it to Tony to inform Kingsley of the Merricks' floundering finances, and to Julia to rejuvenate them—Julia who beneath her charm and simplicity was party to the plan to ensure the future of the Merricks in Waterford. . . .

Julia! he called out in his mind, in his heart where this wound, grievous and unavoidable, had started to fester already.

Julia, so ingenuous, so straightforward, and yet in matters of a personal nature so reluctant, so shy, her reserve completely obscuring what she was after—Julia, who'd led him on charmingly, bit by tiny bit, hiding behind that demureness and dignified modesty which contrasted so startlingly with the eagerness shown by the other young ladies of Waterford, as, no doubt, she hoped it would.

Julia, who understood so many facets within himself—or so he believed—who seemed to understand many of his sensitivities, who appeared to look forward to his company—Julia was only following her father's bidding, willing to offer herself as bait to save her family, and perhaps she really didn't care at all!

Julia, he thought, *you have betrayed me!* The animus of Waterford he'd counted on, the duplicity of his uncle within character—but Julia!

It hurt. It hurt badly, and denying it did not obviate it. But his paralyzed will could not—would not!—accept it. He was good for Julia, he was better for her than anyone else could ever be—he was! Surely Julia had come to see that, too! Wasn't it possible that, setting out to do her father's bidding, she had discovered a compatibility she hadn't realized would exist, that a duty had turned out to be a blessing, that she had discovered in her cousin the perfect complement for herself, been glad of it—was glad yet? Had come to admire him and the qualities of his own that rather well matched hers, had lost her heart to him in the process of setting out to obey her father . . . Tony's telegram only goading her to an act that she had desired but had been too shy, too reserved to initiate before that time? Perhaps Julia had got caught in her own snare, which accounted as easily for her demeanor as any suspicion of duplicity did.

By God, he didn't know. He who believed he understood women pretty well did not understand Julia now; nothing had been as it seemed; he'd allowed himself to be carried along by the appearance of things, instead of sticking to the business at hand, which (remember, Merrick?) had been to show Waterford the kind of man he was, to rule it because it pleased him to do so, to force it to acknowledge and accept him for what he was, whether it wanted to or not, using his uncle as a springboard to position himself where he wanted to be, a plan in which initially Julia Merrick had her part to play—a plan he'd lost sight of because she'd been so charming, because she seemed to so well fill the empty places within him, places that had been empty for a long, long time. . . .

He willed himself to quietness, calmness, standing motionless on the beach, hardly breathing, reaching to find the most reasonable decision, putting away if he could the hurt and anger which only hampered him, closing it off, locking it up, so that it could not interfere.

You've just been carried away, Merrick, he told himself. *You've forgotten where you were going and why, and now you have been reminded. Basically nothing has changed because, after all, no one knows that the illustrious Elijah Merrick is headed for the almshouse, and no one will ever know it if the debt is paid.* And if it were paid, the veneration accorded his uncle remained intact. If it were paid, Kingsley Merrick stood yet to inherit that veneration, that exalted position which, like a mantle, he might slip over his own shoulders, secured for good and all by marriage to the youngest daughter of the house who might—or might not—love him.

Quickly he steered away from that morass, with which he would deal later, in his own time. The question that now must be reevaluated was quite simple: was Lije Merrick's place in Waterford worth paying for? Was Julia's place there worth Lije's indebtedness? Could he as well make his way without that position? Did he want to?

He looked out across the bay, past the brightness that were the cliffs of Eastham, out to the expanse of the Atlantic from whence he had recently come, relinquishing it in favor of this low and gentle land where treachery had met him. Behind him, at his back, there was a whole continent over which the sun would set that night, waiting for any man willing to work for the winning of it, and he was here, in this small part of that continent, and he had chosen it.

He had fared well in that portion of the world with which he had wrestled already, wrestled joyously, yet there had been no satisfaction there. He had understood, months before he'd come to any conclusion about it, that he would return to this narrow land. But he'd not known, really known, until he had succeeded so well in Melbourne, that it was the search for self-respect he was after, a self-respect that money alone couldn't buy because it lay here, where his roots were, where he had been labeled as unworthy of respect without having ever been given the chance to prove himself, because without it, from this place, he could not be whole. Because until he came back he could not be mended, realigned, and unless he came back he would always be running from something he believed bigger than himself, something which must, instead, be made smaller.

But money and power alone could not do it. Waterford could still turn away, disdaining the crass native son, and no matter what he might accomplish, domination such as he envisioned would not be complete. The will of Waterford must reflect his will, his goals must be Waterford's goals, directed by him. With Julia at his side, the respect of the Merrick name his own, the tradition of Grandfather behind him which time and the success of Uncle Lije had smoothed and lifted up, his accomplishments polished, gleaming bright as the ball and vane on the Congregational Church . . . without these things in his pocket, how far would Kingsley Merrick get? And with them, how long could Waterford hold out? What was thirty thousand dollars and the support of six people in comparison to putting to rest the sleepless, nagging fear that Waterford had beaten him, and that for all his life he would be its victim. . . .

Far away, sounding like a wailing gull, her voice carried to him on the wind. Down the beach in the direction from which he had come, small now and growing larger as she hurried forward, was Julia, calling his name, her hand outstretched as she ran toward him, her hair loosened and floating about her face on the breeze, her feet shoeless, he saw as she came closer.

Ungallantly he did not go to meet her, but waited for the infinite distance to be traversed by her. She stopped, a hundred feet away, evidently winded, and walked toward him, her hand pressed against her breast where, no doubt, her breathing agonized her, and he saw that her face was wet with tears, her mouth contorted as she tried to hold the tears back.

My beloved approaches, he thought, and he waited to see what she would say, what role she would choose in this hour of extremity.

She reached out, grasping nothing, clutching nothing, still breathing heavily. "I looked for you and you weren't there," she gulped. "Father is dead."

"I'm sorry," he said stiffly.

She stood as though poised on the brink, her eyes in desperation going over his face as if to discover the thoughts hidden there, unable to understand his aloofness, and her tears started fresh. "I needed you," she sobbed. "And I need you now. I need you very much."

She looked much like a rain-soaked kitten, as helpless and as trusting. He couldn't resist her, her bereft face, her desperation, her fear. He could easily imagine himself in her place with every word deciding her fate and the fate of those dear to her. Indeed, she needed him—and whether he liked it or not, he needed her.

He reached out to pull her to himself and she collapsed against his shoulder, burying her face in the collar of his coat as he patted her back soothingly. She was shaking.

"Kingsley, Kingsley," she wept. "It was awful, not knowing where you were." She gave herself up to crying then, and he stood with her a long, long time until she might get a better grip on herself, felt her slightness beneath her clothing because she was pressed to him so tightly, felt her body without resistance against his own where she sought his strength and perhaps his love to sustain her.

"There, there, Julia," he murmured into her hair. "There, now, be calm, that's it, go easy now, I am here, you have found me now. . . ." Over her shoulder, as he looked across the waters, behind the soft curve of the land and sea lay Boston where he would take her; he kissed the ear beneath her curls and thought, *Perhaps it will work. Perhaps I can make it work, certainly it would be worth the effort!* For as much as he might not care to admit it, much as it was foolish in

211

view of what he knew and in view of what he suspected—rising from the aridity of his heart as a spring from the deep of the earth and as irrepressible, clean, and completely irrelevant of any of his other needs to which Julia might provide the answer, clear and running free of any consideration or speculation or doubt or misgiving, was the purity of truth that neither circumstance nor thought could alter: he loved her.

Yes, he thought, *perhaps I can make it work. . . .*

Four

The Helpmeet

P rissy Pratt looked about the parlor with admiration.

"It's a splendid house," she sighed. "You must be very proud of it."

"Why, yes," Julia smiled gamely. "Of course, I am."

"Don't you get lonesome, rattling around in it?" asked Prissy's sister Caro, who had been outspoken, even as a child. "With servants creeping around and all? I think I would."

"They are people like anyone else," Julia said, patiently as she could. "If you're considerate of them, they certainly respond in kind."

Caro, having never come in contact with Irish people before encountering them in the house of Julia and Kingsley Merrick, clearly did not believe it.

"And as far as being lonely goes, I suppose I am, a little." It was only the second time that summer that Caro and Prissy had come to call, and Julia was lonely indeed. She looked at one and then the other and was aware, within herself, of the yearning, the wishful, poignant, useless yearning for the days, the years when they had been such warm friends to one another without having to struggle so hard, reach so far, to be at ease.

But clearly Caro was trying. Even now she leaned foward, striking a pose of determined brightness, as though she had only, that very moment, remembered the one thing, among many others, of greatest interest to Julia and to herself. (In fact, the conversational flow had been a bit uneven. . . .)

"I believe, Julia, that it would be a very good idea to start a literary club," she said. "I've been thinking about it; there's not so much time for reading now as there used to be—but I'd like to try it anyway." Caro referred to her newly acquired marital status and the duties descending on her which had not been present when she was a maiden.

"I have time to read," Prissy Pratt said. She was yet unmarried, and as custodian of the Ladies Select Library Association, whose collection was held in three shelves in her father's house, she had access to all the books she wanted.

"Obviously Julia has time, too. Perhaps she and I could report on what we've read for the benefit of you girls who find your hands full."

"What a splendid idea!" Gladly, gratefully, she smiled at Prissy Pratt, and tearful affection rose within her at the effort of these young women to find their friend Julia Merrick again. She had suggested the literary club herself the last time Caro and Prissy were here, and she'd been unable to determine then whether or not it would take. Lurking sneakily around the edges was the tacit realization that although Julia Merrick was a married woman, she had servants to take the burdens from her while Caro and others like her did not, and she approached the matter very cautiously, so that no one would believe she sought to flaunt her leisure.

"You never know," Prissy was saying, "when you might find a moment for reading that you didn't know you had, especially when there's an incentive for using it. A lot of the girls thought it was a good idea," she assured Julia.

" 'Fess up, now," Caro teased. "You find us dull, don't you, compared to the city folks, and you'd like to polish us up a bit."

"You are most certainly not dull compared to the people I know in Boston!" Julia declared vehemently. And indeed, they were not! Since she'd married Kingsley, her only companionship in the city was among the wives of his business associates, and in describing them, dull was positive flattery. At dinner conversation dwelt on matters political and financial, in which women were expected only to listen, and after dinner, while the men lingered over cigars and cordials in the diningroom, the ladies in the parlor endlessly discussed things designed to show how rich they were—the Servant Problem, the Doctor Problem, the Dancing Master Problem, and, naturally, Fashion. Mrs. Pettingill affected deafness, in order to brandish about her ear trumpet which was concealed in her elaborately carved ivory fan (she had seen the elder Mrs. Curtis of Beacon Hill with one like it), and Mrs. Wheeler had palpitations, by which means she might, on occasions appropriate, bring out with a flourish a bejeweled salts bottle— she had a succession of them, the gems on which matched any she might be wearing. (She always wore a lot of jewelry.) Mrs. Bricker's joy was her feathers, and she had tons of them, of all sorts imaginable, decorating her gowns, her hats, her capes, and if she had her way, no doubt they'd cover her shoes, one day, and her reticule.

Mrs. Bricker and Mrs. Wheeler and Mrs. Pettingill couldn't

understand why there was no space for them and their offspring in Papanti's schedule, because after all, they could afford to pay for Boston's famous dancing master! And when at last they gained entrance (money did, after all, talk!), they were dismayed to find that the elite were not there; the aristocracy, without informing them, now met at Papanti's hall on occasions exclusive to themselves. Hence the Dancing Master Problem.

The wives of Kingsley's business associates engrossed themselves with their Female Complaints for which no cure seemed ever to be found—the result of which was the Doctor Problem. Their rudeness to their servants, by which means they constantly reminded themselves of their elevated status, led to the Servant Problem (by which means the Irish got back at them, with Julia's sympathy). As to fashion—all you had to do was look at *Godey's Ladies Book*—and they did. They spent hours with *Godey's!* They had never read Mr. Emerson's books or Mr. Longfellow's poetry nor had ever, so far as Julia could determine, entertained a single idea that did not, one way or another, reflect the rise in social rank that their new wealth had brought them. The Pettingills, the Wheelers, the Brickers all lived in the new South End—and Julia couldn't help but wish she lived there, too, because everything was made worse for living on Beacon Hill with Kingsley where she was continually reminded of what she'd missed, and where the clarity of comparison between folks like the Pettingills and the Wheelers and the Brickers contrasted unavoidably with the Leverings, the Abbotts, and the Curtises, where she was unable to put out of mind what she had lost. The vast difference between what she'd hoped for once and what she had eventually got was a daily, hourly abrasion, one which loyalty demanded she ignore and subdue, one which reality told her was only wasteful because nothing was going to change—ever.

And so Julia had come to treasure her friendships in Waterford. Here a tradition and a pride were carried with an unaffected grace, a naturalness, and a simplicity that contrasted sharply with the new rich of the city. And here, Julia was quite sure, a certain brightness could indeed be polished so that Waterford would have a cultural pride as well. All the girls had attended the Academy until they were eighteen; no one in Waterford saw any incompatibility, within reason, between a woman and her brains. It was a matter of nurturing the start they'd been given in life, instead of allowing it to fall into disuse.

But it was not a matter of bringing them forward to attain equal stature with the Boston friends of the Merricks! Waterford girls outshone them by a mile. And if they did not, nor ever could, outshine Beacon Hill . . . well, that was something else again, something Julia did not dwell upon and did not think about if she could help it. There was no point . . . yet come summer's end she wouldn't be able to avoid it any longer. She'd have to go back to Mt. Vernon Street, to take her place at Kingsley's side in the midst of the Beacon Hill scene to which she did not belong, at which she could only peep while having to entertain the Brickers and the Wheelers and the Pettingills—and, without a doubt, she'd have to take her place in Kingsley's bed, too. . . .

Quickly she steered away from this unwelcome thought.

"No indeed, Prissy, you're anything but dull! But no one can afford to let his brain sit idle! I remember that the women used to read a paper of their own at the Lyceum—the *Ladies Star*, wasn't it? And a good way to keep their wits sharpened, too! Do they anymore?"

"Heavens, no!" Caro snorted. "The men are so upset by this secession business that there's no time for anything else. The *Star* fell by the wayside a long time ago. We've had nothing but lectures on slavery and constitutional law and the Dred Scott Decision and the Harper's Ferry thing . . . and the last lecture, just before you came down this year, Julia, was given by an abolitionist who declared John Brown a martyr. Folks got so riled up that the Lyceum hasn't met since."

"That's not true," Prissy declared. "The ceiling fell in. That's why they've stopped the lectures."

"It fell in because of all the shouting."

"Shouting!" exclaimed Julia. "People were shouting?" It was impossible to imagine anyone shouting at the Lyceum!

"Well, it was difficult," Caro tried to explain. "Some people agreed that Brown was a martyr, even if misguided. Others believed he was inspired; all agreed he'd put the fear of God into the South—but some thought it was good that he had and others insisted that it just made matters that much more difficult to negotiate—and of course, it did. There's certainly been no negotiation possible since Mr. Lincoln was elected—and I, for one, think that the Harper's Ferry incident caused the South to close its mind to reason."

"But the shouting?" Julia reminded her.

"Everyone wanted to say something, and pretty soon no one could hear anybody, that's all."

"And then some plaster fell off the ceiling," Prissy explained further, "and the Lyceum was over. But I really think that the dances we've had upstairs loosened the plaster, not the ire below."

"In any case, no more dances either, until it gets fixed," Caro said wryly. "Nor any place large enough to have one."

"If my piano weren't there," Julia mused, regarding it as it stood, mammoth in the far end of the parlor, "and if the furniture were moved out . . ."

"But your piano is there," Caro stated firmly. "And just now, Julia, I think it had better remain."

Caro had meant it as a kindness, Julia knew, but she couldn't keep the tears from rising anyway. Caro had put a finger on a sore spot and it hurt. And Caro, seeing that her good intentions had hit a bruise, leaned forward earnestly, taking Julia's hand in her own, while Prissy considerately looked elsewhere, pretending not to see Julia's distress. "I'm sure everything will settle down in time, Julia," Caro said urgently. "Just be patient, my dear."

It was all Caro decently could say, and in decency Julia could say nothing at all. One did not criticize one's husband in public, nor display the least dissatisfaction with him there. Yet the hackles Kingsley Merrick caused continuously to rise in Waterford redounded unfavorably upon Julia and seemed to build momentum as he went his way, sowing the seeds of ill will broadcast. To hold an entertainment such as a dance could be a complete disaster, Caro was reminding her, drawing together the very people who disliked Kingsley most. A dance, necessarily involving limited numbers, was simply too intimate an undertaking now; even the reception tomorrow evening was a gamble, one for which she could not ask Caro about the chance of success or failure, one which would grind forward, she knew, regardless of its chances. But the saving grace of a reception lay in the very fact of its looseness, with no set time for arrival or departure. A man could come make his manners and leave if it suited him. Kingsley had intended it as a test, a straw in the wind; he had been delighted to learn that everyone had accepted (Julia had written to tell him so). Literally everyone for miles around would come; animosity could be easily buried in a throng, ignored there if need be, for the sake of being entertained in the Merrick mansion, at the first gathering the Merricks had yet held, such an occasion bypassed first in deference to the demise of the honorable Elijah Merrick, and later in deference to the delicate condition of Julia herself.

But a dance, Caro was saying, would be all wrong; the

captains of Waterford had not yet forgiven Kingsley Merrick for packing this spring's town meeting with Mill Village men who had rarely bothered to attend before, but who had arrived in droves to the meeting which would commit Waterford to $30,000 as its portion of extending the railroad from Yarmouth to Orleans under the corporate title the Cape Cod Central Rail Road. Between Mill Village and the sparse support in the town's center, led by Captain Crosby and David Snow, the article had passed. Kingsley had not even been there, but the mariner rightfully saw him as a leading force. His work in Mill Village, done long before, had turned the tide, and well they all knew it. It was part and parcel of Merrick's scheme to elevate West Waterford at the expense of the town's center; it was a continuation of the subtle undermining of Waterford which Merrick had begun by building a higher dam out there in Mill Village and installing turbines, both of which increased the power of the small stream. Rail would cause Mill Village to prosper, it would be another nail in the coffin of sail . . . yes! The Cape Cod Central capped the ill will of Waterford toward the Merrick Mill over which it was dismayed and disgruntled, ill will of which Julia was bearing the brunt now, this summer, when fewer of her friends than ever before had seen fit to call upon her and, despite their affection for her, were uncomfortable when she called upon them. Nor could the blame fall upon them. They were, as Julia was, caught in the crossfire between their husbands and Kingsley, and it was well nigh impossible to ignore it.

Unhappily Julia nodded, to indicate to Caro that she was being patient, would wait, appreciated Caro's unspoken sympathy; blinking her eyes dry, she caught at the thread of conversation.

"How many girls would be interested in a literary club?" she asked. "Have you been able to determine that?"

"Oh, a half dozen, at least," Prissy said lightly, striving to overcome the fact that this was, indeed, a mere smattering, belying once again the lack of ease with which Waterford regarded Julia Merrick. "And more will join once it's underway! Especially if the club discusses interesting books. The library stuff is pretty heavy, though very enlightening. Do you suppose we might slip in a novel or two?"

"Really, Prissy!" Caro reproved her.

"It would be more exciting!" Prissy protested, protecting herself.

"Miss Austen's books and Mr. Dickens's are certainly worthwhile, as well as entertaining," suggested Julia. "And surely it would be a good idea to read Mr. Hawthorne. Mr. Poe I'm not sure about. He's awfully creepy."

"How shall we buy them?"

"Fund-raising," Julia said brightly. It would be good to have something like fund-raising to involve herself with Waterford again. "How else?" She could have bought the books herself, as her friends well knew, but it would be offensive if she offered. "We could have a fancywork fair," she said hopefully, envisioning herself as chairman, surrounded by the busyness of it, surrounded by her friends once more.

"Unfortunately, it's beginning to look as though any fund-raising will have to be in support of the medical supplies and clothing for soldiers," Caro observed.

"Well, you'd better not say so!" Prissy exclaimed. "Not where anyone can hear you, anyway."

"She's right, though," Julia told Prissy. "If you could see the enthusiasm in Boston for war, you'd know she was right. I thought the whole place would go crazy after they fired on Sumter this April."

Prissy clapped her hands over her ears.

"Not another word!" she cried. "The subject is forbidden in Father's house, and the more ignorant I am, the easier it will be to keep my mouth shut."

"I'm afraid Prissy has a point," Caro said. "Just now Waterford's head is in the sand, and it would be better to pass by without disturbing it. I really must go, Julia." She rose and extended her hand. "Thank you for the tea. No—don't!" She waved in protest as Julia reached for the bell cord. "The door's exactly six feet away, and I can get there without assistance, and I can open it unaided, too. Come along, Prissy."

"All right," said Prissy, advancing to kiss Julia's cheek. "I wouldn't mind being let out, though."

"Well, I would!" Caro opened the door without further discussion.

"Until tomorrow evening, Julia!"

"Yes, until tomorrow!" Julia called after them. She watched as their voices drifted away, out of hearing, themselves out of reach, as they walked up her circular driveway and onto the county road. Cousin King's ancestral home lay across the street, occupied now by the Snow family; the Golden Ox claimed the corner and down the street were the two churches, both of whose spires she could have spotted if she tried, but instead she waved in return to Prissy and Caro's wave, the loneliness and isolation that they had held at bay during their visit falling once again upon her as she turned to her huge parlor, thirty feet long and fifteen feet wide, which escaped looking like a barn by virtue of the grand piano at its far end, and by the abundance of furnishings—sofas, chairs (armless, to accommodate hoopskirts), tables, curio shelves, and stands upon which pictures could be displayed. In the corner was a stereopticon with a box of scenic vistas that would appear three dimensional when looked at through the lens; huge potted plants stood about, sulking greenly; the fireplace, more decorative than functional, was framed in black marble, and a vase of ferns, spread like a fan, filled its yawning mouth so that it, too, fitted into the decorative scheme. The windows reaching from the floor nearly to the ceiling were swathed in velvet, caught back by gold-braid cords with tassels, but on the floor there were straw mats, because the Merrick mansion was designed for summer use and heavy rugs to keep out drafts were unnecessary. The mats gave an air of lightness to the otherwise heavy room, gave a certain freedom, lifting the sobriety of the dark furnishings, and beneath them, glimpsed through the interstices, the oak floor gleamed. The doorway to the diningroom was an especially wide one, with much of the diningroom's interior visible from the parlor, giving an illusion of even greater space. It was, quite truly, a fabulous house, one more likely to be found near the city than down here on Cape Cod. Kingsley had intended everyone to be impressed by it, and everyone was. But there its advantages ended. Its elegance imposed a certain restraint, an unspoken reminder of the differences between the Merricks and the rest of Waterford, a restraint that the presence of servants reinforced and that Kingsley heightened by his machinations about town.

At the beginning, the very first summer in which she had lived in this house as Kingsley's wife, she had been able to understand the uneasiness of her friends in the midst of so much grandeur. It would pass, she was sure; certainly her warm welcome—so heartfelt after the first bleak winter with Kingsley's business folk as her only companions, went a long way to dispersing it, demonstrating that she had not changed from the girl who once had lived in a house no different from that of anyone else. Then she had discovered herself pregnant, and as was customary, she withdrew from all save her family and her most intimate friends, Caro and Prissy. It had not helped, being isolated just then.

The following summer, she was barely recuperated from

the birth of Caroline (an experience she preferred to put behind her, its horrors too intense to live with). Kingsley had been busy with his mill, supervising the raising of its dam and the installation of its machinery, its turbines; the house was invariably filled with men and mechanics; weak as she yet was, it took all her strength to see to the comforts of these guests. The balance of her time was spent in attendance upon little Caroline and in seeing that the mud and muss left behind by the men of Mill Village was removed. There was little time for her own friends; the best she could do was to call on them occasionally, at their houses, where, even then, she could see that the Merrick immersion in millworks was beginning to work a wedge between herself and the families of mariners whose prime concern was the sea and who viewed industry as an encroachment on their own domain—and Mill Village was certainly encroaching fast!

The summer after that, last summer, the one in which she might have been able to entertain on a more elaborate scale because a suitable period of mourning had elapsed, there she was pregnant again, unable to lift a hand on her own behalf—the establishment on the Mill Creek running smoothly, to the dismay of Waterford, and Kingsley in his spare moments talking up the railroad, which Waterford did not want, enlisting support for it, which enraged a huge sector of captains—and now, this summer, the railroad having passed town meeting, here was Julia Merrick no longer pregnant, but so far removed from the mainstream it seemed impossible ever to find her way back again, the animus of Waterford running so strongly that only six women wanted—or were allowed—to join a literary club with the wife of Kingsley Merrick. Her eyes filled. . . .

Where will it end? she thought, depressed by the silence and magnificence of the room, pulling the bell cord and gathering up the plates and cups that she and Prissy and Caro had used, piling them on the massive silver tray that held the gigantic silver tea service, an affair encrusted with elaborately molded leaves and curling tendrils and bunches of grapes. *Where will it end, if Kingsley persists in making everything so awkward for us that we can't even converse comfortably, for fear we'll step on something unpleasant. Where will it end, if he continually alienates everyone?*

"Your guests are gone already, Mum?" Delia asked with dismay as she came in for the tray. "Did I miss your call, Mum? I was in the kitchen all the time, I swear it!"

"They preferred to let themselves out, Delia," she explained. "The ladies here are a little more independent than Boston folks."

"Foine ladies!" Delia approved; she'd have gladly opened the door for them. She liked Waterford people, who were better mannered to servants than city folk. That they disliked and distrusted the Irish had not yet registered on her perceptions.

Silly Prissy, who'd like to be let out because it felt good! Independent Caro, who did not care to be catered to! They well represented the ambivalence of Waterford toward the Merrick style of living, an ambivalence she could feel directed toward herself, just as they revealed the ambivalence of Waterford toward war, the underlying tension shown very clearly by the disintegration of the Lyceum and by Prissy's father, who did not want to talk about it. She had been in Boston when Sumter fell, this spring, recuperating from the birth of Augusta, the Merricks' second child. You couldn't miss the fervor there, where everyone was confident that in three months the North could whip the South.

You could see the writing on the wall clearly enough! You could have seen it in the fall, too (though many preferred not to look!), when an obscure politician from Illinois was elected to the presidency of the United States. Even before Mr. Lincoln took office the Southern states, one by one, were up and leaving the Union and were still doing it; since Mr. Lincoln seemed to have had no very definite ideas about what to do with the Confederacy, it became everyone's business to decide the matter for him, and Boston talked of nothing else. Boston, in the main, was hot for war. Not so Waterford, she soon realized, when she came down in June ahead of Kingsley, to open the house.

In Waterford there was only one answer to the problem, quite different from Boston's. Even when the sixth Massachusetts was attacked on its way through Baltimore and the President announced a blockade of Southern ports, trying to force the Confederacy into capitulation without war, there was only one possible hope, as Waterford saw it. For Jefferson Davis, president of the Southern Confederacy, promised retaliation by pillage of the shipping lanes, and it was clear that if there were going to be a war, commerce was going to be in trouble; there was going to be no cotton to carry away from the South and no goods to bring in, no peace upon the routes to Europe and the Far East and probably a decline in trade.

The deep-water captain was not by nature a warrior. He

was a businessman, a master of the sea utterly incapable of sailing under the command of someone else; he belonged under a spread of canvas and not on the deck of a naval vessel, blocking the mouth of a Confederate harbor so that nothing could enter or leave it, left there to rot indefinitely. A war could use none of his talents, would in fact destroy his career; and if there were to be war, Waterford was going to have to pay the price of it. Quite understandably Waterford's answer was the same as Mr. Lincoln's—to do nothing, and hope that the problem would somehow take care of itself, as it had always done before. Despite Sumter, the President had not declared war, was waiting it out to see what the South would do, how far it would go; if Mr. Lincoln waited long enough perhaps the heat of the moment would die down, the Confederacy might succumb to its best interests and forget about secession altogether. And if worse came to worst, if the issue would not resolve itself in some sort of compromise, then Waterford's answer, unspoken, undiscussed, unadmitted, subterranean, unacknowledged, unconfessed—was to let the Confederacy go.

There was not a man among them who sympathized with the Southern cause. It was one thing to contain slavery, quite another to allow it to expand (which the South now insisted upon); despite a long tradition of states' rights, a man of commerce knew a strong nation was good for business; despite certain bruises at the hands of government (tariffs hurt the mariner as well as the planter), the destiny of the nation was a great one, one in which Waterford took great pride, one which Waterford believed invincible, one which offered all possible reason to remain within. Waterford was sure—quite sure—that the Confederacy, once allowed to go its own way, would eventually petition for re-entry. The only possible answer to the present mess was to let the South go, if need be, let the healing passage of time demonstrate its need to belong to the Union for its own good—let it war with Mexico for land if it must—yet it was not an answer in which Waterford took pride. To say as much suggested disloyalty to the Union of which it was a part and which it loved, and so this furtive hope was not mentioned and words were watched carefully; the air in Waterford that summer of 1861 was full of tension and jumping nerves, for in reality the town was waiting for a decision which could well mean its own destruction, a decision that could not be balked nor defended against even in one's own mind, and so the tension was resolved by men like Prissy's father simply by not discussing it. Everyone was waiting for the second shoe to fall, hoping never to hear it.

Much as she didn't look forward to it, Julia knew she'd have to explain this tension to Kingsley when he came down from Boston today. He hadn't been in Waterford this spring; he'd been surrounded by city people hot for war, the streets thronged with volunteers and patriotism on behalf of the Union rampant; he'd been busy stepping things up at Hartland's, because express agencies were crucial in time of war, and he'd have no idea how sensitive Waterford was on the subject. It was one he'd better avoid at their reception tomorrow night, just as he'd be well advised to sidestep the C.C.C.R.R., which he had successfully won without even putting a foot into Waterford at meeting time, so well ordered his campaign for it had been, so well marshalled were its advocates that they could act on his behalf without anyone being able to say he had stood in the wings, calling instructions. So clever that it infuriated Waterford's captains just thinking about it.

But would he avoid these subjects, even if he were warned?

Might he not laugh instead and dive right into the advantages of rail, the necessity of war? He had it in him to ignore Waterford's sensitivities, that was for sure, and she might just be wasting her breath. Besides, she wasn't happy about spending a lot of time with Kingsley, talking or doing anything else. Tonight he would be in Waterford. Tonight he would sleep in this house. Tonight. . . . It had been seven months since Augusta was born, and Kingsley was bound to be getting restless. The less she saw of him the better; the less he saw of her the more likelihood there'd be that he wouldn't be reminded of his wife's recovery, which was regrettably complete now.

She clasped her hands in nervous gesture and found them wet and cold. *Really, Julia,* she scolded herself. *After three years it shouldn't bother you!*

But it did. She was churning inside at the very thought.

She hurried through the hall, past the library which was the base of the tower, to the stairs beyond which circled to the second floor. Caroline's little room lay across from them and next to it the little nursery where Augusta slept, adjacent to her own room so she could hear if the baby cried. Next to her chamber, occupying the rest of the space across the front of the house was the room Kingsley had slept in last summer when she'd discovered she was pregnant for the second time, and fervently she prayed he'd continue to occupy it. She had come down to Waterford ahead of him to open the house and she'd spent a lot of time freshening that front room, hoping that Kingsley would take it as an unstated suggestion that his wife was not yet ready to resume the duties encumbent upon her. Two babies in three years was a little strenuous, it said. *Whether she is recovered from childbirth or not, your wife needs to be left alone!*

In Caroline's room Nanny was reading a story. She looked up and smiled; Caroline, her blonde curls shining like a nimbus, crowed and from Nanny's lap reached out for Julia to pick her up.

"Who is that?" Nanny asked falsetto, but Caroline, ignoring her, regarded Julia in blue-eyed expectation and did not say "Mama."

Julia picked her up and hugged her.

"Is Caroline being a good girl?"

"She's always a good girl," Nanny affirmed. And Caroline was a good child, though so lazy she could hardly be bothered to speak and now, nearly two years old, walked only reluctantly.

"Is Augusta still asleep?"

"I haven't heard a sound from her," Nanny said. "Caroline and I have been listening while we read."

"I'll just peek in," Julia said, intending to give Caroline back to Nanny, finding that Caroline's arms had tightened around her neck, and that her daughter refused to let her go.

She laughed. "Perhaps you'd better check baby," she said to Nanny.

Downstairs she heard Delia opening the front door with exclamations of welcome which fell oddly silent as Kingsley's voice rumbled down below.

He has arrived, she thought. *He's here.*

Something heavy and hurtful fell, deep within.

"Papa is here!" she said brightly to Caroline. "Papa!"

"Pa," said Caroline. It was one of her few words.

"Let's find him," she said valiantly to Caroline, and adjusting the child on her hip, she carefully went down the stairs, feeling for each step so as not to trip. He was still in the parlor, she guessed. She went through the hall to its doorway and looked, saw him and stopped, rooted to the spot.

Kingsley was standing by the fireplace, his clothing disheveled, his cheek covered by an enormous bruise, ugly and purple, his eye rapidly swelling shut. Kingsley, usually immaculate, had been brawling.

"Hello, Julia!" he called. "How good it is to see you!"

227

Caroline, oblivious to the peculiarities of Papa's face, reached for him. "Pa!"

"Hello, sweetheart," he said, his joy in the child shining through his disfigurement. He reached for Caroline, nuzzling her exquisitely soft cheek with the unwounded side of his face.

"Kingsley!" she gasped. "Whatever has happened?"

But Delia was approaching now, basin in hand.

"Take it into the library, Mrs. O'Shea," Kingsley said to her. "And then come and rescue me from this little monkey." Elaborately he made a buzzing sound, burrowing into Caroline's throat, causing her to laugh. "How's Augusta?" he asked Julia.

"She's doing very well," Julia replied stiffly, and waited for Delia to come back, quelling her impatience.

"Now, Caroline, you will go with Mrs. O'Shea in search of a cookie," Kingsley instructed the clinging child, and obediently Caroline reached out for Delia. Kingsley could always get what he wanted from his little girl! "And be sure she does get a cookie," he reminded Delia. "Otherwise she'll place no faith in our promises."

Julia did not remind him that a cookie would likely spoil Caroline's supper. Instead, she followed him into the library and wrung out the cloth.

"Sit down and rest your head on the back of that chair," she instructed. "And tell me what happened!"

He chuckled as though he had not a worry in the world, lowered himself into the chair, winced as she laid the cool cloth across his eye. She tried not to notice the nearness of him, though it was impossible because he put his arm around her waist.

"It seems that I trod on some sensitive toes," he said sardonically. "You could even say I stepped on the tail of Waterford."

She waited as patiently as she could. There was no point trying to hurry Kingsley. He loved to savor a story. But within was a growing dismay. "Yes?"

"I took the Yarmouth stage from the depot, and got off at the Golden Ox, as I usually do," he went on. "And I just thought that the fellows might appreciate hearing the latest news, so I slipped inside."

"What is the latest news?" She removed the cloth which was hot now, rinsed it, replaced it.

"Well, it seems that our glorious army was routed at Manassas. They and the civilian population of Washington who went out to see the fireworks at the river—a little stream called Bull Run—fell all over themselves in their haste to get away, and the Confederates, apparently at a loss without anyone to fight, didn't pursue them. The upshot of it is that Mr. Lincoln has toughened up a little, calling for new recruits, and the Congress is scrambling around, dying to pass any measure it can to strengthen the war effort. The blockade of Southern ports is going to be maintained and strengthened, and even as I was leaving Boston the recruiting offices were inundated with boys volunteering. Naturally, I thought the fellows at the Ox would be interested to hear about it, but it seems they weren't."

There was a heavy sinking in the pit of her stomach.

"Then what?" she asked dully. But she could guess.

"Why, I asked why they showed so little enthusiasm." Brightly his uncovered eye gleamed as he laughed. "I asked where Waterford's recruiting office was—surely, with a strengthened blockade, men of the sea have a lot to offer, don't they? Certainly a lot of men here will want to volunteer, to aid the cause of the country!"

"Oh, Kingsley!" she cried. "It's not that simple!"

"No, I see now that it wasn't! The whole tavern absolutely exploded! Their flasks were about empty; perhaps they'd had too much. They seemed to think I was calling them copperhead! Instantly they were arguing against one another, those that weren't trying to pick a fight with me!"

"Someone succeeded, I see." He smelled of liquor himself, and she wondered about the state of his own flask.

"Sears Bradley—who else! He saw a perfect opportunity and he took it—though his companions prevented him from following through in the field behind the Ox."

"You challenged Sears Bradley?" It was getting worse all the time, and she was feeling quite ill now. Considering Waterford's hostility toward Kingsley, this new blow at its uneasy conscience was terrible.

"I offered him satisfaction if he wanted it. What a pleasure it would have been!" Kingsley sighed in lustful wistfulness.

"Did you accuse the men at the Ox of being copperhead?" she asked in despair.

"Oh, by the time I left, I did! I couldn't very well apologize for wondering what is wrong with them, could I?"

It was impossible! There was no way to redeem it! There was nothing she could do—nothing at all.

Mustering up all her patience, she explained, gently as she could, "This war really does put them in a bad spot,

Kingsley, and you've been unkind enough to strike a raw nerve."

"So it would seem," he drawled. "Though I must confess I was delighted to find a hole in their armor plate, Goddamn them all."

"Coming on top of the fuss over the railroad, I should think it might be quite a while before they forgive you," she suggested, hoping that this would disquiet him, yet knowing it would not. Nothing would make Kingsley sorry; nothing would move him to make amends.

"They don't need to forgive me." He laughed mirthlessly, and she realized that he was making fun of her, laughing at her for thinking that Waterford's good opinion mattered. "They are pompous, conceited, self-righteous, self-interested, Julia, and they don't care that our country faces a grave crisis."

"They stand to lose a great deal," she reminded him. "And if they haven't rushed to enlist, I don't see how you can deride them. You haven't either."

He snorted. "I tried," he said with anger in his voice. "But it seems that my services are more valuable than my life! Express agency employees are exempted; when they learned about my mill down here, they were adamant."

"You went to the recruiting office? You, with a family?"

"Yes, I went. Plenty of men with families will go, eventually. It will be a hard and bitter contest, Julia. This mess at Manassas proves it, and you're either for union or you're against it, unfortunately. War doesn't admit hedging your bets, much as I dislike seeing this thing in such simplified terms. Unfortunately, the time for subtlety is past. Would you care, Julia, if I went away to war? Would you miss me?" His eyes were soft suddenly, and he took her hand.

The flask must be empty, she decided. Kingsley carried his liquor well, and the only way you ever knew he'd had anything to drink was by the sentiment he allowed to show on such occasions.

"Certainly I wouldn't want you to go to war," she said as energetically as she could, frantically seeking a way to turn the conversation away from the snare of intimate implication. "And you shouldn't, either, Kingsley! The mill is a valuable contribution, and so is Hartland's, and you can hire a substitute if it makes you feel any better. You have nothing to be ashamed of." She moved to withdraw her hand but he would not let go. He was hanging onto it, watching her face, seeking her eyes which fled from his about the room, to the books on his shelves, leatherbound in maroon and blue and chocolate, bought by the yard—to the cabinet that held his liquor supply, to his desk with the top that rolled down. . . .

"It *is* good to see you again, Julia," he was saying softly. "I've missed you these two months."

"I've missed you, too," she said quickly, so that he wouldn't suspect she had not. "I've appreciated your letters. I know you don't enjoy writing them."

"I enjoy writing them when it's my wife to whom they're addressed."

"You must be hungry!" she cried. "I'll see how supper is coming along."

He let her hand go at last; his own fell back upon the arm of the chair.

"Jerry will join us at six o'clock," he said stiffly. "So if supper could be had at six and a half, that would work out well. I wrote him early in the week, asking him here so I could catch up on the mill before I go there tomorrow."

He could have seen Jerry in the morning, she thought, at the office he had made there at the mill, but it was his way of foisting West Waterford on her, whom she did not want, foisting it on her as he had done right from the start, crowding out everyone else.

"I'll see to it," she said stiffly, and went to the kitchen to prepare Rose for an extra place at the table. She'd better prepare herself, too, for a long evening, because Kingsley and Jerry were apt to spend a long time in the library after supper, emerging more cheerful than they went in.

Wherever he goes, whatever he does, he balks me, she thought despondently. And the damage he'd wrought in Waterford that day was beyond calculation. It might well take care of every last, feeble friend that she had.

She went upstairs, to choose from among the dresses in her wardrobe one that would make her look as unattractive as possible. A long evening ahead it might be, but there would be an end to it eventually with only the two of them, alone together, unless Kingsley excused her early, and she had a feeling that he did not intend to do so, not a bit.

There was no way, indeed, to stop him. . . .

When Kingsley ushered Jerry out only a half an hour after the two of them went into the library, she knew she was in trouble.

"Well!" he exclaimed expansively, "according to Jerry we're in good shape down there at the mill, and the wool I ordered has arrived to augment our own clip. We're all set to handle contracts now." His eye was completely shut, and he reminded her of a pirate with a patch on. "You've held up well through the meal and all, Julia," he observed. "You must be pretty well rested."

"Reasonably so," she said warily. "But I find I still tire easily."

"Well then! It's time you were abed," he smiled.

Pretending a naïveté she was far from experiencing, she preceded him up the stairs. Delia and Rose, she noticed, were discreetly out of sight.

She paused at her chamber door.

"Good night, then, Kingsley."

"Good night," he said and followed her in.

She'd have to face him, after all. He'd chosen not to take the hint; the wine at the meal, the after dinner stuff, the brief drink with Jerry in the library had made him impervious. *Why*, she thought, *why does it have to be like this?*

He'd closed the door, stood there watching her.

"Do you think, Julia," he asked hesitantly, "that you're well enough recovered that I might spend the night with you?"

There was a twisting in her vitals.

"I suppose I am, Kingsley," she said honestly—for she had been taught to respect the truth. "But I—I don't want another child so soon," she said desperately, wringing her hands although unaware that she was doing so.

He approached her carefully, took her hands in his own to quiet them. "I promised you that I wouldn't let it happen, and I won't."

"There's only one way that I know of to prevent it," she said calmly as she could—which was not easy. "And spending the night in my bed isn't it."

"There are several ways," he said firmly. "I've brought a precaution with me." He released a hand, patted a pocket.

She felt the wave of shock sweep through her. Surely he wouldn't!

"It's called a condom," he said. "If a man uses one, a lady doesn't get a baby."

She stared at him without trying to conceal her horror. Contraceptives prevented venereal disease, and the only occasion they were ever used occurred in houses of ill repute.

"I didn't think you'd like it," he said gently. "But I didn't think you'd like a baby, either."

Hot tears of shame stung her eyes.

"Julia," he said. "I'm trying to do you a favor."

She was cold all over, and the ice in her voice could not possibly escape him. "What kind of favor is it, to bring me to the level of a streetwalker?"

"Nonsense!" he insisted. "I'll admit this device is far from foolproof, but it's some protection for you—for any woman, and it's ridiculous to ban it simply because it also prevents syphilis."

She covered her ears. "It's immoral," she wept.

He wrenched her hands away.

"That's cant and drivel," he said sternly. "Just because everyone says so doesn't make it true. Think of it rationally, Julia. You're a smart woman. It will save you from an unwanted child if we're lucky, and it has no holes in it. Isn't that worth something?"

"You can save me from pregnancy without it," she managed to say in the face of her reticence in discussing such an intimately feminine topic. "The same way other husbands do."

"The same way other men get the clap," he scoffed. "Driving them into the arms of easy women! My dear, it's been thirteen months, more than a year. Do you imagine my manhood simply withers away? Do you want me to have to go to a whore? It's time, Julia! It's time," he said more gently. "And maybe it will be different this time."

He grasped her wrists more tightly than before; he held her steady, firmly, and his eyes held her, too. Kind eyes, eyes with hope in them and she knew it was impossible, that she could say no more. She had put off this hour as long as she could, and now the control had passed to him. She was once more locked into the humiliation of the marriage from which only pregnancy shielded her, and again she would have to suffer impalement on the instrument of his maleness, at his will and at his convenience spread beneath him like an animal staked out for the skinning, suffocating under the rising dread at his touch, doing battle with the terror she'd once known in the Levering coach because the marital assault was, in reality, no different from that one. . . .

She could not refuse, because after all the availability of her body was implicit in the marriage contract. In hopeless despair she knew she would not stop him from using the condom because she could not face pregnancy again—no, not now, not now! She could not escape its conclusion: the threat of death, and the fact of pain such as she had never known existed, but there was a way to escape the fact of sexual intercourse—if she tried hard enough. It took a monumental

233

effort of the will, but she had done it before, and she would do it now, and she clenched her fists and tried to bring her mind, her emotions, under control as she said, "Very well. If you'll let me go, I'll get ready for bed."

He watched as she removed her shoes and stockings; he unbuttoned her dress for her, unhooked her stays, and then, swiftly, she turned off the lamp so that he could see no more as she let her garments fall away from her, quickly slipping on her nightgown which Delia had left lying on her bed, while in the darkness Kingsley rustled about and she knew he was undressing, too.

She forbade herself to flinch when his hand came gently out of the dark to find her, and she clenched her teeth as it traveled up her thigh and past her waist and came to cup her breast and she knew, soon, that he would lower her gown, that she would feel his lips upon her . . .

She wrenched her mind, her consciousness away. It was the only answer, and diligently she forced her thoughts to her linen closet, to the second shelf where the pillow cases were stored, and feverishly she recalled the scent of lavender and pomander and desperately started counting the cases as her mind's eye beheld them: two, four, six, eight, ten. . . .

There was a pause in the dark that lured her mind away, and a fumbling that told her whatever you did with a condom Kingsley was doing, and Julia Merrick was having done to her what was also done to a tramp in a whorehouse. . . .

She lay rigid and full of hate and despair and loathing, counting sheets and then the silver in the pantry until at last he lay still beside her, breathing quietly, more quietly, his body appeased. He reached out as though to caress her. It was too much. She rolled away.

"Oh," he said. "So that's how it is."

He got out of her bed and scooped up what clothing he could find in the dark.

"You're really making this very difficult." His voice was low, and there was entreaty in it. "You make it impossible, no matter what I do, to make our marriage anything but a travesty."

A travesty! *He* would talk of travesty! Her silence was without relent.

"Julia!" he cried. "Talk to me!"

But she could not, even had she wanted to. There was nothing she could say.

"Julia," he said again. "Won't you try to like me a little?"

She wanted to cry out, *Like you! You, who would bring*

such an immoral practice into our marriage (it was immoral, and everyone knew it—everyone!). Like you! With your incessant demands, your insistence on your pleasures. . . .

And yet, she could have liked Kingsley once, she knew. She could have liked him well, had she not married him! He would have been a wonderful friend—but one did not marry one's friend. That sort of relationship did not exist in marriage at all, and it was unrealistic even to wish that it would. No, she was married to him, stuck with him and her role as his wife. He had forced upon her companions whom she could not respect, taken away most of her support here in Waterford. In continually forcing sexual confrontation upon her he might just as well be holding her face over an open cess pit. Now he had denied her protection from dishonor; he had corrupted her with the degradation of a contraceptive device and now, because of it—nothing, nothing would stop him. Nothing! There was no excuse she could offer.

She wondered, in abject misery, if there was ever going to be an end to the despair that living with him brought her.

She said nothing, and did not move. She listened to him, breathing there somewhere in the room as he, too, waited, hoping to hear words of affection, of friendship, of respect—something—but she said nothing, then heard him slowly leave her room, moving about in the one next to it, and she lay looking sightlessly into the dark, listening to the desolate sound of her own heartbeat, and fought to calm her mind so that she could find merciful sleep, and with it, escape.

Obed Stone of Rockford Village lifted the top of a carefully decrusted, fancily cut sandwich and examined the filling. Replacing the top, he tried another, and then another until one met his approval. Slipping it into his pocket for future reference, he took an apple from the artfully arranged basket on the sideboard, causing the fruit to collapse in a jumble, and ambled back into the parlor to take a stance by the potted palm into which he spat a seed.

Watching him from her spot by the front windows, Julia Merrick clenched her fists with anger and despair. She'd been able to watch the whole routine; standing where she did, the diningroom table and the sideboard behind it were perfectly evident. There was nothing, standing here, she could not see! Were she to turn and look out the window, she had a good view of the sweeping driveway, too. But long ago, hours and ages ago, she'd given up looking out there, because it was perfectly clear by now that they weren't coming. Cropping on the lawn, hitched to the dilapidated wagons, were the broken-down nags of Mill Village folk and Rockford people like Obed Stone, scattered over the smooth, immaculate expanses of grass like jackstraws thrown by a careless hand. The Wardens' smart rig, and Dr. McLaren's and the one belonging to old Captain Crosby had been more properly parked by the carriage barn, but they were gone now; they had left as soon as they decently could. Of all the active captains of Waterford, not one had come to the reception, nor had any excuse for their absence been tendered. It was a rudeness greater than Julia had expected; it was blatant and unavoidable and devastating.

"Thank you, Mrs. Merrick, for a lovely evening." It was Mary Ann Stevens and her husband Seth, who was following sheepishly, unintelligibly mumbling his thanks.

"I'm so glad you were able to come," Julia said, shaking Mrs. Stevens's hand, stretching her mouth into what she hoped would pass for a smile. "I'm glad to have met you, too, Mr. Stevens," she said untruly to Seth, who was the brother of Kingsley's boon companion Jon. No doubt Seth, from the smell of him, had just come from the library where Jon and nearly every other man had been drinking with Kingsley all evening.

Mary Ann Stevens smirked. "Perhaps it would be just as well if my husband and I took Stella Hall home," she said importantly. "If we don't she may have to spend the night. Darius, I believe, is nearly out cold."

"Stella will be, too, if we don't get her out of here," Seth remarked. "She's snuck a few."

"In that case I'm sure Mrs. Hall would appreciate a ride," Julia said swiftly, hoping she had not heard Seth correctly. A woman tippling in Julia Merrick's house!

Mary Ann bustled off in search of Stella Hall, leaving Julia momentarily alone with Seth, and for an instant she was tempted to ignore the man. Certainly there was nothing of interest she could say to him—or he to her! But she wasn't going to let herself be dragged into boorishness, just because Kingsley had set her an outstanding example of it.

With an effort she turned to Seth. "It's going to be a hot summer, I perceive," she said stiffly.

"Ayeh," he agreed.

"Do you have a garden, Mr. Stevens?"

"Ayeh," he nodded.

"Then already you must be feeling the lack of rainfall."

"Ayeh," he acknowledged dolefully and belched in his most subdued, restrained manner, as befitted a party.

Stella Hall, thank goodness, was being herded this way by Mary Ann.

"Mrs. Stevens has offered me a ride home, Mrs. Merrick," Stella said carefully, her breath reeking of clove. "So I'll thank you for a pleasant evening and be on my way."

"So nice to have you here," Julia stretched her mouth again. "Good evening."

"Good evening to you," they mumbled in a ragged chorus and awkwardly jostled one another as all three of them tried to escape through the front door at the same time.

There were still an awful lot of Mill Village and Rockford people left, she observed unhappily. She longed for them to go! Obed Stone had finished his apple; the seeds that missed the potted plant gleamed on the straw rug around it. There were tobacco stains and spittle on the black marble of the fireplace, where spitters had missed their aim, and behind a nearby bamboo easel that displayed Caroline's latest portrait there was hidden a jug of home-distilled liquor that someone, mistaking the Merrick reception for a barn dance, had brought as his contribution to the festivity. It was empty now, she suspected.

In the far corner Mrs. Mayo was drawing on her gloves as she talked with young Mrs. Coy from East Waterford (although one never took off gloves at an evening party!), so perhaps she'd decided it was time to quit the Merrick mansion, having fingered the collection of hand-blown bud vases on the curio shelves, leaving her fingerprints all over them, and having gazed to her heart's content through the stereopticon in the corner. The stereopticon's slides were scattered over the surface of the table on which it rested, the order in which they'd been filed in the box beside it utterly disregarded and, no doubt, smeared with butter or spattered with punch.

Rage against these people welled irresistibly from the deep spring of hostility that consumed her, but Julia knew they did not deserve her anger. They didn't know any better than to do what they were doing—but had the mariners of Waterford chosen to attend the Merricks' reception, the manners of the more refined group would have acted as a governor, and at least the outlandish behavior of Waterford's unwashed would not have been so painfully evident. It would have been buried and perhaps smothered beneath the greater weight of numbers.

As it was, the thirty-foot parlor was not so full as it should have been and the air of festivity that only a crowd would give it was notably lacking. The Merrick reception was a washout, a fiasco, and Julia's rage and hostility belonged rightfully to Kingsley who had brought it all about—it had been foolish to have one in the first place, but Kingsley had insisted. . . . Now he'd insured its failure by his taunts at the Golden Ox yesterday, and in the face of it he'd sneaked away, leaving her with the whole sorry mess in the parlor. Seeing the monumental snub given the Merricks at the hands of Waterford Center, he had disappeared into the vastness of his library where his liquor supply was, and there wasn't a man in the house this night who had not loitered there, enjoying his company and his bourbon, leaving Julia stranded with the ladies whom she hardly knew and who were—as they had always been—just a little in awe of Elijah Merrick's gifted youngest daughter. Waterford Center, her only solace, was completely lost through Kingsley's inability—or un-willingness—to understand the pressures under which folk here were living now. They were gone, and Mill Village and Rockford were all that remained!

"Good night, Mr. Stone," she nodded to Obed. "Good night, Mrs. Manning, Mr. Manning. Good night Mrs. Slater, Mr. Slater. Good evening, Mrs. MacFadden, Mr. MacFadden."

Jaws aching and her face clamped into a smile, Julia shook the last hands and closed the door behind her, leaning on it in relief and looking out across the parlor and the dining-room, and the litter of cups and saucers and sandwich plates and little napkins and hearing behind Kingsley's closed library doors, across from the diningroom, murmurs of happiness and drunken joy from the other side.

The disappointment, the cruel loneliness, the icy devastation that the party had brought with it caught up to her all at once, and she knew she'd cry soon. She couldn't stop those tears which had been awaiting her, on the far side of her anger, and she did not want Delia or Rose to see them. Already the girls were picking up in the diningroom while in the kitchen O'Shea lugged hot water from the stove to the sink for them, and so she fled, determined that the servants should not see her distress. After all, belonging to the Great Un-washed also, they'd have no real idea that anything had gone wrong. If the people in the house that night were quite differ-ent from the folks entertained by the Merricks in Boston, still Kingsley's city friends didn't have particularly fine manners, either, and perhaps the girls hadn't seen enough of Waterford Center to know the difference between them and the company tonight. But they'd be on to it in a flash if they saw her in tears, and it would never do to let down where they could see!

Trailed by another outburst of glee from the library, Julia reached her chamber door and shut the noise out, stood with clenched fists and an aching throat, and realized she'd fled directly into the heart of the trap which Kingsley, by design or inadvertence, had set for her. Here in her own bedroom she could not with any dignity nor with any expectation of success lock her husband out, and the bond implied within it made impossible any escape. The vows of marriage held her helpless here, wherein was enacted her submission to his will, from whence all the rest of her submission followed.

And now! Now, she thought, *having completed the destruction of the things I love, no doubt he will come to me again, exhilarated by the admiration of his friends who no doubt see him as their knight, laughing off the mariners as though they didn't matter. Having drunk more than he should, he will seek me here, condom in his pocket, to work further havoc upon me, having reduced me already further than I ever thought it was possible.*

She tried to quiet her racing pulse, the futile beating of her wings in despair. . . . How can it be, she wondered desperately, that the man who courted me and seemed to admire me so consistently reduces me to a mere nothing, a cipher; he proves nothing but his total victory over me with every move he makes. That I am here, under his roof, causes me to follow docilely in the trail of his destruction so that everyone must think I am willing to go along with it, so that he believes it, too. By even being here I indicate that I have subscribed to it all, even to his insult to my person, that I will go along with it—and for as long as I stay, nothing will change. . . .

The idea struck her forcibly.

What if she did not stay?

She sat heavily on her bed, the weight of this idea sapping her strength. She picked at it, daring to think it, expanding it. . . .

If I did not stay everyone would understand that I neither approve nor condone his undermining of Waterford. Most clearly, most important of all, Kingsley would know it, too. He would know that I shall no longer let myself be used and

*abused and debased, I shall no longer let him ruin my life,
nor separate me from those I love.*

A woman deserting her husband, no matter what the circumstance, was asking for trouble—big trouble. There was
absolutely nothing on her side—not law, nor public opinion—and she had never, ever considered it before. She'd understood well enough that she'd simply have to put up with
Kingsley—but now, this evening's party put a tool in her
hands, if she cared to look at it that way. Well Kingsley
might laugh off Waterford's snub, and well it might not matter to him, but if his wife left him now, on its heels, he'd be a
laughingstock, and that, at least, would be intolerable to him.
That was the hole in his armor, and through it, if she acted
now, this night, she would have put him in a vulnerable spot,
so severe to that monumental pride of his that he might well
be made to do nearly anything she asked simply to get her
back before anyone knew and could sneer at him. (Hah!
Waterford would smirk, Merrick thinks he's so clever, but he
can't even control his wife!) And a man who could not control his wife was a man few people respected.

Yes, she would leave; she would do it now, this moment
while Kingsley was in his library with his friends and unlikely
to be listening to the sounds—or absence of them—in the
house. Somehow she'd take Caroline and Augusta, the two of
them, to her mother's house and hide there, herself. When
Kingsley came looking for her, she'd stand firm, dictating the
terms of her return, and unless Kingsley acquiesced instantly,
unless he got her back home before much of the day passed,
Waterford would know she had left him. Waterford would
know that her loyalties lay with it and not with her husband,
and a double blow would have been struck on her behalf:
Kingsley would be diminished, and the sympathy of Waterford would be hers, and it would go a long way to mending
the broken rhythm of her friendships! Yes, whatever the outcome, she was bound to gain, and no longer must she curb
herself to the constraint of passive, patient womanhood which
she'd borne as long as she was able. Those days were done;
Kingsley himself had freed her from them.

She had no doubt of Mama's willingness to harbor her.
When Mama learned that Kingsley had invaded the privacy
of her bedroom only seven months after Augusta's birth, she
would be indignant. And if she had to, Julia could use
Kingsley's insistence on contraceptives as extra ammunition
for the firing of Mama's loyalty. She had no doubt, none at
all, about Mama's reaction to that! No one anywhere held

with the use of such measures in marriage. No one, apparently, but Kingsley!

She opened the chamber door, and listened. The library contingent was singing now, and further in the distance she could hear the chatter and clatter from the kitchen. *Good! Everyone was busy!* She hastened to the next room, where Augusta slept peacefully; bundling her carefully in a shawl, Julia tucked her under her arm and let herself into the quarters above the kitchen, where the female servants slept. She was thankful the house was solidly built, and there would be no creaking to betray her presence. She crept down the servants' stairs; at the bottom to the left was the door to the kitchen, to the right, the entrance to the woodsheds, and straight ahead, the door to the backyard. Quietly, quietly, she let herself out there, into the dampness of the evening and the light of the stars. There was a path here at the side of the yard if she could but find it, that led through the briars and scrub of the meadow to the old house where was safety and Mama, and she searched for it now, picking her way along the shadowed verges of the grass.

There was a sound behind her, at the house. In the billiard room the lamps were lit and the mumbles inside and the rattle of the balls told her the men had decided on a game. A square of light lay flat upon the grass and she froze as she saw Kingsley illuminated in it; he must have come out the back door right behind her. Instantly she stopped, praying that Augusta would remain asleep.

He called unintelligibly behind him, over his shoulder, and a whole covey of men came outside, busied themselves among the bushes, going about men's business, finally went in again, and the game, from the sound of it, began. Frantically she searched for the path and found it, further to the rear of the yard than she'd remembered. She held Augusta high, so that the brambles wouldn't catch on the shawl, and shivered as she hastened along. In her mind's eye was the image of Mrs. Stowe's Eliza, hopping the ice floes to freedom. . . .

Nonsense! she thought. She had never had much patience with militant women; there was nothing wrong with the system as it stood, except that it depended on the goodwill of men. And she would secure Kingsley's! Just one more trip, to fetch Caroline, and she'd be safe in the bastion of Grandfather's house from which she would do battle with her husband—and she would win! *Yes, she was sure of it,* and the heat of anticipated victory drove off the chill as she hurried along. Why, she felt more like herself than she had since she married him, as though she were weightless, and every step a great, leaping bound! She was grateful now, to Waterford, whose snub had put her in a position to defend herself! And she must—she would—use the opportunity to its best advantage—she must be stalwart and unafraid, even though (truth to tell) she was just a little in awe of Kingsley, whom she had hardly ever confronted headlong before.

Surely he did not want her to fear him—to disdain him—to hate him!

Surely, she thought, *he can't be satisfied with things as they are. Perhaps, if nothing else, my leaving him will bring him to the realization that I'm not his chattel, that he can't just have everything the way he wants it. Perhaps Waterford's rejection, and mine, will bring him around.*

The knocking at Mama's front door sent chills the length of her spine.

"I expect that's Kingsley," she said into the uncomfortable silence of the back parlor where she sat with her sisters.

"I'll go upstairs with Jamie and the baby," Ellen said quickly, hurrying away as fast as her six-month bulk of pregnancy allowed. James Duncan was at the Academy; Mama and Caroline and Augusta were upstairs already.

"I'll let him in," Clara offered bravely. The knocker sounded again in the front hall.

"Do you want me to stay, Julia?" Hetty offered nervously.

"No." Her hands were shaking.

"I'll go out to the garden, then. Call if you need me."

With the determination of a ship under full sail, Hetty went. She had only sympathy for her sister, even if she had no idea as to the nature of the quarrel between her and Kingsley. Anyone married to Kingsley had the sympathy of Hetty Merrick! But, now despairing of marriage for herself, Hetty badly wanted to go to school again, to qualify herself to be a teacher—and who but Kingsley could pay her room, board, and tuition? A difficult situation! Still, Julia was her own sister, and her loyalties were firm. She left, and for a moment Julia had the room with its quiet to herself. Upstairs, Jamie rode the toy horse with its wooden wheels that creaked loudly, back and forth and back again.

"Where's Julia?" she heard him demand of Clara.

"Back parlor," she heard Clara quaver, and heard Clara's feet fleeing up the steps. Quickly she took her place by the table in the center of the room, flung back her shoulders. *Be composed!* she told herself, and clasped her hands before her to stem their trembling.

"Hello, Julia." He paused at the doorway, his face set and unsmiling, unrevealing. The discoloration around his eye was fading, the swelling nearly gone.

"Hello, Kingsley," she said with as much dignity as she could muster, her heart beating so hard she could feel it in the pit of her stomach.

He searched her face for a long moment, and when he spoke, his eyes did not waver for even a fraction of a second.

"It seems you've left me."

"It seems I have." Had she looked for it, Julia Merrick would have seen despair and an appalling desolation—but she was not looking.

"Why?"

She hoped her hauteur would sufficiently disguise her nervousness. "Because I didn't care to stay."

"Are you annoyed with me because the more illustrious of our townsmen saw fit to boycott our reception?" he asked innocently. *He was maddening! Surely he must know, must understand what Waterford's snub meant to her!*

"Yes, you could say I'm annoyed," she replied coldly.

"I suppose you blame me for it."

"You called them copperhead. You are most certainly to blame."

"I can guarantee you, Julia, that properly handled they will return."

She restrained the urge to sneer. "You labor under a sad delusion, Kingsley."

"No, I don't! For soon, Julia, I will be a success. This war will make me a second fortune with my mill, and when the railroad is here, to Waterford's profit, then everyone in this town will praise me! They'll come flocking to my door and they'll come on my terms."

"Yes. Your terms."

"I take it from your tone of voice that you don't approve of them."

"I don't even know what they are." She gestured vaguely, because it was all so vague. "I understand only that whatever it's all about, it has to be done your way."

"Well then, let me spell it out," he said with elaborate patience. "If I succeed in bringing Waterford to heel, it will see merit in rail. It will see that our country's future is more important than one man's voyage; it will see that Mill Village has as much worth as Waterford Center, and it will come to

243

see that a man who works with his hands is as worthy as one who doesn't. I propose to give equal advantage to Mill Village, Julia, and I propose to use our house as the point of contact. And since our house is in the middle of it, I clearly need you there. Waterford's various elements need mixing, and I need your help in seeing that it happens."

She shook her head. "They are incompatible, King."

"They are now. But in time they will not be, not if the two of us are working at it."

She snorted, folded her arms, turned away. "Waterford Center won't even cross our threshold," she reminded him over her shoulder. She picked up Clara's embroidery from the couch where her sister had left it, and examined it with exaggerated care.

"All right," he said to her back. "What else is bothering you?"

"We can always discuss your business associates in Boston, especially since they're all that's left."

"They are decent men, Julia. All of them."

"Well, I'm glad to hear it." She sniffed. "I'm glad to hear they are so fine, because I assure you their wives aren't! Their wives are vain and shallow and frivolous and I'm stuck with them while you drink to your heart's content with your decent friends. Just as you do here, with your Mill Village compatriots, while any friends of mine have forsaken me because of your conduct in Waterford."

"My, my," he remarked. "You do have quite a lot on your mind! But you've never said so, Julia."

"What good would it have done?" She faced him again in rising anger. "Would you have stopped throwing me into the company of people I don't care about?"

"Probably not," he admitted. "But I might have told you my purpose in doing so, and you might have been able to work with me in bringing my goals to pass the quicker, and you might not have felt so—isolated, is it? Is that what you feel?"

"That's part of it," she said icily. "But perhaps I don't care to help."

"What else don't you care to do?" he asked politely. He stared at her and despite the poise she was gaining from the bald statement of her grievances, she found herself blushing.

"I must assume, from your reticence, that you find the resumption of our marital relations distasteful."

She felt her face go red and hot.

He paused a long time studying her, a mocking eyebrow

244

lifted. "And perhaps there are other aspects of the marital relation which trouble you, too."

"Perhaps."

"Perhaps an apology for the scene that passed between us when I came home from the Golden Ox is in order."

"Perhaps it is." She held her breath, absolutely without guidance. Where the conversation would lead there was no telling!

"I told you then, Julia, and I will say it again. I was trying to protect you from consequences you apparently can't handle. What more can I do?"

"I told you at the time what you could do!" She said it brusquely, mastering her embarrassment as best she could in the face of this most intimate of topics.

"You find me repugnant?" he asked.

"I'd rather not discuss it," she said stiffly, tense with the anxiety the subject always thrust upon her.

"Julia! Please try! Else we have no hope of being reconciled."

Discussing it was out of the question. It was not something that could be discussed! She stifled the alarm which instantly rose up. "Reconciliation is your idea, not mine," she said, willing to do anything she had to in order to fend him off.

"Well, then, on what terms will you come back to me?"

There was an edge to his voice though no emotion whatever showed in his face. *He was becoming impatient,* she thought—*but he was becoming fearful, too, of losing this contest between them, fearful that, after all, his wife would not do his bidding, and she rather thought she had him where she wanted him.*

"I'll return when you stop bringing your friends to our house in Boston," she said coldly. "I want your Mill Village friends gone from our house here in Waterford, too, so that there's room in it for the people I enjoy. You've damaged everything, Kingsley. Everything dear to me, and I want you to stop."

"The hell I will!" The color rose in his cheeks.

She plunged ahead. "Without some assurance that you'll desist in alienating Waterford, some effort to rectify the wrong you've done, I'm not coming back. Then, Kingsley, you'll be Waterford's laughingstock—and see how far you get! A man who can't even command the allegiance of his wife!"

He stared, shocked at her temerity, and she forbade herself the luxury of even a flicker of her eyes.

245

"So you will use last night's debacle to bring me to heel, is that it?"

"How clever of you, King, to have figured it out," she said with sarcasm.

Slowly, deliberately he pulled a cigar from the pocket of his vest and ambled over to the fireplace where he struck a match. His hands were steady, but there was a pulse beating heavily beneath his dark hair and his eyes, usually blue, were nearly black now, as they were apt to be when he was riled. *Yes,* she thought, *he was quite angry,* and smoking a cigar in her presence was only one evidence of it, because he knew how much she detested them. He leaned insolently against the mantle, blowing smoke in her direction.

"Very well, Julia." His voice was controlled, and without passion. "The party's over. Now we shall consider the facts of life. I can claim custody of Caroline and Augusta, which is one fact you may have forgotten. And if you don't return to our house now, this day, this minute, I shall. And let me point out, as well, that my legal obligation to you ends with your desertion of me. You, and all your family may go to the devil for all I care—which would have happened in the first place had I not married you."

She thought of Mama, of her sisters, of Tony, who labored at Hartland's under Kingsley's heavy hand. She stared at him, at the little puffs of smoke that rose to form a cloud above his head, and could think of not one single thing to say that would not betray the fact that she had, indeed, known it for a long, long time.

"If you think for a moment that I'd kiss the collective ass of Waterford for your sake, you're wrong. If you think you can stay here in your mother's house at my expense and enjoy our children with my blessing, you're dreaming. If you think you can leave me any time it suits you and that I'll come to you begging, you've got the wrong man, my dear. By law I am master of our house and master of you, too, and I'd appreciate it if you wouldn't forget it—ever. You are my wife, and by God you are going to behave like one."

He was perfectly within his rights to take Caroline and Augusta, to withdraw his financial support of her, to send her family to the almshouse until and unless she lay supine between his knees, and her helplessness in the face of these things goaded her anger which rose, high and straight, searing and destructive.

"I should have known you'd resort to force," she said, all her anger, all her spite and venom and frantic rage spilling

246

over into her voice. "You are such a clod, Kingsley. Why, you're just like your father must have been! You are incapable of civilized behavior, either in public or in private. No wonder you have never understood me—or my needs. No doubt your father was such a person, too, without comprehension of the innate delicacy of women, forcing himself on your mother to beget a child out of wedlock!" She pressed on, mercilessly. "Unless, of course, she was not delicate at all. That's it, of course! You have never known what a decent, respectable woman is like, because you lacked the example of one at home. I should have known," she sneered.

His face went white and his eyes, glittering blackly, smoldered, then blazed. He clenched his fists and she realized that he was near to striking her—but before she had time to become afraid, the flame in his eyes flickered and shut down, as though a damper within had been closed, and his features went wooden, as though he were wearing a mask. She realized she'd inflicted a wound far deeper than she'd intended; she stared, horrified, and he stared back with eyes that now held no expression whatever.

"Sit down, Julia," he said, his voice flat. Carefully he threw his cigar into the fireplace. "I can see your distaste for me is deep, and I shall not infringe on it. You shall name your terms within our house and I shall abide by them, whatever they are. Beyond our house is my domain, and the two shall not connect with one another."

"Any terms?" she faltered.

"Any terms," he said without hesitation.

"I don't want your Mill Village friends," she said tentatively despite the wretched, sorry feeling working at her conscience. "They aren't my sort of person."

"All right." His voice held no expression.

"I don't want to be smothered in Boston by the wives of your ill-bred friends, either."

"Since they're all the friends I have at present, what do you suggest?"

"I'll stay here," she offered. "All year. Then I won't have to bother with them. I can concentrate on winning *my* friends back."

"All right," he said. "I'll see to it that heating stoves are installed. Anything else?"

"I think that takes care of most trouble spots. Until such time as you are willing to behave yourself here in Waterford," she said carefully. "And of course I would like you to respect the privacy of my bedroom." *Would he?*

"Oh, indeed!" He smiled unpleasantly. "I wouldn't dream of violating that." He turned away. "You get your friends back and I'll try to keep out of sight. How's that? There'll be times I can hide my light under a bushel—after all, that railroad is bound to begin fairly soon, and Waterford will be reminded of me whether you like it or not. But let's cross that bridge when we come to it. Until then, we shall to all intents and purposes live apart." He looked her over insolently. "I shall visit you the first of each month; I shall expect to see our children, and I shall require your presence too, so that no one will think you're avoiding me." He cocked his head. "Where are Caroline and the baby?"

"Upstairs," she said feebly, exhausted and shaken by the coldness in Kingsley's voice.

"Fetch them, please," he instructed. "We shall take them home now. Nanny is waiting for them."

Tremulously she pulled herself to her feet, headed for the back stairs, encountered Kingsley blocking them.

"I'm sorry you think me such a lout, Julia," he said evenly, with neither anger nor amusement in the least evident. "But I shall keep away from you, my dear, for as long as you want me to."

The look of disdain she managed to drum up was sufficient, she was sure, to tell him clearly and without equivocation that forever was not long enough.

She was neither proud nor happy to return to her house.

While the federal army drilled under McClellen and Mr. Lincoln refused to declare war and Waterford waited for the inevitable, it was a lonely place, because rancor over Kingsley Merrick was not forgotten, nor did men like Sears Bradley allow it to be forgotten.

The Sanitary Commission could have met in the Merrick parlor—indeed, it was the largest one in town—but Julia's offer was politely ignored. The commission met instead in the vestry of the church (now Unitarian in fulfillment of Papa's plans for it). She went to the meetings, rolling bandages and helping pack the supplies collected for the succor and comfort of the federal army should the day ever arrive when General McClellen would decide to use it. Each time, returning home, she couldn't help acknowledging once again the restraint, the distance, that yet separated her from Waterford, that lingered persistently in Kingsley's trail. How polite everyone was! Yet how else could they all behave but with courtesy which eliminated the necessity of having to mention the boycotted Merrick mansion, or those things Kingsley had done and said that contributed to Waterford's rejection of him. There was no choice but to wait, wait patiently and be grateful to her loyal sisters who strove to fill the breach until time would heal it, all except Hetty who was attending the Franklin Academy.

Contrarily, Kingsley's conspicuous absence was a source of unhappiness, too. Assiduously complying to the terms she had dictated, he came to the house only as he had stipulated, the first of the month, otherwise preferring to sleep at his office at the mill when he was in town. His West Waterford friends stayed in Mill Village, and how the Wheelers and Pettingills and Brickers were getting along in Boston without her she never learned because Kingsley made no mention of them; indeed, he only ever inquired politely after her health and spent most of his time with Caroline and Augusta. He was manifestly unconcerned with her; their marriage was one of convenience, just as she'd requested, and she should have felt wonderfully free now, without his shadow constantly hovering over her and spoiling everything she did. He was certainly not the burden that he'd been—and yet, until her friends became comfortable with her again, there was nothing for him to spoil, and his absolute acquiescence to her terms served only to remind her that she got them by hurting him, wounding him where he was most vulnerable. She hadn't known what a devastating blow taunting him through his unfortunate background would be—but that did not excuse it. She should be ashamed—and she was ashamed!—but hardly could she apologize.

She could only hope the sting and malaise of her conscience would ease, and she did her best to help it along by her conscientious mothering of Augusta and Caroline, by her efforts to keep Kingsley's visits cordial and happy so that the little girls would continue to love and respect their father, and she diligently sewed little dresses and hats and coats and tried not to notice that she was terribly lonely. She did her best to look happy when a carriage on Main Street passed by, filled with friends from former times who dared do nothing more than wave; she tried not to be hurt when Caro flatly refused to consider a literary club. Only Caro, among the young women in Waterford, dared to befriend her now—but in secret, where no one would notice. They chatted over spools of thread in Snow's store.

"Don't be silly, Julia," Caro hissed. "It would only give the men another opportunity to get back at Kingsley by refusing to let their wives attend a literary meeting at your house."

"We could hold it at your house," she said wistfully. "And I could just—wander in."

"They could all just wander out, too," Caro observed. "Not that they'd want to, Julia."

"I know," she said sadly. "I understand. I'm not angry. Only hurt, Caro."

"It'll pass," her friend counselled. "The men will forget their fuss over Kingsley, and they'll forget they forbade your friendship to their wives, and everything will be as it ought. Just be patient, Julia."

Yes, she must be patient.

Patience, she told herself, would solve it all. Time would ease her conscience, time would ease the unhappy conscience of Waterford in respect to war, and the Cape Cod Central Rail Road was stalled indefinitely for lack of rail, iron being diverted to the war effort. It would be quite a while before Kingsley would be stirring up that hornets' nest; in the interim, the rancor accompanying it was lulled. And Kingsley, gone so much in Boston, was helping, she was sure, to heal tension by his absence.

Meanwhile the threat of Confederate raiders had become a reality. The *C.S.S. Sumter* had burned the bark *Golden Rocket* of Maine, the *Daniel Trowbridge* of New Haven, the *Eben Dodge* of New Bedford, *Neapolitan*, *Arcade*, *Vigilant*—and all winter had stopped countless neutrals coming out of the Mediterranean. The *C.S.S. Nashville*, a side-wheel steamer, sank the *Harvey Birch* of New York and the *Robert Gilfillan* of Philadelphia. The *Shenandoah* put the fear of God into whalers and in the spring, from the docks of Liverpool, England, Number 290 was launched under the name *Enrica*, later to be armed off Terceira and rechristened *Alabama*. It looked bad, very bad, for the *Alabama* was not simply a vessel converted to the war effort by mounting a gun on her deck. She was built for war, built for the destruction of commerce, and there was no doubt, even in the mind of the optimist, that she would succeed.

It was worse in June, when news of the seven days' battles came in. Thousands—thousands of men had been killed! Nothing like it had ever happened before, and Julia Merrick was as dispirited and solemn as everyone else. . . .

Yet the war itself, directly and indirectly, saved her. Yes, the conditions of war worked for her, unexpectedly drawing her from seclusion because in July Mr. Lincoln issued a call for volunteers—in July her hopes leaped up and took flight, showing her how bored and unhappy she had been all this long and lonely year, because she was neither bored nor dispirited any longer.

Who would have thought it of James, so meek and spindly? Who, for that matter, would have thought it of Tony, always watching out for himself and certainly never indicating any depth of feeling for anything that did not immediately bear upon his life?

Did not Mr. Lincoln call for three hundred thousand volunteers? And did not Tony and James volunteer? They would march away under banners of honor, glory, and admiration! And Waterford however reluctantly recognizing the necessity of war, accorded them the status of heroes. Three other boys in Waterford, inspired by their example, enlisted, too—and the name of Merrick was once again honorable. The fact that Mr. Lincoln had to issue another call in August because response to the first one was so disappointing only served to heighten the nobility of James and Tony, who had not needed to be urged to defend their country. Poor Ellen floated about with tears of admiration and apprehension in her eyes, busy packing all manner of things for James that he likely wouldn't need and couldn't use. *If the government would accept the services of Duncan, puny as he was, it must be in bad shape,* Julia thought, but she set to knitting James a pair of socks and a muffler for Tony, and received the admiring commiseration of Waterford, along with that given Ellen and Mama and her other sisters for their personal sacrifice on behalf of the Union. Tony, quitting Hartland's, stayed with her until it was time to leave, and her house was full of people coming to wish him well, coming to shake Julia's hand, too! In the name of patriotism Tony broke Kingsley's hold on her life and lifted the curse of Kingsley from her; in the confusion, the conflicting loyalties brought on by civil war, the bewilderment and the need to move forward, Waterford of necessity put aside the constraint of former times. Almost without anyone's noticing, Julia was included in the determined effort to cheer James and Tony on their way, and without anyone saying anything, the girls who were once her friends began to look to her for friendship once again and everyone, by mutual if unspoken consent, agreed to forget the local animosity against Kingsley, which, by then, had fossilized into permanence. *Yes, it was time,* she thought, *to begin again. . . .*

But more! Succeeding James at the Academy was David

Pendleton, and when he arrived in town, she was sure that her life would be brighter than it had ever been and that the time had arrived for the polishing up of Waterford.

Tony had taken Cousin Nell Denning out in the carriage and Julia had been at her mother's place the day that Pendleton arrived in the coach and came to find James before he went away with the army, to discover what state James was leaving the Academy in before Pendleton took it over. Everyone was having tea, and naturally they invited Pendleton to share it.

Pendleton, slightly built even as James was, nonetheless was taller and carried himself well and wore his clothes well and more: he had the ability to entertain, the ability to turn conversation into the shimmering lucidity of a sophisticated exchange of ideas; broadly educated, interested in nearly everything, well mannered . . .

Mrs. Merrick, here, was accomplished at the piano? Delightful! He was a fair hand at the fiddle—who else might be got to play an instrument, to join Julia Merrick and himself? It was worth doing, even if no one else ever heard a note. He believed in art for its own sake. Did she?

"I love music," she told him happily. "But as for an ensemble—we shall have to import someone from Boston. The only strings touched here are the lines in the rigging."

"Oh! Of boats, you mean."

"Of ships, sir, of ships," she corrected him gaily. "A ship is not a boat."

"Indeed," observed Pendleton contritely. "I've been told many a mariner lives in this town. I shall have to learn the language."

"It's a fact," she agreed. "Nearly everyone here is a sailor."

"Perhaps one among them plays a Jew's harp?" he suggested.

"Or a harmonica."

"And perhaps one of those things you rig up on the bottom of a bucket?"

"Or, if we lined up bottles with different levels of liquid in them we could play a tune," she laughed.

"When we got thirsty, we could always drink the contents."

"If we used brandy," she observed, "then we'd be happy as well."

"Julia!" Mama cried at this indiscretion. It was like the good old days, all right! Julia laughed, and the conversation passed to theatre, to amateur productions, which, Pendleton believed, were good for everyone. *Would Waterford, in James's opinion, object to stage productions at the Academy? Or would it be considered unpuritan? Dramatic presentations were so beneficial in many, many respects, teaching history, correct English, proper pronunciation, declamation, all in the same breath, but he would not like to project such a thing if it ran counter to folk's inclination . . . no? Splendid! Perhaps adults would enjoy performing, too. Jolly fun for all. The stage was not meant for children alone!*

Somehow, something would have to be done. Somehow, within Waterford or without, people of ability and wit must be gathered so that Pendleton would have a place to shine. Without that, surely he would tire of Waterford and leave it! And if he stayed, surely her own life would have more to make it worth living! David Pendleton liked art. He liked music. Literature. Theatre. . . . All the things that Julia knew were dear to the hearts of Beacon Hill, in the presence of which she had spent the happiest hours of her life.

She still had the balance of the summer and meant to take advantage of it. Her heart in her throat, she issued invitations to a small, intimate reception for David Pendleton such as was quite proper to do under the circumstances, to welcome him to Waterford. Caro and Prissy would surely come, and she would risk Amy and Captain Blake, who had sailed around the world together twice, reading poetry to one another all the way. Captain Blake had come to shake her hand and Tony's; he would not refuse to enter the house of Kingsley Merrick.

Likewise she took a chance on Elizabeth Crosby, her friend from childhood who always talked about Europe which she had visited once, when she was taken there in her father's ship, and Elizabeth's new husband, who collected arrowheads and had once met and talked with Agassiz about anthropology. She invited the masters at the district schools and a sufficient supply of unmarried girls to occupy them, girls whom she knew to be quick as well as pretty, and she invited Mandy Warden, who wasn't Miss Warden anymore since she'd married a Philadelphia fellow who knew—or had known—Mary Cassatt before she'd dismissed high society and gone to Europe to paint. Until Julia met Mandy's husband she couldn't know whether he was interesting or not; certainly Mandy wasn't, but any connection with the Wardens was bound to have interesting results, and the young couple were here right now, visiting the aged Abel Warden.

She avoided the rest of Waterford just then, unwilling to strain her newfound cordiality any further than she had to.

Oh, she had not enjoyed an evening as much as that one in a long, long time—not since the last informal gathering of young people she'd attended with Adam Levering, in which the guests inspired one another to heights before unknown, depths unplumbed.

Those she'd brought together were an especially good mix, Mandy Warden's husband delightful and a fount of information on art, Elizabeth Crosby's husband full of tales about Agassiz, and the unmarried girls positively scintillating. Diverse as everyone's interests were, they were at least interested in something and not one mention was made of ships or storms or even of war.

"How much they enjoyed you, Mr. Pendleton," she exclaimed after the door closed behind the last departing guest, and she had rung for Delia to bring in the liqueurs. If she could keep him here a little longer, perhaps their conversation would drift into desirable channels.

"I enjoyed them!" he responded enthusiastically. "Though to tell the truth, Mrs. Merrick, I am just a little surprised to find such variety and such a widespread interest in—shall we say—life's finer things?"

"I'll confess they were carefully picked," she laughed as Delia entered with the tray. "You were supposed to be impressed."

"I was!"

"Won't you have some brandy?" she asked. "Or, perhaps a little apricot cordial?" She waited by the tray, expectantly.

"Apricot cordial would be pleasant." He sniffed it appreciatively, tasted a minute amount, rolling it in his mouth like an expert. "Very nice," he told her.

"My husband knows his alcoholic spirits." She smiled. "At least, that's what everyone says."

"Everyone is right!"

"Won't you sit down, Mr. Pendleton?" *If only he would, and if only he would relax, and if only she could strike a responsive note within him!* There was a small silence while she cast about to discover the opening she needed. She could find none.

"Mr. Pendleton," she said finally. "You mentioned, at my mother's house, I believe it was—that you believed theatrical productions were as beneficial to adults as to children."

"Indeed they are," he said instantly. "When one takes up a temporary role in a play, it shakes one loose from the role

254

one has been playing every day. Then, having shaken off that everyday role, one is more likely to continue to shake it loose and then one is free to grow, to become a fuller, deeper, greater person. Naturally it requires the proper environment. . . ."

"It sounds wonderful," she breathed. "Do you think we could do it?"

"Certainly we can have a play," he agreed.

"I wasn't thinking about a play so much as providing the environment," she said. "Waterford, I'm afraid, badly needs one."

"Oh?" He scrutinized her carefully, and she thought she had better be cautious. If she painted Waterford in colors too muted, Pendleton might get discouraged.

"My friends who were here this evening have quite a variety of interests—but unfortunately, Mr. Pendleton, there aren't too many other people here in town who have bothered to cultivate themselves. Everyone has been so interested in clippers! But it's different now," she went on eagerly, "because a lot of men aren't sailing, due to the war. And I'm sure they would be interested in doing a lot of things that never appealed to them before—as long as there were things available to do. . . ." she petered out lamely. "Interesting things like musicales and amusing things like cards . . . and theatricals . . . literary things and . . . poetical things. . . ."

He was quiet a long time before he leaned forward, elbows on his knees. "You've been starving in the American cultural desert, haven't you?" He smile sympathetically. "There's nothing here for you, is there?"

Unexpectedly she felt her eyes fill, and he hurried on.

"May I call you Julia? You seem too young, Mrs. Merrick, to be designated by a matronly appellation!"

She laughed shakily. "I'm a matron of twenty-one."

"My age exactly!" he laughed too. "So you must call me David, if you'd like."

"Surely!"

"And then, since we are of an age, and on a first-name basis, let us become partners."

"Partners?"

"Yes! Let us be partners in the creation of an oasis—in the transformation of Waterford."

She stared. "I hope I know what you're getting at, David Pendleton!" she exclaimed, gladness and exaltation rising in her breast.

"It would be interesting, don't you think? To give Waterford some class?"

"It has *some*," she protested loyally. "It's just that there's room for more."

"Quite so," he assured her. "A grand start has been made. Building on that, I should think we might spruce Waterford up a great deal. I'd consider it a challenge."

"I'd consider it a relief," she said frankly. "I *have* been a bit at loose ends here."

"And I'd be happy to have something besides teaching to think about," he confessed. "An unmarried man in a little town can get pretty lonely. But needless to say I'm in no position to change that—teachers make so little money!"

"Marry a Waterford girl," she advised. "No one here is poor. Her father could support you in a manner to which I'm sure you'd like to become accustomed."

He laughed merrily, for a long time. "How do you happen to be here, bless you!" he exclaimed. "I'd expect to find you in an urban environment, not a country one. Your humor alone betrays your sophistication!"

"I once lived in Boston."

"Were you able to indulge your taste for the arts there?"

"Oh, yes!" she said ardently. "If you made alliance with the right people, David, it was really wonderful."

"Well," he said firmly. "The right people are right here! We have only to find them, coax them out of their hiding places. We shall use a variety of bait, both heavy and light— for you mustn't forget, Julia, that people like to be entertained, and different people respond to different sorts of entertainment, only gradually gravitating to deeper and more profound tastes. Yes, we shall ferret them out, we shall coax them, you and I!"

He raised his glass. "To our mutual endeavor!" He downed the apricot cordial.

Two weeks later, under David Pendleton's direction, she again wrote out invitations, but this time to a larger and more varied group than had been encompassed by her party.

Mrs. Kingsley Merrick requests the honor of your presence at her home, 8:00 Wednesday evening to discuss the casting and production of Shakespeare's great play *Hamlet,* to be held at the Lyceum Hall whenever its director, Master David Pendleton of the Waterford Academy, deems it ready.

256

It was a beginning, and she crossed her fingers and hoped—prayed—that Waterford would come.

It did. She kept in the background, supervising the circulation of refreshments while David Pendleton discussed Shakespeare with two dozen townspeople and did it so zestfully that they all decided they'd like to have an adult course of lectures on the Great Bard before they undertook to produce one of his plays. David Pendleton was a born teacher and he could make anything interesting! And he was a catalyst, as well; each person in the Merrick house that night seemed more interesting than he had ever been, better informed, more intuitive, intelligent, eager to learn, to grow—yes, David Pendleton would have them all eating out of his hand in no time!

Only—if only—Kingsley wouldn't ruin it! She would have to tell him, of course. It was his house, after all, and she'd said the Shakespeare class might meet there. She had better introduce Kingsley to David Pendleton and have done with it.

"I told you that I'd leave you free to work out your own destiny," Kingsley said blandly, the beginning of the following month when he paid his accustomed call, spent his accustomed night under his own roof so that no one would know that all was not as it ought to be with him and his wife. "You can entertain Abraham Lincoln if you want to, Julia; I assure you it doesn't matter to me."

"Well, I'm planning gatherings and get-togethers, and I didn't want to move forward and say nothing to you about it."

"A consideration I appreciate." He nodded. "Just see to it that the house is clear when I'm customarily in it."

"You don't care what goes on here? It might be interesting to you."

"It might be. It might not. I trust that nothing improper will transpire in my absence," he said with a wry smile at her embarrassment at his even suggesting such a thing. "And surely you'd rather I kept out of your way, so that I don't ruin everything as I did before."

His gaze was steady, admitting neither embarrassment nor contrition, nor apology.

She could not answer without positive rudeness, which she wanted badly to avoid. She had no wish to be rude to Kingsley! She only shrugged, to indicate that at least she had tried.

And so the Shakespeare class convened regularly at her

257

house, and in the interim David Pendleton came there to hear her play her piano, and admired what he heard, praised it, nurtured her lonely artistry until it was lonely no more. He came and discussed Plato and the Platonic influence on transcendentalism with those of her friends who had read Mr. Emerson, and he talked about that English fellow Darwin in whose theory Pendleton was inclined to believe, even if so many people did become upset to hear they were elevated monkeys. He organized a class in watercolor landscapes under the tutelage of Ned Ballington, who had studied art in Italy and who had come to the Cape to paint portraits, and who had found enough business around Waterford and Yarmouth to warrant staying for a while. The Blakes and the Crawfords, the Pollards and the Dennings, assorted unattached females in tow, trekked out onto the fields and down to the bay with their easels and painted daisies and dories and burnt the tips of their noses and held an art exhibition at the end of the summer, where Clara Merrick won first prize.

By fall a whist club of two tables met regularly at Julia's house, and the feeble literary club blossomed to include eighteen members who planned to raise funds for book purchases. David Pendleton lectured to them about books, and because of him literature was interesting, and poetry, too. He could show them parallels and implications they had not seen before so that they became eager to discover those implications for themselves, and at home the men, unfortunately unemployed these days, browsed through the books, too, although they admitted to it only with reluctance and would not attend a female book meeting. At the Academy, Julia heard, Pendleton's influence was profound. Little boys and girls were inspired scholars now because of him, and one of them, a little fellow of ten, wrote a poem that was published in the *Barnstable Patriot*. Inspired discussions were held in September when the President announced the upcoming emancipation of slaves, upon the breakdown of the Confederate invasion of the North in Maryland. Half a dozen more boys enlisted and Kingsley hired two substitutes. The Presidential Proclamation was a flawed instrument, Pendleton explained, because it still left Negroes in bondage who were unfortunate enough to reside in loyal slave-holding states. But the war, he assured them all, would free every last one of them, even if the President did not.

They discussed it endlessly, earnestly, while the war went badly for the federal cause.

Hamlet was staged at the Lyceum in December, just before

the mutual disaster to both sides at Fredericksburg which dampened everyone's spirits for a while, lifted by an informal concert of the musical society a month later. The whist club grew to include great numbers, and the success of *Hamlet* led to the planning of another production with all sorts of unexpected people clammering for a role, and *Macbeth* was scheduled for June.

For Waterford badly needed diversion. There were more mariners home that summer without voyages than anyone could remember—worse even than when the last panic had stalled trade. In that spring and summer of 1863 the Confederate destroyers were ascendant, and tearing your hair out by the roots didn't do a thing to stop them. The *Alabama*, the *Florida*, and the *Georgia* were on the high seas now; raiders alarmed the North by threatening to shoot at the ports, thus diverting ships from the blockade and permitting escape from it, and worse, the raiders frightened American commerce from the shipping lanes. The *Jacob Bell* of New York was taken and burned by the *Florida* in February, the *Star of Peace* from Boston, in March; *Aldebaran* of New York, *Lapwing* of Boston captured and put to use temporarily as a cruiser, too. The *Commonwealth* from New York to San Francisco was destroyed, the brig *Clarence*—on and on the bad news went, for the losses did not include ships captured and bonded, nor the neutrals bespoken and investigated nor the escape of the raiders from federal naval vessels that added to the humiliation. The *Alabama* by summer had taken fifty-four prizes, and the seas were beginning to empty themselves of the American flag. The effects of the raiders on commerce were exactly what Waterford feared; it did not take long for men of business to put their cargo where it would be safest; under the British flag, which the South respected. British ships carried the bumper harvest of wheat from the American west to Europe where there had been massive crop failures; American ships were being sold or mortgaged to England, in order to fly the Union Jack.

Waterford could only hope that the war would end—for until it did there would be no regaining all that was lost. And if it had once held Julia Merrick at arm's length, it did so no longer because it needed her now. Julia Merrick and David Pendleton had brought new life to Waterford, which reached for it eagerly and even desperately—and Julia could only bless David Pendleton!

It was to the exigencies of war and to David Pendleton that she owed this wonderful shift, David Pendleton of such impeccable manners that no whisper was ever raised to question the nature of the relationship between them, David Pendleton who treated every woman as someone special, who earned the respect of men both by his ability to explain and defend his ideas and by his entertainment, varieties of which kept Waterford in constant delight. Anything, everything, was possible through David Pendleton!

With the need for hope, for laughter once again, little by little Waterford came to her side, the gaiety of the Merricks' house attracting first one and then another. Not everyone, of course. Not Sears Bradley, nor anyone friendly with him who hated Kingsley with the same passion, nor poor pregnant Angelina who, no matter what she thought about it all, was compelled to stand her distance because of her husband, nor the half-dozen other poor, pregnant wives of captains whose delicate condition required that they stay at home. (There were a lot of pregnant ladies in Waterford, because everyone's husband loitered about, waiting for the war to end.) And there were the habitual pessimists, who believed that not even the end of the war would resuscitate the merchant fleet and could not be roused to forget their woes, however momentarily. But there were plenty, nonetheless, who enjoyed David Pendleton and his antics and conversation, who had Ballington paint their pictures just as Julia did, who played cards and sang songs and occasionally read Longfellow aloud to one another.

And just when you thought you'd seen all of David Pendleton's accomplishments—presto!—he came up with a new one and encouraged everyone to come along. He made himself a twanging instrument out of an upturned tub and a broomstick and provided kazoos for everyone else, a hint which turned them all to making improvised noisemakers which they banged away at half the summer, some men becoming quite proficient at the saw. Cynthia Crawford had become hysterical at the last concert of homemade instruments and had fallen off her chair laughing, and Captain Crawford had sprinkled her with gin from his flask, mumbling what he took to be last rites, solemnly assuring them all that it was exactly how the Catholics did it. They had themselves hauled to the outer bar in search of sea clams and made castanets of the shells under Captain James Pollard's direction, who had been to Spain and seen them used there, and they pretended to dance the flamenco.

Parts of Waterford watched these proceedings glumly just as did Hetty, returned from the Franklin Academy and ensconced in her bedroom across the meadow in the old house, from which she peered with glowering countenance. Julia took care to be as unobtrusive as possible—but of course, it was not always possible. And nothing must be allowed to interfere! Nothing did interfere but Kingsley's monthly visits, which she could easily manage because of their predictability.

David Pendleton had literally salvaged her, given her something to live for. Her relief at finding him after having been so long isolated in her unending battle with Kingsley and set apart from everyone gave her life a zest she had never believed possible, and now she, as well as Waterford, sparkled as never before, through the summer of 1863 and the winter as well. The house was filled as it was meant to be filled, with Waterford taking its ease there and occupying itself with something more constructive than useless worry, the sea closed and the war on land grinding on with little to show, one way or the other, and nothing Waterford could do about either one except to enjoy, as well as it could, the cheer and determined goodwill at the house of Julia Merrick, where the hiatus might be passed until the Confederates yielded and Waterford could work on its own behalf once again. Through the spring of 1864 and into its summer David Pendleton and Julia Merrick were sought by Waterford and beloved by it; Julia believed she had never been so happy. The war would surely end sometime and somehow the North would surely win it; Waterford would return to its business on the sea, but she would be firmly established in the center, the inspirer of its arts and graces, the leader of its spiritual life, its spark, the woman most admired by it, the woman who had brought the miracle of David Pendleton to pass. In time, she believed, Waterford would much resemble Beacon Hill in its interest in matters cultural and artistic. Why, Waterford, even when the war was done, was going to be an outstanding little town, and its activity would be directed by herself; she would never be bored or lonely or restless or isolated again . . . or so she thought. . . .

It was a lovely September morning, hazy and somnambulent in the clutch of Indian summer, the leaves on the maples golden early this year, their color in the heavy air diffused, casting an amber glow on the white-painted clapboards of the house. She was on her east porch where the morning sun made her shawl unnecessary; she drank her second cup of tea, having breakfasted lightly on dry toast, and she was happy, going over in her mind the spontaneous gathering at her house the night before when everyone had crowded into her parlor to celebrate the news that Sherman had occupied Atlanta. Waterford rejoiced in this because it would badly weaken the Democrats in the fall election, and the Democrats had plenty of Copperheads in their midst who called for cessation of war at any price. It was to Waterford's best interest that the war should end, of course, but in contrary fashion, cessation was no longer enough. Giving in to the South would be a positive insult after the personal wound the Confederacy had dealt the mariner! No, sir, Waterford, staunchly behind Lincoln now, had a lot to celebrate with Sherman's victory! They'd sung patriotic songs and made rather a lot of noise for such a sedate group of people, and David Pendleton, God love him, had capped the evening by reciting the address of the President at Gettysburg (reprinted in the papers), rendering it so eloquently that everyone began to see that Lincoln had written a nearly undetected classic, however miniscule. The tears had flowed, hearts beat high, the bonds of mutual joy, love, patriotism, sadness, thanksgiving welding them into a tight sentimental unit. Her friends! Hers, and David Pendleton's!

"Good morning."

It was Hetty, coming up the steps of the porch, plunking her stiffly corseted self in the chair beside Julia, mopping her flushed face with a hankie. "What are you sitting here smiling about, all by yourself?"

Julia doubted that Hetty ever smiled about anything, certainly not alone, and she felt sorry for her. "I was thinking about my party last night. . . ."

"Yes, it must have been amusing," Hetty snorted, without letting her finish. "I could hear the amusement, all right."

"Oh! Did we disturb you?" Julia asked with excessive innocence. It was true that everyone was apt to get loud, and last night surely everyone had sung with vigor!

"Yes, you did. My room faces your side, you know."

"Well, I'm sorry, Hetty. I'll try to keep things quieter."

"I'm sure you'll have no trouble, now that David Pendleton is gone," Hetty sniffed, watching Julia from the corner of her eye. "He's terribly noisy."

Gone! He was not gone at all! She expected him to come by this very afternoon! The literary society was due to meet, and he would lead it.

"Gone?" she asked. "He isn't gone, Hetty."

"He's left already," Hetty said firmly, without even a trace of hesitation.

"Are you sure?" Hetty seemed sure, and dismay was rapidly crowding Julia's heart. How could he just up and leave?

"I ought to be," Hetty announced. "I have been asked by the school board to teach at building number four, so that the master there can take over the Academy."

Hardly taking Hetty's words, Julia could only stare at her, protest and despair rising within.

"I'm as qualified as any man," Hetty went on. "And men are hard to come by, with so many of them in the war. Of course they'll only pay me half as much because I am a woman, but it was too good an opportunity to let pass. I'll show them what a woman can do!"

"Hetty," she exclaimed, grasping only one thing. "Why has David left? Why did he leave so quickly?" He could not leave! He must not go!

"Why, they threw him out, that's why," Hetty trumpeted.

She waited. "Well?"

"Well what?"

"Why did they?" Would Hetty ever stop toying with her? Surely Hetty must know how fond she was of David!

"He is not a gentleman," Hetty declared. "The board met last night and decided that. They met again this morning, called him before themselves, dismissed him."

"Why, I've never known a man with better manners," she protested.

"Apparently his manners are not what they should be around young boys," Hetty remarked briefly, but her aplomb faded and her face deepened to scarlet. Her resolve to be offhand melted away as Julia stared.

"With boys?"

Overcome now by embarrassment, Hetty only nodded.

"Do you mean he teaches them naughty language?" Julia asked hopefully.

"No," Hetty croaked. "Come, Julia! Don't be so naïve! Don't ask me to say it out loud, because I can't. It's awful, but I thought you ought to hear it from me rather than from anyone else." The day seemed suddenly quite dark, and a coldness breathed over Julia's shoulder.

"Do you mean—he is—"

"Intimate with boys," Hetty finished for her, blushing furiously. "It's you I feel sorriest for," she said. "Larking about in his company all this time. Your name and his are inseparable now. I don't envy you, when next you go to a commission meeting or to church and have to look everyone in the eye! Julia," she breathed. "How could you!"

Quickly Hetty fled away, so as not to have to look at her sister's stricken face, and Julia, trapped in her chair because her legs refused to move, watched her go in a state of numbness.

David Pendleton was intimate with boys!

She felt her face begin to burn, hot, hotter.

It was a loathsome thing, like a sea worm, which had legs all up and down its sides, its pinchers in front ugly and its muscular long writhing body abhorrent.

Sweat burst out on her brow.

David was deformed. He was repellent, like a midget or a hunchback or a two-headed cow, and unclean, like a leper. She drew her mental skirts away, looking to see if he had soiled them, felt the flood of disgust, of dank and clammy fear in the presence of evil—an evil she had harbored, nurtured—it was like turning a rock over in the pretty garden, to find beneath it crawling, sightless, slimy gray slugs who hid there from day's light, multiplied there, and must be exterminated instantly—as David Pendleton had been exterminated.

Her hands were cold and wet as she sat there in the cruel sun. She felt ill—really ill, and she rose unsteadily, went into the house dark and shaded by its porches.

"I'm going to bed, Delia," she told her servant.

"Are you ill, Mum?"

"Yes. I do feel poorly. Very poorly." Indeed, she must look the part! "You might tell Nanny that Caroline and Augusta may go down to the pond for an hour. Remind her to cover them from the sun."

"Yes, I'll be glad to, Mrs. Merrick. And your guests?"

"My guests?" Why wouldn't her mind work! She couldn't think!

"The literary society?" Delia murmured. "This afternoon."

Oh! She nearly moaned. The literary society.

"Perhaps I'll be on my feet by then, Delia."

"I hope so, Mum. Shall I help you upstairs?" Delia did so, without waiting for Julia's assent, unhooked her, helped her off with her garments and into a robe, closed the shutters, left her in bed to stare at the ceiling where the muted gold lights of the reflected maple leaves moved lazily, haphazardly.

Her mind went round and round. . . .

David Pendleton had betrayed her.

David Pendleton lived under a rock, and no one had known it! David Pendleton was . . . perverted!

No sooner had Delia left than she returned.

264

"This message was just now left at the door, Mrs. Merrick."

It was Clarissa Gray's expression of regret that she would be unable to attend the meeting of the literary club this afternoon.

"Thank you, Delia," Julia said tonelessly.

"There's someone else at the door," Delia said. "Excuse me, Mum."

She waited.

"Another message, Mum."

It was Prissy Pratt's regret. Prissy!

"If any more messages come, Delia, you needn't bring them up. Just collect them downstairs."

"Would you like something to eat, Mrs. Merrick?"

Her gorge rose at the very thought.

"Not just now, Delia. Thank you."

He had betrayed them all, and all of them were in flight, frightened by something they could not understand, something they had been taught to abjure with the strongest of all possible injunctions: the silent judgment of the unspoken, the unmentionable, the unthinkable. Many, like Prissy and Clarissa Gray, would send their formal regrets, but many would not do even that. Instead they would pretend that Julia Merrick did not exist, because if she didn't, then David Pendleton also ceased to exist. The time-honored method of eliminating an unpleasant situation would wipe the slate clean, and wipe her away with it.

They were hastening away, confused, upset, as appalled and frightened as she was herself, and she couldn't blame them at all. In their place she'd do the same thing so that there'd be nothing to remind her of her contact with the unclean, the abhorrent. . . .

But she was not in their place. She could not erase her malaise by fleeing the source of her connection with it. She could not flee herself, but was caught amid the ashes and rubble, the collapse of everything she'd built up, the emptiness that lay ahead, the emptiness of Waterford, the emptiness in the house of Kingsley Merrick where she would be a prisoner, cowering behind its walls to avoid the town's repudiation. She was caught in the haunted shell of herself, where David Pendleton's memory would mock her from its corners, in which, somehow, she must learn to live with the understanding that she had admired, fawned over, cozened a man destitute of decency.

She must live with the abandonment of everything she had

accomplished. If and when Waterford could forget its fears, if and when her friends accepted her again, they would be careful, painstakingly careful . . . never to mention David Pendleton nor any of the things they had enjoyed with him, the mere mention of which would bring him to mind. They would not mention the literary society, nor would it meet again. It was gone, and the musical society would be gone, too, and certainly the amateur theatrical productions if only because none save Pendleton had the capability of staging Shakespeare. The whist players would not gather at her house again, and there would never be a spontaneous party there— if there were to be any social event at her house again (she could not even imagine trying to create one!), the only safe topics of conversation would be ships and storms at sea, or the weather here at home—

Everything was lost. She was alone and empty, and there was no way out of it, and there would be none for a long, long time. She was innocent—innocent as they—yet the responsibility for Pendleton would be laid at her door—and she was alone as she had never been, the loneliness of other times, other days, a mere shadow of this aloneness which began within the core of herself where she couldn't even think of David Pendleton without writhing. No, she was more alone than she had ever been, and nothing Kingsley had ever done to her could compare with it. . . .

Kingsley.

She could picture the look on his face when next he paid his monthly house call. The calm, cool courtesy with which he'd treated her would not falter—it never did—but more than likely he'd look at her and his eyes would flay the pride from her, and in their depths he'd ask: Ah, Julia—am I so repugnant now?

Indeed, by comparison Kingsley was positively desirable. His appetites, at least, were those of a healthy male, and if he'd never attempted to bring them under control, that, at least, was far preferable to this unthinkable, indescribably horrifying craving of David Pendleton of which she could not even imagine the means of gratifying.

Kingsley. He would not be shocked, or appalled, or frightened. He might well be disgusted—but he would not be dismayed. Kingsley was never troubled by things that bothered other people, he would not flap about—not Kingsley! She smiled at the imperturbability of Kingsley Merrick, at the image of Kingsley whom nothing could dismay, whom not even David Pendleton would dismay. No, Kingsley would not run from her in horror and confusion as would Waterford—

Nor would he take her side.

He would not comfort her, nor protect her; he probably would say nothing, simply turn away to play with Augusta and Caroline, turn away just as Waterford would, although for a far different reason: he would not care. And there was no reason why he should.

Their marriage was a facade, their hearth was empty, the embers there stomped on by herself so that there remained no life in them, and as a result, Kingsley certainly had no reason to care whether she was miserable or not, frightened or not, lonely and wretched and in need of comforting—yes, yes— admit it—in need of him, whose dreams she'd laughed at, whose goals she'd repudiated, and whose pride she had demolished in her mother's house, belaboring him with the one thing in Waterford he could not control—his father's unsavory reputation. . . .

She felt tears gathering. Now she had handed Waterford yet another tool for the bedeviling of Kingsley Merrick. It was not fair, of course, to hold him in contempt because his wife had foisted a homosexual (she shuddered at the word) upon them all—but Waterford had never treated Kingsley fairly—never. And never had she.

Oh, Kingsley, she moaned. *I am so sorry!*

Yes, she was sorry for a lot of things. Now that she'd had her own way with her own dreams, seen them come to naught—she was sorry, and growing sorrier all the time, that she'd not given Kingsley's a fairer trial—fairer! She'd never tried them at all!—because certainly they could never lead her into a worse mess than she was in now! And what, she demanded of herself—what was so wrong with them?

Perhaps she didn't like the Pettingills, the Wheelers, and the Brickers—perhaps she never could. But whoever said she had to like them? All that had ever been required was courtesy, for Kingsley's sake.

And Mill Village? Now, there were people who, at least, never pretended to be something they were not. Couldn't she respect them for at least that? Were they so awful, aside from spitting unexpectedly? And had she overlooked the crudities which Mill Village could not help, knowing no better, why, she'd be at Kingsley's side now and the Merrick house would be filled with people and she, Julia Merrick, would still be at the center, welcoming Mill Village and mixing them with the families of mariners because the mariners so badly needed diversion and the mill was a heroic contribution to the war which now Waterford wanted fiercely to win, to make up for its humiliations and its losses. Had she stood by Kingsley, it would be he and she, together, to guide and direct Waterford, not she and David Pendleton. It wouldn't have been easy, or simple, but had she been on Kingsley's side, championing him, in his corner, working to bring his dreams into reality—well, it was at least possible. It was possible because she was not unskillful when it came to manipulating people. It was possible because of Kingsley himself, vital, dauntless, his mind alert and ever churning, his determination of steel and his ability to seize the crux of things and move them as he willed—here in Waterford, or in Boston, or wherever he went—the snap and vitality of life went with him. His dreams, his schemes, his plans—everything that Kingsley had stood for and stood for yet was certainly preferable to what lay ahead for her now. . . .

Kingsley! Suddenly, so strongly, so pitifully, so cruelly she wanted Kingsley, she needed Kingsley—she wanted to run to him, feel herself safe and protected by him as she had felt when Papa died and she had sought him on the beach, the only immovable in a shifting, uncertain world. She needed Kingsley, needed him to care again, to love her, to shield her, to guide her. . . .

Kingsley! she cried in her heart—*I need you so*—

She must make him care!

She must cause him to take her back!

She must seek his forgiveness, beg his pardon, she must go to him, humble, a supplicant—she must beg him to love her again—

She remembered the scene that passed between them at her mother's house; she remembered Kingsley's unwavering courtesy since, his coolness beneath which no glimmer of personal feeling ever showed. She remembered his eyes, so penetrating, yet inscrutable; she remembered the rage that had welled in them when she had flung the past in his face, and then the sudden dying in them, shutting her out.

And when he learned what manner of man she had replaced him with; when he learned that she had given Waterford yet another reason to hold him in contempt; when she begged his forgiveness, cast herself on his mercy—what would she see in his eyes then? What, ever, would move him to forgive her, who had earned only his contempt, and deserved it. What could she say that would ever take away her hatefulness?

There is nothing, she told herself. *There is nothing I can do save telling him I'm sorry, showing him that I am truly remorseful. There's nothing that will guarantee his forgiveness.* To ask for it would be a gamble, the odds unknown. She would have to simply throw herself at his feet, plead for his help, beg for salvation, seek reconciliation on any terms he chose. . . .

She stopped.

Go on, Julia, she commanded herself. *Don't stop now.*

It was not something she could easily face, but she had to do battle with it this instant. Because if she were not perfectly willing to share everything that was important to Kingsley, certainly he would not be willing to share his life with her and open it to her. Unless she allowed herself to be all the things he willed her to be, he'd never lift her over the morass which was her future in Waterford, her future in his house, and there'd be no reason why he should. Acceptance of Kingsley meant the acceptance of all of him. His dreams, his ambitions. And his body.

Oh, God, I can't, I can't, she thought, fleeing in alarm from what had always—yes, always—repelled her.

You must, she told herself. *You must stop this childish squeamishness instantly. You must grow up, Julia! You must think for yourself, instead of hiding behind the standard of female convention. You must ask yourself: Is a man's wanting to gratify himself in respect to a woman the evil that women want to believe it is?*

What she had learned about David Pendleton today—that surely was evil, in comparison to which Kingsley's passions and lusts paled. Wasn't the scorn of woman for sensuality only a facade, a weapon, a tool for controlling men, for limiting their dominance? She shivered. It might well be, for most women. But for herself, she knew, if she were to admit it honestly, it was a façade for the concealment of frigidity—and what lay behind that frigidity, what lay beneath it—was too deep, too obscured, too shadowed to ever know—

But she could not stop there, throwing up her hands, acknowledging defeat. There was a fight to be waged, a fight for Kingsley and she would somehow have to overcome her fears if she were to win him back. She would somehow have to accept his manhood which she'd tried to deny; she must somehow make herself accept and enjoy his pleasure. It was no longer enough to lie, uncomplaining, beneath him, unresponsive while his hands urged her to pleasure, suffering the probing of her tender, unwilling flesh, wishing only that she could forsake her dignity long enough to beg him to stop. . . .

Her flesh crawled, she recoiled . . . and anger reared up. Anger against herself, for making it so hard.

It doesn't have to be that way! she told herself. *It wouldn't seem debasing if you were in harmony with him. If his goals and dreams are yours, if you are working for him and cherishing him—if you accept him for the man he is and not the one you tried to turn him into, why his passion would be more than an expression of domination!* And what was more, if she were to try, really try, to respond to his passion (something she had never done) why, it would be another facet of life they could share, another way of reaching out to him, another way of sharing. . . .

Wouldn't it be worth a try? she asked herself.

Yes! Yes! Oh, yes! Oh, she wanted to try! She did! She wanted Kingsley! All of him! She would give him all of herself, anything he asked, and in return he would lay to rest the ghost of David Pendleton, fill her life which loomed now so full of ugliness, emptiness and futility; he could, if he would, share his plans, his hopes, be the counterpart to her that she would—she would!—be to him.

Yes! She must not think of what she feared. She must not! She must change her attitude about the whole thing. Didn't Kingsley deserve a willing partner in bed, despite the consequences that well could befall her there? And if he could prevent those consequences by using a condom, shouldn't she be willing to accept his help, instead of being paralyzed by polite society's condemnation of contraception? After all, she was his wife! It was about time she began behaving like one regardless of what she felt about it—and if she had to, she could pretend. Pretend pleasure. Pretend acceptance. Pretend anything! Wasn't it worth pretending, considering what she would get in return. . . .

What if he point-blank refused?

She shivered.

She must chance his doing to her what she had done to him. She must offer herself humbly and let him choose, knowing his repudiation would crush her even more than she was crushed already—yet she must risk it or settle for a total loss.

She must change the mortification if he turned away in the face of the greatest of all relinquishment of her being, this greatest of all subjugation of her will to his, the one most reluctantly—yes, most painfully offered.

270

Oh, Kingsley, she pleaded, *help me! Please help me! Forgive me, allow me to make it up to you! Don't turn me away—there is nothing I would not do!*

Her hands trembling, she pulled the bell cord. She listened as Delia's feet slowly trod the stairs; outside the door Delia paused, setting down the water buckets which later she would carry to the water tank on the third floor. Timidly she knocked.

"You called for me, Mum?"

"Yes," she answered, her voice surprisingly strong and steady despite the quaking within. "I need to send a telegram to Boston, to the master. Can O'Shea take it to Yarmouth now?"

"Certainly, if you want him to, Mum."

"If you would find him then, Delia, I'd appreciate it."

"Do you want me to bring you the messages that have arrived since you went to bed, Mrs. Merrick? There's quite a few."

"It isn't necessary, Delia," Julia said gently.

She sat down again to write the message, her stomach knotted and the pain there intense.

What is so bad about being humiliated, she asked herself, *when my pride and self-respect have been so diminished in any case? If he hates me, is it any worse than what I face in Waterford anyway? It is any worse for being spoken? Am I any the more badly off?*

It was worse, and she knew it. It was worse because she'd be asking for something different, revealing that it mattered, that into Kingsley Merrick's hands she put the weapon of her own destruction, the dismantling of all her pride. She had never been so afraid of him before, of his power, and of the greater power yet that she must give over. . . .

Quickly she went out to find Delia, before her courage failed her.

The shutter rattled softly and the light of morning streamed onto the foot of her bed. Its sudden brightness drew her up from sleep, dragging her to awareness of day, the room coming into focus and there, beside her, Kingsley coming into focus, too, materialized as though from her dreams because she'd been dreaming of him in the fragments of the restless night. Towering above her as he looked down, his face composed and quiet, looking at her as he might a stranger, the shreds of sleep departed in the instant, her mind suddenly in the present, the task that lay ahead outlined with

271

the clarity of first consciousness. She gazed back at him, seeing him as she had not seen him for a long, long time. Her heart lurched.

"Kingsley!" Even his name was lovely, and she said it again, tasting it in her mouth. "Kingsley."

He stood motionless, attentive, grave, the mocking smile that he used always, these days, nowhere in evidence. Lying there, looking up at him as though he were a physician who might heal her, she felt small and weak and the whole ordeal ahead too great to conquer. She struggled upright so that she could face him on more nearly an equal level, to assume her maturity in a posture more worthy of it, and the strength it ought to give her.

"Won't you sit down?" she asked shyly.

He was unaccustomed to invitations of that sort from her, and he paid it no heed.

"I got your telegram last night. What seems to be the trouble?"

He was there. He had come instantly, he was asking now—now!—she must go ahead with it. She swallowed, her throat dry and harsh.

"I . . . I've made a mess of everything," she blurted, and the enormity of the mess she had made loomed, nearly overwhelming her. "I need your help, Kingsley, so very badly. I hardly know where to begin. . . ."

She looked closely at him, hoping to find aid, but there was nothing, only his sober, attentive face which was set very firmly, very sternly. She wasn't sure which devastation to attack first; Pendleton, she decided. There was no point going into the emptiness of their marriage if he couldn't or wouldn't look past her failures in Waterford.

"It has just been discovered—I mean, they found out yesterday, or maybe it was the day before—yes, it was the day before, at least they acted yesterday . . ." she floundered. "The board dismissed David Pendleton from the Academy yesterday because . . ." No, she couldn't say it! She had to say it! "Because he has been intimate with boys."

She felt her face flaming scarlet, beating heat. It was awful. It was worse than even she had feared, to come right out with it. She put her hand to her quivering lips to conceal at least that much ignominy, staring at Kingsley who stared back.

"Pendleton is homosexual?" he asked incredulously, bluntly, as he always did.

She nodded miserably.

"Christ!" he swore. "Where in God's name is he now?" His cool aloofness was gone instantly, his courtesy dissipated in the shock of disclosure.

Her own tension mounted intolerably. "Hetty says he's left."

"And I suppose everyone knows of it."

"They must, by now," she quavered. "They must have known it nearly instantly; there are no secrets in a town the size of Waterford."

"And all your playmates have stormed the house, eager to hold your hand and help you mourn?"

"I'm afraid not," she said, trying not to cry. "I'm afraid they are avoiding me. No one has come here." She looked down at her knotted hands. "I am an object of suspicion, Kingsley. I've lost my reputation and my self-respect as well. Through my own lack of judgment," she said, sparing herself nothing. "It's all my fault, and you can imagine what people are thinking about it, and about me."

His eyes swept over her, cold, scornful.

"I guess I can." His voice was carefully contained now. "I know well enough what people will think. A wolf has hidden among the lambs. A viper has been concealed in the bosom of Julia Merrick! The curse that is Kingsley Merrick has been let loose upon the town, in the form of a homosexual nurtured by his wife to corrupt the moral fibre of every person in sight. Oh, it will be meat and drink to them!" He nodded slowly. "Ah, yes, they will suck it dry."

"I'm sorry," she quaked. "It's an awful mess, and an ugly one. I thought you'd better know about it. . . ."

"Yes," he said. "I suppose I had better." He moved slowly to the window and looked out over the dew-spangled lawn, his back to her, straight, unrevealing. But she needed him—needed him badly. She must reach out, plead her cause. She must go ahead—she must!

"There's another mess I've made, Kingsley, and I need to talk with you about that, too. I need to ask your help."

He was still at the window, so far from her, and he made no move to draw closer.

She plunged ahead. "This mess is worse than the last, harder to confess, Kingsley, but I confess it now. I hope you won't laugh," she said, her determination waning. "I couldn't stand it if you laughed."

He turned to look at her, silent, watchful, unhelpful.

"Kingsley . . ." she started, and then did not know how. "Kingsley . . . I have failed you." She averted her eyes from

273

his clear gaze because she could not bear to watch, looked back to him because she knew she must. "I have failed you, and I want to beg your forgiveness, and I need to ask for your help, to show me how I might put right the wrong I've done."

"Oh?" he queried from across the room, as though he had not the slightest idea what she was talking about.

Was he mocking her? She must keep trying.

"I've put you from me. I have repudiated you," she said, and went on before she lost hope, quickly before any remark he might make would impede her. "Now we're strangers, and I don't know what to do. I don't want to be a stranger to you, and it's my own fault. I've been so wrong—I'm so sorry—I don't know how to change it."

Her fear was as great as the loneliness she was trying so hard to banish; she longed for him to hold her, comfort her, but he did not. He was unwilling to make it even a little bit easier, and she could not blame him.

"What brings all this on, Julia?" he asked. "What sort of change would you like to make?"

No, he would make her go the whole way, on her hands and knees. She took a deep breath.

"Now that David Pendleton is gone, Kingsley, it's clear to me that I've been after the wrong things all along. I was so bent on having everything my own way that I never tried to accept what you wanted. I never tried to help you because I was too upset and worried about losing my friends. I never took your side, Kingsley. I can see how wrong I've been. I am ashamed and sorry. I believe that understanding what I understand now I could be a good wife to you—perhaps I could help you in attaining some of the goals you want to reach, whatever they are. I can try. I will try if only you'll have me."

"Well, I'm honored, Julia." Clearly he was not. "It's only because you have nowhere else to go, isn't it?"

She hung her head. "That's true," she said bravely. "There is nowhere, and I have no one. I'm quite at your mercy, Kingsley."

Spare me, she prayed. *Don't use me badly. Don't hurt me.*

"Just how much of yourself do you propose to throw into this new companionship that you conceive yourself ready for?" he asked without inflection.

She quelled the distress rising with the implication of his question.

"All of me," she answered, holding her chin high.

A slow, unpleasant smile came to his lips and she knew she must endure it because she'd asked for it.

"So. Suddenly you've seen that I might, after all, have something worth taking, is that it? And if you ask, I will rush to your side, unsheath my sword, and protect your reputation because you're willing to share what I have to offer. You would even consider intimacy, I take it. The supreme sacrifice. How very generous of you, Julia. A barter of your body, is that it?"

It was an appalling, brutal way of looking at it, and it served to remind her that Kingsley could be a brutal man. But she must not lose her courage now, nor flee the scorn he rightfully heaped on her. She must go the whole way, or not at all.

"It isn't like that," she said quietly. "I would share the things you like, the things you like to do. I would work with you to attain the goals you've set yourself, that are important to you. I would laugh with you, Kingsley, I would hold your hand, I would cherish the scent of your clothes and your wit and ways; I would applaud you and comfort you when you need these things. . . ." How stupid of her, never to have seen before all that she could share and give! "I would love you," she said abjectly, her eyes burning. "I would love you if you let me. But I can't do it alone. I can't do it if you don't want me to. I can't love in isolation, all by myself."

"I don't know why not," he said from across the room. "I've done it quite a while myself."

Quickly she looked up at him, and quietly he looked back without a single expression on his face that she could read.

There was a long, slow pause in which he seemed to gather his forces.

"You tried to leave me," he said in a voice devoid of emotion. "You gave as your reason my failures, here in Waterford, to live in a manner acceptable to your friends. But it was really me you were fleeing, wasn't it? Me and my bed, which was the more available because I could protect you from pregnancy."

"That was only part of it," she protested. "There were other things you were doing—things injurious to me."

"That was the whole of it. Your other complaints merely camouflaged it."

Was that true? She shook her head. "If so, King, I didn't know it. Perhaps you have understood me better than I have understood myself."

"I have understood a good many things," he said softly.

"For instance, I have understood—for quite a while—why you married me."

She felt her skin go cold and clammy. *Oh God, no*, she begged silently. *If I am truthful, it will finish everything.*

"I married you because I wanted to, Kingsley," she said firmly, without faltering. His manhood would never survive the truth, never! And never would their marriage!

He smiled, and it was a smile she was not sure she liked. Perhaps everything was hopeless after all, because Kingsley must have known, early in the game, that Papa had been flying false colors. "Kingsley," she said quickly. "Is that the best you can think of me? Do you truly believe I would marry you for your money, without caring for you at all? Is that all you think I'm worth?"

"You've always run from me," he pointed out. "Right from the start. It's not what I'd expect from a woman who wanted to marry me."

"I shouldn't have," she admitted humbly. "I know it now."

"Then why did you?"

"I . . . I don't know," she murmured, backing away from it.

"That's no answer," he pressed, relentless. There was nowhere to run, nowhere to hide. He waited.

"Please," she whimpered. "I can't talk about it."

"You'll have to," he said quietly. "Because there can be no meeting of our minds unless you do." How hard, how implacable his eyes! His mouth set, his jaw tight, firm.

She must—she must do it.

"All right," she cried shakily. "I am afraid of the sexual encounter. Is that what you want to hear?" She wrung her hands while he waited. "It took away my pride. It made you big, and me small. It made me insignificant, something you could use when you wanted to; you could—you did—break me with it." She balled her fists into tight knots, miserably allowing herself the utter debasement of letting him win. "I hated it," she whispered, "because I felt vanquished each time—conquered, subjugated—yes, raped." *Oh, God, if only she could die!*

But she struggled on, striving to pick up the pieces and make something of them. "And it was stupid. I can see that now. If I hadn't been so busy fighting you, Kingsley, fighting your goals and ideas and your friends and your kin then I probably could have overcome the natural fears of a virgin—I might have let you help me overcome them, as you wanted to do. Instead of that, I allowed our bed to become another battleground, and when I couldn't win that battle, just as I didn't seem to be able to win any of them, I ran away." She was devastated, stripped of her dignity, reduced to groveling; she might as well go the whole way, because he was watching carefully, weighing and balancing in his mind the gap between what she'd said and the rest of what he suspected to be the truth, and she knew it no longer mattered what the truth had been, but only what it was now with the future before them.

"Yes, I rejected you. And your goals, everything—and I was wrong. Please, Kingsley," she pleaded. "Please give me another chance," she begged, without pride. "I'll do anything if only you'll forgive what has gone before. If you can't," she said, fighting back her tears, "I'll understand why." She would not cry! She would not use this woman's tool which so often softened a man because it was only a temporary tool, changing the tenor of the moment but not of a whole lifetime. "I'll accept your unwillingness to do it; I've brought in on myself; I have it coming. But it won't change me. I've wronged you, and I aim to rectify that wrong, any way I can."

"Any way?"

"Any way," she said firmly, suppressing a tremor of trepidation.

He watched her a long, long time, thinking. He turned again, looked out the window, thought further: "All right," he challenged, facing her once more. "Let's see just how far you can go along with me. Let's start with this mess in Waterford which Pendleton has bequeathed us. My ideas to resolve that may not coincide with yours. You may not care for them."

"It doesn't matter whether I do or not, because I will follow your suggestions, whatever they are."

"Probably you'd like me to take you away."

Her heart lifted.

"Would you?" she asked eagerly. "Oh, Kingsley! Would you?"

"No," he said. "You must stay right here."

It was disheartening, disenchanting, a downhill slide of expectation. After so much, Kingsley would leave her here!

"As I see it, unless you stay everyone will think you're running away, as though you had done something wrong."

"Surely I will be held to blame," she pointed out feebly.

"Surely you will," he agreed. "Yet, who hired Pendleton in the first place? It is the men on the board of the Academy who should have been on guard; it's ridiculous to blame you for their error. You are innocent, and you shall not be blamed. You must meet the eye of everyone you see calmly, without apology. When the next Sanitary Commission meeting is scheduled, you will attend it."

"I can't!" she cried in despair.

"You can," he insisted. "And you will. You will promote when you get there a fund-raising project for the library. Whatever is raised, we will match. You will let everyone know it. I realize," he added, forestalling her objection. "I realize they can't be bought. But they can be diverted. You shall divert them. You shall invite all the people you have played about with to a musicale for the benefit of the library, and the doors will be open to anyone who will pay admission. I will bring down some musicians from Boston, and you will play to their accompaniment."

"No one will come," she mourned.

"I'm sure they will," he said firmly. "Because at that occasion I'm going to announce my intention to run for the Barnstable County senate seat. This you shall intimate when you issue invitations, and believe me, they will come. They won't want to miss it."

"Legislature?" she asked stupidly. "What good will it do if you are in the legislature?"

"Because as senator I can best protect the interests of Waterford which is withering now in the grip of the *Alabama* and the *Georgia*. I can push the legislature for the petitioning of Washington for the government subsidy of steam-driven vessels, to be built now for the defense of our shipping lanes and to be used, at the end of the war, for commerce, to better compete with England. Without steam our fleet is doomed and there are plenty of people in Waterford who know it well. Unless the merchant fleet is placed on competitive footing with England, one day soon trade will remain with British ships. The folk of Waterford will not dare ignore me, Julia, because I'll be important to their future, and their support of me will cause them to forget Pendleton and drop any condemnation of you. I can win without them, because I am on friendly terms with mill workers and fishermen and men of the land, people whom the Waterford mariner has not gone out of his way to cultivate. I can move ahead without the mariner—but I can help him, if I am encouraged to do so. He'll be eager to jump on my bandwagon, and when he does, he'll forget, very soon, that it was you who were responsible for David Pendleton's success."

She was impressed, all over again, by the scope of Kingsley's thinking. Despite her concern for her own woes, she could admire his plan simply for its construction and daring—yes, it was quite a plan!

"Will it work?" she asked. "Will petitioning Washington move the federal government to help us build steamships?" Just imagine! Deep-water sailors pleading for steamers! Yet they would, she knew, many of them would—because they'd have to.

"I doubt it," he laughed. "I don't expect Washington will bite, but our friends in Waterford, so convinced are they of their own importance, won't doubt for a minute that the possibility is a good one. And, of course, once I am senator, zealously looking out for the best interests of everyone in Barnstable County, I doubt that they'd raise much hue and cry when I apply a little discreet pressure toward getting the Cape Cod Central going, do you? And certainly a senator can apply a lot more pressure than a plain, ordinary businessman!"

She felt her jaw dropping in amazement, and there were no words available, just then, to express her thoughts. Kingsley wanted the senate seat just to get the railroad moving!

"And I think I need not tell you," he went on, "that a senator, no less than a railroad director, has great need of a wife who knows how to—shall we say—get along with people. All kinds of people. Do you think you can do that, Julia?"

"I certainly will try!" It sounded rather fun!

"Good! Then you might as well know at the onset exactly what it is that I propose to do, here in Waterford, once I am senator and once the railroad is an accomplished fact, and that all this time I have waited for your help in securing."

"Name it, King, name it and tell me how I can help."

"Once I have Waterford where I want it, which the railroad and the senate seat should accomplish, then I want to work on the assimilation of Mill Village."

His eyes challenged her. They had locked horns on this issue before!

"We shall invite the village folks here, and we shall invite the mariners from the center of town, who will not dare to stay away for fear of offending me—I, who represent them in General Court."

"All right," she agreed. "We shall invite everyone."

"I believe they can be mixed, Julia, especially if you aren't ashamed to try it."

"It shall be my aim." It would be. She would make it be!

"When our daughters are old enough, they shall attend district school number three. I would not have them different from or given advantage over youngsters whose fathers aren't rich."

Caroline would start school next year—a fact which Julia dreaded because, it seemed to her, Caroline was not very well suited to learning from books. Caroline was just a little— well, her interests lay elsewhere. But Augusta! Augusta, only four years old, could well begin school now, so bright was she, and all along Julia had been grateful that Waterford's Academy was so fine a one. Augusta, for all she lived in a country town, would be well educated.

She lowered her gaze, so that Kingsley would not see the moment of rebellion reflected there.

"They will get a fine education at district school number three," Kingsley said softly. "As senator, I shall live in Waterford all year round, and as a year-round resident I shall do my part in town affairs. I shall consent to sit on the school board, and by the time I am through, Julia, the education at the public schools will be far better than any available at the Academy. In fact, the district schools will be so good that the Academy will close its doors for want of patronage—and you, in talking with the good mamas of Waterford, will have to reassure them that dismantling the Academy is the only logical thing to do. The building can be used to house the Waterford Library," he went on, grinning wickedly. "Which is a dream that most ladies in town would support readily, I think."

How well he understood the ladies in town!

"Very well," she gulped, her throat dry.

"Next will come the merger of the churches."

"The what?"

"I think it's time the churches united," he said blandly. "They are so near in matters of faith that it's ridiculous to hold separate services, don't you think?"

"I hadn't considered it, one way or the other," she said, perspiration breaking out on her brow.

"I believe it's time that our grandfather's church was enlarged," he said smoothly. "It ought to be refurbished, and it ought to have a new organ, too. The old church is unsafe, and unless I'm badly mistaken, it has bats in its belfry. The Universalist Church can hang the old bell in its own steeple and for the sake of public health, the old building ought to be torn down. Don't you agree?"

He was a very devil! When he talked of bringing Waterford to heel, he was not exaggerating. "It will require a lot of work among the women of the churches, Julia," he said, his glance suddenly sharp, as though ferreting out any suggestion of hesitation. "While I am negotiating with the men, I shall need you to pour oil on the waters on the distaff side. I must be confident that you are working for me, my dear, and not against me."

"I will never work against you, Kingsley," she breathed, staggered by the depth of change he would bring to Waterford. It would be hateful and she knew she would never support it in her heart—but it would place her in a position of leadership again, restoring what David Pendleton had destroyed, and working toward it would give her back Kingsley, whom she so badly wanted. Despite her distaste for his notions, she could not help but admire him and the incisiveness of his mind; he would control not only Waterford's destiny, but also the minds of men, the hearts of women who lived there!

"I'll do everything I can," she vowed.

"I'm glad to hear it." By the window, where he had stood all this time, he straightened himself, squared his shoulders. "That's the public part of our marriage and, I suppose, the easiest. The private part is in your control absolutely; actually, it has always been. If we are to find a commitment to one another it will be up to you, Julia, to sustain it. And you, by God, to nurture it."

"Kingsley!" she exclaimed, suddenly cold, a tremor starting. "There is nothing I want more!"

"Then you'll have to prove it," he said firmly. "And I'll tell you right now that if you want to be part of my public life, such as I have described, you'll have to be part of my private one as well. I don't intend to separate them for your convenience, Julia." He was proud and straight, unyielding and hard, cold and even cruel; his face was inscrutable. "I shall never force you, Julia. Ever. If you want to be my wife, you will be so voluntarily."

Ruthlessly she pushed aside the old familiar upsurge of panic, stifling the anguish that rose to choke her. She must not falter, even now! "Kingsley!" she whispered, seeking to assuage, atone, assure. "I can only try!" She crossed the great distance between them, the terribly long distance. She must show him! She must not be afraid! She would not be! She was not! "Kingsley," she said, and despite the heaviness in her heart and the unwillingness of her arms, she reached out to him, to gather him to her, to hold his dark head on her shoulder, feeling the heat of his face through the frailness of her nightgown, and with firm determination she took his hand and cupped it over her small breast. "Kingsley," she whispered. "I *will* try."

She was still as he removed her gown, unflinching when he touched her, put his arms around her; she met his kiss and closed her eyes, his clothing rough and strange against her bare flesh, and willingly she lay back upon her bed with him, allowing him to lead her as he had always wanted to do, and desperately she willed herself to like it, now that she'd given so much for a chance to do so, waited while he stripped off his own clothing, meeting his eyes as he watched her, waited for his lovemaking, his hands so sure, his lips so strong, waited for the onset of pleasure, of satisfaction. The chill of the fresh morning air swept over her until the warmth of his skin chased it away; the pain imposed by chastity shot through her agonizingly and then gradually, gradually subsided, and she waited for the passion that seemed always to mean so much to Kingsley and that carried him away now, she knew, his eyes dark, fathomless as he caressed her and drove deeper, more deeply and his sweat gleamed on his chest and brow, and now as he kissed her, a lingering, consuming kiss. . . .

In the trees in front of the house birds sang and a cart jangled on the road and a voice rose in greeting to someone unseen; his urgency increased and she matched her motions as well as she could to his and clenched her teeth and tried, tried so hard to catch and capture the ecstasy which should be hers . . . and saw that nothing within her would come to him, meet him, join him. Nothing. Because nothing was there.

Kingsley! Kingsley! Surely she could find, somewhere within herself, sometime, a passion to match his own in the bed she'd so long denied him! Surely in time the united front they would show Waterford would be a total union, a union of body as well as common purpose, a union of passion as well as of love which Kingsley so richly deserved and which she herself so desperately wanted now, too! Surely . . . surely . . . and yet it was not present at that time and in that moment; caught between the frustration of denial and the sweeping tenderness toward Kingsley, whose compassion had redeemed her, she was stunned, and lay in his arms, spent, beaten raw, nerveless.

"Julia," he was whispering, over and over. "Julia! Julia!"

He cradled her, caressed her hair. "I've waited for a long

time," he said, and kissed her ear. "I'd given up! If I've treated you harshly today, I hope you'll understand."

"I only hope that you're sure of me now," she whispered, unable to rely at all on her voice. "I hope you stay sure."

"That rather depends on you, I think." He propped himself up on an elbow. "We'll put what's done behind us," he said gently. "We'll start again. I'm not one hundred percent proud of everything I've ever done, either, sweetheart—so we shall never again inquire too closely about things better left uninspected. I suppose you'll always have to prove yourself," he added ruefully. "But believe me, Julia, I'm willing to be convinced."

She had not fooled him, she thought, about anything—But he, too, understood that they must leave the past behind if they were ever to move forward. How clear of vision was Kingsley Merrick! And how well she admired it!

"I'll convince you!" she said with vigor. Oh, Kingsley, I shall convince you and convince you! She smiled shakily.

He sat up to draw on his clothes. "First we'll take care of the senate seat. That means the musicale. It won't be easy for you to stroll into the commission meeting and casually drop the suggestion that a musicale at our house will be the occasion of my announcement for candidacy—but I'm afraid you'll have to do it, Julia. No one else can."

"I'm not worried about doing it," she told him. "I'm worried about carrying it off."

"You will," he assured her. "You have terrific poise and presence! You'll do very well! When we've buried the remains of David Pendleton, which, I think, you'll find happens very quickly—once you're the wife of the senator!—it'll be up to you to keep my constituency happy, to serve tea to women of all ranks and to welcome them here. And later you can butter up the wives of the Academy directors while I apply the pressure required to make them abandon ship—in good time, of course. It won't do to rush things. We won't even consider the church for quite a while."

Whatever he wanted. She would help him; she would work with him; she would share his life; she would be his helpmeet!

He smiled down at her, his eyes praising her; he covered her with the blanket, kissed her lightly. "Just now I'll get Rose to fix breakfast, and then we'll take Caroline and Augusta for a walk, so that no one will think you're hiding. Later today, if you please, I'd like you to write an invitation to Ed Bricker, to come to the library benefit."

"Very well." Of all Kingsley's Boston cronies she detested Edward Bricker the most.

"Ed's in gravel now, which is a nice place to be when someone wants to build a railroad. Every mile of track laid for the last three years has been in the interest of the war, but Ed, being an old friend of mine, might find some gravel lying around that nobody has claimed yet. And the Brickers have always enjoyed hearing you play, Julia. The musicale would be as good a place as any to soften Ed up."

"I shall write them an irresistible invitation."

"I know you are not fond of the Brickers."

"It doesn't matter!" she pleaded. "We shall invite anyone you want to have, or anyone you need to see!" Yes, anyone at all! She would show him, if it took to the end of her days.

"There's a business contact of Ed's who interests me, too," Kingsley mused. "I've only recently met him, and I suspect he'd be a good person to know. Perhaps Ed will bring the fellow with him, should we indicate it would be appropriate."

"What is so interesting about the gentleman?"

"His job! He's a higher-up in the Syracuse and Quincy Railroad, and the S & O has a stockpile of rail as yet not designated for war. Perhaps it might find its way to Cape Cod! Let's get them both down here for the musicale and the announcement of candidacy—politics always interests men. Then I could show them what the C.C.C.R.R. has in mind while you wow the ladies."

"Well, we can try," she said bravely. "I'll certainly do what I can. I'll admire their feathers and talk about the Servant Problem all they want. And the men can spit wherever they please."

He laughed softly; his eyes sparkled. "Good girl," he chuckled. "I knew you'd be able to do it. I always knew we'd be good for each other, Julia. I've always known there was nothing we couldn't accomplish, if we were working with one another. Just wait and see! There's no end to what we can do!" He kissed her cheek, like a small boy setting out for the day, eager, happy. He searched out his boots and began to pull them on. "Even if you don't like the Brickers, I think you'll approve of Ed's friend with the S & Q. In fact, I think you're already acquainted. When I had lunch with him the other day he told me that he knew you once, when you were a girl in Boston." He straightened his coat; hand on the knob, he threw the door open. "His name is Adam Levering," Kingsley said, and the door closed, and she was alone.

Federal troops under Sherman ground their way mercilessly from Atlanta to the sea, but the South refused to acknowledge defeat.

Union troops under Sherman slashed up through the hopeless Confederacy, seeking total capitulation by waging total war, but there was no capitulation.

The President of the United States, Abraham Lincoln, offered peace at the price of unconditional surrender. His offer was refused; at Appomattox Court House, Robert E. Lee, unable to face more slaughter of his troops, handed his sword to Grant and went home, a broken giant.

Within six weeks the South had surrendered unconditionally.

The American Civil War was done, but Lincoln was dead, and reconstruction ever sought in mercy by him instead was carried forward by the radical, smouldering, distrustful faction of the North which feared that the Confederacy yet lived in the heart and soul of its shattered people. Not for many years was the South allowed to run its own house, not until it legislated what the North deemed good, and by the time it had done so, the pride of the Confederacy had been successfully driven underground where it lived and thrived and was not challenged by the federal government for the next century.

For all the cost, for all the dissension, for all the debt and burden of war, the North had been galvanized to meet the need for steel, transportation, food, and clothing for the army, and the North, now well advanced in the machinery of production, did not falter; men who once thought large thoughts now thought bigger ones. Men of wealth became wealthier, not entirely because of their honest endeavors, and the rising generation sought feverishly to cash in. The innocence of the generation preceding it, a generation which implicitly believed in the perfectibility of man, if only man worked hard enough at it, fell before the evil of war and the reality of wickedness unleashed by its bitter lessons.

The federal government, interested in chastening the South and in the great commercial expansion of the North, the huge potential of the West, was not in the least interested in resuscitating the merchant marine.

There was no interest in subsidizing its conversion to steam, and without such subsidy conversion was not possible. The West, now very powerful in affairs of state, saw no harm in letting Great Britain carry the world's commerce; Western wheat went just as well in English bottoms as American. And then, to finish off what was begun, the federal government decreed that no ship sold or mortgaged in England to avoid the *Alabama* or her sisters would be registered in America again. No ship of foreign make might be used in American commerce. The heavy hand of government, clamping down tightly on the Confederacy, discarded the American merchant marine as ruthlessly as it tore up the Stars and Bars, and the merchant fleet, what was left of it, took up what Britain would not be bothered to carry: lumber, bricks, guano, coal. The clippers were cut down in order to carry more freight, and gradually, gradually, steam-driven vessels took over the tasks of the old wooden sailing ships.

Men of the sea, many of them, went to the cities where the wealth they had accumulated in their prime might do them good in banking, insurance, textiles, railroads. Their sons followed.

Many went West, to the new and upcoming cities there, and their sons followed, too.

A few men of the sea remained on the decks of whatever vessels they could find, because they could not leave the lure of deep water.

George Pullman invented a railroad car to sleep in; the Union Pacific met the Central Pacific in Utah; a thriving little business of sixty-seven branch stores, seeing where the future lay, expanded its line to include spices, coffee, soap, canned milk, and baking powder, and its new name was occasioned by the joining of the seas: the Great Atlantic and Pacific Tea Company.

The 1870 census counted one citizen in every four a city dweller. In Ohio, the Standard Oil Company was formed in order to eliminate "destructive competition," and every effort was made to put a lamp in every room of every dwelling, city or country.

Texas beef found its way east via the railroad; the textile industry was begun in the South, close to the source of cotton, where it should have been in the first place.

In Kimberly, Colony of the Cape of Good Hope, diamonds were discovered and mines opened. England paid fifteen million dollars' reparation for the *Alabama* and those other commerce-destroyers for which blame could be laid at her door. The cities of Boston and Chicago sustained enormous fires; the stock market in New York crashed and depression was inaugurated and people pretended that everything was as it had always been—for surely it soon would be! All it took was faith in America's great destiny—a faith sustained by preserving the appearance of things.

The Gilded Age had begun.

Five

Augusta

The light laughter, the easy chatter, the minute clatter of luncheon dishes being set out on the table under the trees drifted up and through the window, along with the sounds of summer, the rustling of the leaves in the maples beside the house, the birds hopping around in them, the feel of summer, the ease and loveliness of it.

The Fourth of July. Everywhere in Waterford on this fine day people were going on picnics, in their gardens or on the beach. Everyone would eat and drink under the benevolent July sun, the ladies screened from it by large hats and small parasols, and at two o'clock everyone would gather at the new Town House, to be officially opened and dedicated that afternoon and where, ever after, annual meeting would be held, political caucuses convened, entertainments of a large nature contained—and tonight, a dance.

Augusta Merrick, listening to the pleasant convivial party sound out there on the east lawn, knew she must get herself downstairs and into the yard very soon; she looked herself over in the mirror of her dressing table, a mirror large enough to show all of her medium stature, from her soft, high-buttoned and high-heeled kid shoes to her dark, shining hair pinned back and held in place with a wired wreath of artificial lilacs which she'd made herself, her long curls falling from it in carefree abundance. Her deeply blue eyes were made deeper yet by her lilac dress with loosely fitted sleeves which made her look refreshed and cool—but she was far from cool. Her skirts were heavy and there were many layers of them, the top one of which was draped up in front, held in place by pert purple bows, the excess of which was caught up and gathered in a great puff behind her, sustained by a small bustle. The underskirt revealed thus was of white silk, its circumference increased by multitudes of petticoats which would trap heat like an oven.

Yes, she must go down to the lawn party soon. But she lingered, in the attempt to calm herself, to cool the flustered warmth that was not accountable entirely by the manifold layers of her skirt. She must compose herself once and for all, and stay composed, because there were tensions inherent in the afternoon, difficulties ahead in the evening, and she must have her wits about her. She must be tranquil and poised, because if she were not—if she allowed herself to become nervous and full of fidgets—she wouldn't be able to think clearly. And sometime soon, this afternoon or this evening, she would have to make a decision, and regardless of what it was, she would need her composure badly.

She frowned into the mirror, and instantly cleared her brow, pressing on the wrinkles she'd caused with her finger. One mustn't scowl. It would cause unhappy lines which, in time, could not be covered up; she gently pressed the skin, feeling its regained smoothness. Her fingers could not detect, yet, any permanent creases forming. In the mirror her smooth face stared back at her, betraying none of the excitement, the tension, the threat of misery that this day held for her. For surely she would see John Bradley at the Town House! The mirror told her that she looked pretty, that John would admire her if he looked at her from a distance—and if he spoke to her, what then? What would she say? Were she simply polite, he would know to pass only remarks about the weather. Were she instead to look at him honestly, without hiding behind manners, he would know—instantly—that the winter behind them, and the spring, the passage of this summer until now could then be put aside, disregarded as a necessary nuisance.

He might meet her in Emmaline's garden once again, and if he did, he might kiss her again, as he had when she'd seen him there last, when he had cupped her face with his strong hands and kissed her and left her with a racing pulse. . . . To this day—at this moment, in fact—her heart leaped like a doe in the woods, rising swiftly in the air without warning or apparent effort when she brought that kiss back to mind, lived again those brief moments when John Bradley's lips touched hers. . . .

"Augusta?" It was Mama's voice, coming to her through the open window. She went to it, leaned out, her elbows on the sill, looked down at her mother, who was standing below, her lace-covered silk parasol casting filigreed shadow across her upturned smiling face. In the window Augusta was framed by the climbing ivy and trumpet vine that hung

292

around it, no doubt making her appear as a fairy princess looking out over her domain from her castle, an effect, no doubt, that Mama intended. On the lawn, faces were lifted up looking at her: Bax Levering and Tommy Warden and Alex Thayer and his sisters and Sally Sinclaire and the older generation, too, the Leverings, the Thayers, the Sinclaires from Boston, and Cousin Nate King and his wife, Martha, whom he'd married during the war when there was nothing else to do, and Mr. and Mrs. Warden. All of whom, no doubt were thinking how lovely was the youngest Merrick daughter, pure as the glowing orange flowers that grew from the vine about her window, radiant as they.

"When will you be down?" Mama asked. "Mr. Levering has written a poem that we're all waiting for him to read. Surely you want to hear it, too."

"Tempus fugit," Mr. Levering called up, and Augusta waved to him and smiled. Mr. Levering loved to write poetry, and he was apt to commemorate a sonnet to any occasion that might warrant one. He had privately printed his verse in small, leather-bound editions which he gave away to all his friends, and now he was working on another in which today's contribution would no doubt be included.

"I'm coming soon," she assured her mother. "I'll be there in five or ten minutes."

She backed away from the window, from the gay, pleasant scene, from the old and from the young, the stars of Waterford's summer society in whose midst John Bradley did not gleam.

If only Papa were here! If he were, Augusta wouldn't be in this fix because it wouldn't have bothered Papa one bit that John Bradley worked with Captain Barney Blake on his weir and peddled fish all over Waterford in an ice-filled cart, or that John's mother ran a boarding house. In fact, Papa would have approved all the more, because when he was home Papa was especially friendly to folks of more humble estate than himself. He and Mama mixed them all—ordinary people from Rockford and Mill Village, rich captains from Brewster and Yarmouth and of course Waterford Center, city folk from Boston and rural folk from Orleans and even Mrs. Bradley, once Captain Bradley was lost at sea in '68. The captain (inexplicably) hated Papa and had forbidden his wife to accept any invitation to any event the Merricks might be sponsoring; the Bradleys were the only people in all Cape

Cod, it seemed, who did not frequent the Merrick house, when Papa was state senator and director of the Cape Cod Central Railroad, and there was a continual flow of social events, parties, picnics, political celebrations, musicales. But then the coal in Captain Bradley's ship ignited spontaneously, and the captain went down with his vessel (in fact only three men survived, rowing the incredible distance to the Ascension Islands to tell about it) and rather soon after that Mrs. Bradley appeared at the fête celebrating the opening of the Waterford Select Library, housed in the old Academy building. If her appearance was just a little sooner than convention decreed was proper, no one seemed bothered by it.

After that John often came to the Merrick house with his mother. The younger Bradley boys stayed home with the captain's spinster sister, but John fitted right into the social scene at the Merrick mansion; many of the older children came there with their parents because Papa liked young people. Papa thought they kept things from getting too stuffy, and Papa had liked John, too.

"Handsome lad!" he had exclaimed to Mama after the library celebration. "Sears must have been proud to have a son like that!" And then Papa caught sight of Augusta's face, scooped her up in careless abandon. "At least I hope he was proud," Papa had laughed. "Then perhaps he wouldn't have felt so bad, not having a pretty daughter like I have!"

Papa always knew the right thing to say!

He'd known how to get John to his tailor, without offending either him or his mother. The occasion was the merger of the two Waterford churches into one of Universalist persuasion. It was a bargain Papa had sealed by donating a magnificent organ—the best of its kind and the only one like it in Barnstable County, and an expert musician to play it—Mama! Papa wanted John to act as Mrs. Bradley's escort to the fête celebrating the merger—a fête held in an enormous tent set up on the leveled site of the old First Parish Church, across the street from the Universalist one. Papa was mightily pleased with that merger, and he didn't want anyone to miss it, nor the fête celebrating it, and he wanted to be sure the Bradleys were there whether their budget included appropriate clothes for John or not.

John was fourteen then, already taller than his mother, and although Augusta was not even ten years old at the time, she could remember the peculiar lurch, the strange turning over of a vital something within her at the sight of John in his cut-

294

away coat, that afternoon. After that, she was always aware of him, no matter where in the Merrick house he was; he was enjoyable, a good companion—and he admired Papa, which made him all the more acceptable in Augusta's eyes. Particularly she remembered standing beside him, watching Waterford at its hilarious best in the Merrick carriage barn where everyone was celebrating the return of Uncle Tony from North Carolina. Land could be had cheaply in the old Confederacy, and Tony had bought some in order to set up a cotton mill. He had come back to marry cousin Nell Denning, who had waited faithfully for him all the while and Waterford welcomed its child with open arms and plenty of home brew. Papa had matched Uncle Tony drink for drink and was still steady on his feet and able to bow when the occasion required it, while Tony was roaring drunk (Oh, wasn't Mama mortified!). And John had turned to her and exclaimed, "I hope I can hold my liquor like that when I'm old enough to drink." His eyes were bright with admiration as he looked down at Augusta and grinned. "Your father's quite a fellow, isn't he!"

Yes, Papa was that!

Shortly afterward, irrepressible as always, Papa left to seek his third fortune in South Africa. Really, he had insisted, there was nothing to do in Waterford any more. The Cape Cod Central had merged with the Old Colony by then, so he didn't have a railroad to direct. The mill in West Waterford, which had supplied him with his second fortune during the war, burned flat in '69 (a disaster that coincided with the demise of small mills and the rise of huge corporate ones) so that Papa had no business to conduct anymore. He was no longer senator and had no interest in running again; his belonging to legislature had served its purpose in its time and now the time was past. In fact, there was nothing left in Waterford that interested him at all.

But South Africa! Well! The diamond strike at Kimberly was a splendid opportunity, he believed, to get back into coaching—perhaps the last he'd ever have! He had a sizable amount of cash, besides insurance from the burnt mill, to put into it. He could, he was sure, raise the rest. . . .

And, leaving behind all his accomplishment on Cape Cod which now having been achieved no longer challenged him, he sailed for Port Elizabeth and Mama was on her own, able to make her own decisions, wield her own power, and soon enough there was ample opportunity to do so. Shortly after

Papa's departure, Mr. Adam Levering wrote to Mama to tell her his cousin Sally Levering Sinclaire had moved back to Boston. Mrs. Sinclaire had lived in Lawrence, Massachusetts, near the Levering Mills which her husband had bought in the panic of '57, rescuing Sally's father from bankruptcy. Mr. Sinclaire had converted them to wool during the war, and recently had died so that Sally Levering Sinclaire was free to return to the city of her birth. She had expressed to her cousin the hope that she and Mama could see one another again, and Mr. Levering, who had frequented the Merrick house in the days of establishing the C.C.C.R.R. and not much since, hoped to come, too, with his wife.

Instantly Mama prepared to receive them. She sent out invitations to a reception for them, a rather exclusive one because, she said, she wanted to give Sally a good impression of Waterford. More than anything else, Mama wanted to ensure Sally Levering Sinclaire's return and that of Adam Levering. They had been her dear friends, once—in fact the whole Levering family had been Mama's friends, even Sally's brother (who lamentably died in the war) and Mama was sure that in their company would come the wonderful opportunity to enjoy things that she had loved when she was young. Sally Sinclaire and Adam Levering, Mama thought, were the passport to something very special and so she was not going to invite Mrs. Bradley to the reception.

For Mrs. Bradley was a problem. She had recently married a retired captain from Yarmouth, who had taken what was left of her money, combining it with his own, and invested it in a Western silver mine which did not live up to the captain's expectation. The newlyweds, in order to support themselves, prepared to open the Bradley house to summer guests from the city, who increasingly sought the seashore now that they could reach it so easily by rail, and Mama believed that a lady in trade, after all, was awfully undignified. In fact, Mrs. Bradley (now Mrs. Hallet) with something of a social liability and Mama thought perhaps she'd have to drop her altogether. . . .

It was not what would have happened had Papa been home! And when he returned, Augusta knew, he would change everything back again—but soon it didn't matter what Papa might have done because John's mother went and ruined everything. In her anger at being excluded she created a terrible scene with Mama behind the closed doors of Papa's library, and afterward, Mama told Augusta that never would

Mrs. Bradley enter the Merrick house again. A lady would never scream like a fishwife, Mama said acidly, and clearly Mrs. Bradley was no lady. Mama would appreciate it if Augusta never mentioned her name again!

No one else in Waterford mentioned it, either, because no one wanted to offend Mama. And when Sally Levering Sinclaire declared she loved Waterford and would like to visit it often, and brought her friends from the Back Bay with her and the Merrick mansion positively glittered with Boston brilliance and only those Waterford people whom Mama warmly approved were invited there—why, Mama seemed more desirable than ever. Young John Bradley went to work for Barney Blake to earn what he could to help his mother, and no Bradley was seen at any party Julia Merrick attended, nor in the parlors of any people of whom Julia Merrick approved.

Mama rented a house in Boston that winter, on the same street as Sally Levering Sinclaire's house, and Augusta was removed from district school number three in order to attend Miss Jellison's School in the city, where Sally Levering Sinclaire's daughter went.

What Papa thought of it all, there in far-off South Africa, was anyone's guess, because Mama never mentioned his opinion, one way or another. Papa, Augusta gathered, had his hands full getting his business started, and if Mama's life were now directed by her friends in the Back Bay, instead of by Papa—well, there wasn't much, at that distance, he could do to stop her. He couldn't stop her from sending Caroline to a different school from the one Augusta and Sissy Sinclaire went to, so that no one would know how slow Caroline was. In fact, he probably didn't even know about it, and he probably didn't know that the following summer when Mama returned to Waterford, his house was filled with city people who enjoyed dignified receptions and musical events and the reading of poetry and the writing of it and stimulating conversation (stimulating, at least, to Mama and Mrs. Sinclaire), and perhaps he never knew that Caroline very nearly demolished everything by eloping with Tim O'Shea, son of the Merrick coachman.

Augusta had never seen her mother out of control before, never witnessed her crushed and broken, and it was a horrid sight—one Augusta most certainly never wanted to see again! Mama's eyes looked like the diamonds Papa had sent home from Kimberly, diamonds packed in a velvet box lined with emerald-colored silk. Mama's eyes glittered in green splintered brilliance, filled with tears, and her lips were rigid and when she cried, her sobs tore at her throat in deep, ugly rasps.

"What will they think?" Mama wept, and Augusta wasn't sure if "they" referred to Mama's Back Bay friends or her admiring coterie in Waterford. But she knew perfectly well in either case what they would think of Caroline, and it would not redound favorably on Mama. Few families in Waterford Center would countenance the marriage of one of their daughters to the son of a papist immigrant.

Caroline's marriage might well have put Mama beyond the pale in Waterford and in Boston, too, but Mama did not let it. She did not receive Caroline and Tim when they finally returned to Waterford after their wedding flight. She closed the house in September and again rented one close to Sally Levering Sinclaire and sent Augusta to Miss Jellison's, using Miss Jellison as her reason for living in Boston, an excuse for leaving Waterford just then. It was an excuse that permitted her to see her Back Bay friends and further establish her intimacy with them, luring them to her side by the force and brilliance of her personality which seemed to enchant them, and which caused them, as Mama intended it should, to disregard Caroline for her sake and help her get over the shock of it all. Caroline, of course, was never mentioned, and no word was spoken when she died in childbirth in January. You'd have thought it didn't matter to Mama at all. But Augusta knew better. She knew, as no one else did, that Mama wept many hours in the night after that, terrible tears that made Augusta want to cry, too. . . .

"Augusta!" Mama called up again from the yard. "Darling, you must come down now! We all want to hear Mr. Levering's poem, and soon it will be time for luncheon."

There was no impatience in Mama's voice. She approved wholeheartedly of delaying one's entrance until the last possible moment, whetting the interest of those waiting (Bax Levering, notably) and no doubt she believed that interest-whetting was exactly Augusta's plan as she lingered up there in her room.

"In a minute, Mama!"

The table beneath the trees had a damask cloth; damask napkins impossibly folded like swans clustered coyly about the punch bowl as though they were swimming around it, and a beautiful floral arrangement provided a sylvan setting for them. Patricia Hanrahan, who replaced Delia O'Shea, was bringing out the butterballs packed in ice and on the table already were chicken salad and rolls and a lobster salad residing in the lobster's shell, as well as the Merrick silver and the Limoges china. About the lawn were graceful white wrought-iron chairs and small tables, placed there by Patricia's husband, who had replaced Mr. O'Shea, and among them drifted or sat Thayers and Leverings, Sinclaires and Wardens, as well as Crosbys and Kings and Grays, who represented Waterford that day.

She waved, like a princess on the palace balcony, and she was sure Mama was very pleased because it was Mama, after all, who'd set the scene, assembled the guests, and caused everybody to believe that Augusta Merrick was royalty. Probably, had Caroline behaved herself, she'd be the one to reign, the elder daughter, the most beautiful, even if she never had anything interesting to say. But Augusta could carry forward better than Caroline ever could have done. She could and had made up to Mama all the things Caroline should have been and done and much, much more. She had done so willingly, because she was all Mama had. . . .

She'd rigorously accommodated herself to Miss Jellison's school where the academic program stressed excellence after the tradition of Elizabeth Peabody, and where she was kept quite busy. Its social schedule was a bore, but she learned to put up with it, suffering dancing classes and afternoon tea, which was designed to drill the young ladies in its proper observance. The young ladies, themselves, were a bore, too, because they were all the same—a sameness to which she was supposed to aspire and she resigned herself to that, too. After all, it was desirable to be a lady, even if it wasn't very interesting until you got a lot older. And besides, Augusta understood the trouble really lay with her years at district school in Waterford, with the great variety of her schoolmates there and with the greater hurly-burly that was inevitable when young boys were on the scene. District school number three had, truthfully, been far more interesting than Miss Jellison's.

But for Mama's sake she tried, and just as she was getting the hang of it Papa wrote home from Port Elizabeth that he was lonely and not feeling well and wouldn't they all enjoy a trip to South Africa to keep him company for a while!

Go to South Africa! Augusta nearly leaped from her skin at the chance to see Papa—but Mama refused outright.

"No, sir!" Mama declared. "He's just looking for a way to get me out there. Once I'm in Port Elizabeth, for all I know,

I'll never be able to come back." Her face softened in view of Augusta's distress. "If we stay here, dear, he's bound to return. But if we go, he never will! No, I daren't go." Mama's face brightened. "I shall send Ellen instead!"

Yes, the answer was to send her widowed sister, who had nothing better to do than sail away to Port Elizabeth. Aunt Ellen needed to have her time usefully occupied so that she wouldn't be morose. Her husband had died late in the war. Her sons had died of scarlet fever and she had just nursed Grandmother Merrick in her old age. Now that Grandmother was lamentably gone, Aunt Ellen, an experienced nurse, was free to go to South Africa. Aunt Ellen's daughter, her only remaining child, came to Boston to go to school with Augusta—a good thing for Lizzie! Surely the child was getting morbid, having lived amid so much tragedy for so long. . . .

Aunt Ellen wrote to say that Papa was sicker than he'd let on. Perhaps Mama ought to come.

But Mama prevaricated. She did not want to take Augusta out of school, nor Lizzie Duncan either. She did not want to lose the rental of the house in Back Bay, which was a very desirable one; Ellen was to notify her if Papa got worse, in which case of course she would hasten to Port Elizabeth.

Aunt Ellen answered that if Mama were going to come at all she had better do so quickly, and Mama hastened to pack her things and Augusta's, broke the lease, sent Lizzie back to Waterford, raced to New York where the steamer would depart—and when they got there the ship from South Africa had docked and Aunt Ellen's message was on it:

> Kingsley is gone. I am packing his effects
> and will return home on the next vessel.

It was early spring when Aunt Ellen and Mama and Augusta went back to Waterford on the train. The pallid countryside was faintly greening up, the branches on the trees yet bare, the meadows gray and brown. Boggy marshy places were draped with wisps of mist as the water in them warmed in the sun, and her heart and soul were empty. She watched it all sliding by the streaked windows as though the train were stationary and the earth, with all its living, newly breathing things, streamed past in an unending, unwinding ribbon, one she no longer cared about.

Papa was gone. There was no need to wait for the day of his return. There would be no laughing with him any more, no riding in the woods, no warm hand to hang on to, no jokes to share. He was not coming back. . . .

She spent hours with Aunt Ellen, to hear everything her aunt could remember about Port Elizabeth and the express line and the horses and coaches Papa had built, and the house he lived in and the queer plants and trees surrounding it that Papa had looked at every day he'd lived there. Aunt Ellen helped immeasurably to bind up the gaping wound of Augusta's grief, to bridge the gap from life into death. And to a certain extent, the bridge to Waterford was rebuilt, too, there at Aunt Ellen's house. For all her friends, with whom she had gone to school for so many years, came there to share her mourning and reaffirm their friendship and there she saw a lot of Emmaline Snow, who lived across the street from the Merricks in the ancestral home of Cousin Nate's family. It was Emmaline who with her simplicity, her gaiety, her practical ideas and her less practical ones helped more than anyone else to fill the empty spaces in her life just then, helped to pass the time more easily until she stopped hurting.

As for Mama, her friends flocked to her side, all sympathy and understanding, and in time she relaxed and began to smile again, and at the end of the summer the house was closed up and another place in the Back Bay rented. Life, quiet in mourning, gradually picked up its former pace, lurched ahead like a train bumped from the back to couple the cars. Gradually Mama went out with her friends again, and her friends entertained her. Life became what it had been before, with all the people Mama best loved in it, and not those whom Papa had best loved. Now there were the Leverings and the Sinclaires, the Wardens and the Thayers and other elegant friends of Adam and Sally, and Mama bloomed. They were the sort of people who formed a reproduction of Beacon Hill society (so Mama believed) and Mama thrived on it. She guarded it with care and diligence, so that only those she deemed worthy, like cousin Nate and Captain Pollard, Captain Crosby and Captain Denning and their families, were allowed to approach it. And she did all she could to assure herself that it would not ever slip from her grasp as it so nearly had with Caroline, careful to guide and direct Augusta so that Augusta would never, ever jeopardize her standing with her friends as Caroline had—which Augusta inadvertently did because of her friendship with Emmaline Snow.

It was August. Augusta sat in the garden with Emmaline, reading with her in companionable silence, sipping lemonade under the rose arbor to the accompaniment of the hammer pounding out by the chicken shed.

Mama had done nothing to interfere with Emmaline's friendship. She did not cultivate Emmaline's parents socially, although she respected them. Mr. Snow, upon inheriting the Inn of the Golden Ox from his grandfather, had torn it down and replaced it with a more compact structure which sold only general merchandise, without having accommodations for lodgers. He was a good businessman and a respectable one, so naturally Mama did not care to appear unfriendly and she had not objected to Augusta's frequent visits to the Snows' garden behind their house, screened by an enormous leafy hedge. There Augusta often sought sanctuary, as she did this afternoon when Mama was quietly entertaining a few, select Waterford ladies at tea, along with her sisters to whom her obligation might be fulfilled when her Back Bay friends were not in town.

Emmaline was sighing over *Evangeline* and Augusta was poring over a copy of *Godey's* which Emmaline had saved for her (Mama would not let *Godey's* into the house) when the hammering stopped and the quiet afternoon dropped like a curtain in a stage setting.

"He must be finished," Emmaline said, rising to her tiptoes to peek over the roses. "Yes, he is. John!" she called. "Will you have some lemonade?"

"You bet!" he called back, and shortly appeared from behind the honeysuckle that screened the hen house, pausing in surprise when he saw Augusta and then coming forward to sit with them. He carried a wooden tray with a handle on it in which were his tools and he mopped his face and neck with an enormous blue handkerchief. He was large, very tall, and broadly built, muscular and tanned, his golden hair was tangled now around an honest, square face with straightforward, frank eyes. Augusta found herself strangely, mysteriously moved by John Bradley, as though something deep, deep within recognized the presence of decency and responded instantly to it. Were there, anywhere, such warm eyes as his?

There was no extra glass; Emmaline hastily dumped the contents of her own into the roses and filled it fresh for John and squeezed herself in beside Augusta so that John could have the seat opposite to himself.

302

"Thanks," he said, the glass looking ridiculously small in his brown hand. "Just what I needed."

"Hot," remarked Emmaline.

"Hummm," John agreed, and sat back in his seat. A rose protruded from behind his ear and Augusta laughed. He turned his head to look at it and made a growling sound, like a lion. The rose was unintimidated.

He took a penknife from his pocket, cut it away and then another, nearby. "Here," he said, reaching over to give one to Emmaline. "Here," he said, proffering the one remaining to Augusta, and their eyes met as the rose changed hands, and their fingers met, too, in a slight brushing that faintly disturbed her. She fastened her eyes on the rose, and was well aware that John Bradley watched her.

"What have you left to do?" Emmaline asked, but John did not look at her, nor did he appear to have heard.

"What is there left to do?" Emmaline asked again, a little more loudly, and John reluctantly looked her way.

"Barn next," he said briefly. "There's a broken stanchion, your father says, and some shingles to replace on the north side."

"Your reputation as a carpenter is gathering steam," Emmaline assured him. "I heard Mrs. Hall ask Mother the other day if she liked your work, and Mother said quite nice things about it, and Mrs. Hall said she'd get in touch with you soon, that she'd heard other people say the same."

"Good," he smiled. "I'm grateful for the recommendation." Inadvertently he was staring at Augusta again.

"Has this been a good summer for your mother?" Emmaline asked politely. It was Mrs. Bradley's fourth year at taking summer boarders.

"Very good," he said, looking still at Augusta who looked at him, now, too. "A bumper crop," John remarked. "All this financial mess has caused people to flee the city in droves. Are you glad to flee the city, too, Augusta?"

"Which city?" she asked stupidly, dreamily.

Emmaline laughed, full and throaty and delighted.

"I think I'll go into the house and fetch more ice and another glass."

Correctly John Bradley stood as she left and quickly sat down again.

"It's been quite a while since I've seen you," John said, his dark eyes wandering over her face as though it were new terrain to him. His words, which might sound banal and casual, were not. He was telling her that she had changed from the last time he'd seen her, that she had left childhood behind and was a woman now, however young, and that he was a man, startled and pleased to find her here as though they might take up the conversation where they had left it four years ago, the last time he was in the Merricks' house with his mother, before Mrs. Bradley married Captain Hallet, before Papa went away, and before he died, before Caroline eloped with Tim O'Shea, before Augusta spent winters in Boston with her mother.

Where had he been? Why had she not seen him before?

"What have you been up to, John?"

He nudged his tool tray with his toe. "Carpentry, as you see." He smiled, a private smile wherein was no trace of apology for his tools.

"What else?"

"I tend Captain Blake's weir with him, peddle his fish. I have brought some to your house, now and again."

"I never saw you." How amazing, that she never saw him!

"I pick cranberries in the fall. Tend my mother's garden so she can feed her guests."

"You're acquiring a wide range of experience, then." She liked his squarish face with a cleft in its chin, and his hair, curling vigorously; she was instantly at her ease with him.

"Do you go to school in Boston?" he asked.

"I'm afraid I do. I'm not acquiring a broad range of experience, though. I am only becoming learned and a lady." She laughed at the absurdity of being a learned lady, which paled considerably before the lessons learned by John Bradley.

The silence became protracted and she wondered if Emmaline was ever coming back. Yet the silence was not uncomfortable because it was not possible to be uncomfortable with him.

"Do you sail?" she asked.

"Yes, I have a small catboat, anchored west of the old breakwater. I take it out, when the tide is right, on the pretense of catching blues for my mother's table. They don't come into the weir often, and when they do Barney keeps them."

"Do you like to fish?"

"Moderately," he smiled. "I like to sail more. You'd like it, too. Care to come with me sometime?" He asked casually, but he was watching in a manner that was not casual.

"I'd enjoy it very much," she said simply. "But I'm not sure I can." She was thinking of her mother, of course, and the requirements of young ladies that did not include sailing in open catboats, and of course John Bradley understood that instantly.

"I cast off as soon as there's water in the afternoon, generally two hours before high tide, and I come in two hours after high, though sooner if I want to—if I have my catch early, or if my passenger needs to return home." His brown eyes were steady, as though he were concentrating only on his explanation, but in them he was calling to her, calling her to shuck off the refinements binding her soul and body, even as now he was saying, "It's important to wear loose-fitting garments and a hat against the sun."

Emmaline was coming back, loudly clinking the ice in its container.

"I go every afternoon tide in decent weather," he said as Emmaline briskly dropped a chunk of ice in his glass.

"Where do you go?" she asked brightly.

"Sailing."

"Oh! Of course! Fatty Simmonds took me out only last week, me and Crawf and Cindy," Emmaline said, as though it were quite within the scope of things for a girl to go sailing. It was, for a Waterford girl, provided she was home by dinnertime. It was not all right for a young lady from the Back Bay. "Have you heard anything about Tom Slater?"

John told her all he knew about Tom Slater, who had gone to Cincinnati, Ohio, and all about Charlie Gray, who'd gone to Indianapolis, Indiana, and about Everett Stone, who'd gone to Indianapolis, too.

"They're writing a newspaper," he said. "They tell about what's going on out there and what Indianapolis is like, and they send it on to Tom in Cincinnati and he sends it to Lawrence McLaren in Dubuque, Iowa, and so on, each adding his own news and anything he may have heard about anyone else from home, and then sends it to Fatty and we pass it around and write them our news."

"Why can't the girls write in it?" Emmaline demanded. "Those boys are our friends, too!"

"Why not?" John agreed. "I'll bring it over when I get it and you can write to your heart's content."

"I'll pass it around among the girls," Emmaline assured him. "What's it called?"

"The Two Penny Gazette," he grinned. "Brilliant, don't you think?"

"Awful. Maybe we girls can think up something better."

"Women!" he snorted. "Always trying to run things."

"Well, then, we'll leave it as it is," Emmaline offered. "Dull as ditchwater."

"I suppose it is," he laughed. "But we meant well."

He looked at Augusta once more, and his eyes said, I mean well, too. "Would you like to write in it, Augusta?"

"If I'm here when it's available."

"I'll make sure of it," he said firmly, as though he could do anything he set his mind to, including control the U.S. mail. "Well, thanks for the lemonade," he said to Emmaline. "It's been pleasant to chat with you." He said it to Augusta, caught himself in time to glance Emmaline's way, thus including her, and Augusta smiled, a smile which John Bradley returned. He left, whistling as he took his tools away, and Augusta looked industriously at the rose because Emmaline was staring frankly, appraisingly.

"I thought I'd never be lucky enough to witness love at first sight," Emmaline sighed. "But it seems I have."

"Don't be foolish," Augusta murmured. "I've known John Bradley always." She realized she had not denied the substance of Emmaline's statement, but somehow it seemed not to matter.

"Love at first sight doesn't require people to be strangers to one another." Emmaline, ever practical, was direct if nothing else. "It only means that the thing hatches without incubating—if you know what I mean."

"I know what you mean." Softly she rubbed a silky rose petal, remembering the hand that gave the flower to her, the hand that had touched hers.

"What are you going to do?" Emmaline asked, in a question that did not involve actions or answers but, instead, involved Augusta's mother, Julia Merrick, and Julia Merrick's quarrel with Angelina Bradley, which was common knowledge.

"I don't know." Augusta looked at her friend. "I don't know," she said meditatively, quiet with a stillness she had never before known, which put from her, just then, the tensions that would follow.

If she did nothing, it was something. It was a refusal of John Bradley. If she did something, she'd have to do it under cover in view of the fact that Mama had not spoken to—or of—Angelina Bradley for four years. It meant betraying Mama, who was still so protective of her circle and her standing in it, weeding out unsuitable people (like John's mother) in a continuing process. It meant more than that, too—though she resolutely put away what more it might mean and was passive in the embrace of the summer season, following without protest Mama's schedule, Mama's Waterford socials, the hours that she and Mama spent together reading aloud or playing duets on the grand piano, thinking that if the next week of afternoon high tides were filled in such a manner that she could not possibly extricate herself, then there was nothing to decide, and of course, the alternate weeks of afternoon low tides held no decision, either, because John Bradley could not take his catboat out at low water.

Then Mama determined she must go up to Boston. She received a letter from the family lawyer, and it upset her so that she decided to go to the city herself and talk with the fellow. She would stay with the Leverings, and Augusta could come or not, as she preferred. Mama thought that Mrs. Snow would let Augusta stay with Emmaline, or Emmaline could sleep at the Merricks because the Hanrahans would be there. Mama would be gone only a day or so; Boston was dull in the summer; the Leverings, no doubt, would come back down with Mama, and Bax would come, too . . . what might Augusta prefer?

It was a week of high tide.

She didn't want to say it. She wanted Mama to say it, to allow as how Augusta ought to stay on in Waterford because it was cooler, or warmer, or fresher or less fresh or whatever reason Mama might designate, but Mama left it open.

"I'll stay if Mrs. Snow will have me," Augusta said at last. "If it's inconvenient, then I'll go with you."

Guests were never inconvenient; Augusta stayed and she and Emmaline prepared an elaborate picnic the following day, with elaborate explanations to Mrs. Snow about where they were going and when they would return, all coinciding with the tide; Augusta went to the beach and Emmaline wandered away to enjoy the afternoon by herself. She would find a tree nearby and read under it and nibble at the lunch and Augusta would sail with John Sears Bradley.

There was water in the bottom of the little boat, beneath the floorboards; it slurped and sloshed. In the center of the boat was an upright, narrow case in which the centerboard was stored, with a rope attached to let it down when there was sufficient clearance for it. The mast of the stubby little craft was mounted far forward and the sail was huge, its boom sweeping past the stern, and every time they changed direction it careened past her with a wicked thrust, snapping taut when the breeze filled it again and the boat bubbled and foamed through the water. The breeze was gentle and tender; what that sail would be like on a gusty day beggared her imagination.

"Too much for you?" John Bradley asked as she straightened up after the sail had whisked by her head. (She was thankful she had not worn her corset!) "Would you like to have me take you in?"

"Not at all," she laughed. It was ludicrous, undignified, unladylike, sitting on the decking on a blanket he had provided, with the bilge slopping beneath her, and she loved it. John, also sitting on the floorboards because there were no seats on so small a craft, leaned against the steep, capacious side with the tiller braced against his knees. She leaned on the other side, across from him.

"Would you like to steer? We'll be on a straight tack for a while."

"I'd like to try," she smiled, and put her hand on the tiller beside his. Gradually he let go and gradually the tiller pushed against her arm, the sail suddenly going slack and setting up an enormous flap. He laughed and rescued it, putting the boat back on course so that the sail bellied out again.

"We'll go a little further," he said. "And then I'll take in the sail and we can fish."

"Can you anchor so far out?" Land seemed far away, distant in perspective and importance. Beneath a tree somewhere was Emmaline, waiting for her, but she could not spot the blue of Emmaline's dress.

"We're still on the flats," he said. "Look over the side. You can see the bottom."

"We won't tip over?"

"No."

She looked over the edge, and there below was the sand, rippling in the shadows of wavelets, and a crab, a huge crab, scuttled sideways away from the encroaching shadow of the boat and miraculously slid down, under the sand, out of sight.

"I see a crab!" she called. "Now it's gone." She continued to hang over the side, viewing the underwater world that seemed silent and calm and mysterious.

"Here's a good spot, I think," John said. "The herring fry come out here, and the blues come in to catch them. Watch your head." Abruptly he slackened his hold on the tiller and uncleated the sail, causing it to fall in rough, stiff folds on top of her, and he clambered to the bow to tie the sail to the boom in loose, easy loops. The water no longer raced by and a quietness fell as abruptly as had the sail, broken by gulls who fished and the lapping of water against the sides of the boat and the creaking of the mast as they slowly rocked. The anchor tumbled overboard, settling into the sand as had the crab.

"How lovely," she said, feeling the kiss of the sun as the gentle southwest zephyr fanned her cheeks and lifted the brim of her floppy bonnet and let it down again.

"Here's a hook for you," he said, handing her a line upon which a wriggling sea worm danced. "Just put it over your side." He threw his own over his side; the secured and cleated boom divided the boat in half, one part of which was hers, the other his.

"I hope you won't regret coming out with me today, Augusta," he said. "I'm awfully glad you did, but I would be very disturbed if it might cause you trouble."

"If I'm back by dinnertime, no one will know," she assured him. "Though what you must think of me, scuttling about like that crab, I can only imagine."

"I think you've got courage," he smiled. "I'm not unaware of the fact that your mother would not care to see you in my company."

"It's not quite fair of her," Augusta said carefully, so as not to betray Mama, to whom her loyalty belonged. "What goes on between your mother and mine ought to be their business and not ours. I don't know why there's such ill will between them, do you? I mean, surely your mother is free to live her life as she sees fit."

"And surely yours is free to choose her friends," he reminded her. "Both of them have to work out their own destinies. As for mine, my father's death left her financially unstable, he'd lost so much during the war, don't you know. I suppose she thought Hallet would be more helpful than he actually turned out to be."

"That's too bad," Augusta nodded, uncomfortable in the understanding that Mama had not been helpful, either, excluding John's mother as she had.

"It was a bad time, when Hallet's investment turned out so

poorly," John shrugged. "Though for my own intents and purposes it was very fortunate."

"In what way?"

"Why," he laughed, "when suddenly my mother and I were no longer welcomed in the parlors and gardens of nice people because of their discomfort over my mother's entrance into trade, I discovered I was better off not being there—and perhaps I would never have realized it without a little push."

"In what way were you better off?" she asked.

"I don't belong there is all."

"Nonsense, John, you'd fit anywhere."

"I could—but I am happier fishing or building things. I am happier out here than I ever was in anyone's front parlor."

She looked about, over the sands that stretched out along the far-off shore, to the sails of a distant schooner and a piece of driftwood floating past them with the tide.

"Yes," she said softly. "There is a lot here that could make a person happy." She looked out for a while longer, at the spacious freedom of the uncluttered bay.

"I think a lot of us just coast along in the direction we've been set at," John Bradley said slowly, as though he were thinking aloud. "Surely I would have, if my mother hadn't come about and married Zack Hallet. Having been pushed out of your parlor and other parlors like it, I started tending weirs with Captain Blake and learning carpentry from whoever would teach me, and I discovered I liked it. The sea certainly has no future—not as long as England has a monopoly on steamships—but the land, this land, does. I'm only grateful that I found out in time."

"Will you stay in Waterford, then? Doing what you're doing now?"

"If I can figure out enough ways to make a little money. I wouldn't need much—but I can't exist exclusively on clams, either." He smiled. "But yes, I'll stay if I can."

She wondered why. Here on Cape Cod success and advancement passed a man by; only the old captains, retired with their savings intact, like cousin Nate King could live in comfort, dabbling in insurance and banking, the Old Colony Railroad, and town affairs. There was no place in Waterford for a young man, and many young men had left already.

"It won't be easy," he observed. "But I aim to find a way." He was watching her; a response seemed required.

"I should think you might find it a little dull. Nothing much is going on, John."

"And perhaps nothing much ever will. But I suspect that given twenty or thirty years, Waterford will be run by men like me, farmers and fish-weir tenders and clam diggers and herring catchers. These old retired duffers aren't going to live forever! I rather look forward to that day, and I should hate to be in a position where I couldn't be nearby to enjoy it. And between now and then, I will have all this." His arm flung out in an arc, embracing the bay and the gentle land that ringed it on three sides.

"I can't imagine Waterford being anything different from what it is now," she laughed. "Well clothed and self-satisfied."

"Oh! The well-clothed will come here in the summertime! Just as you do, they will arrive in June and leave in September, more and more of them, I expect! They will require eggs and vegetables and fish and ice and boarding houses, and perhaps they will buy a house, and if they do, they'll need carpenters and painters—they will provide the cash, don't you see?"

She began to see indeed, and to feel uncomfortable, designated as a cash crop. She did not like the picture John Bradley drew, of himself tall and handsome and straight, mongering fish to the rich, and of herself, the source of pennies for the poor.

"You are better than that," she said, near to anger. "You can do better than that for yourself."

"But perhaps I don't want to," he said softly. He jiggled his hook to make sure no fish was lying inert at the end of his line. He looked out across the bay and was quiet for a time, and she wondered if she had offended him. She hoped not—but it was true. He could do better for himself.

"Perhaps I would rather stay on this land, where I was born," he said slowly, musing, nearly oblivious to her presence, it seemed. "I confess—yes, willingly—that I love it. I confess to being caught by it, by the quietness of the earth at night and the procession of days by the bay, drummed at by the wind in winter and drowsy in the summer. Perhaps I am only lazy, Augusta."

"If you were, you wouldn't be here," she declared. "It seems to me that it will require a lot of hard work just to find sustenance."

"Perhaps." He nodded. "But the land will support those of us who want to stay. Not richly, but well. Those of us who stay will have the opportunity to live out the dream of

Thomas Jefferson, and we shall not have to go off to the backwoods of Ohio to do it. In my generation and yours, Augusta, Waterford shall revert to a republic in fact, and there it shall remain because it hasn't the resource to beget wealth anymore."

"Thomas Jefferson!" she snorted, and then laughed. John Bradley laughed, too.

"I suppose it does sound a little strange! But I'm only telling you of my expectations—my hopes, really—my future, and why I want it and have chosen it."

He looked landward again. "One day Waterford will be a harbor of refuge for those who want what it has to offer, but long before that day it will shelter me and those of my generation who love it as I do, those of us who are not attracted to cities with their polish nor are lured by the prospect of getting rich, with all its attendant trials."

"What trials?" she asked. "What, after all, is more trying than perspiring in a hay field, bitten by bugs and and itching with chaff?"

"Why," he said thoughtfully, as though he had taken her flippant question seriously, "everything in life has to be bought. The coin isn't always recognized, but it's there. For myself, it's a life of peace and small joys exchanged for labor and dependence on the whim of natural forces, winds and drought and God knows what else! For wealth the payment is tension and tinsel and the giving up of the land and one's roots on it. They're dramatic choices, in my mind, although most people aren't even aware that there is a choice. Everyone's so certain that wealth and the acquiring of it is mankind's only proper good. I have not chosen that." He turned from his line and looked over the cleated, shrouded boom at her. "No one has to choose that, if they don't want to." His eyes upon her were challenging, questing.

Why, she thought, *he has got me out here just to tell me these things.* One could not state these sentiments succinctly in a garden among the roses; the drifting of the afternoon, beneath the sun and in the arms of the bay, caused thoughts like these to wander to the surface and find expression there in a manner that appeared easy and natural, but she had no doubt now that he had done so deliberately, that he had wanted her to know his mind, his purpose, the direction he had chosen for his life, so very different a direction from the one she was traveling now, under Mama's guidance. He wanted her to know it, know what sort of man he was—and what, she wondered, did knowing what sort of girl she was do to him? Did it make him wish he'd chosen differently? Obviously it did not, or he would never have stated so flatly what he intended to do with his life. He'd have modified it, softened it, instead of setting it up, an impenetrable barrier between them that, were it crossed, she would be the one who leaped.

The line in her hands gave a vicious tug.

"Oh!" she gasped. "Someone has come calling!"

"Pull it up! Pull it up, so the hook sets!" he commanded. "Don't let it get away!"

She pulled, up and up, and streaking beneath the water in one direction and then another was a shadow followed by the line she held. John reached over and grasped it firmly and pulled the fish out and into the boat, where it flapped and smacked against the floorboards.

"Oh!" she shrieked. "Catch it before it jumps out!"

He plopped it into a pail under the shallow bow of the boat, where it flipped water around with its tail. She crept forward on her hands and knees to admire her catch.

"How about that!" she exclaimed, forgetting that girls weren't supposed to like fish, slimy and smelly.

He laughed and baited her hook again.

"Here you are," he said warmly. "You've got the lucky touch today. Quick, throw it over. Maybe you'll catch more!"

And laughing with him, she threw the writhing sea worm over the edge and leaned over anxiously to watch its departure for the sandy bottom.

"I don't know how we're going to explain why your nose is sunburnt and mine isn't," Emmaline said. "I hope it doesn't peel!"

"We can say we fell asleep," Augusta decided. "And of course the sun shifted, and I was in it and you were not."

Deception came more easily than she'd realized it could.

"Did you have a good time? What did you talk about? Did he tell you he loved you?"

"We just talked about things generally." It didn't sound interesting, she knew. She did not intend that it should. "I caught three fish."

"Did you! Were they big?"

"Enormous!"

"And what will John be doing tomorrow?"

"Working on your father's stanchion."

"And what will you be doing?"

Augusta laughed, hearty, glad. "Why, I'll be drinking lemonade in your garden, with you!"

Emmaline laughed, too.

Mama, as she'd promised, brought the Leverings home with her from Boston, but she was a changed Mama, somehow. Not different, but more. More brittle, more energetic, more dynamic, more tense, positively bristling with energy and laughter and gaiety and zest. The Merrick mansion filled with guests because it was late summer and no one wanted to miss the remainder of the season; within the month Sally Sinclaire rushed in with her news: she had bought the old Denning house, the papers were passed, the deal was signed, sealed, and delivered. She would live there in the summertime, starting next year, just as Mama did at the Merrick place. Captain Denning was going to Chicago and his family, too, and though Mama regretted that the captain must leave, she was overjoyed to know her old friend Sally would be in Waterford, and wasn't it nice that young Sissy would be there, too, so suitable a companion for Augusta! Dismay crowded her, bumping up against her heart, for if Sissy Sinclaire were permanently ensconced in Waterford, Augusta would have few excuses to visit Emmaline Snow. She would not be able to plead her isolation in Waterford from people her own age, for which Emmaline was the antidote, and who she had used all month as a reason for visiting the Snows' rose arbor, where she met John Bradley.

She came to crave those meetings, though she did not acknowledge, even to herself, that the craving existed. She did not acknowledge that something urgent, something poignant and necessary and sweet and happy was growing, that something within her needed the quiet calm of John Bradley that made her feel whole and secure as she had not felt since Papa went away. She concentrated only on the pleasure of his companionship because what he gave her, she knew, caused her to move further and further away from Mama, a drift she could not acknowledge, a drift which could lead her only to a quagmire—

But it was a quagmire from which Mama abruptly extricated her.

They were putting away summer clothes, piling on chairs the things Patricia would pack to be taken back up to Boston for the winter. Summer was over; school would start in two weeks.

"Enjoy this year as much as you can," Mama was saying. "Next year you'll have a coming-out party and after that, you know, everything starts to get very serious. A small flirtation becomes a matter of great account! Flirt with Bax Levering as you do now, and he'll feel obligated to ask you to marry him!"

"Well, he's very nice," Augusta said noncommittally, folding a ruffled petticoat into a box and sprinkling it with lavender so it would smell fresh next spring when she retrieved it.

Mama sat on the edge of the bed, her hands folded, her strong face suddenly tense. "I don't know, Augusta, if I've ever mentioned to you how high are my hopes for a match between you and Bax."

"Why, no, Mama!" she exclaimed. "You've never mentioned it." And Mama never had.

"Well, you're young—I certainly haven't wanted to burden you with thoughts of the future while you've so clearly been enjoying the present. But I don't have a choice now, I'm afraid. We must, unfortunately, think ahead." Mama stirred. "The panic three years ago has hurt us more than I realized it would. It seems that the income from Papa's stocks is not what I thought it was going to be, and the stocks themselves—well, I won't go into the details, Augusta. Suffice it to say that there are sufficient funds to meet our needs—but there's not enough to take me through my lifetime and yours, too. There wouldn't be enough to support you and any husband you might choose who, frankly, isn't rich or whose parents aren't. If our standard—yours and mine—is to be upheld, dear, you must be the one to ensure it, and oh! I would hate to see you fall in love with the wrong boy, one who can't afford to live in this house, and who is unable to contribute to both its upkeep and its leadership in all the things that make life worthwhile. You'd be separated from your own kind, lost to it forever if you had an unsuitable husband. There's no greater tragedy than that! So I thought we ought to talk about it now. That's why I think Bax is so suitable, you see?"

"Yes," she agreed unwillingly. "I see."

"Of course there may be other suitable young men coming along, too. If you are surrounded by that sort of person. It's one of them you'll choose, don't you see, and it's very important that you choose wisely!"

"Yes, Mama, of course," she'd said, growing numb and unhappy.

John, she saw at once, was not temperamentally or materially suitable. John, by design, planned for a life of simple joys, joys which would not include the cultivation of the arts and social graces. John, she saw, must be put out of mind before any further damage could be done! She was not, after all, the free agent she had assumed herself to be, because Mama herself was not entirely free, either. There weren't sufficient funds in the bank as Augusta had always assumed, to maintain Papa's house in perpetuity. That changed everything. . . .

She sent him away. She saw him in the Snows' rose garden, the rose hips hanging heavy, her hands clasped and her ankles neatly crossed, and told John she would be unable to enjoy his company any longer. And John, standing with one foot on the edge of the seat beside her, looked down at her steadily. John had heard her out, his eyes level and kind as they held her with love in them—yes—love. He had leaned over, when she was done, and kissed her, and had gone away without a word, neither acknowledging her denial of him, nor arguing with it . . . and she had not seen him since, and she had not known a day of happiness nor an hour of joy since. The weeks ground along into months; the desolate satisfaction of doing her duty by Mama faded, to be replaced by sadness and then by mute misery. Bax Levering and Tommy Warden, Van Sinclaire, Tony Crosby and Sally's nephew did not grow more appealing for all her efforts. Try as she might, she could not put away the uneasy knowledge that the damage had gone too far to be remedied.

How much, how much did she really owe Mama! (Everything she had!)

How far did a daughter's obligation require her to go? (As far as was necessary!) This was true of any daughter, and for Augusta even more true because of Caroline. But now, this day, she was sure to see John at the Town House dedication, knowing that she wanted to, and not knowing at all what would happen when she did. . . .

There would be a large table of refreshments, presided over by the unmarried girls with which Augusta would help—on display but out of reach as Mama intended her to be, out of reach but all the more desirable because of it, desirable to any young man whom Mama might find suitable, desirable to Bax Levering, especially. . . .

And John Bradley would be there, John Bradley whom she had been unable to forget—within her was a clamping, a tightening, a tingle of tension, of apprehension, of excitement, of despair.

Carefully she turned from it. Outside on the lawn, she could hear Mama's voice: Whatever is keeping that daughter of mine! There was an edge of impatience in it now, which no doubt only Augusta could hear. She was finely tuned to Mama, after all. She'd had to be, in order to discern how she might best be the daughter Mama needed.

She hurried down the stairs, past the portrait of herself on the wall (Caroline's had been removed), through the French doors in the dining room to the east piazza overlooking the festivity on the lawn, where Sally Sinclaire, bright as a new penny, and Mrs. Levering, quick at repartee and a violinist of great skill; Mrs. Thayer, incredibly learned; and Martha King, willing to listen, to be instructed; and Mrs. Crosby, an authority on English poets—where they and their husbands and offspring awaited Augusta Merrick, upon whom it fell to perpetuate and uphold the tradition of her parents.

Gaily she waved, gaily she called, valiantly she again took up the yoke. . . .

The honorable senator from Barnstable County beamed benevolently on the uplifted faces of his audience. Regrettably the governor had been unable to attend and give a speech, his excuses and apologies tendered at the last moment, but if the senator were disgruntled at being the filler-in, he gave no evidence of it.

He bowed to the selectmen, each of whom had already spoken.

"Honored sirs!"

He bowed to the clergy. "Reverend." Mr. Upton, minister of the Universalist Church of Waterford, had already spoken, too.

Astonishingly, he bowed to Mama whom his practiced eye had picked out from the audience. "Honorable lady, wife of our beloved and deceased senator, Kingsley Merrick!"

To the committee that organized the fête.

To the audience in general, the architect of the Town House in particular, Mr. Jonathan Pollard, newly out of architectural school and, if Augusta read public opinion correctly, well advised to return.

The audience was seated on benches on the spacious lawn

in front of the new building that hovered there in its treeless yard like a great crouching toad; little juts and towers, cupolas and variegated rooflines and projections like random warts, each shingled in different patterns—diamonds, scallops, horizontal rows and staggered ones suggested that it could not make up its mind which suit of clothing it preferred and so had worn them all. But Augusta liked it. It did not disturb her to see such a jumble—it was friendly, she thought—but a lot of people considered it an abomination.

The senator launched his speech, which extolled the past generations of Waterford, the climax of their history apparently culminating in the new Town House which manifested the civic pride of the town. A pride, the senator averred, which had always run strong.

"The fighting spirit of mariners was manifested in bravely ransoming their village during the War of 1812, rather than permitting it to be torn apart by aliens in a contemptuous act of war," the senator declared. "Unable, because of government policy, to defend it, these forefathers of yours chose to beggar themselves rather than let your heritage be destroyed. More honor to them!"

The audience applauded.

"With the deep understanding of the responsibility of one man to another, the forefathers of Waterford established, maintained, upheld their almshouse, their lyceum, their own Academy outstanding all over the county for the excellence of its instruction." He paused as a whispered remark was passed to him from the selectmen. "Maintained until very recently," the senator amended. "And relinquished in order to better uphold the district school, so that all its children could partake equally in the fount of learning."

More applause. *Papa*, Augusta knew, *would be hiding a smirk behind his hand, were he here!*

"Your splendid town upheld as well its duties in the recent war, sending its sons to battle, defending to its last breath the national commitment to equality, commitment to the commonweal *(Papa*, she thought, *would have positively guffawed)*, and now it has erected this magnificent building, demonstrating its continued leadership in the duties of citizenship. I salute you, citizens, for your clear-eyed acceptance of civic responsibility, which is so outstanding an example to every person the length and breadth of our beloved country."

The senator bowed to the standing ovation. Gravely descended from the podium flanked by the town officials, to the carriage shelter on the front of the Town House, where a ribbon stretched taut from pillar to post, and with an enormous pair of scissors, cut the ribbon in half.

More applause. Out of the Town House filed the Britannia Band, marching smartly, striking a festive air while the audience settled itself to listen and a man from the *Barnstable Patriot*, his head covered beneath the shroud of his camera as though he were in hiding like an ostrich, recorded the event for posterity. The maidens of Waterford stole to their posts at the long refreshment table under the trees, and as she ladled punch into little cups, Augusta watched John Bradley, seated with his mother and the other Bradley boys, Todd and David. Would he come over to fetch a glass of lemonade for Mrs. Bradley-Hallet, or would he send one of his brothers? If he came, himself, would he seek her out to speak with her, or would he simply nod acknowledgement of her presence? If he spoke, and did not confine himself to the weather . . .

She could feel herself struggling to breathe as she considered the possibilities of the situation, wondering how best to handle them, totally unable to come to grips with them at all. Emmaline Snow, standing nearby to shoo flies away from the cake, murmured softly, "He's coming this way."

She looked at Emmaline because she dared not look anywhere else.

"What shall I say?" she asked Emmaline desperately. "What shall I do?"

"He's the nicest boy in Waterford, if that's any help," Emmaline hissed. "Wasn't the senator splendid? Hello, John!" Emmaline breezily waved her hankie.

"Hello, Emmaline," John Bradley said, his voice as it always was, resonant and calm. "Hello, Miss Merrick."

She turned to give him a smile such as the occasion both required and permitted, wondering if Mama were watching.

"How do you do, Mr. Bradley?" she asked and found, uncomfortably, that her smile, responding to the expression of his eyes and mouth, was more intimate and friendly than she had intended. John had honest eyes; nothing was ever hidden in them and nothing was hidden now. They admitted frankly that he admired her, could master her if he chose, would be gentle with her always, and meant one day to make her his own if it took him years to accomplish it.

"Will you have some punch?" she asked weakly.

"Thank you, yes. And I should like to claim the privilege of a dance this evening, if your program isn't already filled."

She had not seen him since that day in the garden; then she remembered that Mama did not know about the garden and would not realize that one dance committed to John Bradley would have special significance. John waited gravely.

"Yes," she said. "I would be happy to put your name down for the seventh."

"And, Emmaline, I hope you'll let me dance with you, also!" John was taking the punch carefully.

"Try your luck for the sixth," Emmaline said, and smiled. When the sixth was done, she and John would be near Augusta, wherever she was, so that John would not have to go searching for her, perhaps losing precious moments.

John grinned at them both and left, and Augusta tore her eyes away from his retreating back, its shoulders broad and straight and his neck dark with accumulated sunshine and tan.

"If you could get some other Waterford boys to ask me," Augusta said to Emmaline, "it might help."

"Don't frown! You'll wrinkle. Dickie will ask you, I'll see to it." Dickie was Emmaline's brother. "And, of course, Crawf will be glad to oblige." Emmaline was unofficially engaged to Jack Crawford and could afford to be generous. Waterford boys were apt to be shy of Augusta, for all they admired her. But Crawf and Dickie were tractable, else they risk Emmaline's wrath.

Emmaline lifted the net cover off the sandwich pile so that Captain Crosby could retrieve a morsel. "And how are you today, Captain?"

"Dandy, my dear, just dandy."

A lot of folks decided on refreshments just then, and Augusta was spared further thought.

The meeting room of the Town House was decorated with bunting and red roses and white carnations from the greenhouses of Waterford and massive boughs of blue flowers made from blue silk, donated by the sewing circle of the First Church of Waterford, Universalist, and wired into place along with evergreens by the ladies of the library. The Britannia Band, consenting for extra honorarium to reduce its numbers and play waltzes, was doing a creditable job of it, and around the room were the ever present chairs for those preferring to watch. In the vestibule was the punch table, where rotating volunteers among the ladies took turns supervising it and rotating volunteers among the gentlemen replenished the supply of ice.

Mama was dancing with Jules Thayer, looking handsome as she always did, graceful, supple, stately in her gown of green satin, long emerald ear bobs dangling from her ears. She moved like a girl half her age, enjoying herself with Mr. Thayer. Way across the room was John Bradley, with whom Augusta would dance next. Her hands were cold, her color high in anticipation and through the expenditure of sheer nervous energy, she was more coquettish than usual with her present partner, Bax Levering.

"I shall be finishing Harvard next year," he was saying. "How nice it will be to get it behind me, and get on with life!"

"Yes, I'm sure it will seem very nice," she responded brightly. John and Emmaline were out of her line of sight now.

"And since you'll still be at Miss Jellison's, perhaps you will come to Harvard parties with me, if your mother will permit it." Mama had not, up until now, because she did not want Augusta to appear too available.

"Oh, I'm sure she will!" she exclaimed, looking furtively for Emmaline. "By now she is tired of hearing me beg to go! And now, after all, I am older!"

"Will you go to all of them with me, Augusta?"

Tommy Warden was also enrolled at Harvard College.

"That's a little hard to say, Bax. I can't very well know what I'll be doing each time you want to go to a party."

"Well," he gulped. "What I really wonder is if you'll promise you won't go with anyone else."

"Maybe no one else will ask me," she teased, spotting Emmaline at last, their glances meeting across the crowded floor. "But I'll surely accompany you, Bax, if I'm free to go when you ask."

It was an answer that might, possibly, satisfy Bax, and ought to please Mama, toward whom she inclined her head, to notify Emmaline that it would be as well to end the dance as far from Mama as possible, though it wouldn't be easy since Baxter was supposed to be leading Augusta, and John Bardley was presumably following Bax, and Mama destined to land wherever Jules Thayer deposited her. In relief she saw that Mama and Mr. Thayer were walking off the floor and toward the vestibule. In dismay she felt Baxter's arm about her waist gently pressing her in that direction, too. There was no help for it, and she was soon in the vestibule with Mama and Mr. Thayer and half a dozen other people, including the visiting senator who had stayed for the party and was happily bending Mama's ear now. Mama was nodding at whatever he had to say, as she listened, smiling at Augusta in her own, private way which told Augusta how proud she was of her lovely, charming daughter who was better than anyone else's daughter, and better loved, too. Augusta swallowed hard.

There was a rustling pause on the dance floor as the music stopped, and in the doorway Emmaline was preceding John to the punch bowl, chattering with animation and imperceptibly shrugging at Augusta as if to acknowledge that she'd delivered the bundle as she'd promised but could not take responsibility for the unsuitable place it had landed. A quick glance at Mama confirmed what Augusta knew she would find; at the sight of John, Mama's green eyes went cold and disdainful.

"Did you hear?" Emmaline said in a vivacious burst, "that Captain Pollard was in his dory the other day and hooked a shark that pulled him right out of his boat?" She retreated into the corner furthest from Mama as she spoke, and Bax and John and Augusta easily edged there, too.

"Not really, Miss Snow!" protested Bax Levering.

"Really!" Emmaline insisted. "Ask him yourself if you don't believe me." Captain James Pollard, elegant in sidewhiskers and a cutaway, hardly seemed the sort of man to get pulled from his dory by even God Almighty.

"Not the kind of shark that eats people," Emmaline explained. "A smaller kind—fortunately!"

"What did he do?" asked Bax while Augusta and John tried not to stare at one another. Beneath her tight and restrictive corset her lungs were struggling for air.

"He hung on," Emmaline said. "Until the shark got tired of hauling him about. By then the water was getting low and Captain Pollard walked it in like a dog on a leash."

"I find it hard to imagine!" Bax laughed, as well he might, because it was impossible to picture the captain strolling anywhere with a dog on a leash.

The band was striking up for the seventh dance.

"Who's your next partner?" she asked Emmaline desperately.

Emmaline examined her satin-covered program, dangling from a bunch of flowers at her waist as though her next dance had slipped her mind entirely.

"Why Crawf has it!" she exclaimed. "The scoundrel, why isn't he here to claim it?"

"You'd better keep your eye on him," John Bradley chaffed her. "He's treating you as though you were married already."

"How unpleasant, John, of you to say so," Emmaline retorted. "Do you think I ought to go looking for him?"

"Ignominious," John pronounced. "We'll all go back to the dance floor with you, and when he sees you coming in, the situation will take care of itself." Gallantly he offered his arm to Emmaline, and Augusta clutched at Bax Levering.

"Come on!" she urged. "It mustn't appear that Emmaline is doing more than perambulating the perimeter."

"What perimeter?" Bax asked stupidly, allowing Augusta to drag him along, out of the range of Mama's eyes, onto the crowded floor, where Jack Crawford instantly appeared at Emmaline's side.

"Remember I have the next one, Augusta," Jack winked, and took Emmaline in his arms.

John Bradley bowed. "Miss Merrick?"

It was here, her moment, his moment, and suddenly John Bradley was the only man in the whole world, certainly the only one on the dance floor. She took his hand, large and brown and strong, felt his arm around her waist, and did not look at Bax Levering as she glided away.

She did not know what to say to John, because casual conversation did not belong to this moment. She didn't attempt it. But she met his eyes which she'd been avoiding and found, in relief, that everything was all right. In their steady, calm warmth, she relaxed and at last smiled.

At the rear of the hall, by the bandstand where the music was loudest, he glanced around and, without hurrying, set her into a spin, the end of which concluded out the back door, which John shut firmly behind him. The latch on it clicked in tight authority. There was a little porch with steps to the ground and a railing surrounding it which John leaned against now. The carriage lamps, set at precise intervals across the gravel circle of the driveway, gently lit his face and obscured his dark suit in the shadow.

"Will you walk with me, Augusta?" he asked. "Or shall I take you 'round to the front door again? This one," he smiled, "appears to be locked."

There was nothing she wanted more than to walk with

him, and besides, for all she knew, Mama still lurked at the punch bowl, in full view of the front entrance.

Who will miss me? she thought hastily. Jack Crawford would raise no cry. There was an intermission after the eighth which ought to last half an hour and Dickie Snow had the ninth. Tony Crosby had the tenth, and Tommy Warden the eleventh, but she would surely be back before they claimed her!

"Yes, I'd like that very much," she gambled. "Where would you like to go?"

"How about the field along the path opposite the schoolhouse? It makes a nice walk, and it's close at hand."

He preceded her down the steps, taking her hand when she got to the bottom, placing himself between her and the Town House where the band beat like a pulse. They passed the horse sheds and the band's blare retreated, grew fainter as they left it behind, and the lights of the carriage lamps grew smaller and smaller, like the stars.

To the left of the road John unbarred a section of split rail fence for her to walk through and slid the bar in place again. Beneath her feet was the hard-packed surface of the path, and around her rose the smells of the meadow, grasses and crushed flowers and honeysuckle and rich, damp earth. The voices of the summer singers, the peepers and the frogs and the buzz of night insects and crickets stopped as they passed by and began again quickly, as though they could not bear to miss a note of the season's symphony.

John stopped on the edge of an abutment, below which the land sloped to a shallow basin choked with brush, the water in it gleaming faintly under the stars.

"The path hooks around the bog there, but I can't be responsible for your dress if we go further. The underbrush is really heavy."

"How lovely it is here," she murmured, and it was beautiful in its tangled wildness, so unlike the clipped and orderly lawns of home.

"I have bought it," John said, his eye traveling over the darkened marsh and meadow. "By day, if you stand here, all the boundaries are in sight if you know where to look for them. Six acres. Not much, but all my own."

"You bought it! How amazing, John! Whatever for?"

"Cranberries," he said. "The undergrowth you see is wild cranberry. When I cover it over with sand it will grow bigger and better. There's a spring at the far edge, which I can

324

divert over to the schoolhouse pond, or allow to run into the bog to cover things over in winter."

"It must be a good feeling," she said, glad for him, "to have a piece of land all your own."

"It is," he agreed. "Besides, it will provide me the means to stay in Waterford."

"Just as you told me once you hoped to do."

"Yes." He nodded. "I'm pretty sure now that I can see my way clear to staying. My mother and the captain are doing all right these days. I can maintain the house for them, and I believe my brothers will be loyal. When the time comes, I think they'll do their share. David and Todd will make fortunes—unlike their older brother, they're itching to get out in the world and make something of themselves."

"You'll make something of yourself. In a different way," she said softly. And he would. She could feel the certainty of it.

"I think I'll manage to scrape by," he said modestly. "I'm going to build myself a house here."

"In the middle of a bog?"

"The land slopes up, over there on the far side, facing south." He pointed there. "That's where I'll place my house, so the roof will catch the sun. But first I'll build a barn at the foot of the slope, keep my tools in it, screens and barrels for the berries. Later, when I'm ready to build, the barn will already be in place."

"Why, you have everything all figured out!"

"Yes, Augusta, I do." He was looking at her now. "Have you?"

Something did a somersault at this sudden and direct change in the intent of John Bradley's conversation. The night hung heavy, throbbing, between them.

"I?" she asked feebly, tension knotting within.

"Last fall you told me you could keep me company no longer." He paused, took a deep breath. "I felt then, and I feel now, that it wasn't a decision of your own making. So I thought I'd try to change your mind. I saved enough to buy this land so that you can see yourself what I plan to do and how I plan to do it, exactly what I have to offer, Augusta. I'm not ashamed to offer it. I think you'd enjoy the kind of life I have in mind. I think you'd like the freedom of it, because you're a free spirit, just as your father was. Because you're only half alive now, and will surely die if you give in to the demands of respectability."

325

"Don't!" It came out only a whisper, a plea to stop, because to go further was a burden too awesome.

"You're being smothered, Augusta! And I think you know it. I think you know I can give you something better."

"Don't!" It was a whispered despair, a plea to put from her the rising torment, to save her from a choice too cruel to make.

"You know that I love you." His voice was none too steady now. "I believe that you love me. Am I presuming too much? Augusta!" he whispered urgently. "Do you love me?"

How badly she wanted to answer him—and could not. She should tell him that he *was* presuming too much, that he was mistaken—but she could not. Something within her began to tear, to rip, and it was herself, placed on the rack, full of pain, of longing, of loneliness that only John Bradley could assuage. Inadvertently she reached out; without meaning to she cried out, and instantly his arms were around her, holding her carefully and close, pressing her to himself without regard to her dress. He made a crooning sound, as though to comfort a baby, and he rocked, just slightly.

"I understand," he said into her hair. "Believe me, Augusta, I understand. It's a terrible spot you're in and I do understand it. You're all your mother has, and I know she would welcome no alliance with me. I know that she hates my mother—and no doubt me. But it's not sufficient reason to offer yourself up! The life I would give you—it's nothing your mother will want for you, but it's right for you because I'm right. I *am* right, Augusta."

It was a statement of fact, not a question.

"Yes," she wept, wept now gladly, finally free of all the months when she tried not to think about him. "But she'll never consent, John. Never! She's sure, very sure, that the kind of life she has is the only one worth living." Suddenly Augusta knew it was not the only one worth living, not for her. She accepted his proffered handkerchief, large and dark in hue, coarse in texture. "She expects me to carry on with it. Mama will never understand." Shakily she knew she would abandon Mama, that Mama must carry on by herself, that Mama's hopes were lost, that Mama's traditions would die when she died because Augusta was not going to marry suitably.

"I've realized that," he said quietly. "It's the only reason I was willing to court you secretly last summer."

"Were you courting me?" Seeing John last summer had

been so easy, natural, that she had not thought of it as court-ing.

"Certainly," he laughed. "I was pursuing you! Successfully, thank goodness."

Shakily, she laughed, too. "We'd still have to be secretive," she said sadly. "It would be pointless to confront Mama now, before I've finished school. School is very important to her." She was quite sure that John did not enjoy being secretive.

"I'm willing," he said. "For now, anyway. There'll come a time, Augusta, when I'm no longer willing. And between then and now, perhaps, you might want to change your mind. I'm obliged to give you the opportunity." Her mind, which for so long had been unable to decide anything, was all at once very able.

"No," she said, "I won't change it."

He pressed steadily on. "You seem a lot older than seven-teen. But there's been tragedy in your life and sadness makes a person grow the faster. Still, you're very young. Perhaps it's matured you. I can't ask you now to marry me, Augusta."

"I'm not too young!" she cried. "I've known all winter . . . I knew last summer. . . . I'm not too young!"

"But your mother will think so. I've brought a lot of pressure to bear on you," he said gently. "And perhaps it's unfair that I have."

"John!" she cried. Was he backing away from her, chang-ing his mind?

"We mustn't see one another very often."

Was he growing faint of heart at the prospect of con-frontation with Mama? He could hardly be blamed, if that was so, for Mama was a formidable adversary.

"You've got to be sure, Augusta. Why, perhaps you'll find you don't want to give up pretty clothes, and dancing, and servants, and your father's splendid house. My wife shall live in the house I build for her, here, and it shall be humble. You must understand that."

Hurt, she said nothing.

"You'd have to do a lot of work if you married me. Cook-ing and mending and making do." Into her silence he said feebly, "But I'd help you. I'd lift all the heavy things and help you wash dishes."

She smiled at the picture of John Bradley pottering about in the kitchen of his little house with its low roof, and he must have caught her smile in the darkness. He took her hand. "I love you," he said. "I'll wait, just as I said." They faced one another, a breathless moment in endless time, feeling the beat of the night between them.

"I love you, John," she told him, hesitantly, shyly, tremulously.

He reached carefully for her, taking her shoulders under his hands, bringing her to himself, his lips close and then carefully upon her own, much as his last, only kiss in the garden had been. And then his lips, became strong and his hands on her shoulders tightened and his kiss became irresistible, burning, overwhelming, until he tore his mouth away and stepped back, releasing her, his arms stiff and tense at his sides. He looked at her nakedly in the night and she looked back, shocked and tingling at the new knowledge of what he could do to her, her blood boiling and beating within as she understood a part of herself she had only vaguely suspected before, one nobody ever talked about and that seemed by common conspiracy not to exist. She leaped within, and trembled there, quivered there and sang, wanted to cry out and die all at the same time as she stared at him across the immeasurably infinite space that now lay between them, and she reached out again to him, to know once again the warmth, the tingling and exulting in his embrace, to lose herself again, deeply and more deeply as the summer singers filled their throats and their voices throbbed, ripe and fruitful in the abundance of life.

Thanksgiving. She had longed for it since September, when she left John Bradley behind her, returned to Boston in the autumnal hegira with Mama, returned to Miss Jellison's and the Back Bay and the tea dances and the all-alike girls. She had met John Bradley all last summer, usually with Emmaline's help, and separation from him had weighed heavy and hopeless, relieved only by knowing she would see him again now.

Thanksgiving Day, the last serving of mince and Marlboro pie consumed, the remains of the turkey hidden from view in the kitchen, along with the serving plates of squash and potato and beans and carrots and gravy and cranberry preserve. The family stuffed and happy, filed into the back parlor at Aunt Ellen's house where the coffee and tea would be served. The table in the center of the room was heaped with nuts and raisins and apples and oranges, a decanter of brandy there available for Cousin King and a basket of chestnuts by the leaping fire for the King twins, identical as a brace of quail

328

and as fat. The children would content themselves with roasting the nuts and looking at picture albums placed conveniently near at hand, and would not obtrude. They would suffer the rest of the afternoon without protest, as children were trained to do, and Augusta would suffer it, too, her mind returning helplessly to the Snows' barn where she had met John Bradley yesterday afternoon under the pretext of visiting Emmaline, and where, God willing, she would meet him tomorrow. She had come down on the train with Mama early yesterday morning to share the New England Thanksgiving with Mama's sisters and Cousin King because, Mama thought, one should return to one's roots at that time. Mama and Augusta shared the front room at Aunt Ellen's because the big house was shut up for the winter, and they would return to Boston after church Sunday. They would not come back to Waterford until spring, and Augusta would not see John until then.

"Now for my surprise, with which I've been tantalizing you all day," Aunt Hetty announced, her sharp face wreathed in a smile and her hands rubbing one against the other in expression of her pleasure. She took the chair at the end of the room which she'd reserved for herself by tying a blue ribbon around it; beside the chair was a sizable wooden box which, after the Thanksgiving service at church, she had caused Cousin King to carry downstairs from her room. From within the box she drew a sheaf of papers, neatly sewn on the left margin, looked expectantly around the room to assure herself she had the attention of everyone in it. The children were quiet and Augusta politely folded her hands in her lap, looked down at them, remembering John's hands holding them, holding them tightly so that his own hands would obey the command of his will.

"As you may or may not know," Aunt Hetty began, "several of us here in Waterford have decided to start a historical society, and to that end we meet the second Tuesday of every month, the purpose of which meeting is the exchange of any information we have gathered that will aid us in writing up our family genealogies and history. The net result, we hope, will yield sufficient data to work up a history of Waterford."

"So *that's* what you've been so secretive about!" Aunt Clara exclaimed. She addressed the room. "She was so mysterious about those meetings!"

"I wanted it to be a surprise," Aunt Hetty said benevolently. "And I think you will be surprised, and pleased, too. However!" Aunt Hetty cleared her throat. "Our research is still in its preliminary stages, and another reason for telling you about it is to find out if any of you can contribute to the information I have, or correct it if I am in error."

Aunt Hetty was never in error.

The barn's light was dim, soft, the smell of hay sweet, and John, waiting there in the shadows, stepped out instantly as she came in, his face glad, his eyes bright, tender, happy. He reached toward her and she fled into his arms, where she belonged, to safety, to home, to him.

"I adore you," he said, and his eyes told her that he did.

"I love you," she told him. "Oh, John, I do love you!" Closer and closer they spoke, whispered, until their lips met and within struggled her need of him which must not be allowed to escape the confinement of self-discipline.

"To begin with, it seems evident that by ancestral claim we can safely say that our heritage begins at Plymouth Colony, with Elder Brewster and Governor Bradford and Thomas Prence."

"Truly!" exclaimed Aunt Clara. "What makes you think so, Hetty?"

"Our great-great-great-grandfather, Jonathan Merrick, married Sarah King, back when he first arrived in Rockford from Barnstable town—where he had been a fine, upstanding member of the community and church, I might add—and Sarah King's mother was the daughter of Thomas King, whose mother was one of the children of Thomas Prence's daughter—or was she a cousin? I seem to lose track there somewhere. . . ." Aunt Hetty scowled at her notes. "But as you all know, Mr. Prence came to Plymouth the second winter of its colonization, was eventually governor of the whole colony, and took for his wife the daughter of William Bradford."

It all seemed a little tenuous to Augusta, who tried to look interested.

John's eyes were warm and steady. "I think of you all the time," he said. "It's worse when you're out of town. I long for you, the sound of your voice, the feel of your hair." He touched her hair, followed the shape of her face with his hand.

"Mary Elizabeth Crosby has a genealogy done by her grandmother, and she's been able to verify it all by the church records of births and marriages in Plymouth and Rockford."

"Rockford?" Aunt Clara asked. "Why Rockford?"

Aunt Hetty's face showed her pleasure in this question for which she'd been waiting. "Because Waterford used to *be* Rockford—its north parish."

"Why, I didn't know that!" breathed Aunt Clara.

"The two parishes separated when their population had grown too large to administer from one location. Mary Elizabeth has a paper—a letter, really—telling about it and how relieved everyone was to be rid of the south parish, which was so hard to get to at annual meeting time."

She could not stay long; she was supposed to be visiting Emmaline, and Mrs. Snow would wonder where she was; time was racing by.

"My father's carriage barn is closed up," she whispered to John in the Snows' stable. "The horses are farmed out for the winter. No one is around. Meet me there tomorrow, John! Tomorrow night! We won't have to hurry, to rush, oh, meet me," she pleaded, her longing for him turning over its sharp-edged knife within her.

"What's Mary Elizabeth Crosby got to do with it?" Aunt Ellen asked. "You make it sound like she's the Delphic oracle."

Aunt Hetty frowned at such flippancy.

"Why, she's a King—same as us! Three generations back, her great-grandmother and our great-grandmother were sisters."

"Which great-grandmother?" Aunt Clara asked eagerly, to make up for Aunt Ellen's lack of awe.

"Great-grandmother King. Our grandfather's grandmother. The Merricks, you see, are direct descendants of the Kings; Mary Elizabeth is also a King, through the lineage of the grandmother I just told you about. We share the same heritage, all of us, don't you see."

"So don't the rest of Waterford," Cousin King yawned.

"Exactly," said Aunt Hetty brightly. "A little digging about reveals that all Waterford, at one time or another, merges lines of descent. But the King line is the most distinguished! The Kings were very important to the early settlement of Rockford, and right on through its history, Kings have played a leading role in its development. And you might be interested to know that not only are we their descendants through our father but also that our dear, departed Kingsley was a King not only through his father, but he was a King on his mother's side as well!"

"He was?" Mama exclaimed. "What makes you think that?"

Aunt Hetty smiled at her meaningfully. "Why, we owe it all to Cousin Nate here. His grandparents came to the north parish and stayed but their sisters and brothers remained in the south parish, ultimately to become the ancestors of Susan Slater of West Waterford."

"Well, I declare," declared Cousin King. Mama appeared especially pleased to learn that Susan Slater of West Waterford belonged to the clan of Kings. Between Mama and Aunt Hetty a significant glance was exchanged, a conspiracy acknowledged, set, sealed.

"Who was our mother related to?" Aunt Clara asked.

"The Hall family. Her mother was Olive Snow, whose father married a Hall lady—and the Halls, I must remind you, in their time owned all the mills in West Waterford and prospered greatly."

"How about our other grandmother? Grandfather Merrick's wife?"

"Oh, that's very interesting indeed, and somewhat of a mystery, too. Mysteries are so much fun, don't you think?" She spoke in Augusta's direction and seemed to require an answer.

"Oh, very," replied Augusta dutifully.

"I can't meet you in your father's barn." John looked as though he would like to laugh but could not.

"Why not!" she had begged, and John kissed her, a kiss that threatened to become much more; he broke away.

"That's why," he said. "Oh, Christ, that's why."

"I don't care," she cried. "It doesn't matter!" And she sought John's lips with her own, to further excite him, to tantalize him, to lure him, if she could, so far past his self-control that he would not be able to regain it. . . .

*"Stop it, sweetheart," he said gently, firmly, and held
her, helpless, slightly away from himself, and she
thought she might die. . . .*

"Our Grandfather, Elijah Merrick, married Mary Deems
of Providence, Rhode Island."

"However did he find Grandmother in Providence?" Aunt
Ellen wondered. "From what you say, Hetty, Waterford
people consistently married within the town. Certainly for the
most part they have, right to the present."

"The record is very obscure," Aunt Hetty confessed, "since
Mary Deems is not of Plymouth stock. But I have reason to
believe her lineage was very distinguished; her mother's
family were a fine Quaker couple, and she was an intimate
friend of one Elizabeth Warden of Yarmouth—none other
than the forebear of our own Wardens' family line. Here is a
Bible," Aunt Hetty pulled it out of the box, "inscribed thus:
'With deep affection and the hope of grace from Elizabeth
Warden to Molly Deems.' It is evident that Mrs. Warden and
our grandmother were fast companions."

*"It does matter," he said. "I'm not going to com-
promise you in your father's barn or anywhere else. And
I'm not going to take the chance of getting you pregnant, either. When we marry, Augusta, it will be because
we want to—not because we have to."*

*"I'm sorry," she quavered. "I'm behaving badly. For-
give me, John. I meant it, but I didn't mean to."*

*"I know," he smiled, and fell quiet for a moment. "I
think we're nearing the end of the line, Augusta."*

"Grandfather was friendly with the Wardens, too, though I
don't know how it came about, Yarmouth being so far away.
But he must have met Grandmother through them; unfortunately no record of the marriage is entered in the parish
books. We just have to fit the pieces together as best we can.
But here," Aunt Hetty dived into the box, and removed two
dull and lackluster porringers. "These have come down to us
through our grandmother. On the bottom is engraved the initials 'H.P.' which, of course, are not hers—but may have
been her mother's."

"What makes you think so?" Mama asked.

"Why, because I found them in the attic, under a loose

floorboard, wrapped in a hankie that had her initials embroidered on it—MDM."

"They aren't very attractive," Martha, Cousin King's wife, remarked, fingering the porringers. She was obviously very bored.

"They are pure pewter," Aunt Hetty said. "Properly polished they will be very attractive." Again Hetty dived into the box. "But this necklace is lovely, even you will admit that, Martha." She held it up, a ruby pendant rich as blood, gleaming darkly.

"I certainly will," Martha exclaimed, reaching for it.

"It belonged to our grandmother, though it must have been given her by Grandfather after their marriage, since Quakers aren't given to wearing jewels. Grandmother became a Congregationalist," she added vaguely.

"Where did you find these things?" Mama asked, taking the ruby from Martha. "This is quite valuable."

"It was at Millicent Snow's with a note wrapped around it saying that it belonged once to Grandmother."

"Did Mandy have the Bible?"

"No, that was in the Blakes' attic."

"Why are all these things scattered about Waterford?" Mama asked.

"I am convinced," Aunt Hetty said loftily, "and this is the conclusion of the other members of the historic society, that our grandfather, when he retired, wished to divest himself of the trappings of vanity in order to do what he believed to be the Lord's work—the building of the Universalist society. He sold everything he had—modestly, too, I think. He was a King in the finest of our family's tradition. He never faltered from doing his duty as he saw it, and our grandmother helped him in the performance of that duty in every way that she could. She sold her jewels."

No one, it seemed, ever did anything to besmirch the family integrity. Augusta stirred restlessly.

"Well, it's true that your grandmother did help your grandfather, and did sell all her jewelry," said Cousin Nate. "But somehow I don't believe she did it to attain spiritual perfection."

"Why don't you think so?" Aunt Hetty asked sharply.

"Because of remarks my mother used to make. She was your grandfather's sister, and she knew your grandmother pretty well. I don't personally remember her at all, but my mother did, and when your grandfather set up a store here, in this house, and made your grandmother run it, my mother used to say it served Molly Merrick right."

"She ran a store here?" Aunt Hetty's voice echoed her disappointment in this mundane contribution to the work of the Lord.

"They had to eat," Nate pointed out. "Every penny they had went down with your grandfather's ship, *Sweet Charity*. I can remember my mother saying that charity was all Molly Merrick deserved, and not sweet, either."

"Surely you must be mistaken, Nate," Aunt Hetty frowned. "Though, of course, the new religious society did stir up a certain amount of animosity, as causes of righteousness often do."

"Hadn't to do with the church," Nate said briefly. "My mother said Molly Deems was a witch who cast a spell over everyone, and hoodwinked everybody. But I could be wrong," he admitted hastily at the dismay on Hetty's face. "Perhaps I'm not remembering it right at all."

"Her name was Mary," Aunt Hetty said stiffly, as though this was sufficient proof, indeed, that Nate had remembered it wrong.

"Molly was a common diminutive then," Nate persisted feebly. "A name like that would have gone into the records as Mary, in any case."

But Aunt Hetty no longer cared to consider Cousin Nate's contributions, which did not please her. "I think you'll all be interested to see what other artifacts turned up in the attics of Waterford," she sniffed. She returned to the box, turning slightly away from Cousin Nate as she did so. "These all belonged to Elijah and Molly Merrick, virtually given away by them to free their spirits for the Lord's work." One after another she drew from the box a fine porcelain mug, a blown-glass vase, a half-dozen bright serving spoons, and an enormous ladle with a handle like the stem of a violin.

"Why, Grandfather must have been extraordinarily rich once," Mama exclaimed at the sight of such wealth. "And to think he gave it all away!" She fingered the ladle with a knowing touch, for Mama was accustomed to fine things. "When you come right down to think about it, Kingsley carried forward the family tradition beautifully," she said with satisfaction. "He often had to make his way against heavy opposition, but that never deterred him, and now because of his foresight and integrity of purpose we have a library and a railroad and a church in excellent condition. . . ." She appeared to lean back in her chair, as though she were replete, but of course Mama's back did not touch the chair, because Mama never forgot she was a lady. "Imagine!" she mused happily. "Straight from Plymouth! Right off the Mayflower!" She sighed. "I've just had the most wonderful idea," she said. "And I owe it all to you, Hetty. As soon as I get back to Boston I'm going to order reams of new stationery, and I'll have it embossed with the name Kingsland Manor. In script, simple bronze-colored script. Very elegant, don't you think?"

"Superb," breathed Aunt Hetty. Aunt Clara seemed too awestruck to speak; Aunt Ellen's face was inscrutable, and Augusta's own must have reflected her inability to give this the respectful consideration Mama believed it warranted.

"Referring to the house and grounds in Waterford," Mama said to her, a small tone of impatience edging her voice. "But of course! I must say so! You're quite right, darling. I shall have Waterford, Mass., inscribed also."

"I'm not sure a manor exactly describes our house, Mama," Augusta said.

Mama mouthed the words, testing on her own tongue whether it was an apt description or not.

"Perhaps you're right," she agreed. "Perhaps I've let my enthusiasm run away with me. Kingsland will be enough. Very suitable, too. A tribute both to your father and to our mutual ancestry. How splendid that he bore a derivative of the old family name. Sally is getting a genealogy of the Leverings worked up," Mama reflected. "Hetty, your researches have come at a most auspicious time! Kingsland! We must, all of us, always call it that. Soon it'll be a habit."

She looked happily around the room.

"If we see one another much more, something is going to happen that we might regret. It's about time, I think, for me to speak to your mother."

"Now?" she gulped, going hot and cold all over at the prospect. "This Thanksgiving?"

"In the spring, by God," he said. "No point letting her badger you about me all the winter—but come spring, with you nearly done with school, Augusta, it's then I shall claim you." Then he kissed her again, softly and gently that time, with hurt of a different kind rising in their throats, the pain of promise, of an end in sight that was as yet far away, in the spring of the year.

She would see him tomorrow in Emmaline's barn if nothing happened to prevent it, and then she would not see him until April—it was like the bottom dropping out of a basket, just thinking of that long, long time, impossibly long. But tomorrow when she might see him again was incredibly distant, too, and she squirmed imperceptibly in her chair at Aunt Ellen's, dragging her attention back to the discussion at hand, which, expectedly, was about the heroic, illustrious, noble clan of Kings.

The array of cards was spread on the table like a fan, carefully separated one from another until the ink on them dried. Soft, bright, light washes filled their backgrounds, with holly leaves or fir trees, bows or candles, wreaths or simple seascapes carefully superimposed by Aunt Clara, and across the top of each, in copperplate script, was lightly traced "Greetings of the Season." Aunt Ellen was laboriously filling in the letters now with an exquisite touch; the light was fading fast in the back parlor and Aunt Ellen was bending closer and closer to her work.

"You'll hurt your eyes, Auntie," Augusta said in concern as she hung up her coat, a concern which might, if she worked hard enough at it, replace the lost, lonely feeling that stalked her as she'd walked back from Emmaline's knowing she would not see John for nearly six months.

It's too much, she cried deeply within. *I can't be apart from him for so long!*

"Can't stop now," Aunt Ellen murmured, placing a finished card at the end of the fan and straightening her back which clearly was bothering her. "I want your mother to have a sample of each before you go back to Boston."

"Well, here," Augusta said. "Let me finish. I can do that as easily as you can." Firmly she took the pen from Aunt Ellen's nearly paralyzed fingers.

"I'm not sure your mother will like you to," Aunt Ellen protested weakly. "She wouldn't want you to strain your eyes, either."

"She needn't know about it."

Mama was visiting the Pollards' and would not return until after teatime, and the cards would be finished by then, and when Mama got home again to Commonwealth Avenue she'd casually toss them onto the drawing room table where her friends could not help noticing them, exclaiming over them—for they were pretty—and they would ask Mama if

Aunt Clara could be persuaded to make some more, perhaps two dozen, just like that one with the cunning dogs on it, or that one with a wreath tied to the front door. And Mama would say casually that she'd find out how busy Aunt Clara was, which she had said every year since Aunt Clara began making them (this would be the fourth) and that Aunt Clara charged ten cents apiece for them which made her feel important, don't you know, and gave her something to do that was constructive, gave some sense of direction to an otherwise aimless life with no family of her own in it, don't you know, and for the next month Aunt Clara and Aunt Ellen would labor like any women in any sweatshop anywhere for the pennies the cards would yield. They insisted on doing it! They enjoyed it! And yet Aunt Clara's nerves became bad around Christmas time, and Aunt Ellen's back hurt her. . . .

Augusta dabbed the pen into the ink pot, described an elaborate G on the next card with little spokes here and there and appropriate curls and then knew she couldn't do it. It was too much, too little, her heart was ready to burst and her body, too, and copperplate required more discipline than she could dredge up after an hour with John Bradley, which required all the discipline she had, the two of them carefully avoiding too direct a confrontation which could lead to actions they might regret.

"What will you do this winter?" she had asked, reaching for something—anything—to keep them steady. "Surely it's too cold to go fishing. How will you spend the time? What shall I picture you being busy at?"

"Why, I'll build my barn," he said. "And in the evening I'll sit before the fire and mend my tools and make new ones, roast chestnuts and construct little ships in bottles to sell to the summer folks."

"Can you make a little ship?" she asked. "In a bottle?"

"I surely can. My father taught me how—he was pretty good at it. I've never been to sea, but I can name all the sails and rig them properly, too.

"When we are married, Augusta, you'll have to do your share. What will you make, as we sit before the fire, to sell to the city folk?" He was teasing, but he was serious, too.

"Oh, I shall make—apple dolls," she declared. "I'll make little men mending nets and little ladies with cats

338

*on their laps and corn cob pipes in their mouths and
you'll make a little box to put them in, decorated appropriately—a wharf in the background for the man and a
black iron stove for the lady. You ought to whittle,
John. City people dote on whittled things. Little birds
and rabbits and such."*

*"I shall whittle," he laughed. "Then we shall have a
cup of tea and I'll go out and get more wood for the fire
and bank it for the night." His eyes caught hers evenly.
"And then we'll go to bed upstairs, under the eaves, and
listen to the winter wind. It never stops."*

*"I know," she reminded him. "I've been here in the
winter. I've been here quite a few winters."*

*"Not in a little house with only the roof between you
and a storm."*

*"You shall be between me and any storm," she said
softly. They had stared at one another; his eyes had
golden flecks in them and were kind and thoughtful and
he loved her with them. . . .*

"Those cards will never get done at that rate," Aunt Ellen
observed.

"Auntie, may I ask you something personal?" She bent
over the card so that Aunt Ellen couldn't see her face.

"You can ask," Aunt Ellen said, leaning back in her chair
with her eyes closed, slowly flexing her hands. "I don't
promise to answer."

"You lived here in this house with Uncle James, didn't
you, when you were young?"

"Yes," said Aunt Ellen. "Right here."

"And Uncle James taught school?"

"The Academy. Not the school."

Yes, there was a difference, but Augusta had forgotten it
because the Academy had been gone for so long.

"Did you like living here in the winter?"

"Yes," said Aunt Ellen. "I was very happy here."

"It wasn't dull, or uninteresting?"

"No," said Aunt Ellen. "Not at all."

"That was a long time ago."

"Quite a while now."

"Do you think it's much different today? I mean from
when you were young?"

"You mean, when James was alive." Aunt Ellen's eyes
were open now, watching Augusta.

"Yes, that's what I meant." She had not wanted to say so for fear Aunt Ellen would become tearful as she so often did when James Duncan was remembered.

"I can't see that there would be much difference," Aunt Ellen said. "James and I lived quietly, as the winter population does now. We were just starting our family and had little time for anything else."

"And you liked it."

"Yes," said Aunt Ellen. "What is it that you want to know, Augusta?"

How badly she wanted to talk, to confess her confusions, her needs, her hopes, her despairs. Could she trust Aunt Ellen? Who better than Aunt Ellen would understand the perplexities that beset Augusta now—who better than Aunt Ellen, Mama's own sister!

"I've decided that I'd like to live here all the time," she said, and once having said it, was glad. "When I'm through with school I want to return here to Waterford, and never leave."

"Oh?"

"Mama will be disappointed."

"Yes," agreed Aunt Ellen thoughtfully. "That she will."

"But perhaps she'd be disappointed less if I could assure her that life here in Waterford is not dull, that it has many things to recommend it—things that you yourself could vouch for."

"Unfortunately, your mother and I don't have the same tastes, Augusta. I doubt that my recommendation would make much difference to her. For that matter, I don't think she'd agree to your staying here, either."

"I might do it anyway. I might marry John Bradley, and live here with him."

"John Bradley?" Aunt Ellen searched her mind for the Bradley boy. "The one who works for Captain Blake on his weir?"

"He has done that. Now he's going to raise cranberries."

"You mean he's going to live here in Waterford for the rest of his life?" There was a disturbed quality about Aunt Ellen's voice, furrows appearing on her face.

"Why, yes. Just as you and Uncle James did. John is skilled as a carpenter and picks up quite a lot of work."

"Indeed," Aunt Ellen said, her voice admitting no expression now.

Desperately Augusta plunged on. "He has bought some

340

land down the street, and is starting a cranberry bog, and he'll build himself a house nearby—a house for himself and me, Aunt Ellen! Much as I love Father's house, I don't need to live in it to be happy. In fact, I don't even want to—but I'm terribly afraid that Mama will never understand it."

"You love this man, John Bradley?"

"Oh, I do, Aunt Ellen!" Her eyes nearly filled to overflowing just at the thought of how well she loved him! "He is so right for me! When I'm with John, I never have to wonder what to say next or wonder what he'll think of me when I speak my mind. When I'm with him, it's like my heart were wide open, and my soul, everything that I am is like a flower reaching out for the sun! It's strange, but it's true—I can't explain why, but we have always known one another, always loved one another."

Aunt Ellen stared.

"I don't care if I live in a shanty," she burst out. "Or a houseboat, or a tent—as long as I'm living with John. But, of course, that isn't in Mama's scheme of things for me."

"No, it certainly isn't." Aunt Ellen continued to stare thoughtfully, meditatively. "I wonder, Augusta, if you realize that should you elect a shanty or a houseboat for yourself, you'll be electing it for your mother as well."

"Certainly I won't!"

"You think not?"

"Mama has said so! It's only a question of maintaining her standards and upholding her values, Aunt Ellen, and I am naturally reluctant to flatly deny them—which she will believe I am doing when I tell her that I want to marry John."

"I gather, then, that you believe your mother to be at least financially secure at the present time?"

"Why, yes." There was a sickly fear growing in the pit of her stomach, because it was the second time, in effect, that Aunt Ellen had asked this question. "She told me so!"

"Unfortunately, my dear, she is lying."

A ferocious pain clamped her temples; she could not breathe. Aunt Ellen seemed cold, remote, detached, and Augusta in that moment hated her, wished swiftly that she had never spoken, never asked, never sought reassurance from her mother's sister.

"There is no money, Augusta. None! Your mother is living on borrowed time, waiting for the day you marry well and her burdens are transferred to a stronger back. We, all of us, are waiting."

"You must be mistaken," she gasped, the palms of her hands wet and numb. "There must be something. She told me there was enough to last her lifetime, but not mine, so it fell to me to hold onto Papa's house and land for another generation."

"Oh, well there might have been, had your mother seen fit to conserve her resources!" Aunt Ellen snorted, and suddenly the face that had been cold softened, became gentle, tender, compassionate. "I'm truly sorry, Augusta, if you love the Bradley boy as well as you say you do, because the choices ahead of you are cruel. Either you relinquish this young man, or you destroy your mother."

"Destroy?" she whispered.

"Destroy," Aunt Ellen repeated firmly. "But it's all your mother's doing, Augusta. All because of her selfishness, her vanity. Had she been content to live simply, here in Waterford, after your dear father died, there might well have been enough to last her a lifetime. Why, she spends more in a year than I do in ten: rental of a city house, servants to run it and to run the place here, a fancy school for you, clothing and amusements appropriate to her life with her fancy friends." Aunt Ellen sighed. "I see you are confused, Augusta, so I will tell you plainly as possible. Your papa died before his coach line could succeed. He sold his stocks before the crash of '73 and put the yield into the new business, got backing in Port Elizabeth for the rest. But he was plagued by troubles from the minute he arrived there. Drought and disease to decimate the horses, the long road to Kimberly—700 miles of it, Augusta, most of it not a road at all. Unreliable native help whom he couldn't trust—at one point he was even driving the coaches himself. The strain was enormous, the demands he made on himself relentless, and when he caught pneumonia he didn't stop, because he was not a quitter. Nothing had ever defeated him before! When I got there he was a sick man indeed and it became clear, even to him, that he was not going to get well. He sold the line from his sickbed for what he could get, repaid his debts, but there wasn't much left of his own funds. There was the money in the Boston bank that he'd left there for your mother's use, a substantial amount, Augusta, if not princely. Some insurance. Your mother wasn't destitute! She could have made a decision that would have made all the difference in the world to you now. She could have stayed right here, returned you to district school, lived frugally, and she'd still have a lot of that money. But she did

342

not. She returned to Boston, as though her funds would never run out."

Augusta frowned. Why had Mama done that? And she remembered the humiliation, the shame, and the anxiety over Caroline's marriage that was roaring then like a locomotive at Mama's heels; Mama had labored long and hard over her Back Bay friends. It would have been difficult indeed to reap their sustained loyalty while living frugally in Waterford where Caroline's memory stared her in the face, where the humiliation of Caroline haunted every corner like a ghost while Mama's friends were living elsewhere, living the life Mama had always craved.

Indeed, she had returned to Boston!

Aunt Ellen drove ruthlessly on. "Your father, to repay my kindness in caring for him, deeded this house to me. Your mother wanted me to sell it; I and your aunts and Lizzie should come to live at your house and she could continue her merry way in Boston, the proceeds of the sale safe in the bank for her to use. As if I would! This house, after all, is all I have left of James and the memory of my two dear sons. All I have left to give Lizzie. When your mother no longer contributed to our maintenance we managed, somehow, between James's insurance and Hetty's salary as a teacher and Clara's art lessons and these—" Aunt Ellen made a sweeping gesture toward the cards. "And when last year your mother's lawyer in Boston wrote to tell her that her account was disastrously low, I even offered to help. I told her I would open my house to summer boarders and give her what money I made doing it—Hetty was aghast at the mere thought, I might add—and so was your mother! It would lower her in the estimation of her friends, betray the fact that there was not enough Merrick money to help her own sister, reduce the chance of you, Augusta, finding a suitable husband, so she went up to Boston herself and raised a mortgage on your father's house from the president of Hartland's Express. She asked me to say nothing, so as not to ruin your chance of a good marriage—naturally I have not! Yes, Augusta, your mother is waiting with bated breath for you to marry well. Indeed she is waiting—at Kingsland!"

Aunt Ellen laughed harshly at Mama's pretentions and Augusta gaped, her world now suddenly riddled with subterranean tunnels honeycombed beneath her feet. Mama, returning from Boston in a flush of gaiety, determination, tension, telling Augusta why it was important to marry suitably. . . . But it was not a matter of choosing or not choosing Mama's standards. It had never been. It had never been a matter of perpetuating Mama's traditions for the upcoming generation, but of maintaining Mama now, right away!

It was a question of leaving Mama destitute.

"How much money has my mother got, Aunt Ellen?"

Auntie shrugged. "Who's to know? She spends it so fast! She raised five thousand dollars, but of course she has continued to live exactly as she did before, so that there would be nothing in the way of your marrying that silly Levering boy or that stuck-up Thomas Warden."

"Yes, she's said she hoped I'd marry well," Augusta said miserably. Suddenly, unwillingly, Mama seemed gallant. Gallant in trying to hold everything together against the day that Augusta would save it all for her, holding out against her sisters, her creditors, Caroline's defection, Papa's death, and the diminution of his fortune, waiting for Augusta, who had decided already to defect, too.

No! No! she thought. *There had to be another way out!*

She remembered John Bradley's mouth, his hands, his eyes. *Mama,* she cried. *I have tried to give him up. I have tried already! I can't!*

She was numb all over by now. Nothing within had any feeling whatever, and even her mind was numb, refusing to consider what Aunt Ellen had exposed so ruthlessly in her gentle voice.

"It's all her fault," that voice was saying now. "If she weren't so frivolous, it never would have happened. Gladly would I open my house to boarders, Augusta. Don't worry about us. I wouldn't worry about your mother, either. You have your own life to live. She has her comeuppance due her!" Aunt Ellen nodded in satisfaction.

But Mama was not vain or frivolous. She was—driven.

"Here," Aunt Ellen said, reaching for the paintbrush. "Let me work on those now. You'd probably like to lie down before supper, wouldn't you?"

"Yes," she said. "I think I would."

"I don't envy you, Augusta," Aunt Ellen sighed. "Regardless of what your mother deserves, she is your mother."

There was no reply possible or necessary; wearily she climbed the flight of stairs that seemed so long, to let herself into the dusk-filled room that she and Mama shared. The light of the November day was fading to lemon yellow in the

344

western sky, and it made the contents of the chamber stark, its color gone and only the brass knobs on the andirons gleaming. Now in the pure harsh light it was a simple room, such as might be hers if she married John Bradley and lived with him in a house low to the ground and edging out the numbness was the certainty that a life without luxuries could be fresh and pure and uncluttered if that was what one willed it to be. She thought of John, of his smile, of the little scar near his left eye where a dog had bitten him once, he told her. She thought of John, whose voice she loved to hear, whose large, strong hands were gentle, whose arms she longed for now, and whose life, direct and fresh and honest, she longed to share. . . .

And she thought of Mama, reduced to relative poverty so that Augusta could have the privilege of choosing it. She thought of Mama, reaching for the stars of Beacon Hill society that she had loved when she was young, and which the Leverings and the Thayers and the Sinclaires stood for in a more available and contemporary manner. Yes, Mama welcomed them to her house which she had christened Kingsland, and their company meant so much to her that she had gambled with all she possessed to keep it, and then borrowed more. . . .

That loan was insurmountable! Augusta compelled herself to quiet, to lucidity, to logic. The loan.

Say, for instance, that it could be paid back, between Aunt Ellen's boarders and John's cranberries and the sale of a few articles in the house—the piano, perhaps, and the silver. With the loan repaid, Mama could still have the house and John could see to its maintenance. If Mama lived very, very simply . . .

The house would then be a shell, without servants, Mama inside doing all its work herself with scarcely any time left to enjoy herself. Augusta pictured Mama, having to give up the winter circuit with the Back Bay group, waiting patiently, hopefully in Waterford for them to come to her. Waiting for their invitations to come to Boston to visit them, counting pennies to see if she had sufficient train fare. Genteel poverty was not Mama's style! Never would Mama see it as desirable nor even bearable, nor was there any reason why she should. It did not reflect her soul, and it never would, and scrimp and save and sacrifice as they might, Augusta and John would not be able to give Mama the means to live in the house as it should be lived in. Even if the loan were somehow repaid, Mama living in a shell, empty and hollow, was a problem unresolved. . . .

Could Mama be made to abandon her destiny?

Was, after all, the sale of Papa's house the more logical answer?

Finding a buyer might not be so easy, not with a depression in progress—but there'd be one eventually. Mama could, if she had to, live with John and Augusta while waiting for a buyer, using the balance of the money she'd borrowed to pay the interest to Mr. Livingstone, who would surely be generous and who surely would wait until the house was sold. When it was, why, Mama could buy herself a smaller one, of which there were quite a few in Waterford these days. There would be money left over, especially if Mama would settle for a really modest house.

And Mama would hate it. Modesty was not one of her more outstanding attributes. . . .

You have your own life to live, Aunt Ellen had said. Don't worry about her. She has her comeuppance due her.

But Aunt Ellen did not understand Mama. She believed Mama was only putting on airs—while Augusta, sadly, knew better. Mama was reaching for life itself, as she best understood it. Even should the house be sold handsomely, the mortgage on it paid, Mama with enough funds to live in comfort in a more simple house of her own, it would be a terrible blow, an admission that Mama was not entirely the person she pretended to be. All the folks in Waterford whom Mama had deemed unable to adapt to her ways would surely laugh up their sleeves at her. Mama would no longer reign at Kingsland, and everyone who had been excluded from it would relish the opportunity to cut them. And perhaps her more intimate friends in the Back Bay would withdraw, too, their enthusiasm waning because of having nothing left to attract them.

How loyal, really loyal, were Mama's friends? How much would Mama lose if Papa's house were gone? How much of what Mama wanted for herself, how much of what she had, was tied indestructibly to Kingsland?

Not wanting to at all, she was weeping slowly, painful, hot tears that rose up and spilled over when she closed her eyes and tried to squeeze them away, her throat aching, her nose starting to run. She willed herself to stop. Tears would alter nothing. Crying did not make John Bradley more attainable and they did not change Mama, nor make her a woman simpler, less sophisticated, willing to revolutionize her life, give over her daughter to a man whose goals were not unlike those that Caroline, in her childlike groping for happiness, had chosen as well. Mama would hardly be willing to do that in any case, let alone the present one in which such a choice risked the loss of everything she valued.

But if the present case did not carry such dire consequences? If Mama weren't in debt, if Kingsland could be held intact for her, if someone could be found who would pay for Mama's life . . . relieving Augusta of its burdens, of the gamble. . . .

If Mama herself were to marry!

If Mama herself married someone "suitable."

If Mama remarried, her financial woes would be gone! Her life and friends would continue as they had always done and Augusta's betrayal would be softened, made less harsh because Mama would be cherished and cared for, she would no longer need her daughter to secure for her what she wanted. She would be able, perhaps, to forgive . . . would it work?

There were not lots of men around of Mama's age, waiting to marry her. But you never knew when one would appear around the corner, especially if you were hunting for him. Perhaps right under their noses was a lonely widower, whom they had entirely overlooked because the thought of an eligible man of Mama's age had never entered their heads! And if Mama had someone else to love, she could more easily let her daughter go.

She'd have to start looking, right away! By spring John was determined to speak to Mama, because school would be over. By then someone would have to be found for Mama to marry, that was all. How much, she wondered, was left of the five thousand dollars? How much time actually was there? She didn't know and couldn't find out because then Mama would know that Augusta was on to her schemes, a confrontation would be forced on the spot without any resources on hand to fight for John Bradley, all of which wouldn't matter if Mama found a rich man to marry and hopefully to love! Yes, she'd have to keep her eyes open was all—look for straws in the wind, hope for the best. Hope something would happen. Something, somehow had to happen or she would have to force Mama to forsake the pride of the Kings, and she surely didn't want to do it! No, sir, there was an alternative, after all. There was another way! And Augusta Merrick readied herself to seek it out.

347

The reception room at Miss Jellison's was merry, with carnations gay in their vases and steam rising from the teapots and ladies chatting to gentlemen and young girls flirting modestly as possible with young boys. Augusta stood by Mama's side talking with Miss Jellison, who admired Mama ferociously and tended to lionize her when she could. Just then Mama was content to be monopolized, letting her eye rove about the hall, nodding, when the occasion demanded it, to acquaintances whom she recognized in the distance, and it was she who first spotted Harold Edgerton only moments before a dozen other eager eyes spotted him, a new, handsome face among other faces beginning to look familiar by this third tea dance. He came in with Sam Anthony, and Sam, a nephew of Miss Jellison who habitually provided young men of his acquaintance for the girls to dance with, immediately led Edgerton in a roundabout way to the side of his aunt (the floor was too crowded to come across directly). Sam properly did not introduce Edgerton to anyone along the way because any young man had to be approved by Miss Jellison before such introductions were appropriate. And so Mama and Augusta were the first to meet him.

"Auntie, may I present Mr. Howard Edgerton from Crofton, Canada? Mr. Edgerton, my aunt, Miss Jellison."

"Crofton, Canada?" Miss Jellison smiled formally, correctly, in case Mr. Edgerton were suitable, completely without warmth in case he were not. "Why, what a distance you have come, Mr. Edgerton."

Edgerton was apparently accustomed to polite society even though he lived on the nigh edge of the world, for he bowed in acknowledgment of Miss Jellison's unasked question and proceeded to set her mind to rest.

"Eight hundred miles," he agreed. "It is certainly a long distance, Miss Jellison. So my father and I have come to Boston for the winter. Having traveled so far to get here, we are not inclined to turn 'round and go home in a hurry!"

"Indeed," Miss Jellison probed.

"We are connected to the banking community of Crofton," Harold Edgerton continued. "And of course, Boston being a banking center, there is much we can learn here. We plan to remain in your delightful city for the winter, even if our business is accomplished before the end of it."

"Boston's gain, I am sure," murmured Miss Jellison, still uncertain of Harold Edgerton but impressed with the idea of a bank.

"Mr. Edgerton had a letter of introduction to Dr. Davenport at Harvard," Sam Anthony put in. "I persuaded him to accompany me here when I met him at Davenport's this afternoon."

This was all the reassurance Miss Jellison needed, for a letter of introduction to any respectable family was sufficient anywhere.

"I do hope you are enjoying your visit, Mr. Edgerton," she smiled warmly now. "Where are you staying, sir?"

"Father and I have engaged a suite at the Parker House," said Edgerton, his eyes on Miss Jellison so as not to commit the indiscretion of glancing at Mama or Augusta, to whom he had not yet been introduced. "We find it very comfortable."

Miss Jellison was terribly impressed by an indefinite stay at the Parker House.

"Indeed," she simpered. "Oh! Forgive my rudeness," she exclaimed, as though the thought had only just that moment occurred to her. "I should like you to meet Mrs. Merrick and her daughter. Mrs. Merrick, may I present Mr. Edgerton of Crofton, Canada?"

Mama shook hands with Edgerton, thoughtfully, cordially. "Miss Merrick, may I introduce Mr. Edgerton?"

Augusta smiled and shook the young man's hand. "Welcome to Boston!"

Edgerton bowed formally at each introduction. "Thank you." He permitted himself a smile. "I'm sure our stay will be a pleasant one."

"Where in Canada is Crofton?" Mama asked.

"In the province of Ontario," he told her. Probably Mama knew where Ontario was and probably Miss Jellison did not, but Miss Jellison would never admit such a thing. "How delightful," she nodded. "Perhaps, Augusta, you would be so kind as to introduce Mr. Edgerton to our other guests?"

"Surely, Miss Jellison. If you will be all right, Mama?"

"Certainly, certainly." Mama made a scattering motion with her hand, as though shooing away chickens. "I'll be fine."

"Well, Mr. Edgerton, if you are up to it, shall we proceed?" She smiled up at Harold Edgerton encouragingly, but he seemed not to need encouragement, modestly secure within the fastness of his own being, undisturbed by the necessity to meet dozens of strangers. He was a nice-looking young man, his beard closely, neatly trimmed, his skin above it clear and without blemish, taut across the prominent bones of his face, his eyes light—not quite blue, she thought—they appeared to appraise and instantly catalogue and correctly classify whatever they beheld, accurate upon first survey; those eyes now swept across the dance floor to encompass those gathered for Miss Jellison's tea dance, and Augusta thought that Harold Edgerton would not be discomfited at all.

Correctly she led him to one group and then another, all of it a laborious process because everyone had the same polite questions to ask of Harold Edgerton from Crofton, Canada, each of which the young man answered with identical gravity. The quartet began its tuning as the last person in the reception room was introduced.

"I hope, Miss Merrick, that you'll allow me to dance with you," Edgerton said. "I've been so busy talking to everyone else that I haven't had a chance to talk with you at all."

"Certainly," she answered, and found that he danced well, considering that he came from another part of the world, which was reflected in his speech, clipped and crisp, not quite a British accent, but not American either.

"Tell me, Mr. Edgerton," she began, dredging up the required conversation. "Being Canadian, do you consider yourself an Englishman?"

"No," he said, quite seriously. "I consider myself a Canadian."

"My father had occasion to meet Australians and South Africans," she struggled. "He said they didn't consider themselves English, either. I was only curious to see if Canadians felt the same way, having been connected with Great Britain that much longer."

"How did your father come to meet so many British subjects?"

"He lived in both places for a time. He ran an express business."

"How interesting," Edgerton nodded. "When did he do these things?"

"Why, quite recently in South Africa, in Port Elizabeth, colony of New Hope, to be exact. And in Melbourne from '54 to '56."

"Was his agency in Melbourne called the Clipper Coach Line?"

"Yes, yes it was! How did you know?"

"There are occasions when Canadians leave our continent

350

to see what's going on elsewhere." Edgerton smiled, and he had a nice smile which, Augusta thought, he did not use often enough. "Your father cut quite a swath in Melbourne before he sold out to Cobb and Company. Friends of my father were there at the time; one was present at a farewell banquet given Mr. Merrick, and it seems he never forgot it! How amazing, don't you think, that I should have heard of him as a boy, and now as a man, I meet his daughter! Your father was highly respected, Miss Merrick. May I ask what he is doing now?"

"He died four years ago." She found that it hurt to say it. "In Port Elizabeth."

"Oh! I am very sorry!" His voice told her that he meant it and was not simply being polite. "I know that it's hard to lose a parent. My mother died two years ago. Father and I still can't get used to it."

Instant tears of sympathy and commiseration sprang to her eyes. She shook her head, to indicate that no further words could possibly add to nor express more fully the profundity of such shared sorrow, and they danced quietly for a brief moment, until it came to her—quite suddenly—that the senior Edgerton was a widower. She continued to look at Harold Edgerton's boiled shirt and the studs marching down its front, a miniscule diamond in each, and glanced at the hand which correctly cradled hers, because she'd have sworn she saw a ring there, before, though she couldn't see it now because of the position of their hands. Were she not mistaken, it was a star sapphire, set in a heavy, chaste gold frame; the Edgertons were spending their time at the Parker House and they were well enough established to simply vacate Crofton for the winter. The Edgertons were rich.

"Actually, one reason we came to Boston this winter was to escape our house at Crofton," Edgerton said after a suitable pause. "Father's bank can easily manage a season without him, and it's surely true that establishing closer rapport with American lines of credit is both sensible and astute and should have been done before. But actually Father needed the interval to pull himself together, and a season in a new atmosphere, I hope, will help to get him moving along again. He has been withdrawn, altogether too quiet, not like himself at all."

"I take it you work with your father."

"Yes," he confirmed. "The bank has been in our family for three generations. It started as a trading post, at which my great-grandfather sold food and clothing and bullets and such which he brought in across the Great Lakes in the clement months. And sometimes of necessity, he extended credit or gave out loans with tracts of land as collateral—security if you wish."

"I expect not everyone could repay their loans," she remarked, now in a good position to know, indeed, that occasionally someone could not pay back a loan.

"How astute of you, Miss Merrick. Indeed, my ancestor was land poor, as they say, until the demand for lumber rose in your country. But tell me of your family," he politely changed the subject. "Are you a Bostonian?"

"Practically speaking, I suppose I am. But we are really Cape Codders; our home is in a small town on Cape Cod, about one hundred miles south and east of Boston."

"East of Boston seems quite wet," he remarked in grave wit, and dutifully she laughed. Really, he was ponderous!

"Do you think this winter in Boston will truly help your papa?"

"Oh, yes, I'm sure it will. Tonight, for instance, he's playing whist at the Oyster League, and he hasn't been interested in any sort of play since Mother passed away."

If the elder Edgerton were admitted to the League, his connections were excellent, and he was no mediocre businessman of obscure breeding. It became important—terribly important—to meet and know Harold Edgerton's father, and the route lay surely through Harold Edgerton himself. Her progress was already good, she was sure, and in the next few minutes she'd have to come to a judgment that could matter a great deal. She must decide on the proper course of action to insure seeing him again, and in Edgerton's case, "proper" more than likely was the exact key. He was extremely proper, and although other girls with whom he might dance that afternoon would simper and flirt, she guessed she'd have to gamble on being strictly proper, too, and hope she'd assessed him correctly. He must not be allowed to forget her, nor must he forget the sympathetic bond already sprung up between them.

"I regret," she murmured, "that this dance is nearly over. I could tell you about so many interesting things in Boston that would entertain your father and help to lift his sorrow. Let me see if I can't quickly think of a few. The Lowell lectures, are marvelous, and a lot of music is played in Boston now, some of it excellent—my mother is the best judge of that, actually. She is an accomplished artist at the piano, even writes music when she has the time. Opera and theater, of course . . ."

"Perhaps you could tell me more upon another occasion," Edgerton said, and beneath his courteous words she believed she detected a trace of eagerness. "I know it's not done, but since I am a foreigner perhaps my gaucheness would excuse my asking you to dance again with me."

"It might excuse you, Mr. Edgerton," she laughed. "But it wouldn't excuse me."

"No, no, of course it wouldn't," he said quickly. A faint blush tinted his fine skin. "If an apology is in order, I hope you'll accept mine."

The music stopped.

"No apologies, please," she said gently, with a suggestion of sympathy for his position. "Most certainly you have not offended *me*." She smiled, seductively as she dared.

Fortunately Bax Levering had arrived just then, so that there was no awkwardness nor hunting about for something to say that would not break the subtlety of her remark, which suggested that she both recognized his invitation as a token of esteem, and welcomed it even while etiquette required her to put it in its proper place (they had only been introduced, after all, this very afternoon!). Still smiling, she introduced Bax and acknowledged Edgerton's bow of departure with a small tilt of her head, not a formal nod but an informal dismissal, a friendly one, and as she turned to Bax for the dance she saw, from the corner of her eye, that Harold Edgerton had not immediately asked another girl to be his partner, but had retreated momentarily to the sidelines with Sam Anthony.

"You're late, you rascal," she said to Bax. "Here I've been looking everywhere for you."

"I'd judge you hadn't even noticed," he said with a pout in his voice that was not reflected in his face because he'd been taught better. "Who is this fellow Edgerton?" he demanded suspiciously, and Augusta judged that her friendliness to Edgerton was apparent indeed. Fervently she hoped she had not overdone it, that Bax was only hypersensitive.

"Visiting dignitary," she suggested.

"Looked like a pompous ass," Bax said indiscreetly.

"Why, Mr. Levering!" she laughed. "Your language!"

"I suppose I'd better apologize."

"No need," she said gently. "We surely know one another

353

well enough—and surely always will—to drop the formalities. Don't you think so?"

"Why, I suppose we do," he said in some confusion, unable to decipher her intent. A promise? A subterfuge? A suggestion? He gave up trying to understand Augusta Merrick, just as she intended he should.

"A pleasant dance," he remarked. "And a good crowd, too. Sam Anthony must get paid a dollar for each fellow he totes in."

She laughed, relieved for the reprieve from Bax Levering's interrogations, and saw that Harold Edgerton was dancing with Maddie Pettingill, whose competition never worried her. "Sam will be a rich man one day," she said merrily to Bax. "More power to him!"

A sheaf of roses arrived the following morning, with Edgerton's card enclosed.

"My, my," Mama breathed. "Isn't that nice!"

"Isn't it?" Augusta agreed. "You're better at arranging than I am, Mama. Won't you take them?"

"Nonsense. They aren't mine to begin with, and besides you arrange flowers very well, Augusta. You must have more confidence in yourself. Was Mr. Edgerton pleasant?"

"Very," she said. "Well mannered, too."

The roses were expensive, and fresh loads of them arrived every other day for two weeks, to replace one another in fast-wilting, brilliant succession.

"Oh, my," exclaimed Mama. "I think you have made quite an impression, Augusta."

"Mr. Edgerton's doing all right for himself, too," she laughed, tossing them into the vase with abandon, now that she was getting to be an old hand at rose arrangement. "Do you suppose I ought to drop him a note at the Parker House, expressing our appreciation?"

Mama frowned. "Normally, of course, you wouldn't. . . ."

"I'll bide my time, then," Augusta said quickly. She must play it exactly right, because if she did, John would be there at the other end. . . .

"We wouldn't want Mr. Edgerton to get discouraged," Mama suggested just as quickly. "After all, he's a stranger here."

"If not acknowledging the roses is the proper response then that's what I'll do," Augusta said firmly. After all, however

354

slight was her acquaintance with Harold Edgerton, it was more extensive than Mama's. Harold was proper!

A brief, formal note was at last enclosed. "If I may be permitted to call at your convenience?"

They decided on the following Saturday afternoon, and Augusta labored an hour over her reply.

Dear Mr. Edgerton [she wrote]. First let me express my appreciation for the roses you have so thoughtfully provided us. They are exquisite and we have enjoyed them to the fullest.

It was a little strong, but she let it go.

My mother and I would be pleased to receive both you and your father at our house for tea, Saturday next at three-thirty P.M.

Should she put in an extra line about his papa, how glad the Merricks would be to meet and entertain him?

My mother will, at that time, cause to be concocted cranberry tartlets, a delicacy native to our own Cape Cod, with which you may not be familiar but which you will both enjoy, I am sure.

The senior Edgerton could scarcely refuse to come, knowing that the hostess was going to extra effort on his behalf!

Looking forward to welcoming you and your father, I remain

Sincerely yours,
Augusta Merrick.

Should she copy it on Kingsland stationery, recently arrived? Perhaps inappropriate because she was not writing from Waterford, yet it would give an appropriately elegant impression, suggesting that the widowed Mrs. Merrick lived in some splendor and comfort not unlike the Edgertons' own, and would surely not be fortune hunting!

She did it, and was pleased to receive instant acknowledgment of an acceptance by both.

Now she began to understand her mother's anxieties of the recent years! Now she glimpsed the concern of the parent for

355

the child, for the daughter who must make a good impression at all costs, but who must not be told to do so, in case she balked or became clumsy for trying too hard. No, the parent must sit back in an attitude of genial relaxation, exuding confidence that the course of nature would naturally direct the attention, nay, the affection, of the proper people to one another, and Augusta found herself waiting for the doorbell to ring that Saturday afternoon, so tense and wrought up that she wondered if she had the necessary stamina to carry on with it at all, worried because Mama had chosen to wear purple, not her best color, and was carrying herself with the decorum of a dowager ready to inspect the young man who intruded himself in their midst—when all the time another, older suitor would be present whom Mama, her gaze directed toward young Edgerton, would not bother to notice.

She had not yet told Mama that the senior Edgerton was a widower, but she wondered now if she ought to, so that Mama would try to be a little charming; thought the better of it, in case this knowledge had the opposite effect, stopped herself on the brink, uncertain, flustered, apprehensive as Patricia let father and son in downstairs and ushered them up to the drawing room. *Here we go,* she thought, and advanced to meet them.

"How nice to see you again, Mr. Edgerton," she exclaimed with carefully moderated pleasure, and found her jitters gone because the curtain had opened, the play was on, and the stage fright vanished because one need not worry any longer, one need not anticipate. She shook Harold Edgerton's hand.

"May I present my father?" Harold asked courteously. "Father, I should like to introduce Miss Merrick."

The elder Mr. Edgerton wore pince-nez, which he instantly removed and tucked into his vest pocket and took Augusta's hand warmly in his own. "A pleasure to meet you, my dear Miss Merrick," Mr. Edgerton said in a firm, well-modulated voice. *Ah,* she thought, *Mama will like his voice, which is quite musical!*

"I am happy to meet you, sir." She smiled at him. "And may I introduce you to my mother?" She turned to Mama, looming large and purple in the center of the room. "Mother, this is Mr. Edgerton of Crofton, Ontario. My mother, Mrs. Merrick, sir!"

"How do you do!" The senior Edgerton bowed as men of his generation did on every possible occasion. "Permit me to express my pleasure, Mrs. Merrick, at meeting the wife of the

Clipper Coach Line's founder, whose reputation for honor and ability far outreached his native land."

Mama was pleased. "Why, Mr. Edgerton, I am moved at your remembering my husband. Perhaps you'll tell me how you came to know of him." Graciously Mama moved to the couch and indicated that the gentlemen might be seated, while Mr. Edgerton told her all he'd heard about the illustrious Kingsley Merrick, whose contributions to the British domain were not forgotten nor, he assured her, would ever be. Once the newness wore off, Augusta could see that he was a cheerful sort, quite chipper really, now telling Mama of the farewell banquet given Papa in Melbourne which, Mr. Edgerton was saying with a twinkle in his eye, was truly quite an event, from what he'd heard. Mama produced a silver humidor, inscribed on that occasion, for Mr. Edgerton's inspection.

She seated herself in a chair nearby young Harold, and said softly, so as not to disturb any favorable impression that might be moving forward between Mama and Harold's father, "How have you fared these weeks in our city, Mr. Edgerton?" and with half a mind listened to his sober recital while she worked to catch the drift between Mama and Harold's father (whose name, she learned, was also Harold, though it would be a long time before Mama ever called him that!). *Had any spark been ignited there? Not that it would show!* But she knew Mama pretty well, she guessed, well enough to sense if she were merely pretending interest as Edgerton now described the Crofton scene, or whether her interest were real, because of the gentleman himself. And it did seem to her that Mama enjoyed the elder Harold Edgerton very much. But it was hard work, listening to two conversations at once, and she was exhausted when Patricia brought in the tea.

"Won't you pour today, Augusta?" Mama said instantly, to put Augusta in command of the next hour.

"Oh, no, Mama, you pour," Augusta demurred as eagerly. "You're so good at it."

"So are you," Mama insisted. "And it's time you relieved your poor old mother of some of her duties. Even the nice ones!" Mama smiled at Mr. Edgerton in acknowledgment of the graceful reticence of her daughter who would not knowingly usurp her mother's place. "I'll be interested to see what our Canadian friends make of our native Cape Cod berry," Mama went on smoothly, cutting Augusta off from further protest and forcing her to the tea table so that there would be no awkward gap. "It's quite tart—almost sour—and takes getting used to."

The Edgertons dutifully bit into the tartlet, unable to contain the grimace that cranberries brought to even the practiced palate, and Augusta couldn't help laughing aloud although it was bad manners to do so and Mama shot a stern glance at her.

"Forgive me, gentlemen," Augusta exclaimed, and tried to put away her smile which refused to leave her lips. "Cranberries startle nearly everyone." The elder Edgerton chuckled; whether he was laughing at himself, all puckered up, or at Augusta struggling with her manners it was not possible to know—his humor didn't help to bring her giggles under control, and she rather thought that young Harold was not amused, either with the tart or with her, or his father, either.

"Very interesting," he remarked, looking at the rest of his tart with certain displeasure. "Very interesting, indeed."

"They have grown wild for a long time," Augusta behind the silver teapot explained, hoping to hide her gaffe. "Recently they've been put under cultivation by adding lots of sand to the beds and flooding them, if need be, to protect them from winter damage. Freezing doesn't hurt them, but frost does."

"Really, Augusta?" Mama asked. "I didn't know that."

"I'd judge nothing could hurt them," Harold Edgerton pronounced. "They're impregnable."

Then it was proper to laugh, and happily she did, relieved that young Harold could occasionally say something that was actually funny, and the balance of the afternoon seemed to pass more easily, although she was glad when the hall clock chimed five and the Edgertons rose to depart.

"Perhaps, Mrs. Merrick," Edgerton senior said, "you and your daughter would enjoy accompanying my son and me to the theater Wednesday next?"

"Why, we'd be delighted, I'm sure," Mama said gladly, not bothering to consult Augusta.

"We'll come by at seven-thirty, then," Edgerton announced. It seemed clear enough that the older gentleman was picking up nicely in the new environment of Boston. He was looking for entertainment, for friends; he was quite a lot of fun and would be easy to please, to draw from bereavement—he was surly a very fortunate find! For who could be more suitable than the senior Harold Edgerton of Crofton, Ontario, Canada!

The trail of their murmurs disappeared down the stairwell, echoing as though in a museum, and below, Patricia helped them with their coats and canes, hats and gloves. Augusta and Mama listened silently, each with private thoughts and hopes of her own. Elaborately they picked up their needlework to wait for dinner, assiduously avoiding any discussion of their visitors and talking, instead, about the play they were to see, what they would wear to it, and finally they sought refuge in Mr. Clemens's novel about a boy called Tom Sawyer which Mama thought remarkable, although some of her friends believed that in this book, as it was in others, Clemens was guilty of sinning against good taste. It was an argument the critics had not, after two years, yet resolved—but Mama had settled the whole thing. The fellow was a genius, she believed, and goodness knew there were few of them in American letters these days. Mama's friends were beginning to come around to her way of thinking, because Mama's opinions were well regarded in the Back Bay. . . .

The spring sun was caught in the chandelier above the dining room table at Kingsland. Patricia Hanrahan had cleared the luncheon dishes, and now, freed from Patricia's presence, Mama could speak her mind. That something had been on it all through the meal Augusta did not doubt; Mama had hardly eaten anything at all.

She smiled encouragingly. "Well?"

But Mama did not smile back. Instead, she spread out on the table between them a letter. "I'd like you to read this," she said.

The rainbow twinkles from the chandelier glanced off the heavy paper where, in elegant script, was written Harold Edgerton's expression of disappointment, his steadfast loyalty and willingness to wait—forever if need be—until Augusta changed her mind and consented to marry him.

"I know I shouldn't have read it," Mama said, looking embarrassed but determined. "I—I just couldn't help myself, dear. I was so sure he was proposing to you, because he mentioned to me that he wanted to!" Dismay, disappointment, desperation crowded her face, chasing the embarrassment away. "Darling," she whispered tensely, leaning over the table. "Why did you refuse? When did he ask you?"

Augusta looked at the heavy, expensive paper without

seeing it, desperately wishing this had not happened. For if Mama had remained in ignorance about young Harold's proposal, the discussion that must go forward now could be evaded. But now it was unavoidable, and she knew anger, both with Mama for opening a letter not intended for her eyes and with young Harold, who had asked in the first place for the hand of Augusta Merrick in marriage. Drat him!

The whole winter in Boston lay behind her, spent in the company of the Edgertons, whom Mama had introduced to all her Back Bay friends, a winter spent in mutual approval, so it seemed—but now as she thought of it, also seemed probable that Mama had consented to see the senior Harold Edgerton so that Augusta would be thrown into the company of his son. Mama had outdone her!

Now the winter was over, and the Edgertons were to visit Kingsland in a few days; Mama and Augusta had come down with Patricia to open the house, and Mr. Murphy had come, too, in order to fetch the horses from their wintering barns and reaccustom them to the saddle or shafts should the mistress or her guests care to ride. The weather was warm enough now to warrant a visit, and the visit would last five days. The Thayers were coming, too; everyone would stay at Kingsland and hopefully the senior Mr. Edgerton, pleased by its grace and the enchantment Mama could weave around it, would want to be part of it all and would propose to Mama before leaving for Crofton, which surely could not compare to Waterford. He would retire soon; he would live here with Mama, pay the bills . . . oh, yes, Augusta had it all worked out! Mama would be proposed to and would accept without even knowing that young Harold had been refused and Augusta could then slip away to the arms of John Bradley. . . .

But Mama knew all about it now.

"When did he propose?" Mama asked again.

"Before we left Boston," Augusta said. "He took me rather off guard, Mama. I couldn't think straight. So I told him no. I didn't know what else to say. Certainly I don't want to marry him!"

"That is really too bad," Mama shook her head and sighed. "I'm sorry, I truly am," she said. "I can see that you're upset. Your eyes are nearly black—your father's eyes used to do that. I didn't realize you'd be so disturbed that I opened your mail, but I had to, Augusta! God knows you're too young to carry everything, but I'm at the end, and I had to find out if Harold were proposing to you!" Mama covered Augusta's hand with her own. "There are a few things I had better tell you," she said slowly, reluctantly. "A few things you had better understand. And then you'll see why this letter was so important to me."

Augusta waited, easily able to guess what Mama would say now, and knowing not at all what she would say in return.

John! she thought, swamped in angry desolation. *I had such hopes! Still,* she thought, *it's not too late! Not if Mr. Edgerton proposes to Mama when he comes to Waterford. Nor if I make it clear to Mama that she had better accept him!*

"Surely you know, Augusta, that the panic a few years ago, and now the depression, have made things very difficult. I've mentioned before, I think, that we have fewer resources at our disposal." Mama paused as though in genteel reluctance to discuss anything so crass as money. She swallowed. "There is even less now than there was when I spoke of it last, Augusta. Money seems to fairly melt away."

Mama made no mention of Aunt Ellen's offer to open her house to summer boarders, nor did she mention the style of living she'd chosen, and which had landed her in the spot she was in.

"It was all very sad, Augusta. The fact is, in order to pass your birthright on intact, I have had to borrow money, using Kingsland as collateral. Do you know what collateral is?"

"Yes," said Augusta tonelessly.

"It means that if I don't pay it back," Mama said as if she had not heard, "then Mr. Livingstone of Hartland's, who holds the mortgage, is privileged to sell the house and take what portion of the proceeds will satisfy my indebtedness."

She paused, waiting for Augusta to be dismayed that Kingsland was mortgaged and might be lost.

"Do you think the house could be sold? I mean, would there be anyone willing—or able—to buy it, do you think?"

Mama stared. "Why, I don't know, dear. That's not the point! The point is that Kingsland would be gone! Your birthright lost to you! It's all that's left of your father's life work. Perhaps I haven't made that clear, Augusta darling. We're on the brink of losing everything."

Burning in the back of her brain was the image of Mama when Caroline ran away, Mama weeping, broken, hurt, defeated, an image she had taken such care to see never would recur, one which now, more than likely, would happen all over again despite her efforts. Damn Harold Edgerton! But it was going to be Mama, or it was going to be her, and if she wanted John badly enough, she was going to have to sacrifice Mama for him, tell Mama that she loved John better than anything or anyone else and if Mama wanted to secure Kingsland for any reason at all she'd better see to it that the elder Mr. Edgerton proposed to her. She would have to tell Mama that her daughter Augusta was lost to her already, just as Caroline had been lost.

She took a deep breath. *John,* she thought. *Never doubt that I love you. I do this to my mother for your sake.* Her hands were sweating, her throat ached.

"I think there's a certain confusion in your mind, Mama," she said. "I think we need to look more closely at what you conceive my birthright to be."

"Why, this house, of course!"

"And the way we live in it."

"That, too. A way of life our house makes possible."

"Well, Mama," she said, her voice distant in her own ears, "I think you lack candor. I think that what troubles you most is your having to live more simply, in a manner you don't choose, unless I marry a rich man. It's your way of life you're interested in preserving, not my birthright."

"That is most unkind," Mama cried, drawing back as though stung. "And untrue, too!" Mama looked at her defiantly, her head high, her eyes not wavering even fractionally, and it was Augusta who finally looked away.

"I am not going to marry Harold," she told the sideboard firmly. "I don't love him."

"What has loving him got to do with it?" Mama urged. "You can learn. He's an excellent young man and his father says that he plans to stand for parliament in a few years. That would be fun, Augusta! You'd live in Ottawa!"

She could see Mama was impressed by that, and would be pleased to make reference to her son-in-law, Harold Edgerton, M.P. She could see she must get on with it because not loving someone was insufficient reason for not marrying him—not when destitution hung in the balance.

"I rather hoped you'd end up marrying Harold's father," she said tentatively. "Then you'd be able to save Kingsland, Mama. Mr. Edgerton would surely pay off your mortgage!"

"I? Marry the senior Edgerton?" Mama's face registered dismay and distaste, as though an offensive odor had just drifted into the house.

"It's one of the more infallible means of separating a man

from his money," Augusta pointed out ruthlessly, distastefully, since Mr. Edgerton deserved better than this! "It's surely the answer to your mortgage problem, Mama."

Mama looked her over carefully. "Just how long have you had up your sleeve the notion that I might marry the senior Mr. Edgerton?"

Mama had her! There was nothing to do but confess it.

"I've had it in mind all along."

"Am I to gather from that the implication that you have known about the mortgage all along, also?"

"Since Thanksgiving. Aunt Ellen told me."

"Ellen!" Anger blazed a trail across Mama's face.

"She was trying to explain certain things to me, Mama. An explanation I asked for because . . ." she steeled herself, "I am going to marry John Sears Bradley, Mama, and Aunt Ellen wanted me to understand what my marrying him would mean to you."

Mama seemed cast of stone, and her pallor turned a stony gray, too, as she sat there without so much as a muscle stirring.

"And, having understood," Augusta pushed on, "naturally I saw right away that Mr. Edgerton would be exactly the answer to your dilemma."

"John Bradley?" Mama's voice was not her own.

"John Bradley," Augusta said strongly. "I am going to marry John Bradley."

"I hope you aren't serious." Mama was recovering, her skin regaining a little of its color. But the little lines around her eyes and mouth seemed deeper than they had been.

"I am entirely serious, Mama."

"Has Mr. Bradley asked you to marry him?"

"Yes."

"You've been seeing him, then. Obviously."

"Yes."

"In secret, since I've known nothing about it."

"Yes."

"Skulking about."

"If you put it that way."

"How long?"

"For nearly two years."

Shocked, disbelieving, Mama for once was stopped cold.

"I tried not to think about him after the conversation we had about who would be suitable for me to marry. I understood John wasn't, because he could not carry Kingsland for-

363

ward as you so badly wanted. But I can't help it, Mama. I couldn't put him out of my mind."

"Two years," Mama echoed. Her eyes seemed unfocused. "I . . . I can't quite picture him receiving here, Augusta, in your father's place."

"He won't be living here, so you need not worry about it."

"He won't? He doesn't want to?"

"He will build a house of his own."

"Which you propose to live in with him."

"Yes."

"Forsaking the house of your father."

"I like what John offers," she said firmly, though mention of Papa made it more difficult. "I like what he offers very much."

"A common, mediocre life."

"I suppose it would look like that to you. It is simpler, that is true. It is grounded in different values. But those values, Mama, are the ones I have chosen."

"And Kingsland, and I, may go to the devil."

How ugly Mama's face was!

"I am not interested in the way you live, Mama. If it means so much to you, then you had better marry Mr. Edgerton because I am going to marry John Bradley. Mama!" she urged, veering off on another tack, the only other alternative. "If marrying Mr. Edgerton is so repugnant to you—though it ought not be, for he is charming—why, if you are so averse to the idea, perhaps, Mama, you might consider selling Kingsland after all. Surely you can live on the remains of the sale, and live very comfortably, too. And the Leverings would come to visit you, and the Sinclaires, and you could visit them in Boston . . ." She faltered, staggered to a stop, looked closely at Mama to see if this suggestion was having the desired effect.

"Sell it!" Mama's eyes became fierce. "Sell it! After everything I've done, after everything I've been through to hang onto it, you would have me sell your father's house. . . . I would remind you that buyers are not beating at the door—" Suddenly Mama was laughing and crying all at the same time. "I can't believe it," she gasped. "My one hope—you! And you would not only leave me destitute, but would do it for the sake of Angelina's son!" With effort, Mama struggled to bring herself under control, took a deep shuddering breath. "There are a few more things, perhaps, that I had better tell you."

364

"Perhaps I don't want to hear." Suddenly, desperately, she wanted not to hear!

"I shall tell you, anyway." Mama was trembling all over, shaking visibly, and her terrible tension made Augusta shake, too. "I shall tell you why your marriage to John would destroy me, Augusta. I will tell you why I hate his mother and why she hates me—I will tell you a lot of things, all of which converge in one single fact—Angelina Bradley was your father's mistress."

The room spun a moment, stopped. Mama firmly clasped her hands before her on the table and studied them.

"Do you remember when Papa and I were estranged?"

"Estranged!"

"I didn't think you would. We were separated for three years, when you were a tiny girl—it was an arrangement of my own making. But then certain events here in Waterford showed me that I had erred grievously in alienating your father as I had, and I begged for reconciliation, and he forgave me." Mama closed her eyes as though she saw something painful; she opened them again. "I swore I'd make everything up to him and that I'd help all I could to see his goals were reached—and I did! Your father had everything the way he wanted it, after that. He became senator. The railroad was built. His fondest dream, that Mill Village should meet and mingle with Waterford Center on terms of absolute equality, came true. Everyone's child got the same education; everyone attended the same church, had access to the fine little library which he expanded greatly.

"And I did everything he wanted me to do. I forbore for his sake the things I needed and craved—among them the company of friends that I have now, and Boston itself, which I love. For your father preferred the company of the Brickers or else his friends in Mill Village. He didn't care for the Leverings and he didn't want them to be important in the scheme of things, though he brought Adam here himself when he needed help with the railroad. He wanted me to welcome to our house the people that *he* wanted there, to put into the minds of Waterford women the ideas that he wanted passed on to Waterford men and he did not want the Leverings to be important to me. And so I made no move in their direction, contented myself with the few occasions when they did come to Waterford. It wasn't easy, Augusta!"

She could well imagine that it had not been.

"I told myself that I owed it to him, and when he wanted

365

me to go to South Africa—that I owed him that, too. I told him I would come when he was ready for us, whenever that would be, and he left.

"Then—then Mr. Levering wrote to say that Mrs. Sinclaire had come back to Boston, that she was eager to see me. The prospect of renewing my friendship with Sally Sinclaire was a far more pleasant thing to contemplate than the thought of moving to South Africa, all Boers and black people! How much I looked forward to that visit!" Mama's face lost some of its tension as she remembered her joy. "I wanted badly for Waterford to appeal to Sally, so that she'd come back often. But Waterford was feeling the aftermath of the war and the loss of shipping and a lot of successful men were leaving, seeking an alternative to the sea, and Mill Village people were moving in because with the mill burned down and gone, there was no reason for them to stay in West Waterford. In fact, our town was beginning to look just a little like Mill Village used to look, with shops on the main street. Why would Sally want to come here if she thought Waterford common? Or worse, if she suspected that it was dying on the vine. It wasn't! There were still plenty of worthy and interesting people left, and it was those people I wanted her to see. I didn't dare ask Mrs. Bradley, for fear Sally would think that the best company I could dredge up would be a woman who ran a boarding house! And so I did not."

Mama was kneading her temples as though they throbbed, and Augusta watched, wishing she could make her stop, knowing nothing would stop her now.

"I hadn't realized that our parties and picnics and receptions had meant so much to her. She was like a child who had starved all her life and then been admitted to a full table, and in the middle of the feast had been asked to leave. She was afraid she was going to be excluded permanently because of her fallen estate. She was livid; she wanted to hurt me, just as she conceived I was hurting her. And she succeeded very well. She told me all sorts of things I hadn't known. And she enjoyed it to the hilt, believe me. She laughed at me, derided me, scorned me. For all my airs, she said, and all my pretentions weren't worth a damn—all they did was to hide the fact that I couldn't satisfy my husband in bed. I had failed, she said, the most important test of a woman—and how it pleased her to inform me that she could—and had—provided Kingsley with what I was unable to give. Indeed, she provided it for years."

"No, Mama!" she whispered. "I don't believe it!"

Mama gripped the edge of the table.

"But she can prove it, Augusta! She can prove at least that your father loved her once and loved her well, because there is young David Bradley! The boy was born during the war when Sears was home and out of work, as captains were then. Naturally it never crossed anyone's mind that David wasn't Sears Bradley's son. But he is not. He is Kingsley's child, Augusta, conceived during the time your father and I were still separated. Look at him carefully if you don't believe me. Beneath his fair hair and blue eyes is your father! The only thing I can be thankful for is that hardly anyone remembers what Kingsley looked like anymore. And I took pains to have the portraits here altered slightly so that there's no chance anyone will make the connection."

Augusta started, and Mama laughed harshly. "You never realized that his portrait was changed, did you? But I could have managed to live with what I knew," Mama went on, sparing herself nothing. "After all, I handed Kingsley to Angelina on a silver platter, estranging him as I had. But I can't swallow the facts of our reconciliation. I can't. Here I'd believed his forgiveness, and acceptance stemmed from love which I, in my stupidity, had never allowed him to express. Yes, I believed he gave me another chance because he loved me. But it wasn't true. It seems I crawled, I groveled, I licked his boots only in the appeasement of his pride and the securing of his dreams, and if afterwards he saw to it that I fulfilled my marital duties, it was only to prove that he had the upper hand—because you see, Augusta, he kept right on being Angelina's lover." Mama's lips trembled. "I could not, I did not, win his love. Angelina had it. She had it all along and never lost it, and to top it all off, she came to our house, to enjoy the social life only I could offer—she came here to be received by your father and me, to kiss my cheek and pretend to be my friend and all the time they were lovers! How they must have laughed at me! The signals they must have exchanged behind my back! What a fool they made of me!"

She could not bear the torment in Mama's face.

"No!" she whimpered. "It isn't true. She made it up to hurt you."

Surely Papa wasn't like that!

"I have only Angelina's word for what went on after our reconciliation, that's true. But I believe her." The color rose in Mama's face at the mortification of her belief. "I believe her because I am no good with a man, Augusta. Once your father and I lived together again I tried with all my heart to give him what he wanted, and I couldn't. I was unable to respond to him no matter what, and I knew it would be hard to hold him. Why shouldn't I believe Angelina when she told me—with details more intimate than I care to relate to you—how well she satisfied him, how well he satisfied her— that they were lovers right up until the time he went to South Africa and, having lost him finally, she settled for Zack Hallet. Why should I try to delude myself? What had I to offer Kingsley Merrick whom, Angelina was happy to inform me, was both insatiable as well as incomparable in bed? A fact which I, in my frigidity, would be unable to appreciate."

The hurt in Mama's eyes was like a sword.

"Once I saw what a fool the two of them had made of me, I was under no compulsion to remain loyal to your father's dreams. That was why I would not go to Africa, Augusta, when he was ill. Were it not for the appearance of things, I wouldn't have attempted to go even when I knew he was dying. What could I say to him? I . . . I cannot hide it, my dear. Knowing what I know has hurt—hurt badly—so quite naturally my friends have become important to me. They could give me what once I valued above all things and what I value yet. They have stayed by me despite your father's indifference to them while he lived, and they overlooked Caroline's transgression for my sake. Through them I have brought style to Waterford, and to our life. Quality is not served by equality, Augusta! If it seems I spent what money I had foolishly, just remember it was spent on things that are priceless, beyond value. Does it really mean so little to you? Do I? Would you really have me marry Mr. Edgerton, live far away, unable to nurture what I have begun, have my life once again directed by the whim of a man while weeds grow all over everything here that I've worked at to keep shining and clean—so that you can marry the son of my husband's mistress?"

"Mama!" she cried. "I didn't know!"

Mama caught her breath, collected her poise. "Of course you didn't, dear. And I didn't want you to." Mama looked out onto the side piazza, to the sodden, thawing lawn, as though to recall the parties and picnics held there, as though to bring her mind back to the matter at hand. "We have a good life here, Augusta, and we can keep it going by continuing to play music and write poetry, lifting ourselves up from the mundane—which really is what life should be all about, and usually isn't! We can continue perpetuating our traditions and our roots and our heritage, the things that ought to make us proud and which unfortunately require money to maintain, in order to keep them from falling into the common dust of the mediocre. . . ." Mama's mouth began to quiver, but she persevered. "I have kept it for you. Along with this house I bequeath you the parlors of the nicest people in Waterford and Boston, people whom it is a pleasure to know, who make life abundant and joyful. I can only tell you that Kingsland is something you will always regret should you lose it, because there is no way to replace it. I've done as much as I can, carried it as far as I can go. . . ."

Mama's eyes shivered behind the tears glistening in them, and she looked at Augusta with a gaze that neither faltered nor wavered. She rose then, proudly, her shoulders thrown back, and she swept away, up the stairs, firmly, regally, without hurrying, and without a backward glance.

Augusta did not move. Before her was the letter of Harold Edgerton, and around her the shattered sunlit afternoon, and within the old numbness was creeping, seeping back.

"Would you like a cup of tea, Miss?" Patricia stood beside her, and without interest Augusta wondered how long she'd been there, if Patricia had been lingering near the dining room door all this time and heard everything. Not that it mattered. Not that anything mattered.

"No," she said. "I'd like to go for a ride. Tell Mr. Murphy to saddle Scamper, please."

"Yes, Miss." Patricia stole away, to return uncounted, unending minutes later.

"Murphy's outside with the horse, Miss Augusta."

Numbly she followed Patricia into the kitchen. On a peg by the door was a shawl which she wrapped absently around her shoulders. "That's not warm enough," Patricia protested. "Let me fetch you a better one."

"I don't want a better one," she said, and went out without shutting the door behind her, let Murphy help her into the saddle where she hooked her knee over the angled horn.

"If you'll wait a moment, Miss, I'll saddle Ranger and come with you."

"Thank you, Mr. Murphy," she said. "But I'd sooner go alone."

Digging Scamper viciously, she wheeled and rode faster than her saddle permitted for safety, hurtled down the drive with its clamshells flying and out onto the main road over to the intersection, past Emmaline's house, past the Golden Ox, down the Rockford road until she reached the overlook at the Flax Pond, and there she stopped, giving Scamper a chance to catch his breath.

Papa, Papa! Within her rose the silent keening as the old wound of his death opened up again under the assault of seeing Papa as she had never seen him before, a man less noble than she had believed, a man not so honorable as she had supposed, a man who, perhaps, was not worthy of Waterford's veneration nor of hers. . . .

Unworthy.

Papa! Papa! she grieved, seared by the white heat of losing him again, a second time, of losing her respect for him and—yes!—her love, too. For perhaps Papa did not deserve it.

Papa, she mourned, *how could you have hurt her so?*

Across the road from the overlook lay the track to the heartland of the Cape, where were scattered the Merrick wood-lots along with those of every old Waterford family, scrambled in a tangle of obscure deeds and lost landmarks so that no one was sure anymore exactly where his boundaries lay or, indeed, how many lots his family had. There were no boundaries there anymore, just as there now seemed to be none, anywhere. All the boundaries that ever had defined her life seemed dissolved, as though a fog had fallen with its silent suddenness just as she was traversing territory she had never crossed before. . . .

She had ridden that heartland track with Papa, many times. He had praised her skill at riding, a superb horseman himself. . . .

She kicked Scamper into action again, fleeing the heartache that caught up to her everytime she paused. She circled the pond through the woods that surrounded it and headed west on a path that once, Papa had told her, had cut through one enormous pasture stretching from West Waterford to Rockford on the south shore, so large that it was simply bared at either end with a view to keeping the sheep out of town rather than inside their own domain. That had been within the span of her own lifetime, but she could not remember it. Once the war was over, the demand for wool dropped, the sheep were consumed for mutton instead of clipped for their worthless fleece. Worthless, the little mills that had sprung up to meet the wartime demands now bankrupt, and Papa's mill burnt. . . .

Oh, no, she thought. *Oh, Papa, no!* But it was true. She knew it as surely as she knew her name. It had been a fire of convenience. And as a consequence of it, Papa had the insurance money to help finance his fiasco in South Africa, and there was not even a shred of doubt in her mind that he'd planned it that way because Papa was the sort of man who took what he wanted, what he deemed belonged to him . . . just as he had taken another man's wife. . . .

Oh, Papa, she thought. *Mama tried so hard. Is that all she deserved, to be made a fool of by you and Angelina Bradley?*

The path through the pasture was becoming obscured now, because the brush was growing back fast, overtaking it. Perhaps she would lose her way, or an accident befall her far from help. It was lonely out here in the raw spring breeze, in the silence of the abandoned meadows. . . . She trotted Scamper briskly, heedless of any danger to herself because it didn't matter what happened . . . trotted although trotting was not pleasant in a sidesaddle.

In the middle of nowhere, as she neared the chain of ponds that lay south from the mill stream, the land was cleared to reveal marshes that had been hidden, untouched and unnoticed, beneath a tangle of bull briars and the low snarled bushes that abounded in the Cape's sandy soil, and the marshes were brought under cranberry culture by unknown hands whose owners walked the necessary miles to dig the trenches, to dump sand on the vines, to prune—there were quite a few bogs, she noticed, on either side of the path, but thankfully no people were working in them. Perhaps their labors for the season were finished. Or perhaps not yet begun. . . .

She could see Jerry Slater's ice houses, one on each of the ponds. All of them, do doubt, stuffed with ice and sawdust. Jerry had done well with ice since the mill burned. Papa had given him the money to get started. Papa always gave every advantage he could to Mill Village people, some of whom were his kin, all of whom, he believed, could achieve what any captain had achieved, given the same advantages, because one man was as good as another in this life. Or as bad, and you had to judge them by their intrinsic worth as human beings and not by their achievements which, all too often, a quirk of fate had made possible.

She dismounted, stood beside the gaping foundation of the mill. Its stones were forever blackened, and vines were beginning to grow over them; wild flowers were poking up through the rubble on the floor and a strong stand of grass grew now on the land surrounding the old place, raked clean, the debris of the fire hauled away. Across from the holding pond was the old Hall mansion house, square, hip-roofed, cumbersome, which had been a hostelry in the days of the coaches, Papa had told her. He'd turned the house into his office in the day of the mill; it was vacant now, watching the road sightlessly from its blank windows in an impersonal, unjudging stare.

Just around the corner, out of sight, was the modest Greek Revival house of a more contemporary Hall, empty now because its inhabitant had died. Most all of the other houses, little low cottages they were, stood vacant, too, and the roof on the tannery across the road had fallen in, and the old gristmill was never used any more because there were no chickens to grind corn for.

Mill Village was returning to nature, just as the mill had, and soon there would be nothing left to show for its having existed. It was returning to nature, just as Papa had returned, and perhaps there really was nothing left to show for Papa's having lived, either. For all of Papa's great contributions to the town of Waterford or Mill Village, they could have gotten along just as well without him. The same things would have happened had Papa never lived. He had not accomplished anything that wouldn't have happened anyway, given the passing of sail which depleted Waterford Center and given the loss of the mill in West Waterford. The Academy would have closed, the churches would have united because neither were luxuries Waterford would have chosen to afford once its living was taken from it. And the mill in West Waterford only delayed a process that began again as soon as the mill was no longer there, for the place had begun to die as soon as Warner Hall no longer spun cotton there, years and years ago. . . .

It was futile. The whole thing was futile, and Papa's life was an exercise in futility, if you looked at it that way—

But suddenly Augusta could not look at it that way. She could not, because in her grief she remembered Papa more clearly, more cleanly than she had in some time. She remembered his love for her manifested in so many ways—the hours he spent with her playing chess, teaching her to handle the cue in his billiard room, riding in the woods. She remembered how large he seemed, so much bigger than ordinary men, one who accomplished more, saw farther, lived more deeply, gave more fully, who respected men for what they were and insisted that others do the same, and whom often Augusta had seen looking at Mama when Mama didn't know it, with eyes fond and full of devotion—the kind of devotion that had nothing to do with a woman's performance in bed. Suddenly she could not believe that he betrayed Mama a second time with Mrs. Bradley. Not a man so deep, able to love so deeply, who saw so clearly into the heart of life and of people. The first time, perhaps that was so, and perhaps with some reason, but the second, after the reconciliation Mama described—no, Augusta did not believe that Papa would do that. If she had to choose between Mrs. Bradley's account of the years following the birth of young David and the man she believed Papa to be, why, there was nothing to choose from! After all, anything Mrs. Bradley had told Mama about her liaison with Papa could apply equally to the early relationship as to a later one. No, no it was Mama's understanding of her failures that caused her to believe Angelina Bradley! Mama's own limitations which made her doubt Papa's love! It had nothing to do with Papa at all. He had not deliberately hurt her, and there was no need to justify his having done so.

There was an upward surge of joy, of gladness, of thanksgiving, the bitterness ebbing fast and the peace of amnesty filling the place where the bitterness had been, and she let her eyes drift over the flatness of West Waterford as it stretched out toward the bay, and the bay itself, reaching out and out and she saw Papa's life and the things he had done reaching out and out, too, like waves that touch one another, on and on. . . .

She saw Waterford Center humming vigorously now with the life blood pumped into it by Mill Village. She saw that Mill Village filled a vacuum created by the departing captains, a consequence that Papa could not have foreseen but which he had made possible. Mill Village had rescued Waterford from its fate as a listless, lifeless shell, and very likely none of it would have happened without the hand of Kingsley Merrick, because the mill had given West Waterford an enormous economic advantage. Such a great advantage that Mill Village men could buy the houses of captains, and Mill Village smithies and carpenters could set up their little shops and businesses in the center of town, and Waterford Center began to take on the appearance of Mill Village as it once had been. . . .

Mama, of course, preferred to concentrate on Captain Gray, who sold Mutual Life Insurance, and Captain Pollard, who sat on the board of directors of the Old Colony Railroad, and Captain Crosby, who was serving as a selectman just now, all of them retired, living off the fat they had accumulated before the war, and from that respectable element she had chosen company for her Boston friends. She did not care to see John Stevens' cabinet shop in the Winslow barn on Main Street. She was sad to see Captain Blake mongering fish, and she resented Jerry Slater, who was rich on ice, living in comfort in the old Sears place. It embarrassed her that Captain Hall had to sell coal and kerosene from his front parlor because his savings didn't quite reach far enough. Mama believed these things to be a shame. The consequence of them was to make Waterford common; she did not like to see such diverse elements rubbing elbows in such absolute equality—an equality that Papa had made possible.

In fact, Papa would have understood very well John Bradley's dream for Waterford, which paralleled and perpetuated his own, and Mama would not understand it at all, just as Mama had not understood Papa either, a man full of zest, of joyfulness, a man virile, restless, irreverent, utterly indiscriminate when it came to people, a man ruthless, Augusta now saw, somewhat cruel in the pursuit of his determination, perhaps amoral . . . and whose dreams were more right than Mama's because they were more grounded in reality (though there were plenty of people who would see neither right nor reality in them)—and whose dreams did not need Augusta or John Bradley to perpetuate them because they were impervious as right things were impervious, and would come to bear, in their own time. . . .

She climbed back up on Scamper and rode through the West Gate which was no more barred, back toward the center of town, by Cousin Nate's house at the west end of the town proper, close by the intersection of the low road and the town cemetery where Papa's monument was planted. But she did not want to see that. The ruined foundations of the mill were monument enough. . . .

Dusk was falling fast, and she was cold; and the breeze generated from Scamper's gallop didn't help as she rode quickly by the Waterford Library and past the house of John Stevens, where he made cabinets and chairs in the tradition of his father. At her left was the district school, and across from it was the field of John Bradley with its cranberry bog in the center and his small barn near the bog which he'd built this past winter, to hold the tools and equipment needed to maintain cranberries. The building seemed to stand as a token of the future that John Bradley intended to take for himself, and it seemed far away, very distant, a long, aching distance from Augusta, who watched it on Scamper's back and then fiercely rode on, past the Sinclaires' house, which once had belonged to Captain Denning and the McLarens' next to it, past the First Church of Waterford, Universalist, which proclaimed its unity in a sign out front and raised its steeple, with its ball and vane and the bell from the old meeting house, to catch the sunlight that lingered high up in the trees in the last glitter of that day.

And then there was the house of Kingsley Merrick, large and imperial behind the maples that lined the driveway. The house and the monument in the cemetery, the library and the organ in the united church—these were the residue of Papa's estate, respectable monuments, munificent ones, shined up and clean under Mama's care so that no one knew to this day that Kingsley Merrick, president and founder of the Merrick Woolen Company, director of the Cape Cod Central Railroad, senator of Barnstable county, director of the public schools, patron of the library, pillar of the church, died a pauper. No one would know that Julia Merrick lived in the shadow of financial extinction and spiritual annihilation. Moving ahead diligently and with courage, Mama had not allowed anything to get in her way; not even Caroline had disrupted her labors nor prevented Mama from moving inexorably forward to what she conceived as her destiny—no, not panics nor depressions nor failures in business. Her destiny, founded in reality or not, was Kingsland, with all its lamps lit now as though expecting its usual throng but quiet because there was none. Over the front piazza was the new, neatly elegant sign that Mama had caused to be nailed there, with gold leaf in its letters at how much cost! Kingsland, which John Bradley did not want. Kingsland, for which Mama lived and which Augusta Merrick could take or throw away.

John. John . . .

She did not need to guide Scamper to the carriage house because he was heading there anyway, where above it stretched the bronze weathervane, a pacing horse reaching for the nonexistent road beneath its feet, which Papa had commissioned to be made especially for himself and of which he had supervised the mounting, pleased to see a bronze representation of the beast he loved so well. Flaunting it

375

proudly over his barn instead of the clipper ship most places in Waterford raised to the wind . . .

Within the barn the small lantern told her that Murphy was awaiting her return.

"I was starting to worry, Miss," he fretted, helping her off Scamper and steadying her until her legs, stiffened from so long on the sidesaddle, could be depended on. "Did you have a pleasant ride?"

"Very nice," she said politely, shivering beneath her shawl. "Very nice, thank you." And she walked toward the house, to the monument her father had raised, to the pride of the Merricks, the pride of the Kings, to its walls stout and strong and its tower rising four stories above, its ghosts and it secrets, its grace and its splendor, its future and its past with the hopes it had stood for and stood for yet, if Augusta Merrick were to shoulder her mother's burdens and make them her own. She shivered and ran to the warmth within and the shelter there and the woman inside whose pride had held it all together and whom Augusta Merrick did not have the heart to destroy.

In the library were crammed her wedding gifts, elaborate and lovely. They had arrived every day all summer long, each to be opened and exclaimed over, tagged, entered in a white kid-bound book, placed on the tables lining the room for the inspection of the curious. Tea and coffee service, sterling and china, damask napery and napkin rings of gold, finger bowls and soup tureens, carving knives and demitasse sets and nutcrackers, crystal goblets and vases and gleaming trays and decanters and ice buckets, pickle forks and gravy ladles. She had three forms of thank-you notes which she copied on Kingsland stationery, thus saving herself the chore of having to gush creatively. One to close friends of the Merricks in Waterford and Boston, one to strangers in Crofton, and then a cordial yet rigidly correct one for people like the Brickers and the Wheelers and the Pettingills and folks in Waterford whose favor Mama did not encourage. Gifts from Crofton flowed with the same abundance and fine taste as did those from Boston and Waterford, much to Mama's satisfaction, because it proved that Crofton knew quality and could afford it, and therefore must not be too bad a place to live. In fact, Mama was fond of saying, Crofton must be a gem.

Yes, all things considered, Mama was well pleased. Having assured herself that Crofton would be a splendid place for

Augusta to live, she immediately began planning for the great event which would signal Augusta's departure for this far distant jewel and had been in her element all summer, and now, with the encroachment of autumn, in fact this moment, with the wedding not twenty-four hours away, Mama had spun off to even greater heights of organization and was out right now seeing to the red carpet which would be rolled out to the road from the Universalist Church. Papa's Concord coach had been repainted, and Augusta would ride in it and from it would alight to walk with her attendants, who would line up to escort her, and her dress would not once touch the dust of the earth. Mama had engaged an organist from Boston to play upon the occasion, because, unfortunately, it was not appropriate for the mother of the bride to play at her daughter's wedding. Mama had gone to considerable trouble locating an organist whom she believed would do justice to the occasion, thereby incurring the eternal indignation of Miss Susan Blake, who customarily played the Universalist organ whenever Mama was out of town. Blithely Mama dismissed Miss Blake from her mind. Apparently Mama had arranged for the weather, too, because it was a sparkling day, of the sort only Cape Cod could produce, and tomorrow promised to be another like it. All would be well for the wedding of Augusta Merrick.

She dipped the pen in the inkwell at Papa's desk and began yet another note of appreciation, the form of which she knew by heart.

Dear Mr. and Mrs. Pettingill, [she wrote] Let me take this occasion to tender my thanks and those of Mr. Edgerton for the gold-filigreed oil and vinegar cruets you have so thoughtfully sent us. They are truly lovely.

Bilge! she thought. *They are horrid.*

Instantly she put this thought away, pushed it into the appropriate place where other like thoughts were, which must never see the light of day. The place for such thoughts was becoming uncomfortably filled, and Augusta quickly put down the pen, lest the ink left in its nib drop onto the Pettingills' note, and clenched her hands tightly in her lap, waiting for the surge of impatience, of frustration, of aggravation and rage to pass, because all these things would pass if she were patient. They would pass because they must, but accommodation must be made for them. . . .

Waiting, she raised her eyes to the bookcases filled with volumes Papa had never read. On the opposite wall hung a picture of Papa's father, who wore a cravat with a stickpin in it and whose suit was dark and beside it a picture of Papa himself, a picture in which there was little resemblance to Papa as he had been, and certainly none to young David Bradley. In it Papa smiled warmly, fixedly, and a team and wagon trotted off into infinity, glimpsed behind a half-pulled curtain just behind Papa's left shoulder. Had his face been unaltered, the resemblance to David Bradley would have been remarkable, Augusta knew. She had watched young David very, very closely when she'd seen him in church the week that the Edgertons visited Kingsland. She had not even the least doubt that David was Papa's child. That did not alter her belief in Papa himself. But unfortunately her belief did not mitigate the failures and humiliations and mortifications that dogged Mama's footsteps and, of course, it did not pay the mortgage on Kingsland, either.

Kingsland, which soon she would leave, because tomorrow she would be married.

Lizzie Duncan would be her maid of honor. Cousin Nate would stand in Papa's place to give the bride away; six all alike girls from Miss Jellison's, including Sissy Sinclaire would be attendants; and six Edgerton males from Crofton, of varying ages, would be the groomsmen. Folks from Boston filled Waterford now and more would come on tomorrow morning's train, departing on the one in the evening. Many, many people from Waterford Center would witness the wedding; oh, indeed, Waterford was chock-full and brimming with a cup honeyed and joyful. The wedding of Augusta Merrick would not be soon forgotten! Every house in Waterford this day was filled with Merrick guests from out of town; young Edgerton and old were staying with Aunt Ellen; Aunt Edgerton representing the female side of Harold's family, properly lodged here at the Merricks and just now resting upstairs, in the old nursery, Mr. and Mrs. Livingstone of Hartland's Express were staying in the spacious front room that Papa used to sleep in, although just at this moment the Livingstones were out in Mama's carriage, seeing Cape Cod under Murphy's guidance. Their presence here gave Mama pure, unadulterated joy because not even they understood how thin was the ice upon which Mama had been skating. The mortgage held by the Livingstones was repaid already.

"Harold," Augusta had said, "there's a debt hanging over

our heads, and I can hardly marry you without your knowing of its existence. I wouldn't have the courage to confess it later."

"I knew, my dear, that your late father had encountered difficulty in his last venture." She seized this casually offered reason, stifling any shame she might have felt at so using Papa.

"Yes," she said. "There were some debts outstanding. . . . Mama has raised five thousand dollars with a mortgage on our house, as I understand it. . . ."

"I shall repay it," Edgerton promised. "Immediately."

And he had, leaving Mama with the balance of the money she had borrowed intact, and he proposed to send Mama a small sum of money every month, just for her pleasure, so that Mama wouldn't doubt that her new son-in-law regarded her fondly. It was quite a small sum of course, because Harold Edgerton had no real idea that Mama was in need—but with an allowance there would never be (God willing) any reason to have to tell him.

Harold Edgerton was decent—so decent he might have inspired the original definition for the word, and Augusta was ashamed, heartily ashamed, of using him. Fortunately, he inspired a kind of devotion in his own behalf, which would make easier her use of him because she aimed to be a good wife, and she aimed to make up to him, for the rest of his life, the using of him. Were he not the sort to cause devotion to arise spontaneously, it would have all been much, much harder.

"I think it's obscene," Emmaline choked, Augusta's betrothal announcement crumpled up in her hand.

"It can't be helped," she said firmly, not betraying by even the slightest nuance of the sorrow and aching within.

"I hope you don't ask me to be a bridesmaid."

"I wouldn't dream of it." She had not intended to sound haughty or disdainful, but that was the way her words came out, and she had as surely driven Emmaline away as if she had deliberately tried to. Perhaps it was just as well, because it was imperative to retreat, to lock herself up in a merciful numbness past which the days marched swiftly by, approaching her wedding and her departure to Crofton, Canada. It was important to put Waterford away from her, as far away as possible, to remove herself from what was happening until it was over, and so she had allowed herself to be carried along, attending parties given in her honor and smiling and chatting with the streams of well-wishers who came to take tea at the Merrick house. She did not restrain Mama from all her elaborate plans nor abet them except to choose between lemon or vanilla wedding cake, white roses or pink in the church, champagne or sparkling burgundy at the feast tonight, catered and held at the Town House, at which all Crofton guests would appear, and those selected from Waterford Center, and of course the Leverings, and the Sinclaires; Bax would be there, but he would have little to say and would only cast a reproachful glance or two at Augusta and try to make the best of a situation which disappointed him.

She had no regrets on behalf of Bax Levering. She had never wanted to marry him, and now, being unable to, she was not cast into a pit of regret or recrimination. She still did not want to marry him, and in fact was relieved that, since she could not marry John Bradley, she would not have to stay in Waterford at all. Bax would be continually returning here!

If there was any place that Augusta did not want to be, Waterford was it.

She fastened her attention fiercely on a robin who hopped in the grass, listening for worms. In the bushes at the edge of the lawn a towhee was jumping about into the sun, which heightened its patchwork of white and russet and brown. It reminded her of Mama's sewing room upstairs, in the third floor of the tower, when it was picked up and neat as it was today. The room had a maroon plush chair and white walls and maroon curtains and its floor was dark and it was cheerful and chipper and neat like the towhee. Only this morning had it been returned to this pristine state, the wire forms of Augusta and Mama put away in the closet, pins replaced and threads and snippets of lace, silk, muslin, and cotton swept away. Upstairs in that room Mrs. Stevens had sewn Augusta's wedding gown and the pink silk she would wear tonight at the prenuptial banquet and all her undergarments and night-clothes and a dozen new dresses to wear in Crofton, Canada. The trousseau, sewn, pressed, and packed, was on its way to Crofton, where Augusta would catch up with it after a brief honeymoon at Niagara Falls.

Tomorrow night. Tomorrow night she would lie in a man's arms and she would yield to him her maidenhood and it would not be John Bradley to whom she surrendered it . . . but this, too, was an inappropriate thought which must be banished even before it formed, and quickly she returned to the task at hand. . . .

Again, thank you for your kind thoughtfulness

Sincerely,

Augusta Merrick

The house was silent, unusually silent, because nothing was happening in the kitchen, where generally there arose clinks and clatters and muffled Irish exclamations.

Tonight everyone who mattered would dine at the Town House. The dinner would be catered and wine would be served the multitude, toasts made. Presumably the dinner would honor Augusta Merrick and Harold Edgerton—but when you came right down to it, most of the people there would be friends of Mama's, and it was, in truth, Mama who would shine tonight. Yes, Mama had got everything her own way. . . .

She wandered out of the library into the parlor just as Mama opened the front door. Mr. Edgerton—Harold—was escorting her, and Augusta ducked behind the doorway of the dining room, unwilling to be seen by him just then. He would be at her side this evening, and tomorrow she would be permanently bound to him, and an extra five minutes of cordiality right now was not entirely necessary, although this did not reflect any distaste for him. In fact she was fond enough of Harold Edgerton, grateful to him for being such a fine companion, thankful that he had, in so many respects, provided a way out.

Once Mama was safely inside and Mr. Edgerton was safely on his way back to Aunt Ellen's, she stepped out from beside the dining room door.

Mama was looking very pleased, and when she saw Augusta, her pleasure took on an overlay of surprise.

"I thought you were resting!" she whispered, careful not to break the peace and silence, thereby disturbing Aunt Edgerton and causing her to come downstairs to be entertained. "You're supposed to be preparing yourself for tonight's festivities."

"I had a thank-you note to write to the Pettingills," she whispered back. "So I thought I'd get it out of the way."

"Oh, yes! What a horrid cruet set! I have something wonderful to tell you, darling. Let's go back into the library. No one will hear our voices from there."

They found two chairs and placed them by the window. Around them gleamed and glittered the offerings of the Merrick friends.

"I have had a most satisfactory afternoon with your fiancé," Mama said with evident content. "He sought me out at the church. We walked—and talked." She waved in benefaction. "I've been wanting to speak with Harold about you, and your new life in Crofton, and how he could best insure your happiness."

"It wasn't necessary, Mama. I know I shall be happy there."

Mama brushed on by. "As it turns out, Harold has been wanting to speak to me because he reasoned I'd know better than anyone else your tastes and preferences. He's a little worried about uprooting you and carrying you so far away. Quite naturally. So we talked, and he promised me that he'd get you a piano right away, Augusta, when I told him how well you like to play."

"Hardly worth the expense," she observed, patiently as she could. "I'm hardly good enough to warrant it."

"You certainly are," Mama said briskly. "And it will comfort you, if you get lonely. Of course, I'll be in Crofton myself in several months time—we talked about that, too. Harold says that when I come at Christmas, I must stay until spring, and in May he will allow you to come back to Waterford with me for a visit. Won't that be fine?" Mama's face was beatific. "He agreed to it without any difficulty at all."

She watched Mama, remote and detached. "However did you manage that, Mama? After I'd told him how happy I'll be to get away from Kingsland!"

"Well, it was a close call!" Mama laughed. "I wish I'd known you said such a thing! I had to talk pretty quickly when he mentioned your present dislike of the house—honestly, darling, you should have kept me informed!"

"Who could know that the subject would even arise?" she asked dispassionately.

"Once I caught on," Mama continued, "it wasn't too difficult. I simply convinced him—and it wasn't so hard, either—that after you were married to him for a while, the happiness you would surely experience with him would nullify Papa's loss, and Waterford would be as important to you as it had ever been, it being your ancestral home and all. He seemed to accept that. He said if, indeed, you were homesick

382

for Kingsland he'd see to it that you had ample opportunity to visit. And I rather believe him, don't you?"

"Certainly. If that's what he said, that's what he meant."

"I wondered how you got him to propose!" Mama laughed. "You told him you didn't like Kingsland anymore—and that suggested to him your readiness to be part of another, more distant scene? Not bad, darling! Not a bit bad!" There was admiration in Mama's voice, an acknowledgment that when it came to the manipulation of men, Mama had met her match. No doubt Mama would have enjoyed more details, but Augusta did not gratify her. . . .

She had stalked Harold's father with the aid of Papa's billiard table.

Mama had taken everyone outside to examine the newly budded bushes; Harold's father stayed behind, disinclined for the sake of courtesy to risk the only pair of shoes he had brought, and Augusta politely asked him if he would enjoy a game of pool. It was an opening she had been looking for throughout the Edgertons' visit.

"I'm very good," she warned him, smiling.

"I'm pretty good myself," he laughed indulgently.

He put the balls in the wooden rack, courteously offered her the break. She fingered the cue lightly, chalked it and broke the balls in a manner of which Papa would have been proud. "Number six," she called, and sank it, and eight and ten besides. "Twelve," she announced, and it went in the middle pocket.

"So that's the way it is," Edgerton murmured, eyeing her, as she had intended, with respect. It was a ploy that would fail with a young man—but which well might work with an older, more self-assured one, one who might not need a woman to diminish herself for the feeding of his self-esteem. Excellence an older man would notice, and appreciate, especially if he happened to be excellent himself. Edgerton was. They played for two hours.

"You know, Augusta," he said, as they finally hung up their cues. "As Harold's father, perhaps I might be a little presumptuous without offending you. I know he has asked you to marry him, my dear, and I surely wish you would. I have a billiard table at home, and you could be my live-in opponent."

He smiled, so that she would understand his words were in jest—those concerning billiards, in any case.

She looked quickly away.

383

"Harold is a fine young man," she murmured. "And I'm sure he'll make some lucky girl a fine husband."

"But not you."

"No. Not me."

"Why not, if I may ask?"

She paused, and when she answered, her voice was steady, her words deliberate. She looked him squarely in the eye.

"Ever since my father died, Mr. Edgerton, I don't seem to be very much attracted to young men. I refused Harold because it didn't seem right to accept, on the grounds that one day I might be glad I did. Probably you think I'm being foolish."

"Certainly not! It wouldn't be wise at all, my dear, to marry against your inclination."

"And do you think my inclination is also unwise?"

"It exists, Augusta," he said kindly. "There would be no gain in denying it. But, perhaps, given a few more years, you'll find it has diminished."

"Yes, that's more than likely true!" She smiled. "Unless," she added softly, "I can in the meantime find a mature man to marry!"

Quickly she went off to find Mama and young Harold and the others, letting Mr. Edgerton meditate on her words, and she did not treat him, during the rest of his visit, in a manner any different than she would any other of Mama's friends. He was neither coquettish nor grave, but carefully made sure that she was near him so that unobtrusively they could get to know one another better, so that he would grow accustomed to her presence and grow to need it, so that he might watch the young girl whose fancy led her to a preference for mature men. . . .

The day before the Edgertons were due to leave, Harold's father challenged her to another game of pool.

"I insist we lag for the break," she said. "I think I've demonstrated the lack of necessity to place yourself at a disadvantage by observing courtesy."

"All right," he chuckled. "I will." His lag lay closer to the foot spot than hers, and he broke the balls, their colors flashing in the sun that streamed onto the green tabletop.

"It's a lovely afternoon," she said after several matches during which she had been carefully attentive to the play and not to him and had made sure he won by the narrowest of possible margins. "I think everyone's walking outside. Perhaps you'd like to join them."

384

"I think I'd rather stay here." Together they looked out the window at the afternoon.

"If only your visit were longer!" she said wistfully. "You could teach me billiards. I'll bet you're good at it."

She hoped she was not pressing too hard.

"I'd like to stay longer," Edgerton said. "We've enjoyed ourselves very much. Your place here is charming, but unfortunately there is business at home I must see to."

"I'm sorry to hear that!" she said. "With you here, Mr. Edgerton, Kingsland seems a lot as it was when my father was alive. It takes a resident man, I suppose!"

"You really miss him, don't you?"

"I'm afraid I do," she admitted. "I've almost come to dislike returning here, because it is so empty without him."

"You're a loyal daughter."

"I don't think it's a question of loyalty," she said quickly. "It's not that complicated. It's only that something that should be here isn't, that's all. Kingsland has just seemed empty. So I am empty."

"That's a shame," he said. "A girl young as you are shouldn't be empty, Augusta."

"I suppose not, but I haven't felt empty this week and I have you to thank for it, Mr. Edgerton. And I do thank you! Perhaps you'll come back again, though Crofton is so very far away. For that billiard game!" she twinkled.

"It is quite a distance." There was a long silence. "Perhaps it would have some appeal for you. Crofton, I mean. The empty space that your father left wouldn't seem so apparent there, because everything would be different, strange, ready to begin fresh."

She turned from gazing out the window to staring at him, a man whose hair was thinning, whose beard was salt and pepper, whose eyes were surrounded by gentle crow's-feet, and the lines around whose mouth betrayed a life of smiling. She did not speak.

"I rather hate to leave you behind, Augusta, feeling empty. Would you like to come to Crofton with me?"

There was nothing in his question or in his demeanor which could open him to offense or wounded pride should she laugh. He was, at that point, only seeing if she wanted a way out.

"Why, yes," she said tentatively, speculatively, as though this were a new idea. "Yes, it would be very nice to go to

Crofton. I'd enjoy seeing what it's like. I'd play pool there with you, too!"

She met his eyes alertly and he stood straighter, moved closed to her very deliberately, very carefully taking both of the hands watching to see if he frightened or offended her. "I didn't have in mind your coming along as an adopted daughter."

"I can't be your daughter," she pointed out, "because I'm already someone else's."

"I didn't have in mind your coming as a guest, either, Augusta."

"Not even a permanent one?"

They regarded one another for some moments, and she greatly admired his poise, his deliberation, his consideration. A mature man, perhaps, did have a lot to offer!

"Marriage to someone as old as I has its drawbacks," he said conversationally. "Though many a girl has married a man old enough to be her father and it seems to work out pretty well."

"There's no reason why it shouldn't," she said gently. "Especially if the man in question isn't continually reminding himself that he is old."

"You'll consent then?"

She paused, counted to five.

"Gladly," she declared quietly. "Yes, gladly."

It was Mama who took care of young Harold. It was not uncommon, she told him in her next letter, for a young girl to prefer an older man to one more nearly her own age. Augusta, Mama told young Harold, had never, ever gotten over her father's death, and Harold Edgerton, Sr., standing in Papa's place, was the only possible choice for a girl bereaved as Augusta had been.

Augusta heard those words falling often from Mama's lips, whenever she thought Augusta was out of earshot. By now Mama believed it because she wanted to. Why, the widowed Mr. Edgerton was right as rain for Augusta—yes sir, right as rain! Mama needed to believe it! The implications of Augusta's marriage to a man old enough to be her father rang loud and clear in Mama's mind, but of course Mama said nothing. There'd been enough ugliness stirred up in the dining room the week before. All summer Mama assiduously looked the other way, but it was time now that Mama understood the implications—all of them. Mama had claimed enough! It was understandable that she should, and Augusta did not shrink from Mama's claims—but they could be extended only so far. Mama's claims, and Augusta's loyalties, in fact, were extended just as far as they would go.

Mama was laughing happily. "Why, I believe, Augusta, that with a few well-placed remarks it won't take long at all before Harold agrees that you should spend all your summers here, and once that is accomplished—well!—it portends very well for the future—the not-so-distant future, either!—when Harold retires, it seems to me that it won't be hard at all to persuade him to live here. The weather will be more clement, the house certainly sufficiently spacious for all of us—and your happiness, of course, insured by such a move. He is very ardent in the cause of your happiness, Augusta!"

It was hard to control the urgent need to shout, to scream the contents of her mind, but Augusta hung on.

"I think it only fair that Harold should spend the years left to him, after he retires, where he'll be happiest," she said firmly. "After all, Mama, he's always lived in Crofton. He'd be lonely here, away from his own people."

"That's very considerate of you, dear, and I'm sure Harold will appreciate it. But it won't be necessary, don't you see? He will do it your way, I just know he will."

"And I shall do it his."

"My, my," said Mama sarcastically. "I didn't know you'd conceived such affection for Harold, such concern for his well-being."

"I learned."

"Augusta! He does not want to deprive you of your heritage," Mama said, a little stridently. "It's as important to him as it is to you. Or at least it will become so, now that my well-placed remarks can be used to further the idea."

"But Mama," she said softly, wickedly. "It isn't important to *me*."

Mama, taken completely off balance, struggled to regain her aplomb.

"Nonsense, darling. You're just tired. You should have been napping, this afternoon, instead of writing notes. You're cross and irritable, not unusual for a bride. One does get the fidgets!" She rose, as if to escort Augusta up the stairs, to her bed where she might catch forty winks before the banquet tonight to restore her equilibrium.

"Sit down, Mama," she said quietly. "I am not going to take a nap just now." The enormous authority in her voice

387

caused Mama to drop back into the chair. "And I am not going to visit here next summer, away from my husband. I shall not come here upon any occasion unless Harold himself wants to come."

"I'm sure he can be persuaded, Augusta!" Bewilderment was clear in Mama's voice.

"*I* shall not persuade him." Her eyes held Mama's steadily. "I shall go to Crofton and I shall stay there at Harold's side, making him as happy as I can, and I shall not encourage him to retire here, at Kingsland, because he must live where he is happiest. I can't help but feel that Crofton is that place. He deserves happiness, Mama, and he shall get it. And as for me, I don't plan to come back to Waterford any more often than I must."

Her eyes locked with Mama's and what could not be spoken was said in them. Across Mama's face came the unwilling acknowledgment of what she had not wanted to acknowledge, and an understanding that there was no reason now not to say it.

"You chose Harold because he will die before you are old, didn't you?" she whispered. "You chose him because it might yet give you the chance to have John Bradley if you wait long enough. Didn't you!"

"I did," she said firmly.

"That is despicable, Augusta!"

"Is it?" she asked gently. "Is marrying Harold Edgerton, Senior, whom I respect and enjoy, more despicable than marrying his son, whom I detest? Is my marrying Harold Edgerton any more despicable than your refusal to do so? Is my willingness to make him happy in exchange for his security any more despicable than your attempt to dupe him, by wheedling me away from him in the summer and by coaxing him, using me as bait, to retire here so that we can live in luxury and he can pay the bills till the end of his life?"

Mama went white.

"I can't predict what will happen. Perhaps I'll die before Harold does! Perhaps John Bradley will marry someone else. But I think it only fair to tell you, Mama, that Kingsland could again be jeopardized in the future. If fate favors John and me I shall not hesitate. You have your reprieve now, and you deserve it. But if another chance comes my way, I shall not refuse to take it. I wanted to warn you now, Mama, and warn you fairly."

"Augusta!" Mama cried. "You sound so cold, so angry! You sound as though you hate me!"

Her voice trembled, her eyes were full.

"Well, I don't. I only thought it would be unkind to go off to Crofton, leaving you to labor under the misapprehension that somehow my love for John Bradley has simply evaporated. Or to think that you are forever safe. You aren't, Mama. You're safe for as long as Harold lives—and then everything will all be up in the air again. So any scrimping and saving you might do now will help you in the future, and I sincerely recommend that you pinch your pennies as tightly as you can. You should have done so years ago—though, believe me, I understand how it happened that you didn't."

"You don't care?" Mama wavered. "Kingsland means— nothing?"

"I guess it doesn't, Mama." It was cruel, and harsh for Mama to know how little it mattered. But in the long run it was better to let Mama know how little Kingsland meant, that nothing had changed—that Augusta Merrick loved John Bradley and always would. "I'm sure everything will work out," she said, kindly as she could, to hide the fact that toward Mama and toward Kingsland, at this time only indifference was possible.

She returned her mother's anguished stare calmly, and Mama, her face disfigured by shock, staring as she tried to read beneath the expression on the face and behind the dark eyes of her daughter Augusta Merrick backed slowly out of the room, carefully closing the door behind her as though the library now housed a bier with candles at either end, as though any sound might disturb the respectful silence the living owed the dead, and she listened to Mama's slow, rustling ascent to the second floor, where just as quietly her bedroom door closed.

The tower was on the west side of the house, and by turning her head slightly, craning her neck a little, Augusta could see Main Street lined with poplars and elms, and in the distance, through the tracery of leaves (some of which had already fallen) winked the ball and vane, gold and bright, on the Universalist church, and on the vane roosted a sea gull that watched over Waterford with a proprietary air. Along the road came Barney Blake's fish cart which stopped at the Snows' house across the way to deliver freshly trapped dinner. Captain Pollard's carriage with the captain and his wife inside trotted past it, the two of them on their way to Cousin

King's house where, no doubt, they would enjoy a cup of tea and late afternoon chatter before joining the wedding dinner at the Town House. Dressed to the nines and jaunty, the captain saluted Barney as he passed, a man more fortunate than the other at this point in his life, but respectful of Barney Blake's past when he had sailed the seven seas with the best of them.

She sat once more, folding her hands as might an old woman without anything to look forward to anymore, who simply waited . . . waited to see what would happen next because there was nothing anymore that she could do on her own behalf, as though, like an old woman, everything that could be done had been done and now she must be willing to drift, to let the years take her where they would, just as one allowed sleep to overtake one, because there was nothing left to do until morning.

And in the morning?

Time worked in its own way, she knew. She knew it well! Time made resolutions unnecessary. Fulfilled some promises, broke others. Made neither hope nor wishful thinking wise nor profitable. . . . Yet she knew, sitting there, she knew, beneath the poised exterior of herself and beneath the reconciled interior, that morning was twenty years hence or thirty, even forty, when Waterford would be peopled by the ordinary, the humble, the mundane, who got their living as best they could and ran their town to suit themselves, who dug clams and fished and farmed and kept in sound repair the houses of the summer rich and who lived out—perhaps (probably!) without awareness—the dream of Thomas Jefferson. . . .

Morning was the time when conceivably she would be set free, to return to Waterford her own agent, and time, only time, would reveal the manner of her return and would determine whether she would stay and in what capacity. . . .

The church bell began its hour's telling. In another hour the groom would arrive, and on the floor above the bathtub was being filled with a trickle of cold water from the tank on the third floor, and in the kitchen the buckets of hot water from the stove being filled, carried up; she remembered telling Patricia she would bathe at four. It was time to put on the pretty pink dress, to be driven to her wedding banquet, to smile upon her betrothed, to whom she would remain true with all the strength and nerve she possessed—Harold Edgerton, whom she had chosen instead of John Bradley—John, to

390

whom she could not admit her reasons for choosing an old man to wed instead of one far younger. She had not needed to admit it, of course, because John knew.

"What can I say, Augusta?" he asked her, angry, despairing. "Anything I say will only make me ashamed."

"Perhaps I make you ashamed," she suggested softly. They were standing in John's barn, with its neat racks of tools and stacks of barrels, piles of screening, waiting for the oncoming season. "If I do, it's a consequence I'll have to accept. But it may make you feel better, John, to know that I do like Mr. Edgerton very well. He's kind, very kind, and rather fun, in many respects quite delightful. Since I must choose between one or the other, I can cling to him with far more integrity than young Harold who is, quite frankly, a bore." And it was true. Her integrity, such as it was, remained intact in the hands of the senior Edgerton.

John Bradley's quiet face reflected pain only in the lines of strain around his eyes, and in the depths of his eyes themselves. "I shouldn't ask, but I will," he said, searching her face, her soul. "What pressures did your mother bring to bear on you, which so profoundly overrode mine?"

She could not tell him about David his brother, who was her brother, too, nor about Mrs. Bradley, who had wounded Mama past mending, who in fact had ruined everything past repair.

"Our house is mortgaged," she said simply. "Unless the mortgage is paid my mother will lose it, and there will be nothing left. What could I do, John?"

"How much of a mortgage?"

"Five thousand dollars."

John Bradley did not have five thousand dollars, nor could he ever accumulate it; there was no circumstance under which Mrs. Merrick would accept help from him even were he able to give it. He clenched his hands and watched Augusta, refusing to move his mind to the years ahead because it shamed him to consider them, angered him to speculate on the time of another man's death, dismayed him to behold the hard calculation hiding in the heart of Augusta Merrick whom he loved.

"If you think I have degraded myself, there's nothing I can do about it," she said helplessly. "If you are unable to accept my resolution of my situation and my mother's difficulty there's nothing I can do about that, either. Hate me if you will, John. I shall marry Edgerton in any case, because I have to."

The tortured, twisted, white-hot pain seared her, made her want to pound something, break it or destroy it, but she hung on, fiercely passive in the embrace of his decision, speaking only with her eyes. *I love you, John Bradley, I adore you, I would die for you, I am dying . . .*

"Whatever happens will happen, John. Thinking about it changes nothing! Hope for nothing, and then you'll be free from guilt, as I am free." She seized his hand, and restrained herself from kissing it, a token of fealty, homage. "I shall think of you as little as I can help, and you must not think of me. But love me now, oh love me!" she whispered. "Love me in good conscience, and then let go, and let time and destiny take care of the rest. I believe I could be happy, knowing that you stood by me now."

Could he ever, ever know how well she loved him?

There were no promises that could, in good faith, be made, and they did not make them.

There was no future to be shared that in good conscience they could share, and they did not try.

There was nothing but that moment, which they could give to one another, and they gave it.

John!

The seagull had flown away, disturbed by the bell, and Barney Blake had left the Snows, had driven off down Main Street and out of sight. The bell signaled the passage of time, the approach of night and a long sleep, during which she would not behold John Bradley nor see his eyes and face nor hear his voice, and not until morning would she be free, free to unlock her heart and let it fly high and soaring and undiminished. . . .

John!

Quickly she ran for the door, hastened up the staircase, ready now to set her feet on the path that she had chosen, upon which a few faltering footsteps had been made already, footsteps that would have to be firm from now on, without hesitation. But she could do it. She would do it, and she would wait for morning.

"I'm coming, Patricia," she called. "Is my bath ready?"

THIS IS THE HOUSE

by Deborah Hill

**"THE KIND OF NOVEL
YOU CAN'T PUT DOWN!"**
—*El Paso Times*

**"AN ASTONISHING NOVEL . . . EVERYTHING
GONE WITH THE WIND HAS!"**
—**Pamela Hill**
author of The Malvie Inheritance

*Very carefully, beautiful Molly Deems
learned all the ways in which her irresistible
charms could use a man's aroused appetites
to feed her hunger for wealth and position. When
Elijah Merrick offered Molly his name and
his growing fortune in return for the sensual
pleasure she brought him—the passionate
response she pretended, the lie she lived as his
wife—her rise in the world was assured.*

*But Molly Deems was also a woman—a
woman with blood that ran too warm and a
pulse that beat too fast for the one wanton,
devastatingly attractive man who tantalized her
burning desire, and intoxicated her with the
most dangerous dream of all—a dream
of wild, fiery, rapturous love. . . .*

The following excerpt is
from Part One of *This Is The House*

1

They were years of mourning, and of joy.
They were years of despair, and of affirmation.
They were years of tumult, and of tremulous prayer.
And, at the end, the war with England was done.

From one village to the next, across the farmlands and the hills of New England, over the gentle rises and falls of the Delaware Valley and the Shenandoah, onto the sprawling fields of the Southland, the news of it spread, and thanksgiving rose up. Men embraced, and women wept the gentle, cleansing tears of joy. For now the farmer might return to his land, the fisher might return to his nets, the maid and the man in peace might beget the next generation of the new nation. Now the ships might pursue their destiny, lifting their sails to the sun and sea, unrestrained by the mighty hand of Britain. Now a man might speak his mind and will without committing treason. The war in which America rarely won a battle was finished. The old questions, the old loyalties, the old loves, all were laid to rest, and the new taken up in a new land.

Then the flood of thanksgiving that had risen ebbed as men turned themselves to living in a land guided only by themselves. And from the leaf-bare forests of the South to the snow-laden freeholds of the North came the slow understanding that the shoals of bankruptcy and poverty lay close at hand.

The American Confederacy was born.

2

John Deems had followed Washington to New York. With tenderness he had kissed his wife farewell and had wished never to leave her. They had been married only half a year, and he loved her with his whole heart and his whole soul. But he went.

There were many men who did not go that year. There were some who never would. There were some who would enlist only between harvest and planting. There were some who would drift continuously between the lines of battle and home, unable to make a firm commitment to either.

Hannah Deems knew this; she knew John did not have to go. And yet he was perfectly placed, without a large family to encumber him and possessed of a burning zeal for the cause of that new entity—the United States of America. Already had he quarreled with his father over it and broken his bond with his parents. For the Deemses were Loyalist. And because they were and he was not, and because Hannah agreed with him that the American cause was just, he went south with the Army and left her behind in Providence with her parents.

It was an unhappy arrangement for her, yet it was their only recourse. It was awkward because her parents were Quaker; they refused to support the war and would not fight it. They upheld their faith with quiet dignity, even at the risk of being labeled Loyalist, and Hannah, forced to live with them again, thought she would never be able to summon the restraint needed to be a peaceable member of the Pinckham household.

She had married out of Quaker meeting, for John Deems belonged to the Church of the Standing Order, Congregational. If she had not married his church, she had, nonetheless, become wed to a new standard of values. To this extent she had broken with her parents when she became his wife.

Because the Pinckhams were people who believed in peace, they welcomed her back and forgave any pain she had caused them in marrying John Deems in the first place. But because she was young and rebellious, she dreaded it. To go back to their house, there to find herself pregnant and helpless until the return of her husband was, to her mind, her personal sacrifice to the cause of Independence.

Her parents had not berated her, nor had they tried to force her into their beliefs as the price of refuge; since they were Quakers, this would have been repugnant to them. But they stood solidly in opposition to Hannah, gently firm in their refusal to discuss the war or anything connected with it. They waited, instead, for the time when their daughter would listen to the voice of the Lord, who, they knew, spoke lovingly to her even if she would not listen. As far as they were concerned, they would know when she had heard, for then she would return to the pacifism of the Quaker faith.

The Continental Congress was notorious for delay. Paying the armies was the last on its list of priorities. John Deems' wage lagged, and he sent Hannah nothing. The months passed, and soon after the birth of Hannah's baby it was clear to Pinckham that he could not support his daughter and granddaughter by himself. John's Army pay seemed a dream, and the family savings had shrunk disastrously. Pinckham's little business was bankrupt; as a forger of iron he would do nothing that would find its way to the Army. He had thought to serve only the people in Providence, shoeing their horses, making nails for their houses and tools for their farms, but they would have none of him. Without any income, he was hard pressed.

When Hannah had recovered sufficiently from childbirth and still no Army pay had come from her husband, she saw that she must somehow help. Food for the Army was critical, and she found work at the outskirts of town at the farm of George Gorman, who was engaged in beef production. Although his meat was for the Army—and the Army was an entity they would not support—her parents closed their eyes to the destination of Gorman's produce and its consequent undermining of their beliefs. They cared for the baby, Molly, while Hannah, toiling at the Gormans, brought in the much-needed money. It was heavy work, carrying feed and buckets of milk, churning endlessly for butter, scouring the pails and containers, but she was diligent, and the Gormans appreciated her willingness. They often complimented her industry and declared they could never, never get along without her. Hannah began, at last, to feel secure; she felt that with the Gormans a small measure of permanence and safety was hers.

Then it was gone when her father declared he would stay no longer in a place where he was so unwelcomed, even though Providence had been his home for many years. Most Loyalists had by then left the country, fleeing either to Britain or to Canada; those who were not committed to the rebel cause wisely kept their thoughts to themselves, and those who had no commitment because of their apathy were not men of Pinckham's ilk. He eschewed the war because of his religious principles, not because of his politics—which were very much in sympathy with the colonials. The strain of being in the minority without having a readily understandable reason for it became a burden Pinckham no longer wished to bear.

"Daughter," he said to Hannah, "Mother and I cannot remain peaceable people any longer. Wherever I go everyone wants to argue, and I am lucky if they do not turn their arguments into fistfights. The rabble controls our city, and I feel more under fire here than your John must feel facing the redcoats."

"Poor Papa," she said with genuine sympathy. She could well imagine he felt threatened, for he would probably not have defended himself, even under attack.

"Papa," she said, trying to swallow the lump in her throat, "are you going to live with Jared?"

Jared was Pinckham's oldest son.

"Aye," Pinckham said. "Will thee come?"

"To western New York? Papa, you are daft! I would sooner take my chances on a battlefield. Any battlefield. Papa, you must not go there." Her heart constricted in a spasm of fear.

"And why is that?" he asked kindly.

"Indians," she whispered. "The Mohawk Indians. They hate whites."

"Jared writes me that he has been getting along with them very well," her father said complacently. "But of course, he holds love for them—great love. And they know it. Love, daughter, is God's way, and it works every time."

"Not every time," she said emphatically. "Naturally it is up to you, Papa. If you want to join Jared, certainly you should. But I must stay here; how else will John know where to find me?"

"He will find thee all right," her father insisted.

But Hannah was as firm as her father.

"Here I stay," she repeated, and the next day she asked George Gorman if she might live at his house. She and the baby would occupy a room together, she said. She would need no pay for her work; the money had gone to her father for her support, but it was no longer necessary since he was leaving Providence. Instead, would Gorman not accept her labor in exchange for her room and board and that of little Molly?

Gorman, a good man and happy to help when he could and when such help did not cut too deeply into the muscle of his life, was more than willing for the two to board with his family. So again the security that seemed inherent in her position with Gorman was reestablished, even though her parents were absent. The baby, Molly, then one and a half, followed her mother from task to task, watching silently and making no demands. Even as a toddler Molly seemed to sense that no demand would be fulfilled.

Soon after the departure of the Pinckhams, Hannah received official word that her husband had perished at Valley Forge. Now she was alone, very much alone in the world, with a baby to care for, and the realization of it paralyzed her. She wrote desperately to her parents. She would risk all and take her chances with the Mohawks.

But there was no answer.

She wrote again.

And again.

The path to New York was tortuous, long, exhausting. Hannah understood that it would take a long time for any message to be relayed and pinned her hopes on those riders of rafts, plying their goods to the inland over the waterways, who knew so well the settlements on the rivers and the trails leading to ones farther into the forests. But the Indians were raising havoc in some far western homesteads, they told her. They tried, with as much kindness as their sort permitted, to tell her to hope for little.

When definite word finally reached her, there was no hope at all. Her father, her mother, her brother, Jared, and his family had perished out there on the edge of nowhere in a Mohawk raid.

She tried to stem the welling up of panic. There was no one she could turn to for help; she had renounced the Quaker community of Providence when she married John Deems, and in its turn the meeting had renounced her. Her father had enraged the citizens of the town, and there was no help to be had from that quarter either. She wrote letters to the Continental Congress requesting her husband's Army pay, which was due her, but there was no answer. There seemed to her nothing she could do to help herself, aside from staying at the Gormans' and hoping that the war would be fought indefinitely or at least until John's Army pay caught up with her. She told herself there was nothing to fear as long as George Gorman made a profit from the war—and there was no way he could *not* profit from it, so high were the prices for beef. As long as hostilities continued, there was nothing to worry about.

The Army wage never arrived, and then one day the war was done. And the next, and the next, and the next, prices for farm produce fell, and men who profited from the demands of war found their profit gone, with taxes absorbing what they had saved. There was no work for Hannah. She and Molly were existing on George Gorman's charity. Their clothes were threadbare; they had no money. Food was scarce.

Her fear grew.

Molly was six years old.

Their situation was becoming more and more intolerable as each day passed; Hannah had nowhere to go, yet she could not stay. The pressures to force her out increased to such an extent that George Gorman began talking of the widow's vendue—the sale at public auction of bereft women who had no support. It was a practice not uncommon in early days and recently revived—at least in tavern discussion—as a means of dealing with the helpless. Gorman could no longer extend his charity to Hannah. It was cutting into the muscle now.

If the Continental Congress had paid its bills, such measures would have been unnecessary. But Congress, with no taxing power of its own, was at the mercy of each individual state, and as a result, its own coffers were bare. The soaring tax rate imposed by the separate states hardly collected enough to pay the interest on the national indebtedness, let alone to pay wages due Army widows.

There was no one to help Hannah and Molly Deems, even if the will was there.

Then, abruptly, Seth Adams, lean, short and slightly stooped, arrived on his way back from war, stopping to ask for shelter in the barn if nothing else could be provided. No one knew Seth Adams, but this was of no consequence; many soldiers stopped on their way home, and if they could not be fed, they could at least be housed.

Seth Adams was cruel. Seth Adams was scum. No one knew it. No one would have cared, even if it had been known. For he offered to take Hannah with him, back to his place on Cape Cod, near the town of Barnstable.

"I am interested in that woman," he told George Gorman "Who is she?"

"Her name is Hannah Deems. She's a widow. She worked here during the war, while she waited for her husband. But he fell at Valley Forge."

"And what becomes of her now?" Seth Adams asked, his small eyes alert.

"I wish I knew." Gorman sighed. "For I can no longer keep her."

"I'll take her."

There was a startled silence.

"You'll—take her? Just like that?"

"Just like that," Seth Adams said, his mouth curling into a small smile. "My wife run off. Before the war. I don't know where she's at. But I need a woman for my farm—and here one is, all broke in."

"I—I am not sure of the propriety of it," Gorman said uncertainly. "Though the vendue's never concerned themselves with being proper."

"If you mean, will I marry her, I can't," Adams said. "I'm married already. I don't need two wives. I need a woman. I'll feed her, house her. What more can she want?"

"She has a baby girl," Gorman said, feeling that the situation was wrong, but powerless to right it in the face of his waning funds. "You will have to take her, too."

Adams shrugged. "Why not?" he cried.

Gorman told Hannah she was lucky not to starve. He could not, and would not, do any more for her. Adams would help; she must leave. Now. And Hannah saw that for her there were no alternatives left that were any better. The vendue and the humiliation of it before so many folk who already disdained her family were, for her, the ultimate in mortification. If Adams was an unknown entity, at least he was there and willing. Weakened by her helplessness, bereft of hope and now nearly broken by fear, she went— her only bulwark the small child, Molly. Whatever the future might hold for them both, it would lie in the Narrow Land.

Cape Cod had, during the fifty years preceding the English war, left the farm, whose earth it had used up, and had gone to sea, fishing. It had grown dependent on the sea, and when it was taken, it returned to farming knowing the land would not feed it. And it did not.

Cape Cod, which had not seen a battle or fired a shot, emerged from the war with England as broken as though every skirmish had been fought on its poor soil. Its shipping had disappeared, its vessels rotted, and its people weak from lack of food while trying to provision the Army.

The seas were now free; there was no longer a blockade. But neither were there ships. Nor was there money. The Cape was forced to stay on its farms yet a little while. Food was, for the moment, money enough; corn passed for currency.

It was an endless walk from Providence to Barnstable. Gorman gave Hannah a broken-down cart into which she bundled Molly and their few belongings—patched clothing, worn blankets, some trenchers and porringers her mother had given her. By night Hannah cradled Molly while they slept under the stars on one side of the cart, Adams beneath his blanket on the other; by day they wordlessly walked the dusty road, on and on, as the land became more sandy and the trees took strangely twisted shapes from the winter winds. After seven days of travel they stopped in Barnstable village for supplies—food, seed, a spade, some rope— and by midafternoon they left the edge of the town far behind. They tracked into the heartland of the Cape, still heavily forested, and in the center of a sizable clearing they found his cabin.

The door was unlocked, and Hannah wondered that Adams would leave his home without even bothering to secure it. Inside she saw why. There was nothing to take. There was a fireplace in the middle of the room; a cot without a mattress lay behind it.

A table and chair stood in one corner; rows of shelves lined the back wall. A ladder beside the fireplace reached to the attic—and that was all. It was dark and moldy from lack of use.

Hannah tried desperately not to feel that she had been committed to prison. She tried gamely not to be afraid while she waited for Seth's instructions.

Under his direction she unloaded the cart and put its contents on the shelves, and while he restrung the cot with the rope they had bought in the village, Hannah and Molly gathered leaves in a blanket. When it was sufficiently stuffed, they laid it on the cot, and Seth, testing its comfort, stretched out his full length and grunted his satisfaction.

"It'll do," he said. "Fix me a bite to eat, woman."

With Molly huddled in a dark corner and Seth watching from the cot, boots on the blanket and a chew of tobacco in his cheek, Hannah grilled a piece of pork. The cabin showed no evidence that a woman had ever been in it. The hearth was spoiled and soiled with an accumulation of grease no woman would have allowed. She wondered if Seth Adams had ever really had a wife. She set the pork on a trencher of her own and took it to him.

When he was through, Seth smacked his lips and belched with gusto. He made no move to leave the cot.

"Perhaps the child had better go look for more leaves," he remarked, "if she wants something comfortable to sleep on."

"I'll help her," Hannah said, taking another blanket off the shelves.

"She can do it herself," Seth said.

"She's too little. It won't take long if I go with her. I need some for myself."

He swung himself off the cot with a swiftness she had not yet seen in him.

"God damn it, woman, I said she's to go herself."

Hannah stiffened, fear leaping suddenly within her. She spoke low in Molly's ear.

"Stay outside until I call you, little one."

Molly whimpered and held back, but Seth raised his hand, and Molly ran out quickly, holding the blanket tight.

The quiet of the cabin was terrible, and Hannah hardly dared breathe. In the dimness she saw he was watching her. Then he threw some small branches on the fire, and the room became brighter. He moved to confront her and struck her face so quickly that she had no defense against him. The blow dashed her against the wall. She wailed in terror, and he struck her again, then caught her wrist and held her fast.

"Don't yell," he said. "I don't want no one running in here, wondering what's going on." Hannah thought desperately of the loneliness of his cabin and knew no one would hear. "I don't want that brat of yours carrying tales to anyone either. So you just shut your mouth."

He released her wrist and she backed away.

"When I tell you to do something, I want it done. I don't want no arguments about it. I didn't bring you here to argue with. I brung you to help me. Understand?"

"Yes," she whispered. He turned away and seated himself at the table.

"Make yourself some victuals," he said, stretching and clasping his hands behind his head. "Feed yourself and the child. Then fix up the attic the best you can for her. You and me will sleep here." He indicated the cot behind the fireplace.

Hannah stared at him, horrified.

"I can't sleep with you!" she gasped, forgetting his injunction.

"Why the hell not?" He was sitting in absolute stillness, but she had the sense of his readiness to spring.

"I'm—I'm a good woman," she stammered.

"You're a poor woman. You're a penniless woman. With a child, whom I have offered to feed. You had nowhere else to go." He watched her face. "Did you?"

"No," she whispered. "Nowhere."

"And I've taken you in. Both of you. Without me the child would starve. Isn't that so?"

"Yes," she whimpered. "Please, please, Mr. Adams, pity me. I shall work very hard here to somehow repay you. Please, let my labor suffice."

But her heart grew heavier with each word. It would not work. She should have known that coming with him was, in fact, a bargain that included her body.

"I think I should get a reward for being so nice. I would rather that you gave it, instead of me having to take it."

He waited while she struggled with herself. "Let me share the attic with her," Hannah said at last. "You sleep here. I'll come to you anytime you say. She's a heavy sleeper; she'll not know." And Hannah tried to swallow something too large for her throat.

"Now," drawled Seth Adams, "now that strikes me as some inconvenient. Mighty inconvenient. You wouldn't be trying to duck out on me, would you?" He was on his feet, and she backed away in terror.

"No, no, I'll do it, I will. I just want her to be a nice girl, Mr. Adams, that's all, so she can get on in this world. I don't want

her to learn things too early in life that might make her—well—
not nice."

"You must mean I'm not nice," he said, pleasantly enough.

"I didn't mean it like that," she said, and wrung her hands, her
eyes filling and her face a mirror of despair.

"Now, Hannah, my girl, don't you get so upset," Seth Adams
said softly. He approached her; she was too close to the wall to
move away. "I guess I scared you some—I shouldn't have hit you
so hard. I'm a man with a temper—you may as well know it. But
if I'm content, I ain't so bad. If you make me feel good, I'm even
a nice person."

He reached for her, and she shivered and shrank from him.

His face clouded.

"Now, woman, it angers me mightily to see you try to avoid me.
I won't hurt you none if you don't make me mad. All I want is
someone to clear up this pigsty. I want someone to do my bidding—a man likes that, too."

He reached for her again and said, "I like a woman to let me
have my will. I want that you should obey me. Right now, I want
you should hold still."

With enormous effort, she made herself stand quietly, without
resistance. He unbuttoned her dress and drew it over her shoulders, past her waist and hips, and let it fall to the floor. He removed her pantaloons. He stepped back to admire her in the
flickering light.

A tear slipped down her cheek.

"I like it that you don't wear no chemise," he said. "I'll clothe
you, but promise you won't wear a chemise. I like it, knowing you
got nothing on under that dress."

Miserably she nodded, and Seth, satisfied for the present, turned
away. He was canny enough not to press too far. If she became
too fearful, he reasoned, she would be unable to give him the
sustained pleasure he envisioned. It cost him dearly to restrain
himself, but he knew she would pay him in full. For now, the
important thing was to show who was the master of the household and of her.

"You can dress now," he said. "Then make the child comfortable. Fix yourself a bed upstairs, too. As soon as she's asleep,
you come to me. But I warn you, woman, don't make me wait too
long."

She ran from the cabin, buttoning her dress as she went, and
found Molly scrambling among the fallen leaves beneath a nearby
oak.

"Here, my dear one, here I am. I'll help you."

"What did Mr. Adams want, Mama?" Molly asked.

"He said we could sleep together in the attic," Hannah said, steadily as she could. "We'll get lots of leaves and make ourselves a big, puffy bed. That will be nice, don't you think? We can keep each other warm."

"Oh, yes, Mama. That will be very nice!" Molly set to the leaves with pleasure, but her short arms dropped as many as she gathered.

Hannah drew the little girl to her.

"Dearest," she said slowly, carefully keeping her voice light, "you must always do what Mr. Adams tells you. You must try always to help, as much as you can. And say nothing to him unless he asks a question. Do you understand?"

Molly nodded. "Will he hit me?"

"Not if you do everything as you should. Then he will have no reason to."

"Will he hit you, Mama?"

Hannah blinked and tried to answer in a clear voice.

"He may. But you must not mind it, Molly. For I do not. He will feed us and give us clothes to wear. So I am grateful to him. We must try very hard to please him. And Molly?"

The child was attentive. "Yes, Mama?"

"If you should ever wake in the night and find I am not there, you must stay in our bed and keep it warm for me until I get back."

"But where will you be?" The little face drew up in concern and worry.

"I will be downstairs with Mr. Adams, helping him plan our work for the next day," she lied gallantly. "But you must not call for me or come looking for me. That would make him angry. Do you understand?"

Molly nodded, and the two of them filled the blanket with leaves and carried them up to Seth Adams' attic.

ABOUT THE AUTHOR

Deborah Hill was born in Newton, Massachusetts, and grew up in Toledo, Ohio. She lived for six years in the Cape Cod locale that forms the setting for THE HOUSE OF KINGSLEY MERRICK as well as THIS IS THE HOUSE, the first book in her projected trilogy about the Merricks. Many of the characters and events in both books are based on real people and real happenings discovered through research into diaries, genealogies, records and Cape Cod history, which lends her writing its tremendous authenticity. Deborah Hill was trained in philosophy at Villanova University. She lives with her husband and two sons in Vermont, where she is at work on the final novel in the Merrick trilogy.

More Bestsellers from SIGNET

☐ **LORD OF RAVENSLEY by Constance Heaven.**
(#E8460—$2.25)†

☐ **THE PLACE OF STONES by Constance Heaven.**
(#W7046—$1.50)†

☐ **HARVEST OF DESIRE by Rochelle Larkin.**
(#E8771—$2.25)

☐ **TORCHES OF DESIRE by Rochelle Larkin.**
(#E8511—$2.25)*

☐ **MISTRESS OF DESIRE by Rochelle Larkin.**
(#E7964—$2.25)*

☐ **THE RICH ARE WITH YOU ALWAYS by Malcolm Macdonald.**
(#E7682—$2.25)

☐ **THE WORLD FROM ROUGH STONES by Malcolm Macdonald.**
(#E8601—$2.50)

☐ **SONS OF FORTUNE by Malcolm Macdonald.**
(#E8595—$2.75)*

☐ **DANIEL MARTIN by John Fowles.** (#E8249—$2.25)†

☐ **THE EBONY TOWER by John Fowles.** (#E8254—$2.50)

☐ **THE FRENCH LIEUTENANT'S WOMAN by John Fowles.**
(#E9003—$2.95)

☐ **SONG OF SOLOMON by Toni Morrison.** (#E8340—$2.50)*

☐ **ALOHA TO LOVE by Mary Ann Taylor.** (#E8765—$1.75)*

☐ **SO WONDROUS FREE by Maryhelen Clague.**
(#E9047—$2.25)*

☐ **SWEETWATER SAGA by Roxanne Dent.** (#E8850—$2.25)*

* Price slightly higher in Canada
† Not available in Canada

Buy them at your local

bookstore or use coupon

on next page for ordering.

SIGNET Books for Your Reading Pleasure

☐ **LILY CIGAR by Tom Murphy.** (#E8810—$2.75)*
☐ **MOMENTS OF MEANING by Charlotte Vale Allen.**
(#J8817—$1.95)*
☐ **BEDFORD ROW by Claire Rayner.** (#E8819—$2.50)†
☐ **JUST LIKE HUMPHREY BOGART by Adam Kennedy.**
(#J8820—$1.95)*
☐ **THE DOMINO PRINCIPLE by Adam Kennedy.**
(#J7389—$1.95)
☐ **HOW TO SAVE YOUR OWN LIFE by Erica Jong.**
(#E7959—$2.50)*
☐ **FEAR OF FLYING by Erica Jong.** (#E8677—$2.50)
☐ **KINFLICKS by Lisa Alther.** (#E8984—$2.75)
☐ **OAKHURST by Walter Reed Johnson.** (#J7874—$1.95)
☐ **MISTRESS OF OAKHURST by Walter Reed Johnson.**
(#J8253—$1.95)
☐ **LION OF OAKHURST by Walter Reed Johnson.**
(#E8844—$2.25)*
☐ **FURY'S SUN, PASSION'S MOON by Gimone Hall.**
(#E8748—$2.50)*
☐ **RAPTURE'S MISTRESS by Gimone Hall.** (#E8422—$2.25)*
☐ **WARWYCK'S WOMAN by Rosalind Laker.**
(#E8813—$2.25)*
☐ **RIDE THE BLUE RIBAND by Rosalind Laker.**
(#J8252—$1.95)*

* Price slightly higher in Canada
† Not available in Canada

Buy them at your local bookstore or use this convenient coupon for ordering.

THE NEW AMERICAN LIBRARY, INC.,
P.O. Box 999, Bergenfield, New Jersey 07621

Please send me the SIGNET BOOKS I have checked above. I am enclosing
$_____ (please add 50¢ to this order to cover postage and handling).
Send check or money order—no cash or C.O.D.'s. Prices and numbers are
subject to change without notice.

Name _____

Address _____

City_____ State_____ Zip Code_____
Allow 4-6 weeks for delivery.
This offer is subject to withdrawal without notice.

Recommended Reading from SIGNET

- [ ] **THE DOCTORS ON EDEN PLACE by Elizabeth Seifert.**
  (#E8852—$1.75)*
- [ ] **THE DOCTOR'S DESPERATE HOURS by Elizabeth Seifert.**
  (#W7787—$1.50)
- [ ] **THE STORY OF ANDREA FIELDS by Elizabeth Seifert.**
  (#Y6535—$1.25)
- [ ] **TWO DOCTORS AND A GIRL by Elizabeth Seifert.**
  (#W8118—$1.50)
- [ ] **TWINS by Bari Wood and Jack Geasland.** (#E8015—$2.50)
- [ ] **THE YEAR OF THE INTERN by Robin Cook.**
  (#E7674—$1.75)
- [ ] **COMA by Robin Cook.** (#E8202—$2.50)
- [ ] **EYE OF THE NEEDLE by Ken Follett.** (#E8746—$2.95)*
- [ ] **FLICKERS by Phillip Rock.** (#E8839—$2.25)*
- [ ] **LOVE, LAUGHTER, AND TEARS by Adela Rogers St. Johns.**
  (#E8752—$2.50)*
- [ ] **MAKING IT by Bryn Chandler.** (#E8756—$2.25)†
- [ ] **DAYLIGHT MOON by Thomas Carney.** (#E8755—$1.95)*
- [ ] **JO STERN by David Slavitt.** (#J8753—$1.95)*
- [ ] **PHOENIX by Amos Aricha and Eli Landau.**
  (#E8692—$2.50)*
- [ ] **WINGS by Robert J. Sterling.** (#E8811—$2.75)*

  * Price slightly higher in Canada
  † Not available in Canada

Buy them at your local

bookstore or use coupon

on next page for ordering.